THE UNMAKING

FSC
www.fsc.org

MIX

Paper from
responsible sources

FSC® C016245

ENVIRONMENTAL BENEFITS STATEMENT

Coteau Books saved the following resources by
printing the pages of this book on chlorine free paper
made with 100% post-consumer waste.

TREES	WATER	ENERGY	SOLID WASTE	GREENHOUSE GASES
20	**9,255**	**9**	**619**	**1,706**
FULLY GROWN	GALLONS	MILLION BTUs	POUNDS	POUNDS

Environmental impact estimates were made using the Environmental Paper Network
Paper Calculator 3.2. For more information visit www.papercalculator.org.

www.coteaubooks.com

LAST DAYS ⊕F TIAN DI

THE UNMAKING

BOOK TWO

CATHERINE EGAN

Edited by Laura Peetoom
Designed by Jamie Olson
Maps by Jonathan Service
Printed and bound in Canada at Friesens

Library and Archives Canada Cataloguing in Publication

Egan, Catherine, 1976-
    The unmaking / Catherine Egan.

(Last days of Tian Di ; book 2)
Issued in print and electronic formats.
ISBN 978-1-55050-559-7 (pbk.). –ISBN 978-1-55050-560-3 (pdf). –
ISBN 978-1-55050-744-7 (epub). –ISBN 978-1-55050-745-4 (mobi)

    I. Title. II. Series: Egan, Catherine, 1976- . Last days of Tian Di ; book 2.

PS8609.G34U55 2013   jC813'.6   C2013-903654-7
                                                   C2013-903655-5

Library of Congress Control Number   2013940632

COTEAU BOOKS

2517 Victoria Avenue
Regina, Saskatchewan
Canada S4P 0T2
www.coteaubooks.com

10 9 8 7 6 5 4 3 2 1

Available in Canada from:
Publishers Group Canada
2440 Viking Way
Richmond, British Columbia
Canada V6V 1N2

Available in the US from:
Orca Book Publishers
www.orcabook.com
1-800-210-5277

Coteau Books gratefully acknowledges the financial support of its publishing program by: the Saskatchewan Arts Board, the Canada Council for the Arts and the Government of Canada through the Canada Book Fund.

FOR
MEREDITH EGAN & LUCY LIBERATO
AS THEY COME INTO THEIR OWN POWERS

Map of Tian Xia

Map of Di Shang

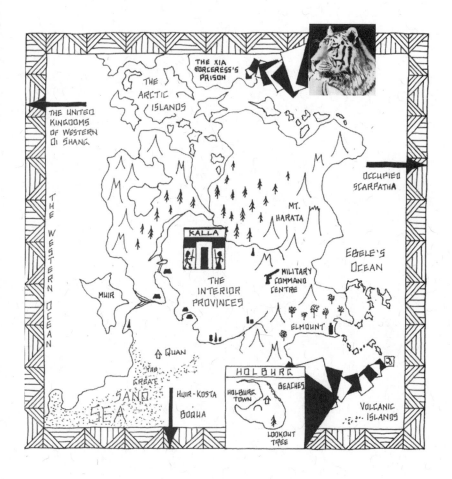

THE XIA SORCERESS'S PRISON

THE ARCTIC ISLANDS

THE UNITED KINGDOMS OF WESTERN DI SHANG

THE WESTERN OCEAN

OCCUPIED SCARFATHA

MT. HARATA

KALLA

EBELE'S OCEAN

THE INTERIOR PROVINCES

MUIR

MILITARY COMMAND CENTRE

QUAN

ELMOUNT

THE GREAT SAND SEA

MUIR-KOSTA

BORWA

HOLBURG

HOLBURG TOWN

BEACHES

LOOKOUT TREE

VOLCANIC ISLANDS

CHAPTER

1

Abimbola Broom was worried. He rarely had cause to worry and was finding it most uncomfortable. He looked out the window of the car at the dark, wet streets flashing by. It had been raining for days now and the weather matched his mood. His driver, Miles, took the corner hard, turning onto Victory Avenue, and the long black car roared up the hill to Abimbola's estate. Only when the car pulled up at his front door did Abimbola stir from his anxious reverie. Neglecting to say goodbye to Miles, who was standing in the downpour to open the car door for him, he trotted up the front steps holding his briefcase over his head to keep off the rain.

Abimbola fumbled with his keys and opened the front door. Most of the house was dark but there was a light coming from the Visitor's Parlor. There, Abimbola's wife, Nekane, was sitting in the most comfortable chair and reading a book. This irritated him unduly. It seemed all she ever did lately was read romances and he didn't see why she had to do it in the most elegant room in the house. Nekane got up to greet him. As always he was struck by how beautiful she was. Having her at his side had been one of his greatest joys once, and it had been easy in those days to delight her with expensive gifts and exotic vacations. She had seemed to admire him then, to enjoy having a powerful and influential man as her husband. But over the years she had grown cool, indifferent. The kiss she placed on his cheek was dry and perfunctory. He despised the groveling unhappiness her disinterest caused him and this made him treat her cruelly.

"Are the girls asleep?" he asked, glancing disapprovingly at the book she had left open on her chair.

"Yes," she answered, adding pointedly, "It's late."

It was an invitation to quarrel but he was too beset by other anxieties to engage with her tonight. Without another word, he turned and went up the broad, carpeted stairs to his study. He had forgotten to eat supper and was quite hungry. He would call the maid and have her bring him a drink and something to eat.

Abimbola's study overlooked the city of Kalla, the great capital of Central Di Shang. Tonight it was a maze of lights hunched against the November rain. He used to look out over the city in triumph, a self-made king in this kingless republic. But the more you have, Abimbola thought glumly, the more you have to lose. Abimbola's father had become wildly rich in the early years of the long war, selling fake charms supposed to protect the wearer against Magic. "One man's tragedy is another man's opportunity," his father had been wont to say. The lesson was not lost on young Abimbola, who started up a newspaper, peddling horrifying, apocalyptic stories of the havoc wreaked by the Xia Sorceress, her inhuman allies and the treacherous Scarpathians. He outsold all his competitors easily. Within a decade, he owned most of the major news outlets and TV stations in the Republic, as well as stock in a great many other businesses. His finances and multiple businesses were run by people who were eminently competent and, more importantly, terrified of him. Abimbola inflicted anxiety and fear on others as a matter of course. He was not used to experiencing them himself.

Another peculiar feature of great wealth, Abimbola thought, was that the more one had, the more one seemed to need. The things Abimbola considered necessities expanded as fast as his tabloid empire – the estate with its swimming pool and tennis courts, the extravagant parties and vacations, the fleet of sleek, aggressive cars, the private jet, his second and third homes on the coast and the 100-foot yacht he never used. For Abimbola, there was no such thing as enough. He depended heavily on his investments but did not like to gamble. He liked to know exactly what he could expect. He liked to know things that no one else knew. To the rest of the world, Abimbola's financial decisions seemed prescient. He was lauded for unerring instinct. But it was not instinct that told him when to buy or sell stock. It was the Cra.

For obvious reasons, the Cra were among the most hated of the beings that had ever crossed over from Tian Xia. While many of them remained in Tian Xia feeding off small animals, the bolder among them refused to be denied their natural prey, the human infant. They came to Di Shang and raided hospitals, orphanages, undefended villages. Since the end of the war, however, the military had become increasingly skilled at hunting them down. The situation became desperate for the Cra.

Though neither their Magic nor their physical strength was very great, the Cra did have particular skills that were useful to Abimbola. They could fly. They were swift and stealthy. They were adept in basic spells, particularly the enchantment of objects and hypnotism. In other words, they were ideal spies and thieves. The exchange of services was simple. Abimbola controlled information. To a certain extent, the news in the Republic was what he said it was. If an attack by the Cra was not in the news, there was no public outrage, hence no government funding, hence no military counter-strike. He kept the Cra out of the news as much as possible and funded several fake orphanages and a fraudulent adoption service in Huir-Kosta, through which he provided the Cra with a relatively steady supply of unwanted babies.

The Cra repaid him royally. They soared, dark shadows down gleaming hallways, enchanting sophisticated alarm systems, charming open locks and safes, hypnotizing guards. They brought Abimbola the most secret information of the most powerful companies in the Republic. He knew where to invest, when to sell. If the company was corrupt, bribery was a simple matter. For years it had been the perfect partnership and Abimbola had come to depend on it absolutely. Doing honest business was no longer possible. But now something was going wrong. Something or someone was decimating the Cra.

It was not the Special Forces. They would be trumpeting the

news to all Di Shang if it were. It was not the Mancers either – the Cra were not being banished, they were being killed, sometimes one at a time, sometimes in large groups. Their numbers were dwindling and fewer and fewer among them were crossing over for fear of this new, mysterious enemy. The Cra had demanded that Abimbola, with the vast resources he commanded, discover who was hunting them down and put a stop to it. It was an ultimatum – until he found and destroyed their enemy, business as usual would not resume. Abimbola had a number of high-stakes deals hanging in the balance at the moment and could not afford to make any decisions without the information only the Cra could provide. He had been stalling for weeks now and had uncovered nothing. He had only the terrified rumours that were spreading among the Cra to go on. Some believed it was a bereft mother whose grief had transmogrified her into a vengeful witch. Some said she rode a giant raptor. Others said it was a dragon; still others said a gryphon. It was whispered that she had a dagger carved from the claw of a dragon, but Abimbola discounted this outright, knowing full well that dragon claws, being harder than any other substance in the worlds and also impervious to heat, could not be carved. Some claimed it was the Shang Sorceress, but others insisted that they had delivered this very girl into the hands of the Xia Sorceress more than two years ago and that, in any case, she had been but a powerless child.

Abimbola's stomach rumbled and he remembered that he should eat. He turned away from the window and went to his desk to pick up the phone and call the maid. As he did so, a shadow stepped out of the opposite wall and said a single word in a strange language.

He tried to scream. He opened his mouth but no sound came out. He tried to reach for his phone and found he could not move. Abimbola Broom had never before in his life had cause to feel truly afraid, but he was afraid now.

"You should be happy, aye," said a young, female voice. "You were just wondering how you would find me and here I am."

She came closer. He could see her face now, a brown, beaky little face under a mass of disorderly curls. Why, she was not even a grown-up! She was a girl of no more than fourteen or fifteen. Her hair and clothes were wet, as if she had recently been out in the rain. She was dressed quite ordinarily for a girl her age, in a pair of slim trousers, laced black boots and a long winter coat, perhaps dark green, although it was difficult to tell in the unlit room. She wore a shard of white crystal around her neck. She did not appear frightening until she reached into the coat and drew out a dark blade the length of her forearm.

"You're wrong that it's impossible to carve something from a dragon's claw, by the way," she said. "There are mystical ways of moulding even something as hard as this, if you know a great deal about Magic and a great deal about dragons. I dinnay know much about either, as it happens, but I know someone who does."

Abimbola could not breathe or think. His mind was a roaring black cavern. He was going to be murdered, he understood that perfectly, and had not imagined himself capable of the terror he was now experiencing.

"I'm nay going to kill you," the girl said impatiently. "Though you dinnay deserve any better. But Di Shang has its own kind of justice for men like you. I'm going to hand you over."

Free of the fear of death and given a moment to recover from it, Abimbola's mind began to race. There was nothing that could be proved against him, nothing at all.

"Lah, you're wrong there," said the girl, circling him with her awful black blade pointing towards him at all times. "You may be able to mix a messy little potion of invisibility and creep around unseen to your meetings with the Cra, but there are more kinds of Seeing than you can imagine. You dinnay know much about Magic, of course, so I'll share a few facts with you. For example, did you know that I could touch your coat and discover its entire history? Everywhere you've been, everything you've done while wearing that coat — I can find out about it with a simple spell. I could do the same thing with your shoes or your briefcase or your wife's diamond necklace. Then there's the Vindensphere, which you've never heard of, but which could be used to show a judge everything you've been up to for the last eight or nine years. Of course, *I'm* nay going to go marching into a court of law to testify against you. I think one of the Emmisariae of the Mancers would be better suited for that, lah. Nobody would question what a Mancer said. And yes, the Mancers know about you, and yes, they want to see you prosecuted and convicted for the murder of innocent children, and yes, I am the one who has been hunting down the Cra. My name is Eliza."

Abimbola Broom was dizzy. Whatever invisible force had been holding him immobile lifted suddenly and his knees folded beneath him. He crashed to the floor and found his voice.

"My children," he managed to say. "I have two daughters. Without me, what will become of them?"

Eliza's face clouded over. "I dinnay know. I'm very sorry that they will grow up without a father and that they will have to be so ashamed of you. But I cannay undo the things you've done."

"I beg of you," he said, "I will find a way to...atone. I have given a great deal of money to charities, you can see the receipts in my desk, thousands of –"

Eliza interrupted him with a brief command and once again his voice was gone.

"I cannay listen to you," she said, disgusted. She put away her dagger and unlooped a coil of slender brown rope from her belt. She uttered brief commands and as she did so he found himself getting to his feet and putting his hands behind his back for her to bind. She bound his feet as well. The cord did not feel tight and it did not look strong but he could not move his limbs where it bound him.

"That's better, aye," she said. "Now I dinnay have to concentrate on keeping you still."

She strode to the window and threw it open. The rain was thunderous now, crashing down onto the city.

"Charlie!" she called. A giant winged creature swooped past the window and Abimbola gave a little scream. Eliza tugged the rope that bound him and he skidded to the window. She was about to push him out into the dark when there was a tap at his door. He looked down at Eliza, wide-eyed, and she looked back at him, her expression impassive. The door opened, revealing Nekane, silhouetted by the light of the hallway behind her. She had come, simmering with resentment, to say goodnight and a few other things, the exact wording of which she had been working on all evening with the unread book open on her lap. But her face changed now. She stared at the young girl at the window and her husband, bound fast.

"Nekane," said Abimbola desperately. He wanted to shout for help, he wanted to tell her to do something, to stop the girl, but what came out of his mouth was what he least expected – "Forgive me."

Then Eliza gave him a swift push and he tipped out the window. Something hard and bony closed around him, stopping his fall. When he dared to open his eyes he found himself looking at the powerful chest of a gryphon that had caught him in its talons. Eliza jumped out the window onto the gryphon's back and they soared off over the drenched, shimmering city. If Abimbola had been able to see into his study as they flew away, he would have realized that the expression on his wife's face was one of unmistakable relief.

In spite of the rain Eliza enjoyed flying over the city, its countless lights swimming beneath her like phosphorescence in the sea. She was terribly pleased with herself for having captured Abimbola. Charlie had drawn her attention to the Cra's unusual activities months ago and had taken the guise of one to discover whom they were working for. When he told Eliza about the arrangement they had with a wealthy businessman, she had hardly believed it. How could a *man* be responsible for organizing such slaughters? She didn't understand it and she didn't much want to. She would hand him over to the Mancers and they would deal with everything from there. Of course, she wasn't foolish enough to think they would be pleased with her. But who were they to argue, when she had been out doing what they had neglected to do for years?

Abimbola, nearly crushed by the gryphon's grip, had begun to gibber with fear. Eliza slipped upside-down towards him, hooking her leg over the gryphon's neck and getting a firm grip on its foreleg with one hand. She stuck a piece of the rope in Abimbola's mouth to still his tongue, then pulled herself back upright with her leg. They left Kalla behind them, flying south across the Interior Provinces. Cities were scattered below like twinkling pools of light in the vast darkness of the plains. She was soaked through but exhilarated, she and the gryphon one in their joy of flight. Only the bound man was not enjoying the journey. Dawn glimmered on the horizon as the lush plains dried out into stony, unforested gullies and ridges. Further south was the Great Sand Sea, home of the Sorma, her father's people. She could go that way and deliver this man to their care to be sent on a spirit-quest and have the poison taken from his soul. It would be better for him. If he survived, he would be whole. But she wasn't interested in what was best for him. She wanted him to be punished, not healed. They flew over the great river Noxoni, a brown torrent with a swathe of green on either side of it, and the gryphon veered west.

Less than an hour later, on the ragged lip of a vast canyon, the Citadel of the Mancers came into view. The Citadel formed a square with towers at every corner enclosing the grounds, which were startlingly green in contrast to the arid world outside. The Inner Sanctum loomed at the centre, a giant white dome. As the gryphon swooped down towards it, Eliza began to mutter under her breath, requesting entry in the Language of First Days. She could feel, as always, the slight surprise and annoyance that came in response to her request. They didn't like the way she came and went, as she was well aware. But they always let her in.

Eliza and the gryphon landed in the grounds by the south wing. The early morning sky was bright and cloudless. Her beloved teacher, Foss, was waiting for her, shaking his head.

"You are soaking wet!" he scolded, sounding so motherly that she laughed out loud. He looked rather offended and turned his attention to Abimbola Broom.

"Who is this and why in the worlds have you brought him *here*, Eliza Tok? A human. And bound with the Onbeweglich Cord! Rather extreme, is it not?"

"I didnay want him being difficult," said Eliza.

Abimbola Broom spat out the piece of cord that was lodged in his mouth and gaped around him. Although he had never seen a Mancer, he was certain that was what stood before him, towering and gold-skinned with pale hair and eyes like suns.

"Sir," he began, his voice shaking, "I have been most abominably treated! I have been *kidnapped* while my family slept and I pray to the Ancients that you in your infinite wisdom will be able to rectify –"

Charlie, who had ceased to be a gryphon and become a boy again as soon as they landed, interrupted this speech by bending down and sticking the bit of cord back into Abimbola's mouth, silencing him. Being a Shade, Charlie could take any shape he chose, but he kept Eliza company by appearing most frequently as a boy her own age. She thought it was unnecessary and a bit vain of him to insist on being such a good-looking boy but didn't say so.

"He should be put in the dungeons with a barrier," said Eliza. "I'll show you what he's been doing, aye. Then the Emmisariae can take care of things."

Foss sighed. "If you want to put a human in the dungeons, Eliza Tok, you will have to speak with Kyreth. He is expecting you, by the way."

"I know," said Eliza. "Will you keep an eye on him, Charlie?"

"Aye aye, Cap'n," said Charlie, settling down in the grass next to Abimbola.

"Dinnay call me that," said Eliza, and then smiled at him involuntarily. "Nice flight, nay?"

"Wet," Charlie came back flatly.

"Perhaps you should change into something dry first," said Foss to Eliza, only just managing to refrain from saying *before you catch your death of cold.*

"I'm almost dry. But aye, you're right, I should get cleaned up anyway. Come on, walk with me. Have you nay missed me at all, Foss? I've been gone for weeks!" She looked up at his brilliant face, his eyes much brighter than when she had last seen him, and she remembered that they were approaching winter, his strongest season.

"I would have missed you more and worried less if I'd had any idea what you were doing. Although, as it turns out you were terrorizing and kidnapping a human, I think I would have worried even if I had known."

"He's been in league with the Cra, Foss," said Eliza as they made their way into the south wing and up the marble stairs, in the direction of Eliza's bedroom. "He's been *planning* their attacks and making sure they didnay get reported!"

"The Cra." Foss's shoulders slumped noticeably. "I have mentioned, I believe, that none of us are terribly happy about you going into battle alone with so little training. And I am understating the case quite dramatically." He looked as if he was about to say more but decided against it.

"It's just the Cra," protested Eliza. "It's hardly dangerous. And lah, besides, I always have Charlie with me."

Foss shook his head. "Kyreth will not be pleased," he said.

CHAPTER
2

Foss was right. Eliza spent the morning rehashing the same argument she always had with the Supreme Mancer Kyreth, which, as usual, left them both even angrier than when they had started.

"It is beyond irresponsible! You are a fool, Eliza, a foolish girl. When you are sufficiently trained and you have a daughter, that is the time to fulfill your duty as the Shang Sorceress. But to put yourself in danger so *deliberately* – you are too much like your mother, and will meet her fate or worse if you do not learn to obey those who hold your interests at heart!" Kyreth paced back and forth behind his heavy marble desk, hands locked behind his back, his eyes blazing so white-hot that Eliza could not look him in the face. The room hummed with his anger. Behind him one of the blank Scrolls hanging from the wall wrote out swiftly *too much like your mother*, and another Scroll wrote *her fate or worse*.

"I was *not...in...danger*," Eliza ground out between her teeth for what felt like the twentieth time. "Charlie was with me the whole time, aye. Anyway, I can *handle* the Cra. I can *handle* a man. Lah, if the Mancers had ever bothered to deal with the Cra then I wouldnay have had to do it in the first place!"

"Do not be insolent!" Kyreth flashed with rage, making Eliza wince. "Is it your belief, Eliza, that the Mancers spend their days in idleness? Answer me!"

"Of course nay," she protested. "But –"

"Then is it your belief that to separate the two worlds is an easy task, requiring little of our power?"

"No." She became sulky now.

"And do you think it is effortless to maintain and build upon the barriers that hold our enemy, that Arctic fiend, a task made infinitely more strenuous since you delivered to her the Book of Barriers?"

This was a sore point. Eliza fell into furious silence. *Infinitely more strenuous*, wrote one of the Scrolls, as if to rub it in.

"Eliza?" he demanded again.

She could barely get the word out, "No."

His voice softened. "I know that you mean well. You wish to rid Di Shang of the evil of the Cra and this is most commendable. But there is no end to evil, Eliza. Evil will keep coming. And if you were to perish now, the line of the Shang Sorceress would end. The world would be bereft forever, the power of the Mancers stretched beyond what we can achieve alone. For the time being, the military is responsible for beings that cross over from Tian Xia. The Mancers are responsible for separating the worlds and keeping our terrible enemy imprisoned. You, Eliza, are responsible for learning what you can of Magic, for studying in diligence and obedience. When you are ready, and when you have produced an heir, you will perform your duty and guard the Crossing. But now is not that time."

"How can I wait until I grow up, while the Cra —"

"Now is *not that time*," thundered Kyreth.

Eliza leaped to her feet and found herself slammed back into her chair hard by Kyreth's Magic, which only angered her further. "Tell that to the mother of some child the Cra have stolen!" she shouted at him. "And dinnay try to tell me you're just too *busy* to take care of it. That's the worst excuse I've ever heard in my entire life!"

"Enough!" Kyreth struck his desk with his fists. The room shook and the word *Enough* spilled down each of the Scrolls on the far wall except one, which wrote, much to Eliza's surprise, *The worst excuse I've ever heard*. When Kyreth spoke again his voice was very quiet. "Listen to me, Eliza Tok. If the man is what you say, the Emmisariae will arrange to have him prosecuted. We will keep him in one of the guest rooms until then, with a barrier on the door. I will speak to Aysu about the Cra and see what can be

done. This is what you wish, is it not? But you must make con-
cessions too. You must accept that we have rules and that there
are good reasons for these rules. Eliza, I am most concerned that
you have been killing. It is not for you to decide whether a being
should live or die."

"If you only banish them, others just keep coming," said Eliza
unhappily. He was right but she knew no better way to deter the
Cra from crossing over. "Lah, if you could make some kind of
barrier to stop any of them from ever crossing over..."

"You do not understand what you ask," said Kyreth impatiently. "If it were so simply done, we would have done it! What
can you infer then? Answer me."

"That it's nay easy," said Eliza sullenly.

"Impossible, given the many demands on our Magic," Kyreth
shot back. "I will speak to Aysu about the matter. Now go, Eliza.
You hear nothing that I say and I am weary of speaking to you."

Eliza was still seething when she left Kyreth's study and went to
find Foss in the Old Library. Charlie was with him and they both
looked bored.

"I have been instructed to tell you that the Shade cannot have
free rein of the Citadel," Foss said. "If you bring him here, he is
to remain supervised at all times."

Charlie rolled his eyes.

"Fine." Eliza plunked herself down in a chair. "Where's
Abimbola?"

"Under guard," said Foss, with a hint of a smile. "I understand
Aysu and Kyreth are meeting this afternoon to discuss the matter
of the Cra."

"You know I'm right, Foss," said Eliza, eager to make her case
again. "The Mancers should have done something about the Cra
ages ago. I think you're all too used to relying on a Sorceress, aye.
Ever since my mother disappeared, the Mancers have just had
these big missions, like finding me, or maintaining the Arctic

barriers, or separating the worlds, but you've nay paid any attention to evil beings that are still crossing over and hurting people."

Foss frowned. "Mancer policy is a complicated matter and not for us to dictate," he said. "But I am interested in your choice of words, Eliza Tok. Do you believe the Cra are evil?"

"They kill *babies*," said Eliza, shocked.

"An unsavory practice, to be sure," said Foss. "Is a human who dines on veal evil, then? What of the wolf who kills the lamb?"

"Wolves are just animals, aye. They dinnay make choices like intelligent beings," said Eliza. "And eating veal is nay the same as murdering a baby."

"So the Cra are evil because they are intelligent, self-aware and feed on other intelligent and self-aware beings?"

"I spec so. Foss, I'm tired and I've nay had breakfast and I cannay think about this right now. Are you saying you dinnay think the Cra are evil?"

"I have no fondness for them," said Foss. "A human life is indeed a precious thing and the Cra should be kept from Di Shang, without question."

"Lah, so?"

"It is a mere matter of definitions. What is evil? Can a thing be evil in nature? Or does evil reside in choice? The Cra are what they are and cannot choose to be otherwise, in spite of their intelligence. Abimbola Broom, on the other hand, made a heinous choice. Are they both evil? Is one, having an irremediable nature, more evil than the other, who goes against his better nature?"

Charlie put his head down on the table with a thud. "I define evil as the pointless debating of philosophical questions while one's friends slowly starve," he said.

Eliza laughed but she was troubled. "Lah, evil is just a word. The point is that the Cra murder babies and have to be stopped." She paused and added, "Kyreth called them evil, too."

Foss nodded sadly. "Let us go to the kitchens and see if we can find some food for the two of you."

"Hooray Foss!" cheered Charlie. "You'll find redemption for your twisted soul yet!"

Charlie left at dusk. Eliza went out to the grounds with him to say goodbye. A large raven swooped down and landed nearby. It was promptly joined by another.

"You'll be back in time, nay?" Eliza asked him, glancing at the ravens. "Even a day or two late will throw everything off."

"You can count on me, Cap'n."

"Stop calling me that."

"But it suits you! Dinnay worry, you'll nay be stuck here."

"Why dinnay you stay?" she suggested hopefully. "It might be fun, aye. Or relaxing. Like a vacation."

"A vacation where everybody hates me except you and you're too busy to spend any time with me. Tempting, but I think I'll take off for a while."

Eliza sighed. "Where are you going to go?"

"Just exploring a bit."

Charlie never told her where he went when he wasn't with her. She liked to imagine that one day she would be free enough to see more of the worlds with him but that day seemed far in the future. Another raven dropped from the sky and landed at her feet with a sharp squawk.

"I dinnay know how they get through the barriers," said Eliza, looking at it uneasily. "Kyreth doesnay like it. They're nay supposed to be here."

"I think letting you in means letting them in," commented Charlie, unfazed as three more ravens descended. "Lah, I'll leave you with your friends. Take care of yourself, Eliza. Nice work with whatsisname, by the way."

"I couldnay have done it without you. Be careful, Charlie!"

"Self-preservation is what I'm best at," he said with a wink. His face changed all at once, feathers bursting from his head and neck, his body lengthening out into the golden, muscled body of a lion. Huge wings unfurled from his shoulders. No matter how many times she saw him change, it never ceased to amaze Eliza. She could feel the barriers around the Citadel making way for him. He surged into the air and away, leaving her in the grounds with the six ravens.

For months now they had been appearing around her in twos and threes and sometimes more. At first, she had eagerly assumed that her Guide was being made known to her. Every Sorceress had a Guide that took the form of an animal. In Tian Xia the Faithful had tattooed a raven on her left palm and a dagger pointing towards her on her right. She had tried to speak to the ravens in the Language of First Days but they showed no sign of understanding her and did not respond. Kyreth counseled her to be cautious. It was possible, after all, that they were spies or some new trick of the Xia Sorceress. The Mancers had done what they could to block Nia from contacting Eliza through dreams and visions as she used to do. The idea that the Sorceress might have found another way to watch her made Eliza feel a bit queasy.

They stood now, their feathers bright black, peering at her expectantly. She had no idea what they were expecting, though. She sat down in the grass and looked back at them, waiting, until the sky was entirely dark, pricked with stars.

"Eliza."

A Mancer was approaching. She could not see his face but from his stride, smooth and confident, and the tenor of his voice, she recognized Obrad of the Emmisariae, manipulator of earth.

"Hello," she said.

"We are all very glad you have returned," he said.

"Aye, Kyreth couldnay stop gushing about how happy he was to see me," said Eliza.

Obrad laughed, rather forcedly, she thought. "He is concerned for your safety, as are we all. And yet what you did was motivated by noble intentions."

"Thank you." Eliza was surprised that Obrad, of all the Mancers, should voice such an opinion. She had always felt awkward with him, more so than with the others, because he had been intended for her mother Rea, a great Sorceress before Nia took her power and all her memories. She imagined that he, even more than the others, must feel stingingly how much stronger her

Magic would be if he had been her father. Of course, she wouldn't have been Eliza at all in that case but some other girl, a powerful Sorceress raised with Magic from an early age. Perhaps that non-existent girl would not fight with Kyreth so much. No doubt they would all prefer that girl who didn't exist. Maybe even Foss.

"I personally will take care of this matter with the man," he continued. "I have already contacted Judge Adil in Kalla and informed him of the case."

"Thank you," said Eliza again. The ravens hopped closer to her, forming a tight little circle. Obrad noticed them but said nothing. She wondered if she was expected to say more, but she couldn't think of anything.

"It is good to have you back," said Obrad at last. "Eliza."

"Thanks." Eliza was beginning to feel like a broken record. "Goodnight."

"Goodnight."

The odd conversation left her feeling she needed a bath, so she got up and headed back to the south wing. The ravens hopped aside so she could walk unobstructed and did not follow her, remaining a dark clump on the lawn, watching her disappear into the Citadel.

It was good to sleep in a bed again. She dreamed of flying, the world far beneath her, and Kyreth's voice shouting at her the whole time from somewhere she couldn't see. She woke, or thought she woke, in the middle of the dream to see a woman standing over her. She was dressed all in black, with cropped white hair and darting hazel eyes.

"Why are you so angry?" asked the woman.

Eliza sat up in the bed, reaching instinctively for the dagger under her pillow.

"Who are you?" she demanded, her voice still thick with sleep.

"My skin is full of wool and fleas or I would show you," the woman said plaintively. "My eyes are full of broken glass and my tongue is caked with earth, I cannot *see*, I cannot *tell*. It's difficult.

This is not the finest room. My room is not fine at all. No, I should not say so, it is very fine, very fine indeed, I am like a queen there, queen of what realm? But I do not like stones and I do not like the air much at all, there is no rest, there is no rest."

Eliza did not know what to make of this strange speech but the woman looked somehow familiar. She had seen her before but could not think where.

"Dinnay I know you?" she asked.

The woman laughed, and then looked startled by the sound she had made. "Did you hear that?" she asked Eliza, and her eyes rolled about wildly in her head. "It was so unexpected. When I am quiet I think I am in the garden and he is kind to me and we have nothing to fear. Silence, silence. I long for it, my ears are buzzing always, there is no rest. How will you get there without a Guide? Oh, you mustn't get lost in the woods, child. It isn't safe. All manner of beast will prey on such tender flesh."

"I'm nobody's prey," said Eliza coldly. "It would be a foolish beast who'd take me for such." But she let go of the dagger.

"Have you seen my snake?" The woman asked, looking around. "We are often apart these days because we are not happy, not clear, and sometimes there are many and I don't know what to do. It never rains here and my room is fine but not the finest of all and the stones are cold and he is sad when he sees me. Look, I have been bitten, by mice or bats perhaps. They live in my bed between the sheets and they gnaw at me all night long. I cannot sleep."

The woman showed Eliza her bare arms covered in bite marks. They looked as if they had been made by human teeth, and indeed when Eliza noted the angle of the marks it was obvious the woman had bitten her own arms. Eliza frowned and looked up into her face again. "What's your name?" she asked.

"I have a present for you but I've forgotten it," the woman replied, suddenly backing towards the door, her eyes wide with alarm. "It will be colder before spring comes. Lost, poor thing. Have you no pity? I did not give it to you, it was a good day but then I forgot it. I will go and get it and you will make it all right. Promise me, child, you will make it all right."

"Wait," said Eliza, scrambling out of bed. "Where are you going?"

All at once it came to her. She knew where she had seen this woman before.

"Hurry, hurry, it will be colder and all the songs will be sung twice over before you find it, I know that, I know, and she is coming. No pity. What? What will you do?" With that, the woman turned and fled the room. Eliza chased after her down the hall. The woman was tall and long-legged and in spite of her white hair she was much faster than Eliza. Eliza lost sight of her on a set of stairs but continued chasing her footsteps. When she reached the southeast tower the woman was gone.

"Where are you?" Eliza called softly. There was no reply. She did not go back to bed. Instead she rounded the tower and made her way through the darkened portrait gallery of the east wing. Far below, on the lower floors of the east wing, the manipulators of wood slept in their chambers, but Eliza was not worried about being found wandering at night. The Mancers rose and went to bed with the sun and it would take a great deal to wake them now.

There were more than twenty stories of portrait rooms, the size and shape of each room varying depending on which kind of Mancer was depicted therein – manipulator of fire, water, metal, wood, or earth. The portraits depicted all the Mancers, living and dead, going back as far as the Great Mancer Simathien, and in vast halls on the upper floors, all the Shang Sorceresses, including Eliza. It was to the most recent of these halls she went, to the one that contained her portrait and her mother's. She knew the way by heart, even in the dark, for she often came here to look at the images of her ancestors. She murmured a spell and a tiny light appeared at her shoulder. She sent it up along one of the portraits to illuminate the face. There she was, the woman who had come to her room. In the portrait she had short fair hair and a steady gaze but it was unquestionably the same woman. Selva. Her grandmother. At the bottom of the portrait, the inscription read, *Killed in Battle.*

"I saw my gran last night," Eliza told Foss bluntly the next morning. They were in the Old Library, with its marble cliff-like shelves of books towering above them, hung with ropeways and ladders and amber lights. Foss thought the power of the Early Texts would help or inspire Eliza during their lessons and she was too polite to complain about their rather distracting smell.

Foss seemed preoccupied by something else and gave Eliza an impatient look. "What do you mean you *saw* her? In a dream? What a thing to say, Eliza Tok! Rea used to tell me her dreams. She thought to parse them for meaning no doubt, but the frequency with which she dreamed of cake suggested to me that –"

"It wasnay a dream, Foss. She came into my room and talked a lot of nonsense...ranting, aye, as if she was crazy, and then she ran off down the hall. I chased her but she disappeared near the southeast tower. I thought my grandmother was killed in the war. Is that nay what you told me?"

"Not in the war," said Foss, the light of his eyes fading and then flaring up again. "Not exactly, although it was the same time as the war. She went to Tian Xia on a mission and she did not return. I am not privy to the details, but Eliza, I am sure you did not see her."

"I did see her," said Eliza. "What kind of mission was it?"

"I have heard tell...well, it is only hearsay. You must ask Kyreth if you wish to know more," said Foss.

Seeing how anxious he was, Eliza dropped the subject immediately. Foss's position among the Mancers was still tenuous after he had let her escape the Citadel more than two years ago and she did not like to put him in a difficult position. If it was a matter of rooting out secrets, there were other ways.

"I'll ask him, aye," she said.

Foss looked grateful. "Then let us begin the lesson."

Since the summer they had been working on the basics of Deep Listening and Deep Seeing. She was pleased with how easy it had been to Listen to Abimbola Broom's thoughts, though of course it was only because he was human, like her, and hadn't known she was eavesdropping. She had been stretching the truth, however, when she told him that she would be able to find out what he had been doing by touching his coat. In theory it was possible, but Eliza's grasp of this Magic was shaky at best. She was able to catch glimpses of an object's history, things that had happened in the vicinity of the object, but she could not control the Magic enough to look methodically for a particular moment. Before her latest excursion, she had been practicing with the library table where they had their lessons. Foss had concluded that it would be a useful method of review to try and find particular lessons he had given her in the past by Deep Seeing through touch. She placed both her hands flat on the table, and then lowered her forehead to the table as well, as this sometimes helped her.

"I want you to find our lesson on simple barriers from last spring," said Foss now. "If you are going to run about chasing down the Cra, that would be a useful one for you to review."

The little jab irritated Eliza and she was still thinking about her grandmother appearing at her bedside, so it took a while for her to clear her mind and utter the words of the spell Foss had taught her, asking that the table reveal to her its past. She stared into the wood and it opened into nothingness before her eyes. It was as if she was peering through a gap in the table at herself and Foss in the library, seeing the present moment from somewhere outside time. But it was only a flash. She could not hold onto the moment or keep her concentration steady. She was swept into a storm of images of Mancers and books and fair-haired, serious Sorceresses, chanting and speaking incantations, a thousand voices clamouring together. Then, all these sounds and images burst into a black cloud of birds and scattered. One raven remained staring at her through the table, its eyes like little black stones. It opened its ugly beak and said, *She's coming.*

Eliza yanked her head off the table with such force that she fell over backwards in her chair. She lay on the floor in shock, her heart hammering against her ribcage, until Foss's face appeared above, looking down at her.

"It would appear, Eliza Tok, that the table is still stronger than you are."

"I need to talk to Kyreth *now*," she said.

Kyreth agreed with Foss that the trouble was her own mental weakness, her inability to control what was revealed to her. He put it rather less delicately than Foss, too.

"I know that and I'll work on it," said Eliza, struggling to remain patient. "But what about what the raven said? *She's coming.* What could that mean but Nia, lah?"

Kyreth shook his head thoughtfully. "We are working hard to maintain the barriers and I see no sign that she is any nearer to freeing herself than before. I will take what you saw as a warning to be even more vigilant, but it seems most likely that your own fear was taunting you, lost and overpowered by the spell as you were."

"Praps you're right," said Eliza hopefully. "Lah, it's the first time a raven has spoken to me. Even if it wasnay a real raven. I wish I knew if it was my Guide or not."

Kyreth stood and took a stack of heavy books down from his bookshelf.

"I have been waiting to give you these," he said. "I think now is the right time. These are the eight volumes of the Chronicles of the Sorceress. You will find some information here about Guides. Like the Guardians that enforce the limits of all things, of Magic, of Life, of Space and Time, they are mysterious to we who live in the worlds. They do not have desires as we do, but they have purpose. If the ravens are your Guide, it will become clear to you. In the meantime, take care, for they may signify something else."

"Will we study these books together?" asked Eliza, daunted by the pile on the desk before her.

"No, Eliza. These are for your private study. We will continue with the thirty-seventh commentary on Simathien's *Book of the Ancients.*"

"Oh."

This commentary was a very dry tome, which outlined the genealogy of all living beings, extrapolating from Simathien's statement that the mortal beings in Tian Di were Mancer, Mage, Demon, Human, and Animal. It was much impressed upon Eliza that the Mancer line had remained pure, but that mingling of the others had given rise to the vast diversity of beings in the worlds now. The Cra, she remembered, were part bird, part demon. They had left off last time tracing the elaborate lineage of Centaurs. She felt weary just thinking of it. Kyreth was scanning the shelves for the book. Unable to think of a natural lead-in, Eliza asked simply, "What happened to my gran?"

Kyreth's eyes flamed a little hotter as he turned them on her. "You know the answer to that, Eliza Tok."

"Nay the *exact* answer," said Eliza. "Only that she was killed."

"Why do you ask me this now?"

"Because..." She considered a moment and then lied, though she couldn't have said why. "I dreamed about her." She was not a good liar and had to look down at the desk as she spoke.

Kyreth leaned forward, suddenly intense. "What did you dream?"

"I dreamed she came to my room and talked a bunch of nonsense and then ran away. I chased her down the hallway, aye, but I couldnay catch her. Lah, the dream felt very...real."

Kyreth's eyes bored into her. She kept her own gaze trained on the Supreme Mancer's great gold hands, lined and powerful, folded together on the marble desk.

"Your grandmother Selva is dead, Eliza," said Kyreth in a low rumble. "She was felled by a Faery Curse, attempting to retrieve an object of great power jealously guarded by the Faeries."

Eliza continued staring at the table mutely.

"What did she say to you, Eliza? In this dream?"

"I dinnay remember much of it," admitted Eliza. "She kept talking about stones and snakes."

"Her Guide was a serpent," murmured Kyreth.

"She said she had a present for me. Oh! And she also said 'she's coming'. Like the raven!"

Kyreth sat back and the fire of his eyes dimmed enough for her to look up at his face. It was full of sorrow and she remembered that her grandmother Selva had been his wife. It was never really possible to think of Kyreth as her grandfather, though she knew it to be true.

"The spirit world is the greatest mystery of all," he said. "I do not know if this dream of yours was of your own creation or indeed your grandmother reaching out to you from the land of the dead. I cannot know. The very strangeness of her speech may be due to the difficulty of coherent communication between the living and the dead. In any case we should not ignore what she has said to you, most particularly since the vision of the raven has echoed it. You are being warned, and yet...*she is coming*...it may indeed refer to our enemy. It is well to be wary."

"Who else could it refer to?" asked Eliza.

"Perhaps your Guide," said Kyreth, with the faintest trace of a smile.

That night Eliza returned alone to the southeast tower. She walked the narrow corridors around it, brushing her hand against the walls. She could feel the heavy enchantment on them. All the towers were protected in this way. There was no use even trying to conjure a door here. Of course, she could cut right through the wall with her dragon-claw dagger, but that would be a desecration of the Citadel and she dreaded to think what the consequences would be. She leaned against the wall, pressed her cheek to the cool stone.

"Are you there?" she whispered.

The night was silent and still, and gave her no reply. As she made her way back to her bedroom in the dark, all the things she did not know and all the things she had to fear seemed terribly near, massed against her and invisible behind a wall of secrets.

CHAPTER

3

The weeks flew by, then a month, and then two months. With January came a biting frost, unusual this far south. The sensational trial of Abimbola Broom began in the capital and the Emmisariae were frequently gone but Eliza scarcely had time to pay attention to it. Her days were filled entirely with her studies. She spent mornings in the strenuous practice of Deep Seeing with Foss. After lunch she went to Kyreth's study and they ploughed through dense Commentaries until dusk, when he dismissed her. By evening her head was pounding and her eyes were swimming. Even so, she could not resist picking up the Chronicles of the Sorceress and reading until her eyes would not stay open any longer. Here at last was a book that might tell her something about herself, her heritage, who or what she was.

The book began at the very beginning of the Worlds, when it was still One World. Faery Dominion in the Early Days of Tian Di had been near absolute. Humans slaved in their mines, the Demons formed their army, and the Mancers were their Scribes and Record-Keepers. Though Mages often lived solitary lives in far-flung places, they too had to answer to the Faeries when called upon for a potion or a spell. Everything changed when the Great Mancer Simathien organized the Mancers to build a Citadel deep in the Irahok mountains and began in secret to assemble a Library there. He married a human Sorceress by the name of Zara and she was his partner in this task. Refused entry and jealous, Zara's twin sister Morhanna told the King of the Faeries, Amadeo, of the Citadel and the Secret Library. When the King laid claim to it, Simathien persuaded the Mancers to erect barriers around the Citadel to keep out the Faeries and their Magic. Outraged, the Faeries sent their army of Demons to destroy the Mancers. The Sorceress Zara turned herself into a giant brown bear with an impenetrable hide and in this form she decimated the Demon army. The story of the battle took up several pages and Eliza skimmed through it to the part where Simathien and Zara bore a daughter, first in the long line of Mancer-born Sorceresses. They named her Quyen. When Quyen was three years old, a hawk came and carried her off to the Yellow Mountains. The Mancers were appalled, Zara bereft, but Simathien told them not to pursue the hawk. A year later the hawk returned with the child. She knew all the ways of birds and grew up to be a powerful Sorceress. From this time on, the Sorceress was always trained by, and later married to, one of the Mancers, while the mystical Citadel moved about the farthest reaches of Tian Di to elude the ever-wrathful Faeries.

As winter set in, Eliza came to the separation of the worlds. She read huddled under her covers for warmth until she hadn't the strength to maintain her tiny conjured light and it faded and winked out. The Sorceress Ebele begged the Mancers to give aid to the humans, who were rising up against the Faeries in futile and bloody rebellions. In the final, greatest act of Old Magic in all the history of Tian Di, Karbek initiated the separation of Tian Di into two worlds, Di Shang and Tian Xia. Karbek was the first Mancer to bear the title of Supreme Mancer and Ebele the title of Shang Sorceress. Her Guide was a lynx and it was written that her mother gave birth to them together, as if they were twins.

From then on, the Chronicles dealt with the great feats of Sorceresses who guarded the Crossing, how they turned back and banished all would-be invaders. Some Sorceresses had lived in relatively peaceful times and were dispensed with in a page or less that recounted who she had married, when she had given birth and how she had died. Every Sorceress, it seemed, met the same end. She won every battle until she lost one. Some of them were quite old when they finally fell, but no Sorceress retired. Eliza woke most mornings with her face pressed against the pages of the open book and was wracked with guilt when she found she had drooled all over a page about Freda's banishment of a cohort of invading giants in the late Middle Days.

At last Eliza came to her grandmother. Selva's Guide was a serpent that had been found wrapped around the baby in her cradle just days after her birth. Eliza read that while her great-grandmother Minorr fought valiantly in the war, banishing a great many of the Cra, giants, trolls and harrowghasters, the various mixed descendants of the vanished Demon race who flocked to Di Shang to prey on weak humans, Selva was sent to Tian Xia as soon as she had given birth to a daughter, to obtain something called the Gehemmis. She lost her life under a Faery Curse, and was greatly mourned, was all the book said. Eliza stared at the page, stunned. The Chronicles recorded in elaborate detail the final battle of each Sorceress since the Middle Days. Whether the Sorceress was felled by a horde of half-hunters, a giant with enchanted weapons, Faeries or evil wizards, the how and the why was written down in the most reverential language. And yet here, nothing at all.

Eliza had seen the word *Gehemmis* in one of the earlier books. She flipped through the pages until she found it. Indeed, four thousand years ago a famed Sorceress named Lahja had gone to Tian Xia, faced the Horogarth of the North, and brought back one of the four Gehemmis . Three other Sorceresses were said to have died or disappeared in Tian Xia on a quest for one of these Gehemmis.

At the end of the eighth book, Eliza read in Kyreth's hand, *The Sorceress Rea was seen from a young age in the company of a fox. At that time it was a pet to her. As she grew older, she became possessive and secretive regarding her relationship with the fox and would not speak of it but it was assumed to be her Guide. Her power outstripped that of the Sorceresses for a thousand years or more but her devious character led her into difficulty. She married a human in secret and bore a daughter by him. The damage to the line of the Sorceress was irrevocable. She hid this daughter for reasons unknown. Her greatest accomplishment was holding the Sorceress Nia in battle for one hundred days while the Mancers built her prison.* The next line, *She gave her life in this act of heroism,* was crossed out. The text continued: *When she was stripped of her power by the Sorceress Nia, she was stripped also of her Guide. There has been no sign of it since her rescue. Rea lives out the remainder of her life, crippled, amnesiac, and powerless, in the Great Sand Sea with the Sorma.*

There was nothing in the book about Eliza. She tried to imagine what might be written about her one day, another young Sorceress far in the future perhaps reading about the Sorceress Eliza. She couldn't think it would be terribly flattering. The first Sorceress without a Guide. Fathered by a mere human. Tricked by Nia into giving her a powerful book. Would she be given credit at least for finding out Abimbola Broom, for combating the Cra? What would be *her* final battle?

Eliza was looking through the table at her first lesson with Foss more than two years ago. It wavered unsteadily before her eyes. She could not hear anything but a rush of wind or wings. Foss looked distorted in the image, his eyes shooting out beams of startling light, and she herself looked terribly young and on the verge of laughter. There was a sound behind her and then her grandmother was looking at her through the table.

"No pity, then?" she said sadly, and her face fell away, a chasm rushing up to meet Eliza. She raised her head from the table, gripping its edges to steady herself.

"Pardon my interruption," said Aysu, standing next to Foss across the table from Eliza. Aysu was considered the strongest of the five Emmisariae. Like Foss, she was a manipulator of water. Winter was her Ascendency and so her power was now at its height. During this season, she was second only to Kyreth. Eliza was surprised to see that she looked weary, her face drawn and her eyes somewhat dimmer than usual.

"I would like to show you something," she said to Eliza.

Foss and Eliza exchanged a look and followed Aysu out of the

Library. She led them in silence down to the ground floor of the north wing, and then further down the winding stone steps that led into the dungeons.

Eliza smelled them before she saw them – the putrid scent of damp feathers and oily skin that she had come to know so well. It made her skin crawl. She did not need to conjure a light, for the brilliance of the Mancers' eyes lit up the dungeons. The small stone cells were full of the Cra, crouched and hissing and spitting, their wings straining against the invisible barriers that held them, their sharp-clawed fingers pressed up against unseen walls. There were hundreds of them. Eliza knew she should be elated. Instead, her mind was flooded with memories of all those mornings she had crouched by rivers and streams, washing their sticky black blood from her dagger and hands, gagging and weeping with disgust.

"Kyreth will not see you this afternoon," said Aysu once they had passed right through the dungeons and re-emerged on the ground floor, where the manipulators of water had their chambers. "There is much to do."

"We will continue our lesson, then," said Foss. "Perhaps outside. We could use some fresh air."

Aysu left them and Foss and Eliza walked out into the chill winter air, breathing in deeply to rid their nostrils of the stench of the Cra.

"You have persuaded Kyreth to do a good thing," said Foss carefully, after allowing several minutes of silence to pass. "But do not think it was indifference that kept him from doing it before. The Emmisariae are powerful and we have been forced to do without them these past many days as they rounded up the Cra. Given the necessity of maintaining the barriers in the Arctic, it was a calculated risk to let them go. Kyreth had been divided on the matter for some time and at last concluded it was necessary for *your* sake, to keep you from placing yourself in harm's way and taking justice into your own, may I say, *inexperienced* hands. That is a dangerous thing to do, Eliza Tok."

"I know," said Eliza. She wanted to tell Foss how much she had hated hunting them, how relieved she was to have it finished, but somehow the words wouldn't come. "I've been reading a lot," she said instead. "About the Sorceresses before me."

"Yes, you mentioned. The Chronicles." Foss seemed relieved to have a change of subject. "For some years now I have been working on a Commentary on chapter six of the final volume. You must understand, Eliza, that the earlier texts were written long after the fact and are therefore not entirely reliable. They are myths, essentially, legends passed down for thousands of years. Did Zara ever exist? We believe so but Simathien himself mentions her only once in his Book of the Ancients. Some believe she is a composite of more than one Sorceress. Morhanna is called her twin sister, but how can this be, when each Sorceress bears only one daughter? Were they the first Sorceresses? Have there been two lines of Sorceresses from the beginning, as the Book of Origins suggests, or did one line separate into two at some point? The Chronicles raise as many questions as they answer, in my opinion, but provide *fascinating* reading all the same. Yours is a complicated heritage, Eliza Tok, and one to be proud of!"

He looked ready to continue for some time and so Eliza had to interject her question quickly, a skill she had perfected by now, "What about these Gehemmis that get mentioned? Sorceresses going to Tian Xia to get them?"

"An example, Eliza Tok, of the unreliability of the Chronicles. The Gehemmis, supposedly, are gifts of the Ancients guarded by the Four Immortal Powers of Tian Xia. They are said to be endowed with the essence of Old Magic, possessing untold power. But do they exist, in fact? In the records of the Mancers you will find that sending a Sorceress on a quest for a Gehemmis has always been terribly controversial, quite simply because many Mancers do not *believe* in the Gehemmis." He gave Eliza a sharp look suddenly. "Have you spoken to Kyreth about this?"

"Nay about the Gehemmis, exactly," she said. "But he told me my gran died of a Faery Curse, aye, and it says in the Chronicles that she was trying to get one of the Gehemmis from the Faeries."

"Yes," said Foss, relieved. "And one Sorceress is said to have succeeded and obtained a Gehemmis from the Horogarth four thousand years ago."

"I read about that. Her name was Lahja," said Eliza.

"And yet, where is this Gehemmis? If she obtained it, why do we not have it here in the Citadel? And is it possible that a mere Sorceress, pardon me Eliza, could truly face the Horogarth, one of the children of the Ancients, and take something from him? I am skeptical, Eliza Tok, I am very skeptical."

"Lah, then so am I," said Eliza, smiling up at him. At that moment, a large raven flew straight at them, screaming, its beak wide. They both ducked, covering their faces, and then it was gone.

"I dinnay think they're friendly," said Eliza, her voice shaking, looking around her for the vanished raven.

"It is too soon to say," replied Foss with a frown. "Let us return to the Library."

Early the following morning Kyreth summoned Eliza to his study.

"The Shade approaches," he said dryly. "Have you made plans?"

Eliza's heart leaped but she kept her voice steady and answered as politely as she could. "When I asked you in the summer, you gave me permission to spend Winter Festival with my parents and the Sorma. Like last year, aye."

"I remember," said Kyreth. "But Winter Festival is still two weeks away."

"I know. But I've nay seen my parents in months and the journey is tiring," she said.

"The Festival lasts six days, does it not?"

"Yes."

"That is a long absence, Eliza. And you have only recently returned to us."

"When I come back, I promise to stay and study without interruption until the summer," she said.

"I will hold you to that, Eliza. Remember that you are under our protection and need only to call us if you need us." He indicated the crystal that hung around her neck. Eliza touched her hand to it and nodded.

It was their little ritual. He couldn't stop her, really. She would not be kept against her will. As long as she was free to come and go, she studied hard. But for the sake of politeness she pretended to ask permission and he pretended to give it. Before leaving the room, she made herself look into his terrible, blazing eyes.

"Thank you for bringing in the Cra," she said.

Kyreth made a sign in the air and the door swung open behind her.

The gryphon circled upwards, leaving the Citadel far below, then veered northeast, towards Kalla. Eliza felt lighter by the second. She flattened her body against the gryphon's back to keep warm. She loved the sense of absolute freedom she got when flying with Charlie and it was only heightened by the fact that nobody knew where they were going. She had not been entirely lying to Kyreth when she said she was going to spend time with her parents. She would indeed go to see them in the desert. Just not immediately.

They took a winding route through the sky, avoiding cities and highly populated areas, flying low over the rich farmland of the interior provinces and stopping frequently to build fires and warm themselves, for the air was bitterly cold. In spite of the gryphon's speed, it took them a full day to reach the capital. They spent the night in an abandoned barn they had used for shelter before, an hour outside of Kalla. This far north the ground was thickly covered with snow, and even with the blankets they had stored in the barn they had to keep the fire going all night, which meant sleeping in shifts. This didn't always go as planned. Eliza woke just before dawn, stiff and shivering, the fire dead beside her. Charlie had nodded off.

"Wake up," she said crossly, nudging him and giving him an angry look. He sat up and looked from her to the dead fire a couple of times.

"Sorry," he mumbled. "Should've been a polar bear, aye."

Shivering uncontrollably, she found the duffel bag they kept hidden in the barn. She pulled out a girl's school uniform and ducked behind a broken-down tractor to put it on – a navy flared skirt and jacket and a striped silk tie over a crisp white blouse.

"Come on," she said. "We dinnay want to miss breakfast. Lah, but I'm frozen!"

"Sorry," Charlie mumbled again. He stumbled out of the barn and morphed into a gryphon, more slowly than usual. Awkward and terribly cold in her skirt, Eliza clambered onto his back and he took off. It was important to reach the school while it was still dark. A girl on a gryphon would hardly go unnoticed in Kalla.

Ariston Hebe Secondary School, the most prestigious school in the Republic, was a large ivy-walled compound with rolling grounds. They landed in the snowy arboretum and Charlie turned into a boy wearing a navy school uniform. They waited there, shivering, until 6:30. When the breakfast bell rang, they ran for a supply closet window they had jimmied open months earlier, crawled in, and cautiously opened the door. The hall was full of students still putting on their jackets and doing up their ties as they hurried to the Dining Hall. Charlie and Eliza were able to slip into the mob unnoticed. The Dining Hall was a very grand room with crystal chandeliers hanging from the ceiling and paintings of famous alumni on the walls. They scanned the crowd hopefully, slowly warming up, until somebody crashed into Eliza with a squeal, crushing her in an embrace. Eliza stumbled and laughed and hugged her best friend back.

While Eliza loved Holburg, it had always been too small for Nell, and she had found her way off the island as soon as possible by winning the only scholarship to Ariston Hebe offered to a student from the archipelago. Eliza had worried at first that her friend would not fit in but Nell took to citified sophistication like a fish to water. She remained top in all her classes, excelled in sports, and had a following of hangers-on as ardent as those she'd left behind in Holburg. Life in the elegant old school, with more students than the entire population of the island she'd grown up on, was a dream come true for Nell, and all of Kalla was just outside the gates. A closed gate and a mere wall were no great impediment for a girl like Nell.

The three friends filled their breakfast trays with eggs and sausages and toast and joined Nell's class at one of the long mahogany tables. Nell's school friends were wildly curious about Eliza and Charlie, who turned up on occasion and gave the impression of not having school or parents or homes or anything normal themselves. Only Nell would be so audacious as to steal uniforms for outsiders and then have them in for breakfast. When they asked Nell who these mysterious friends were, giggling about Charlie, who always caused quite a sensation, she said coyly that they lived outside the city but liked to drop by. She could have made up a convincing story about them but it was so much more fun being secretive. Eliza sat next to Nell and Charlie slid into a space across from them, delighting the girls on either side of him.

"Have you heard about Abimbola Broom?" Nell asked meaningfully as they sat down. Her shiny chestnut brown hair was cut in a stylish bob that framed her face perfectly and her violet eyes were sparkling. "His daughter used to go here, aye. Isabella Broom."

"Basically an imbecile," one of Nell's group chimed in, eager to contribute.

"She was pulled out before the trial began," said Nell. "Nobody knows where she's gone."

"Poor girl," said Eliza.

Nell shrugged. "If he's so awful, lah, she's better off without him. Listen, you're both coming to Holburg for Winter Festival, nay? You have to!"

"I'm going to try my very very best," said Eliza. Nell pulled a face. Eliza's very very best was not what she wanted to hear.

"We'll be there," said Charlie firmly. Eliza gave him a look. He shrugged and said, "I'll be there, anyway."

"It depends on my parents, lah," said Eliza. "I dinnay know if I can convince them."

At this, all of Nell's group looked very curious and waited for more. But there was no more.

"What about your family?" one of Nell's friends asked Charlie flirtatiously.

"Oh, them," said Charlie vaguely, and left it at that.

"How have you been getting on at school?" Nell asked Eliza. Their breakfast conversations were always coded in this way.

"Lots of new stuff," said Eliza. "But Kyreth and I are still arguing a lot."

"He's the principal at her school," Nell tossed off by way of explanation to the others.

"You argue with the principal?" one of the girls asked, perplexed.

"*All* the time," said Eliza. "But the librarian is a prize. Lah, but you know what's strange? I ran into...the *agriculture* teacher a couple of times, and he was being sort of...friendly, aye."

By this she meant Obrad, the manipulator of earth. Nell picked up on it immediately.

"Oh-oh," she said, making a little O with her mouth. "That cannay be good!"

"What do you mean?"

Nell shot Charlie a pointed look. He sighed resignedly and struck up a separate conversation with the girls around them so that Eliza and Nell could talk more freely.

"What do you mean?" hissed Eliza again.

"I mean that he missed his chance with your ma when she snuck off and married your da," Nell whispered. "But praps he thinks he can still marry a Sorceress. As in, *you!*"

This had never occurred to Eliza and she was left quite speechless with horror. Charlie heard it even though he was carrying on another conversation, and exploded, "WHAT?"

This caused a number of the students at the tables around theirs, as well as a few breakfast monitors, to look over at them. "*What?*" he hissed, more quietly.

"That's how it works, nay?" said Nell. "You *are* supposed to marry one of them, lah!"

She glared at Charlie, who went back to his conversation with the startled group of girls. "Anyway, the royal family of

Boqua doesnay want anybody to *know* that their son was born with six fingers on each hand because they're very superstitious about that kind of thing down there..."

"It's a great honour for the Mancer in question, nay?" Nell whispered into Eliza's ear, around a mouthful of buttery toast. "You said Obrad wasnay happy about being passed over before. Do they let you have any say in it, lah? Are there any young and handsome Mancers or are they all hundreds of years old and scary looking?"

Eliza had gone quite white. "I feel sick," she said, pushing her breakfast tray aside. Having finished her own breakfast, Nell piled Eliza's plate on top of her own and began on what was left of Eliza's.

"You should rebel, aye," said Nell. "Your ma had the right idea."

"I agree," said Charlie, interrupting his own story again.

"Lah, and speaking of young and handsome, there's Julian." Nell waved over a blond boy with his tie still undone. "He's my boyfriend, aye. I'll introduce you."

"WHAT?" Charlie exploded again.

"Stop it. Everybody's looking at you. He's in the year above me. Top in Math in the school, aye, and the fastest swimmer in his year. A coup, nay?"

"Is that...allowed?" asked Eliza, quite unprepared for this. Julian sat down with them, smiling in a friendly, half-awake sort of way. Eliza and Charlie eyed him suspiciously. After that, of course, they had to talk to Julian about the swim team and his plans for Winter Festival.

Nell had classes after breakfast and so Charlie and Eliza rested in her room. When the cleaner came by they hid in the large oak wardrobe, Nell's dresses hanging down around them, trying not to breathe too loudly. As soon as they heard the door click shut as the cleaner departed, Charlie said, "What did you think of Julian?"

"He seems...nice," said Eliza uncertainly.

"She's never mentioned him before, lah."

"No. I spose he's a new...development."

"Why do you sound like that?"

"Like what?"

"The way you sound – 'He seems...*nice.* He's a new...*development.*'"

"It's just...surprising."

"Yes. That's what it is, aye. Surprising."

They sat in the wardrobe a minute longer, until Charlie said, "Why are we still sitting in here?"

Eliza got the giggles and they pushed the doors open and scrambled out. At noon, Nell burst in with some lunch for them.

"By the Ancients, they're piling on the tests before Winter Festival!" she groaned, flopping onto the bed. "Were you two horrendously bored, cooped up here all morning?"

"We kept ourselves entertained, lah," said Charlie. "I turned into a river goblin to scare the cleaner. That was fun."

"You didnay," Nell grinned. "And I wouldnay have approved if you had. Esta is my source of insider gossip. Now, I need to talk to Eliza privately for a minute."

She looked pointedly at Charlie, who stared back at her, confused.

"Could you leave the room, please?" said Nell politely. "Just for a minute."

"What for?" asked Charlie.

Nell sighed in exasperation. "Just wait in the hall." She slid off the bed and shoved Charlie towards the door. He looked shocked but didn't protest, stepping out into the hallway and staring in at them. "Just stay there," said Nell, shutting the door on him. She turned back towards Eliza with a huge smile.

"Lah, I have a present for you," she said, and pulled a little parcel of pink paper out from under her bed.

"Thanks," said Eliza, unwrapping it. Inside were two crisp white bras with lace flowers on the straps. "Oh!" she exclaimed.

"You need them, aye," said Nell matter-of-factly. "I spec between the Mancers in the Citadel and your parents in the desert, nobody thinks of these things for you. Does your mother remember things like bras?"

"I dinnay think my underwear is high on anyone's list of priorities," said Eliza dryly. She should have been expecting something like this. It was Nell she'd turned to for supplies when she started menstruating, feeling quite unable to ask the Mancers.

"Good thing you have me," said Nell, pleased with herself. "Somebody who actually lives in the world! Try one on."

It was impossible to be self-conscious with Nell. Eliza took off the tie and shirt and awkwardly put the bra on. Nell did it up swiftly at the back.

"Better. I knew it would be the right size. How does it feel?"

"Sort of constricting," said Eliza. She put the shirt back on and fumbled with the buttons.

"You'll be grateful next time you have to run down a flight of stairs," said Nell. "And you'll get used to them, aye. Here, put this one away and I'll let Charlie back in."

Eliza stuffed the other bra hastily into her skirt pocket and shoved the paper back under the bed. Nell bounced over to the door and threw it open. Charlie was standing in the hall with his arms folded, frowning.

"Come in," said Nell grandly.

"What was all that about?" he demanded.

Nell gave him a look. "Dinnay you know what *private* means, Charlie?"

He ignored her and sat down on the bed with Eliza, who quickly did up her tie. To avoid his gaze, she picked up the book on Nell's bedside table.

"What's this?" she asked.

"Physics," said Nell. "It's one of my stronger subjects, but the Mentor really seems like he's *trying* to trip us up in the tests."

"I should get you to tutor me a bit, aye," said Eliza. "I dinnay learn any of this kind of thing anymore. I'm going to grow up knowing lots about Magic and nothing about anything else."

"Lah, I think you'll probably survive without Wennot's Sixth Law," said Nell.

A bird hit the window suddenly, hard, and fell out of sight. They all jumped.

"How horrible," said Nell, wincing. "I hope it's nay badly hurt."

Eliza was shaken. It had been a large, black bird. "Tell me about Wennot's Sixth Law," she said, ignoring the look Charlie was giving her. "See if your physics is as good as you say."

"It's one of the laws of motion," said Nell lazily. "Equal and opposite force, aye. It's why we dinnay float off into space or fall through the ground, for one thing. If you go and push on that wall, it will meet whatever force you push against it with an equal and opposite force and nothing will happen. You press your hand against the wall, aye, but the wall is also pressing against your hand with the same amount of force, in the opposite direction. Neither you nor the wall will give way."

"But if she uses Magic something will happen," said Charlie. "She could conjure a door between your room and the next, just like that, nay, Eliza?"

"P'raps," said Eliza.

"Of course you could!" said Charlie. "You're *excellent* at making doors! You should have seen how great she was getting into that creep's house!"

"Aye, tell me about *that!*" cried Nell. "So much more interesting than Wennot and his laws of motion!"

They became so absorbed in their conversation about Abimbola Broom and eating their lunches that the ruckus outside had been going on for quite a while before they became properly aware of it. Charlie suddenly leaped off the large bed with its quilt embroidered with the school logo and went to the window. The girls became aware of the yelling and cawing outside as he did so. They followed him to the window and the three of them stood and stared.

The grounds were covered with ravens, black as ink on the white snow. They were on the ground, in the trees, all over the wall and the gate, hundreds of them, cawing furiously. Students were shouting and pointing and a few teachers were waving sticks at the ravens to try and frighten them away but the ravens were not in the least frightened. One raven flew past the window, looked straight at Eliza, and opened its beak in what was almost a scream. Then all the ravens took to the air *en masse*, swirling before the window like a dark tornado, shrieking and cawing.

"What by the Ancients is going on?" whispered Nell.

"I dinnay know," said Eliza hollowly. She turned away from the window and covered her ears. Charlie drew the curtains firmly.

The noise continued all day, with ravens covering the roof of the school as well, as Nell reported later. Charlie and Eliza left under cover of dark, promising Nell they would see her again soon. The mob of ravens followed them like a black cloud through the night sky, cawing, from Kalla all the way to the Karbek Mountains, the longest mountain range in Di Shang and home of the volcano Harata.

CHAPTER

4

As the sun rolled up over the horizon, Foss knelt in his chamber and let his mind slip into the morning trance with the ease of long habit. Waiting for him as always was the black crab on the dark, wet sand. The crab scuttled up the sand, away from the water, to where five blackened, twisted stones stood upright, stretching towards the sky. The crab moved among them sideways, his black fore-claws waving and snapping. Although the sky was clear, the air tasted heavy with rain. Beyond these stones were more stones and they grew taller and more plentiful until he found himself in the midst of a forest of black stones, tortured and charred like lumps of cooled lava. He could feel how they strained from within. There came then a deep cracking sound from all around and the stones splintered and fell away. At the core of each was a Mancer, unmoving, silent. They stared out with sightless eyes and then slowly, slowly twisted and darkened into stones once again. The sky groaned deeply and seams appeared in the blue. Something dark as blood began to seep through and spill downwards in smoky threads. With his claw, the crab wrote in the sand, *Kyreth does not trust you*, then fled back towards the sea.

Foss opened his eyes and sighed. This was hardly news to him. When Eliza fled the Citadel two and a half years ago, Foss had spent a short time in the dungeons for letting her go (colluding with her, they'd called it – a bit of a stretch but he had not tried to defend himself) and he had been threatened with expulsion. The power of the Mancers was uniform, interwoven, and dissent was dealt with harshly. Even though he had been officially restored to his position as Spellmaster upon Eliza's demand, he was shut out of the inner workings of the Citadel, no longer invited to important meetings. If he went to Kyreth and told him of today's trance, omitting the coda of course, how would Kyreth interpret it? It was an unsettling vision, and once he would have reported it immediately. But today he decided to keep it to himself until he understood it better. If something were much amiss he would not be the only one to have sensed it.

The gong rang and he left his chambers, joining the manipulators of water filing out of the north wing and across the grounds towards the Inner Sanctum. They took their places and, when Aysu gave her command, the manipulators of water began to call upon the power of the seas and the rains. Anargul gave the same command and the manipulators of wood began to call upon the trees that covered the earth. Then Ka called out his command and the manipulators of fire called upon the interior of the earth, the sun and the stars. Trahaearn called out and the manipulators of metal called upon the ore that flowed in the veins of the earth. At last Obrad called out and the manipulators of earth called upon the Earth itself. Foss felt within him the deep, eternal pull of the ocean, vast and secretive. He felt the gathering of rain and the swift rushing journey of rivers making their way from the mountains to the sea. There was something in this too large to be called joy but it was a kind of joy nonetheless. In a single voice they spoke the old words, made themselves conduits for the forces of water, and the power that was drawn into them was pushed out again as Magic. Now it was for Kyreth and the Emmisariae to guide this Magic to its purpose. Kyreth had already begun the lengthy and difficult recitation of the Sperre-Tahora, the Barrier Incantation. Foss lent his entire will, his very self, to the task of channeling the Magic, and in his mind the ever-moving, overlapping layers of the Xia Sorceress's prison came into view.

He had once tried to explain to Eliza, as a sort of Deep Math lesson, the structure of this prison. It was largely his own design and he was prouder of it than of anything he had ever done. A single barrier, no matter how strong, would eventually fall before the Magical onslaught of a Sorceress as powerful as Nia. Instead, they had created a multi-layered series of barriers, not merely flat walls but grids and spirals and cones, an infinitely complex maze that was never still, each piece following its own pre-determined rotation. At the centre of all this was the approximately fifty square feet in which the Arctic Sorceress had lived for twelve years. She had of course sent spells of seeking into what gaps she could find, to try to unlock the secrets of the maze, but there was no way out. The Sorceress's seeking spells were lost in the continuing orbit and infinitely varied geometric patterns of the barriers. It was indeed a thing of beauty. It was, Foss believed, a mathematical perfection.

This daily task of strengthening the barriers had become more critical and also more taxing since the Sorceress had used Eliza to steal the Book of Barriers. While her thousands of seeking spells swirled and eddied, lost among the barriers, she began to make holes. Even with the Magic outlined in the Book of Barriers, she could only make a hole in one layer at a time and, because of the complexity and constant movement of the barriers, this did her little good. The layers shifted levels and slid to and fro, so that a hole she made in the layer nearest to her might soon be lost somewhere near the centre of the barriers, entirely inaccessible, useless.

However, the Mancers knew better than to underestimate the Sorceress. They were concerned by the holes. They sealed up as many as they could and added continually to the barriers. Foss had mapped out the Sorceress's efforts on charts in the Library and often pored over them with Kyreth or Aysu late into the night, trying to determine a pattern. Her choices seemed to be entirely random. It was possible she was simply trying to alarm and distract them, to waste their power in patching holes while she worked some other Great Magic to bring down the barriers. But strong as she was, the barriers of the Mancers were nigh unbreakable. Today, as every day, with the four directions of the compass and the five elements they drew upon, the Mancers poured all their power into the task of strengthening and rebuilding the barriers, protecting themselves and the worlds from the most dangerous foe they had ever known.

In the afternoon, Foss was summoned to speak with Kyreth. The Spellmaster was surprised and more than a little apprehensive. Kyreth spoke to Foss rarely these days and only to lay out Eliza's curriculum. He stood before the Supreme Mancer stiffly while Kyreth looked down at his marble desktop.

"Eliza left yesterday," said Kyreth.

Foss wasn't sure if this was a question or a statement. He said nothing.

"How does she seem to you?" asked Kyreth.

"Much as usual," said Foss, taken aback by the question and the apparent sincerity with which the Supreme Mancer asked it. "She is diligent and makes good progress considering how late she has come to this. Her natural ability is not remarkable, for a Sorceress, but I think it is sufficient."

"I am referring to her manner. How does her *manner* seem to you?"

"Why do you ask?"

"I am concerned. She seems unstable to me. She is a deeply angry child, do you not think?"

"I think..." Foss paused before continuing, unsure of how blunt he should be. "I cannot claim to be an expert on human girls but I do not think she is unusual. She is fourteen years old and grew up without the discipline of her foremothers. What may strike you as excessive belligerence or even anger is, I believe, a result of ordinary adolescent turmoil. Not altogether ordinary, of course. She misses her father. Her life is anything but normal. But the attitude you refer to should not, I think, concern us unduly. She will outgrow it."

"And what do you think of her killing the Cra?"

"I do not weep for them."

"That is not what I asked."

"Where did she learn to kill? You left her at the mercy of a hound of the Crossing once. That was her first kill, was it not?"

Kyreth looked annoyed. "It was a test, and a necessary one at that. But self-defense is not the same as *hunting*. She has no self-control; she is too emotional. Anger drives her and she acts, pity drives her and she acts. She comes and goes as she wishes, she makes imperious demands of us. How are we to impress upon her the importance of her duty? Of *restraint*?"

"It is difficult for her," said Foss. "She was not raised among us. If you are asking me for advice, I can only say I believe she is doing her best and requires our patience."

Kyreth did not look satisfied but he nodded his head.

"Thank you, Spellmaster. I wished to hear your honest opinion and you have given it. She trusts you, I can see. You have great influence with her."

Foss laughed dryly. "I think it is an exaggeration to say I have any influence."

"She listens to you. She respects you. Tell me, have you ever spoken to her on the matter of an heir?"

Foss was quiet for a moment and then said simply, "She is still too young."

"I realize that. I am not saying she should be married now. Only that it is best she be prepared."

"We have not spoken of it," Foss replied.

"When she returns, I hope you will speak with her," said Kyreth. "We cannot risk another debacle such as Rea's marriage. You may go, Spellmaster. Chart the new holes in the Barrier and inform me immediately if anything worries you."

Foss hesitated, wondering if he should tell Kyreth what he had seen in his trance. But Kyreth was already turning away from him, towards the Scrolls, and so he bowed and left the study, saying nothing.

Di Shang was pockmarked with secret, hidden points of entry and exit to the Crossing, that mystical divide between the worlds. There were gaps in the atmosphere that led not into space but to the Crossing, so high up in the sky that they were not, as Charlie put it, human-friendly. There were other entries through boiling vents at the bottom of the ocean. There were whirlpools in rivers that might leave a drowning human or animal stranded on the shore of the Crossing, unable to go back. The Mancers maintained their own access to the Crossing through the dark wood of the Citadel but, of course, Eliza could not use that one without their knowing. The safest way was through certain volcanoes. Harata was a land-locked volcano, several hours east of Kalla. It was a dark red, towering hulk of a mountain, flat on top where its peak had exploded centuries ago.

The flight there was made horribly stressful by the trail of ravens pouring after them. Eliza could not shut out their ugly voices. She buried her hands and her face in the feathers of Charlie's neck and willed the journey to be over. When they reached the great lava beds of the volcano, the gryphon did not pause for an instant. He headed straight for the crater and plunged into a vent barely wide enough for his wingspan. The ravens did not follow further but circled and swarmed around the mountaintop. Eliza clung to the gryphon's neck as they shot through the darkness and heat. He landed on a sharp lip of rock that hung over a pool of steaming water and became a boy.

"Do your mojo," he said, breathless.

Eliza nodded and struggled to regain her composure. Even without the pursuit of the ravens, entry into this volcano was harrowing and working Magic afterwards was not easy. It was a law known to all who crossed over that something of great personal value must be given to the Boatman. Only beings of great power could command him. Eliza was the Shang Sorceress and so she ought to be able to command the Boatman, but so far the Boatman did not agree.

In the utter blackness of the cave, a white misty boat began to form. Eliza called to it in the Language of First Days, "*My power spans the worlds and that between the worlds, my power spans the skies and seas of Tian Di, my power is undivided. Where I walk is the ground and what I speak is the truth. The tide will come to me when I beckon, the moon will sink when I point to the horizon. Here I demand a bridge, here where I stand, here I call upon the Boatman of the Crossing, passage to be mine.*"

The boat came closer, solidifying into a long sloop with a single mast and sail. For a moment Eliza felt a little surge of hope, until she saw the Boatman at the bow. Translucent flesh stretched over knotted muscle and flowing blood; he was not easy to look at. She glimpsed a ghastly, mocking grin on his face. As always, Eliza could not meet his eyes, did not even know if he had eyes, so powerful was the Magic that kept her from looking at them.

"Dinnay you think she's getting better at it, lah?" Charlie asked the Boatman. "I thought that was quite convincing."

"Command me, will you, would-be Sorceress?" jeered the Boatman, as he did every time, ignoring Charlie. "Think you I need no payment? If you wish passage, how will you pay?"

"I willnay pay," said Eliza crossly.

The Boat began to fade.

"*Stay,*" Eliza commanded, which worked, but it didn't mean the Boatman would take them. Half-faded, he waited for the inevitable next step in this dance of theirs.

"Try again," Charlie said encouragingly.

"I cannay," said Eliza. Her limbs felt like wet noodles, she was damp with sweat from the flight down the vent, and she didn't have the energy to do it again. She sat cross-legged on the hard, hot rock and squeezed her eyes shut, reaching down into herself for the gift her mother's old friend and teacher Swarn had given her. When she spoke again, it was not with her own voice but with the command of the Warrior Witch, "*Bring me the Sorceress, Boatman.*"

The boat came clear again, and the Boatman stepped aside with a nasty smile, indicating that Eliza could board.

"And how will you pay for your passage, Shade?" sneered the Boatman.

"Dinnay pester Swarn. You know I'm included," said Charlie. The Boatman let him on as well.

"Lah, you dinnay *have* to give us a hard time," Charlie added.

"You know we're going to get across anyway."

"I will not be commanded," said the Boatman harshly, "by those with no power to command."

Eliza half wanted to apologize, for she thought it must be very annoying indeed for the ancient Boatman to have a girl like herself trying to boss him around. Instead she turned her back on him, breathing deeply as the boat sailed fast away from the rock and the black pool and Di Shang.

At sundown, Foss stood in the Library and inhaled. As his breath entered him he let the image in his mind filter into the air in his lungs. Then he exhaled slowly and a milky haze came out of his mouth, forming a square-foot replica of the Arctic barriers. He felt a surge of pride and joy when he saw it. It was an unsolvable puzzle in constant motion. He rotated the replica into the position it had been in when the Sorceress completed the most recent hole and froze it. He was impressed by her speed and precision. Because of the constant motion of the barriers, she had to move with them and work quickly in order to complete the shape she wanted. She did not allow for any careless rips or jagged edges. Each hole was a perfect circle, six feet in diameter. There were a great many of these holes but not enough of them to compromise the barriers as a whole. Each hole penetrated a single layer only. He left the replica frozen and with his breath created another, freezing this one where the previous hole had been made. The first one was bored through the centre of a giant sphere, which spun in a difficult-to-decipher orbit through the mass of barriers, then spun up to the top and rolled in a shrinking spiral over the top of the barriers before falling back to the centre. The second hole was through a flat, hard sheet that moved, along with several hundred others, very quickly back and forth across the bottom layer of barriers, intermittently rising up a few layers when a gap allowed it. These looked a bit like flying piano keys under invisible fingers. Foss looked carefully from one replica to the other but he could not work out a relation between the two holes.

He had two years' worth of charts marking out the trajectory of the barriers and the holes the Sorceress had made. Regular study of these charts had never revealed any logic or pattern to the holes. But his trance this morning had disturbed him. It may have been no more than a personal warning regarding Kyreth but the fear had been somehow greater than that. The charts were not three-dimensional and did not simulate the motion of the barriers. Perhaps in looking at complete moving replicas of the barriers, he would see something he had missed. It was not likely that the Sorceress was acting without a purpose. Breathing deeply, he brought forth another, then another. The sun set and he felt the pull to rest but he was too intent upon his task to obey it. It was the season of his ascendancy and he was strong enough to continue working his Magic through the night. The ghostly replicas filled the long passageways between the bookshelves, hundreds of them hovering at chest height in the air. Once he was finished he walked from the first to the last, examining each one closely. He set them into orbit and they began to spin and swirl and shift. Again, he went from one to the next and though he could not pin it down something unsettled him. There *was* a method to her assault on the barriers; he felt more and more certain. This was no game, no accident, no mere distraction. There was another puzzle now embedded in the puzzle he had made. She was cleverer than he was. She had understood perfectly the Deep Math of her prison. She was toying with it now in ways he did not understand and the fate of the worlds depended on his understanding. When dawn came he felt it like a tap on the shoulder and startled. He had no time to retire to his chamber, so he sat on the floor of the Library amid the barrier replicas and fell too quickly and uncontrolled into his trance.

The world was a ruin. The black crab leaped among the battered rocks and the sky crumbled overtop of them. Fire fell like rain.

Eliza looked up at the tatters of red cloud swirling in the sepia-coloured sky, that pitiless, unfriendly Tian Xia sky she had come to know so well. She was watching for something she did not see. Then she spotted it, falling fast towards her, a ball of light. In one fluid motion she pulled her bow taut and raised it to the sky, letting her Deep Knowing guide her arms and calculate the speed at which the object fell. She released the bow and the dark arrow shot through the ball of light, exploding it into a shower of sparks.

"The aim is good," said Swarn, who was standing back and watching with her arms folded. "But you lack force in all you do. You are precise, but weak."

They were standing in the middle of the dark marsh dotted with skeletal bracken. Swarn's house was a little hump in the distance, not really recognizable as a house at all from where they stood.

"It takes everything I've got just to fix on the right spot, aye," said Eliza. She wondered if Swarn could tell she was wearing a bra. She wondered if Swarn was wearing a bra. It seemed unlikely somehow. Definitely not a bra with lace flowers on the straps.

"Then you practice. Grow stronger. The aim should be easy by now, it should require nothing of you. When you face an opponent, you cannot just tap it between the eyes. You need to go right through the skull."

Eliza grimaced a little at that. Swarn bent and snatched up one of her long red spears. In her arm, lean and brown and muscled, it seemed to weigh nothing. She tossed it to Eliza effortlessly but Eliza knew enough to brace herself. The spear was enchanted iron and very heavy. Catching it nearly knocked her over.

"You are using your physical strength again," said Swarn impatiently. "You are a fourteen-year-old human child, Eliza! There are few beings as physically weak as you are. But you are not only a girl. You *are* the spear. You *are* the air. You *are* the ground. Are you not?"

Eliza inhaled slowly and raised the spear over her shoulder.

"Let it flow, let it flow," chanted Swarn. It was a feeling Eliza loved – when she could muster it. She felt like rushing water, a force of nature, and the spear in her grasp was subject to this force, a twig in a torrent. She could exert on it the same power as the sun did over the planets. It would follow its course, unresisting.

"Take care," warned Swarn. She read Eliza's feelings well, for Eliza was tempted to unleash this power she felt, to send the spear as far as it would go. But that was not the purpose of the exercise. She caught a flash from the corner of her eye and pivoted, hurling the spear straight through the ball of light. The spear plunged into the marsh several meters away, dripping fire.

"Better," said Swarn. "Much better."

Now that it was done, Eliza felt drained and weary. "I need to rest," she said.

Swarn shook her head.

"You do not push yourself hard enough, Eliza. How will you get stronger if you stop whenever you are tired? Here."

She tossed Eliza another spear and this time Eliza caught it easily, but the surge of power faded fast. She saw the ball of light too late this time and tried to throw the spear, but her aim was poor and her strength gave out. The spear made an ungainly crash to the swampy ground just a few feet away. Eliza's knees buckled and she sat in the mud. Swarn looked at her as if she was an insect.

"I'm nay as strong as my ma," said Eliza rather angrily, because she knew that was what Swarn was thinking.

"That is not the issue," said Swarn. "You barely try."

"I *am* trying." Eliza could have wept with frustration. Whenever she left Tian Xia she was amazed at how much she had learned from Swarn, what leaps forward her Magic had made. But while she was here she felt only the exhaustion and misery of training under someone who seemed to have no experience of pain, hunger or weariness. She forced herself to her feet again.

"I'm ready, aye," she said.

Swarn threw her another spear and it knocked her over into the mud.

At first, Swarn had taught her potions. Foss had books of potions and endless jars of supplies in the Mancer Library, but Swarn was a witch and she knew of potions no book told of; she needed no reminding of the materials or enchantments necessary. She and Eliza had hiked great distances through the Dead Marsh, even into the Ravening Forest and the Irahok Mountains, to find the right herbs or stones or creatures. There were no jars of tidy powders and dried herbs. Eliza learned herself how to cut open a frog or a foot-dragon and take the parts she needed, how to find the right roots and dry them in the sun, how to recognize different types of volcanic rock or obtain the saliva of certain cliff-dwelling birds. There was a great deal of clambering about with nets and baskets and it reminded her a bit of playing with Nell on Holburg when they were children, although this was much more strenuous and dangerous. As they searched for their ingredients, Swarn told Eliza all about the mystical properties of the thing they sought and what other materials might serve in their place in an emergency. She came to understand, on these long rambles, the underlying theory of potion-making. Now, if Swarn told her "invisibility" or "confusion" or "forgetfulness" or "rage," Eliza could set out with her equipment and find the necessary ingredients, prepare them and mix them in a potion that would do the job, if clumsily. Some time later, Foss had decided to teach Eliza a few potions. She had been so efficient, so confident, so expert, that he had just watched her carefully and then moved on to something else. They had never returned to potions and she wondered if he guessed where she had learned so much.

After potions, Swarn had taught her to forge weapons. For this they had gone to the cliffs of Batt, where dragons nested, and Swarn had showed Eliza a pool of white-green flame in a dark cave whose walls were carved with ancient runes. Here Swarn had given shape to Eliza's dragon claw, forging a dagger from it, showing her how certain spells combined with mystical elements could be used to mold the most indestructible materials. Together they had made a spear out of spells, layer upon layer, a spear that would fly true and break whatever Magic stood in its way. It took such a spear to kill a dragon, Swarn had explained, or to drive through a barrier. They made swords and spears and knives and arrows. It was sweaty and confusing work, not nearly as enjoyable as looking for things to put in a potion. Eliza had expected to continue with forging spells this time around but suddenly Swarn had decided to teach her to use these weapons. Eliza was thrilled – at first. Now the day was only half-over and she was worn out. It was the most difficult thing they had done yet, by far, and she couldn't help thinking that perhaps she was not ready for it.

After piercing balls of flame with arrows and spears, they went on to dueling with enchanted swords. Eliza's sword had a will of its own and she had to impose her will over it. Tired as she was, she found the sword controlled her more than she it and that she was darting and dodging to accommodate its movements. Swarn was most dissatisfied and lectured her about balance. When the sun was sinking down towards the horizon and the red clouds had faded to dark grey, they turned and trudged back to the hut.

They had left Charlie sleeping by the fire that morning but he was gone now. Though he didn't stray far, he tended to stay out of Swarn's way. Indirectly, he was the cause of the quarrel between Swarn's sister Audra and the Sorceress Nia that had ended with Audra being killed more than half a century ago. Though he could hardly be blamed for it, he knew well enough that Swarn didn't like the sight of him. Swarn told Eliza every time that she would happily send a dragon to meet her at the Crossing but the truth was Eliza liked to have her friend with her. The dragons were loyal only to Swarn. She had profound respect for Swarn but the witch had three times come close to killing Eliza early on in their relationship. Eliza felt better knowing Charlie was nearby.

It was part of Swarn's peculiar regimen of training that Eliza became a sort of servant when she stayed there. She swept the earth floor of the hut, maintained the enchantments on the fire, walked an hour and back every morning to the spring for fresh water, cooked their meals and rinsed the dishes. Now Eliza chopped marsh vegetables on a rough, worn strip of wood while Swarn sat, back straight and legs crossed, hands on her knees, staring into the green fire in the hearth at the centre of the room. A large black cauldron hung over the fire, rigged from the ceiling by chains. Eliza winched it up close to the ceiling so it was out of the way and set up a short iron stand for the frying pan. The frying pan was black and battered but still serviceable. Eliza stirred the vegetables and herbs together with some oil and a handful of dried marsh minnows in the pan. The mixture began to sizzle.

"How is your mother?" asked Swarn. She was not looking at Eliza.

"Same as usual, I spec," said Eliza carefully. When Swarn did not reply, she added, "You should come visit her sometime, aye."

"No," said Swarn, her voice harsh.

"You'd be welcome," said Eliza.

"No," Swarn said again, nearly whispering this time. "I could not bear it."

"Praps it's easier for me, because I dinnay remember her the way she was before," said Eliza.

Swarn cut her off. "Tomorrow we will practice deflecting barriers."

"Barriers?" Eliza was startled. "What for?"

Swarn said nothing in reply to this.

"My dagger can cut through barriers," said Eliza. "Why do I need to deflect them?"

"Suppose you were held by a barrier that prevented you from moving your arms," said Swarn crisply. "How would you reach your dagger?"

Eliza paused and let this sink in. She could not think why Swarn would suggest such a thing. First and most obviously, she was not ready. It took Magic far greater than what she could yet perform to deflect the spell of another. But stranger than that, barriers were Mancer Magic, and the Mancers were Eliza's sworn protectors.

"Do you really think the Mancers are some kind of threat to me?" she asked at last. She asked this not out of concern, but out of disbelief. Eliza felt sure Swarn was doing the Mancers a great injustice if she believed they might hurt their own Sorceress-in-training.

Swarn looked up from the fire, locking eyes with Eliza. Her brown eyes were almost lost in the wrinkled folds of her eyelids.

"I do not believe the Mancers wish you harm. But they have

their own agenda, and for your own sake it is best that you never be powerless among them."

The vegetable and minnow mix was smoking a little. Eliza let the subject drop and scraped a portion off for each of them, filling up the white dragon-bone bowls. The mix of roots and plants and dried fish was bland but surprisingly filling. They ate in silence, seated cross-legged on coarsely woven mats on the cold earth floor. When they had finished, Swarn handed her bowl rather imperiously to Eliza. She washed the dishes in the bucket of water reserved for that and set them aside on a mat to dry. She threw the dirty water outside, then took off her clothes and the new bra and washed herself in the doorway with a rough cloth and cold water. The night sky was full of the monstrous screaming shapes of dragons casting their great shadows over the moon. Her clothes were thick with mud and so she rinsed them off too and then hung them over the fence to dry. She wore the black tunic that was the costume of the Shang Sorceress mainly as a nightgown these days.

When she came back inside, Swarn was already lying down with a rough blanket pulled around her, her shoulders rising and falling steadily with her breath. Eliza unrolled her own sleeping mat and lay down gingerly, sore and bruised from the day's training.

In her dreams the house was crowded with ravens. They were all jabbering at her, their nasty beaks snapping open and shut, and what she heard them saying was *"Making, Making, Making."*

CHAPTER

5

After the day's work in the Inner Sanctum was done, Foss went to Aysu's chamber and requested an audience. They sat facing each other across the low stone table inlaid with ebony crabs.

"I did not wish to trouble Kyreth with this, as it may be nothing," said Foss. "But I believe the holes our enemy is making in the barriers may be more dangerous than we realize. I cannot decipher the pattern and yet there *is* a pattern, some kind of Deep Logic, I am certain. I catch hints of it, but cannot link it all together."

"Is it perhaps only fear, or weariness, Spellmaster, that makes you think so?" Aysu suggested softly. "You did not sleep last night. All the manipulators of water were disturbed."

"Forgive me," he said humbly. "I became overanxious. It is not only due to my examination of the holes. My trances have been full of disturbing images. Disaster. Is no one else seeing such things?"

"No, Spellmaster. You are the first to say so."

"Then perhaps it is nothing," said Foss, relieved. "If something were truly amiss, you too would have sensed it."

"Perhaps not," said Aysu thoughtfully. "The barriers are your design. It may be that you are more sensitive to the damage being done to them. It should be looked into further. I will inform his Eminence."

"Thank you," said Foss. He rose to go but Aysu made a gesture inviting him to sit again.

"Spellmaster, you know that in seven years, I will pass on."

"Yes. You will be missed."

"You are very kind to say so. The matter of my successor is not yet decided."

"No. You will appoint a successor with Kyreth's approval three years before your passing."

"For many years, it was common knowledge that you were favoured. You are the Spellmaster; your knowledge is unparalleled and your power respected by all."

"I thank you. But circumstances have changed. I understand well that it is not for me to become an Emmisarius. I am content."

"Good. The matter is quite out of my hands, Foss. But you still have *my* respect. That is what I wished to tell you."

"I am most grateful," Foss said, moved. "Convey my greetings to his Eminence when you speak to him."

"I will do so."

After they had eaten breakfast, Eliza said to Swarn, "Tell me about Making."

Swarn gave Eliza a look of such scorching intensity, it felt almost like the gaze of a Mancer. "An odd request from a girl who can barely conjure," she said.

"I dinnay mean teach me how to do it," said Eliza, irritated. "I mean tell me about it, lah. What is it, exactly? I know the Ancients Made Tian Di, but do other beings have the power to Make?"

"It is exactly what it sounds like – the creation of something that did not exist before. As you say, it is the power of the Ancients and I could not teach it to you even if I were mad enough to wish to. Why are you asking me this, Eliza?"

"I had a dream, aye. Or...lots of dreams, praps. Ravens kept saying *Making* to me, over and over again. It seemed to go on all night."

Swarn stood up in one fluid motion and paced in a circle around the small earth hut. "That is very strange," she said at last.

"Aye," said Eliza dryly. "What do you think it means?"

Swarn shook her head.

"I don't know. Making lies at the root of all Magic. What we call *Magic* is, in fact, the residue of the Ancients in their creation, for no being can separate itself from what it Makes. The Magic of Making, the power of the Ancients, is still in the earth and the air and the sky and our own blood and breath. We call upon it for all our lesser Magic."

"So no beings since the Ancients have actually *Made* anything?" Eliza asked.

"Some have," said Swarn. "We have only myths and stories to go by. The story of Making that is most widely believed harks from the Middle Days. There was a wizard who lived with the Immortal Dragons in the East. He was called the Great Dragon Mage. It is said that he quarreled with the Lord Dragon and stole from them the sacred flame that was the source of their power. He fled the Dragon Isles and came to Tian Di, where he used the sacred flame to Make the mortal dragons. They were his creatures, bound to him. They served him and did his bidding. But as they procreated and their numbers grew, their power became equal to and then greater than his. They drew upon his life force, his essence, to increase their own strength. Though he tried, he could not sever the link between them and was absorbed by them entirely. I do not know if this story is true but it is certain that there were no mortal dragons before the Middle Days, and since those days the Immortal Dragons have not been seen in Tian Di." There was a strange gleam in Swarn's eyes as she spoke. She seemed to be looking at something far beyond the small, dark room. "There are some other stories in the Mancer Library I expect," she finished. "You would be better asking them to tell you about Making. I have told you all I know now."

"Something is happening," said Eliza, frowning at the fire. "I cannay ignore these visions and dreams, the ravens following us all the way to the Crossing. They're trying to tell me something, aye, or they're trying to harm me, I dinnay know which. But I cannay just wait for it to come clear. I need to find out."

"And how do you propose to do so, Eliza?"

Eliza looked up at the witch and for a moment Swarn thought

she saw, for the first time, some slight resemblance to Rea.

"I want to speak to the Oracle of the Ancients," said Eliza.

Turning away from Eliza and from that flash of her old friend, her love, Swarn said curtly, "We will leave at once."

Swarn and her dragons turned back towards the Dead Marsh while Rhianu welcomed Eliza at the Temple of the Nameless Birth. The first time they met they had been unable to communicate but Eliza was now able to speak haltingly in the Language of First Days. It was not a language that lent itself to conversation, however, so much as to proclamations and flowery inquiries.

"Your hospitality is an ocean of dandelions," said Eliza, then frowned and bit her lip. That was certainly not the correct phrase.

Rhianu laughed and embraced her, replying, "We are honoured and humbled that the Shang Sorceress should again grace our inadequate hallways with the soles of her blessed feet."

Like all the Faithful, Rhianu wore a long black robe. Her head and face were covered with a beaded hood and scarf so that only her pale, lidless eyes were visible. The red beads on her hood indicated rank. She was a priestess of the Ancients and loyal servant of the Oracle. The Faithful believed that the Ancients had written the story of the worlds in signs, that the future was laid out already and would come to pass as They had ordained. They believed also that the Oracle was the messenger of the Ancients, through whom the Ancients communicated with the beings they had left behind. Whether indeed the Ancients spoke to or through her, nobody in Tian Xia questioned that the Oracle knew and could see things that no other being in the worlds could. Eliza had met the current Oracle before, but she had been in danger of being killed at the time and would not have known what to ask at any rate. It was time they met again.

The main temple was a giant dome of red earth, honeycombed with vividly painted chambers and corridors. Wooden walkways and stairways snaked all around the outside of it. As they made their way up one of these stairways, Eliza could look out over the tops of all the smaller red earth temples branching off from this one to the black cliffs that encircled the lake of the Crossing. The Crossing was both the centre of Tian Xia and its edge.

"I pray to the Ancients that you prosper in the light of day and by the shadow of night," said Eliza, which was the closest thing she knew to saying, *How are you?*

"Your kindness is to me like a boundless sea of persimmon petals," said Rhianu pointedly, for that was the phrase Eliza had been looking for to match with hospitality.

"Lah, yes! Persimmon petals!" exclaimed Eliza. They ducked into a narrow entryway and Rhianu led Eliza down the hallway to the central spiral staircase, which formed the spine of the structure. Rhianu had not asked and likely would not ask Eliza why she had come but Eliza thought she should explain. It was not easy and she was not helped either by the dizzying descent down the spiraling staircase, where she could only ever see the dark tip of Rhianu's hood ahead of her as she vanished around the curve.

"In ancient days I came here to meditate upon the Great Truth," began Eliza. Of course, it wasn't correct to say *ancient* days but she didn't know how else to express *before now*. "The Faithful welcomed me with persimmon petals." She heard Rhianu snort ahead of her. She was making a horrible muddle of it. "Now I come to this sacred place to...respect...honour, and I am inadequate, a wish deep as the ocean and wide as the sky to consult the Great Oracle of the Ancients with my...question."

Rhianu was silent in response to this. Eliza followed her the rest of the way down the stairs. They stopped in a small chamber for Eliza to leave her weapon and put on the robes of the Faithful. Then they continued along a sloping, unlit passageway so narrow that the walls on either side brushed against her shoulders. Eliza could not see Rhianu ahead of her in the darkness but followed the gentle slap of her footsteps and the steady intake and release of her breath.

The footsteps stopped and there was a slight rustle of clothing. Eliza stood still in the dark. Rhianu began to croon something in the Language of First Days. It sounded like *The greatest secrets of your servants are ever protected* but the words for protect and remember were rather similar, as were the words for secret and truth, so it was hard for Eliza to be sure. Then Rhianu stood and took Eliza by the hand, pulling her down towards the floor. Eliza felt along the flagstones with her hands for the one that had fallen away. She reached through the gap until her fingers touched the rope ladder.

"Thank you," she murmured.

Rhianu's footsteps retreated back the way they had come. Eliza felt a clammy ripple of fear creep along her skin. She had been here before and the Oracle had not come that time. She was not much looking forward to what might be simply a long, pointless wait in the dark, alone. But she climbed down the ladder and stood in the darkness. The ground was packed earth, the walls cold stone. The last time she had come here, she had been entirely powerless, with the Mancers hunting her. So much had changed since then.

By measuring it out in paces, she found the centre of the octagonal room and sat down cross-legged there. She stared into the darkness, thinking about the ravens and what she would ask the Oracle. Her concentration was occasionally interrupted by unwanted thoughts, such as what might be looking at her now in the dark or how outraged Charlie had been at the idea of her marrying Obrad. She tried to shut that memory out, as it just confused her. She was the Shang Sorceress, not a schoolgirl. She had more important things to think about, she told herself scoldingly.

As it turned out, she had a great deal of time to think. When she began to be terribly hungry, the flagstone above was lifted quietly and a dark package sailed down, landing at her feet with a thud. Then the opening was closed up again. She undid the package. There was bread, cheese, dry fruit and a flask of water inside it. When she was tired, she stretched herself out on the earthen floor and slept.

Calculating by her meals and the times she slept, three days passed in silence and darkness. The difference between sleeping and waking began to close. She sat upright in a sort of half-dream for hours at a time. Her body ached with stillness. She had almost forgotten what she was doing there when on the third day a blaze of light startled her, the walls groaned, and there before her was the Oracle of the Ancients.

"Oh," said the Oracle, recognition dawning in her cold crystal eyes. "It's you."

Foss had not slept in three nights when it happened. A few days earlier, he had shown the Emmisariae and Kyreth his replicas of the barriers. Foss had hoped that the Supreme Mancer or the powerful Emmisariae would be able to see clearly the answer that eluded him but they were as baffled as he was. Whatever reservations the other Mancers had about him, no one doubted that he had the sharpest mind regarding Deep Mathematics. Kyreth pardoned him from the work in the Inner Sanctum and asked that he focus entirely on solving the riddle posed by the Xia Sorceress's holes. He had spent the past three days and three nights on the brink of understanding and yet it never quite came together. There *was* a pattern, but it was a pattern that simply didn't make sense. She had understood *their* pattern, the orbits and rotations of the barriers, that much was clear. She had solved the puzzle and so she knew there was no way out. She continued making the holes in an elaborate pattern of her own and yet the pattern revealed nothing. Foss paced and racked his brain and did not sleep. No solution presented itself.

And then one morning she struck.

It was a great blow to the barriers. Every Mancer in the Citadel rocketed from their sleep. The gong sounded twice, summoning them to the Inner Sanctum. Only Foss did not obey. Shaking, he breathed out a replica of the barriers as they were now.

Some terrible force had radiated out from within the prison, striking the barriers in nine places. The barriers were far too strong and complex for any amount of force to break them all. But she struck now with nine blows so powerful and so precise that they altered the motion of the barriers. Orbits changed. Rotations reversed. Another nine blows came and he felt it like a violent kick to his heart.

The Mancers ran to the Inner Sanctum. Kyreth stood in the centre of the main hall, shouting out commands with his Emmisariae around him. They bent all their concentration to the barriers. But there was no time. Mancer Magic was slow and whatever was happening now, it was happening very quickly.

Foss, in the Library, knew it was too late. Another nine blows struck and they all felt it. Everything was changing position. For a brief moment, as he watched his replica, his horror was surpassed by a profound delight. This was miraculous. It was beautiful. It was pure genius and he would never have imagined it possible. As the barriers spun and shifted, her pattern came clear. It was simply unstoppable. Foss strode across the Library, threw open the window, and called a small bright bird to him. It sat alertly in his palm and he spoke to it briefly in the Language of First Days. Then it swooped off in the direction of the dark wood in the northwest corner of the grounds. Time was short. He turned to watch it happen. He could not resist. The barriers spun, and for a mere few seconds all of the holes came into line, creating a circular passage, six feet in diameter, out of her prison and into the world.

The Oracle came towards Eliza on her eight golden spider's legs, her upper body tattooed with the elaborate characters of the Language of First Days, her crystal eyes severe.

"I have questions," said Eliza, forcing herself to meet the Oracle's eyes.

"Ask them," replied the Oracle. Her tone was light and mocking.

Eliza held up her right palm, with the tattoo of the dagger pointing down.

"What does the dagger signify?"

The Oracle tilted her head back as if listening to something.

"Struggle," she said after a pause. "Violence."

"Why does it point towards me?"

The Oracle's eyes were alert with interest. "*Sacrifice,*" she said, as if it pleased her. "Victory will only come at a price for you."

She couldn't help herself. She asked, "What price?"

The Oracle waited for a moment and then bared her tiny pointed teeth in a chilling smile. *"You will cut out your own heart."*

Eliza stared at the Oracle, radiant and haughty, moving to and fro slightly on her golden-furred legs. A deep shudder took hold of her. The Oracle was watching her hungrily, as if eager for her tears. Eliza knew that once a question had been answered, there was no point asking for clarification. She should not have asked such a thing in the first place. She forced her spine straight, drove her chin up, pushed aside all the new questions that clamoured within her, the panicked chorus of *when* and *why* and *spare me*, to ask the question she had come here to ask.

"What are the ravens to me?" she asked shakily.

"That which you seek," said the Oracle with a disappointed scowl. "That which you fear."

It was a pointless riddle of an answer. Eliza pressed on, "Are the ravens my Guide?"

"Only if you follow them," said the Oracle.

"What are the ravens trying to tell me?"

"A warning," said the Oracle.

"What is the warning?"

"She is coming," cawed the Oracle in the voice of a raven. *"Making."* She looked confused by this and annoyed with Eliza for bringing forth so baffling an answer.

"Who is *she*?" asked Eliza, her heart tightening in her chest as she neared the point of it all. "Is it Nia?"

"Yes," said the Oracle, her expression darkening. She fixed her eyes intently on Eliza, waiting for more, for this concerned her also.

"When is she coming?" asked Eliza.

The Oracle's eyes widened with fear. She whispered, *"Now."*

The Mancers stood dumbfounded in the Inner Sanctum, uncertain of what had happened. They had all felt the gap in the barriers. Now it was gone, the barriers continuing in their new and uncontrolled movement.

Kyreth spoke in a terrible voice. "Emmisariae, go now to the Great Sand Sea. Find Eliza and bring her here. The rest of you must do your utmost to strengthen the barriers around the Citadel and prepare some defense. I will consult the Scrolls."

They all obeyed him and he went quickly to his study. Now there was much to do. Getting Eliza here was the most important thing. Why had he let her leave? He would also need to call upon the Triumvira of Tian Xia for assistance, and he would need to do it immediately. There was no time to waste.

In his study he did not sit down but said to the Scrolls, "Is the Sorceress Nia free of the barriers?"

A single gold character appeared on each of the Scrolls: *Yes*.

"Where is she now?" he demanded.

Here. It was written over and over again.

His heart froze. "In the Citadel?"

Yes.

"How?" It came out a shallow gasp.

Magic.

He would need to convey this to the Emmisariae without delay. They must not bring Eliza here. They must take her to Tian Xia and put her under the protection of the Triumvira. But so transfixed was he by the horror of the moment that he did not act immediately and found himself asking instead, "What does she intend?"

The golden characters wrote themselves in a graceful sweeping row down one of the Scrolls: *No more than you deserve*.

This shocked him so deeply that for a moment he could not formulate a thought, let alone a question. Golden characters spilled down the next Scroll in a great hurry.

You were a fool to think you could hold me bound and disempowered forever.

He took a step back and his blood ran cold. The Scrolls filled with words, one after the other.

Do the Mancers know what you did?

Do they understand the war I have with them?

Or do they follow you without question?

"How?" he said again. It didn't matter. He began to murmur a spell to create a barrier between himself and his enemy but the words came out quite wrong, jumbled in his mouth, nonsensical. Somehow, without his realizing it, a Confusion had taken hold of him. He could not move to tear his eyes away from the characters on the centre Scroll, which began to flow rather differently, in long sweeping lines, outlining the form of a woman in gold ink. The ink became flesh and the Sorceress Nia stepped out of the Scroll into the study. Kyreth's tongue was stilled, his hands frozen.

"Hello, Papa," she said, planting a kiss on his cheek.

CHAPTER

6

Eliza hammered on the walls, shouting, but no one came. She turned back towards the Oracle, seated on her eight legs in the middle of the room, eyes glassy and vacant.

"Get somebody to come and let me out of here," she begged. "I have to go!"

"She will come for me," said the Oracle faintly. "She will come for me here."

Eliza's mind was hurtling along a trajectory of worst fears and nightmare scenarios. She needed to get out and she needed her dagger and she needed Charlie.

"Rhianu!" she screamed, pounding the wall again.

"The Chamber shall not be entered or left while I am here," said the Oracle in a faraway voice. "They cannot open it."

"Then leave," said Eliza furiously. "I need to get out!"

"She is coming for me. I will remain here. We cannot flee our destinies," said the Oracle.

"I have to warn the Mancers," pleaded Eliza.

"They will fall before her," said the Oracle. "I have seen it. I have seen my death today."

Eliza stared at the spot where she thought the opening should be. She felt her way up the walls with her Deep Knowing to the ceiling and the flagstone that had opened before. She pushed at it with all her will but the presence of the Oracle was like a magnet holding the room tight together. Eliza was not strong enough to break it.

Around her neck she wore the shard of crystal Kyreth had given her long ago. He had told her she could use it to summon the Mancers if ever she needed them. For all her battles with Kyreth, now, when her greatest fear was materializing, she wished desperately that he were here. Nothing terrible could happen if only the powerful Supreme Mancer were watching over her. Why had she left the safety of the Citadel? She closed her fist over the crystal around her neck and squeezed it, begging, "Help me, please." The crystal gave a sudden, dramatic flash. Light poured out between her fingers but the light struck the walls and bounced back without penetrating them.

"You *have* to let me go," said Eliza again, more feebly. It was no good. She sank to the earthen floor and buried her face in her hands. The Oracle's voice hissing that she would cut her own heart out came back to her. She choked back a sob and leaped to her feet again. She would *not* wait in this hole for Nia to come.

In this way the night passed, and much of the following day. She swung between despair and grim determination. The air was getting thicker and her head was pounding from hunger and thirst. As long as the Oracle remained, nobody would bring her food or water. At this rate, she might be dead before Nia even arrived. She thought she was dreaming when a sudden groaning and straining sounded from overhead. The Oracle stared furiously at the hinged flagstone, which trembled as if some great force were trying to shift it. Then the flagstone dropped away and the Oracle leaped to her feet, spitting. Eliza backed against the far wall with the Oracle, assuming it was Nia come for them, but instead Swarn's face appeared above.

"Pardon my intrusion, O Oracle of the Ancients," she said in a rather perfunctory tone. Eliza was so flooded with relief she could have wept.

"Insolence," hissed the Oracle.

"Eliza must come with me," said Swarn. "I have received a message."

"We are doomed," the Oracle replied in a dead voice, not budging. But Eliza leaped for the arm Swarn extended her and Swarn pulled her up and out of the pit. She drank back the fresh air outside it, the fog in her brain clearing as if in a sudden breeze.

"It's about Nia, nay?" said Eliza, her heart hammering in her chest. Swarn gave her a sharp look.

"What about Nia?"

"She's coming," said Eliza. "She's free of the barriers."

"I did not know," said Swarn quietly. "A messenger bird from the Citadel came to me with two words only – Eliza Return. It was sent in great haste by your Spellmaster."

"So Foss *did* know where I was all along," said Eliza. "And they must know about Nia already, aye." Her panic was beginning to subside. This time, she would not have to face Nia alone. She had the Mancers and Swarn on her side.

"Yes. You will be safer with them than with me, I expect. Your friend the Shade is waiting outside. Come."

The daylight was so bright after her days in the Chamber of the Oracle that her eyes watered. Rhianu was waiting with Charlie and Swarn's dragon in the shadow of the Temple. She handed Eliza her dagger and Eliza took it gratefully.

"It's Nia," Eliza told Charlie immediately. "She's free."

His face tightened slightly but all he said was, "You look thirsty, aye." He gave her a flask and she drank it dry before turning to Rhianu.

"Your hospitality..." she began, but she was too agitated to think of the right words. "I'm sorry to leave this way," she said. "Thank you."

Rhianu bowed and said, "Your Destiny awaits you."

Eliza did not find this particularly comforting, given what the Oracle had told her of her destiny, but again she said, "Thank you."

"This is for you," said Swarn gruffly, untying a long, bright spear from her dragon's spikes. "It is deeply enchanted. When the time comes to use it, aim for the heart." She strapped it expertly to Eliza's back. Eliza could feel its power against her spine. Then Swarn pressed a small leather gourd into her hand. "A potion, also. Should you need it, it will give you some extra hours of strength when all your strength has been sapped."

Eliza put it in the pocket of her robe gratefully. Such a potion was very potent indeed and she happened to know it required the mucus of a giant, no easy thing to come by.

"I wish I could have stayed longer," said Eliza. "What will you do?"

"Warn the Faeries," said Swarn. "When you arrive, Eliza, tell Kyreth we await his call and are ready to join the Mancers in Di Shang if need be."

"I'll tell him," promised Eliza.

"May the Ancients keep you safe and guard you always," shouted Rhianu as they took off, heading for the black cliffs around the lake of the Crossing, where Swarn commanded the Boatman to take them home.

They disembarked on the silvery beach and headed in among the trees. No reply came to Eliza's request for entry and no barrier stopped them as they passed through the dark wood into the grounds of the Citadel. She had a sudden, panicky urge to flee with Charlie to the desert and her father. But that was foolish. She was safer with the Mancers. Perhaps in her exhaustion she had simply not felt the usual acknowledgement of her arrival, or the barriers may have been down in expectation of her.

"Something feels different, aye," said Charlie. "I dinnay like it."

"You dinnay need to stay," said Eliza.

"Lah, I'm not leaving you here alone," he said grumpily.

When Eliza's eyes fell on the Inner Sanctum she gave a cry of surprise, for its usually gleaming white dome was black and spiked. It was a moment before she realized it was covered with silent ravens. She and Charlie exchanged a horrified look and approached it together. Eliza had never been inside but the ravens covering it looked at her hard as if *willing* her to go in. Whether that meant she should or should not enter she couldn't say but curiosity won over prudence. She drew her dagger.

"We're nay supposed to go in there," Charlie said, but Eliza ignored him. There was no door barring the way, just an arched opening tall enough for a Mancer leading down a gleaming marble corridor. She followed the corridor all the way to the main hall, where the Mancers worked their Magic, and there she stopped. Horror pooled live and cold through her veins.

The Mancers stood in formation, more than two hundred of them. Their arms were raised, their eyes looking up towards the domed ceiling. But they were made of stone. All of them. Eliza ran from one group to the next. Here were the manipulators of wood and water and fire and earth and metal, frozen into statues. The manipulators of earth formed a pentagon around an empty centre. This was where Kyreth and the Emmisariae ought to be, Eliza assumed, but they were missing. She noted with a mixture of relief and trepidation that Foss was not among the manipulators of water.

"Forsake the Ancients!" Charlie whispered, entering behind her. "What happened?"

"She's *here*," said Eliza. Her voice sounded odd to her, like somebody else's voice. "She must have taken them by surprise, aye. They had no time to...act."

"We've got to leave," said Charlie urgently. "Come on, Eliza. We have to go straight back to Tian Xia, find Swarn."

Eliza's mind was as frozen as the Mancers around her. She could not force it into action.

"Eliza!" shouted Charlie, grabbing her shoulder and shaking her. "You need to get *out* of here! Let's go! Now!"

Eliza pulled away from him. "I need to find Foss. We'll look in the Library."

"Have you lost your *mind*?"

"Lah, she might not be here anymore. But if she is, she already knows we're here and it's too late. I need to know if Foss is all right."

"We could still escape," insisted Charlie.

Eliza shook her head. "Too late. You know that."

She swung Swarn's spear from her back. It comforted her to have something flowing with such power in her hand. Charlie became a half-hunter, a ferocious, thick-skinned beast, part-lizard, part-hound, that walked on two legs and bore weapons. Although she knew an enchanted spear and a half-hunter would be no match for Nia, Eliza was glad to have the hulking creature at her side. They left the stone Mancers and the raven-shrouded dome behind them and headed across the grounds back towards the north wing. The usual birdsong in the grounds was silent. There was no sound at all, in fact, until they approached the Old Library and heard a hollow sort of *thunk*. They both froze, but there was no further sound. The half-hunter sniffed the air, then nodded his great head at Eliza, baring teeth as long as daggers. Cautious and alert, they continued a little further. A human-sized hole had been smashed through the thick marble wall. They stepped through it into the Library.

The Library looked as if a giant had been rampaging through it. A great number of the vast, marble bookshelves had been pushed aside, some of them collapsed against the next stacks like toppled mountains. In the space created at the centre of the Library there was a large pile of books. On top of this pile stood Nia, wearing a red dress and a white fox-fur coat. Her hair was loose, spilling in red-gold curls over her shoulders and down her back, and she wore a jaunty white fur cap. She had a book open in her hand and was running her fingers along page after page very rapidly. The pages fluttered aside under her touch. She seemed to be concentrating deeply and didn't notice them for a moment. Eliza saw Foss frozen against the wall, stone arms raised before his stone face as if fending off a blow, and her heart broke.

Without thinking what she was doing, she found the spear was flying from her hand straight for Nia's heart. Nia's head shot up. She reached out and caught the spear with one hand, stumbling back on her pile of books as she did so. There was a groaning moment while Nia clutched the spear, straining against its Magic without dropping the book in her other hand, and then it snapped in two and Eliza felt the Magic crumble.

"Why is it that whenever I see you, you're terribly angry with me and in desperate need of a bath?" asked Nia, tossing aside the broken spear. "As a personal favour to me, next time you come for a confrontation, *please* have a shower first. Honestly, what have you been doing?"

"Speaking to the Oracle," said Eliza grimly. Nia had not changed at all from Eliza's memory of her. She was still utterly bewitching. There was no point running away from her now, so Eliza stood her ground.

"Fascinating, I've no doubt," said Nia, arching an eyebrow at her. "I suppose that explains your outfit. And you're still hanging about with the Shade – sweet. You know you can't trust those things, though, don't you?"

Eliza said nothing. A low growl rumbled deep in the half-hunter's massive chest and he drew two short swords from his leather harness.

Nia laughed and looked Eliza up and down appreciatively. "Look how tall you've become, Smidgen! And your hair...well, your hair is still a fright but it's lovely to see you anyway. I assume that since you greeted me with a less-than-friendly spear throw, you aren't here to help me take my revenge."

"Why are you taking revenge on *Foss*?" cried Eliza. She couldn't bear to look again at her teacher made stone.

"Oh yes, have you seen the others too?" asked Nia. "I know it's hard to tell the difference, but if you look at them *very* carefully, you'll notice that they're ever so slightly slower than usual."

Tears spilled unexpectedly from Eliza's eyes. Nia's face fell.

"Go on, that was *funny*. You don't feel *sorry* for them, do you, Smidgen? Look, these beings have kept me locked away in the Arctic for more than twelve years. Why should I take pity on them now?"

Eliza wiped her tears away angrily. "They had no choice," she said. "They had to protect people." It was absurd, really, trying to rationalize things to Nia.

Nia tilted her head on one side and smiled warmly. "One of these days, Smidgen, I'm going to have to enlighten you about your friends the Mancers. But that's not what I want to talk about with you right now. Something has been baffling me ever since you snuck off the last time and I've just got to know – how in the worlds did you lay your hands on *Faery blood?* I've been *dying* of curiosity for more than *two years* now!"

It had not occurred to Eliza that, of course, Nia didn't know she had stabbed the King of the Faeries and so her escape must have remained a mystery. Sealing her inner thoughts away tightly, she said, "The Mancers and the Faeries are allies. They help each other."

Nia shook her shining curls and laughed scornfully. "Eliza, please! Don't insult me by suggesting that Faeries are giving their *blood* to the *Mancers!* They only tolerate each other at all because they're all terrified of *me*. No, Smidgen, the Mancers don't have a secret stock of Faery blood. And yet *you* had some. I haven't been able to figure it out."

"Lah, let me know when you do," said Eliza, struggling to keep her voice steady and calm.

Nia laughed again. "I couldn't stop thinking how clever you'd been. Just a little girl really, not even able to use your Magic, and yet you escaped from *me*. And look at you now, so much stronger and more confident! Oh, I know better than to underestimate you, Smidgen, I've learned my lesson. It's left me with a difficult decision to make. I could come for you first and take your power the way I always intended, but then my enemies would have time to get ready for me and I do prefer to keep the element of surprise on my side. So I settled on the second option – crushing them all as quickly as possible and then coming back for you when I'm done. But starting with revenge meant that I had to come up with something to keep *you* entertained and out of the way in the meantime. You see, I've been *terribly* busy since we last saw each other! So many things to prepare and the timing had to be perfect."

Eliza drew her dagger and waited. She didn't trust her own voice, she didn't trust what words might come out of her now. She was feeling that familiar, awful, irresistible tug, the helpless desire to be embraced by Nia, to do as she said, to be as she wished. It took all her strength not to drop the dagger and run to fall at her feet.

"I intend to be merciful towards two of my enemies," continued Nia, "and give them quick deaths. For the other two, I have something more elaborate in mind, something along the lines of eternal torment. Nothing so easy as oblivion. And then *you*, my lovely Eliza, will live on in me always! It's going to be very jolly. I should be getting on with it but I got a bit sidetracked here. The Library of the Mancers! I know the place will be crawling with every kind of horrible fiend once the word is out, so I thought I should get what I can while this place still exists. Watch this!" She tossed the book she'd been holding over her shoulder and it landed with a *thunk*. She picked up another book, opened it wide so Eliza could see, and ran her fingers across the pages. The pages flew aside rapidly and as her fingers passed over them the ancient ink disappeared, leaving them blank. Foss had taught Eliza such a deep reverence for the books here that to see them drained in this way was like a knife to the heart.

"You cannay," she gasped, relieved for a moment that Foss couldn't see what was happening in his cherished Library.

"For *millennia* the Mancer Library has been revered in both worlds as the greatest Library ever to have existed," said Nia cheerfully. "Even the Faeries coveted it! And now...most of it is *here*." She touched her temple with her fingers and tossed the empty book with the others. "Smidgen, are you all right? You don't look very well."

Eliza was not feeling very well either. She steadied herself with a hand on the half-hunter's shaggy arm. The destruction happening here, the erasing of thousands of years of lore and history, was unthinkable.

"Are you frightened?" asked Nia sympathetically. "Fear is so unpleasant, isn't it? I believe it's the worst sensation there is and it's best to banish it altogether. If you fear nothing, you're truly free. As long as you're afraid, everything requires *courage*, and courage is an exhausting thing to maintain."

Eliza gripped her dagger tighter with her right hand.

"Get on with it, aye," she said. "Whatever you're going to try to do to me, stop talking and just do it."

Nia laughed aloud at that. "Quite the teenage attitude you've developed," she said incredulously. "Well, Smidgen, if you're so impatient, I won't bore you any longer. I *could* just turn you to stone like the Mancers or shut you up in a barrier while I take care of my other business, but I have far too much respect for you to do anything so prosaic. Instead, I've spent a great deal of time and energy making something very special just for you, something to challenge that sharp little brain of yours. Would you like to see it?"

"Show me," said Eliza.

Nia tipped her head back and opened her mouth wide. Suddenly it was as if all the air had been sucked out of the room. A dark shape was crawling out of Nia's mouth. It grew larger as it emerged, expanding and stretching, massive limbs reaching for the ground. It kept coming from somewhere inside her, a mass of darkness and flame, until it landed on smoking hooves, towering over Eliza. She took in curling horns, a myriad of spiked arms, the powerful thighs and hooves of a horse. Charred flesh flamed and smouldered around a colossal skeleton broken in too many places to count. Its eye-sockets burned in a face like molten rock and its immense wings were black and veined with fire. The hideous thing let out a roar that left cracks in the walls and showcased the bright white of its ribcage between the broken, burnt flesh. Then it lunged at Eliza. A part of Eliza that was faster than sight or sound spoke a barrier spell. It was a feeble barrier and the spiked fists scraped along it and tore it open but it gave Eliza just enough time to dodge its grasp and drive her dagger into its side. Lava poured out over her dagger. Before she could cry out for Charlie to stop, the half-hunter drove both his swords into the beast and made for its throat with his teeth. He emitted a strangled airless howl as lava poured down his face and the thing drove its razor-sharp spikes into his chest. The half-hunter crashed to the ground while Nia applauded from her vantage point on the pile of books. Eliza pulled her dagger out of the beast's side, stumbling back, lungs bursting. The monstrous thing left its two foes on the floor and bounded to a tall window at the back of the Library, crashing through it and taking flight, black wings beating hard and trailing sparks behind him. Once he was gone, Eliza found herself able to take a breath. It was like emerging from the sea after diving too deep. She couldn't gulp the air back fast enough.

"Isn't he *horrible!*" exclaimed Nia, delighted. "I don't like to brag, but I am *brilliant*, aren't I? Do you know where he's going now, Smidgen?"

And Eliza knew, with a heart-plunging-into-the-stomach kind of knowing, that everything was about to get even worse.

"He'll stop in a few towns on the way and smash everyone in sight to bits," said Nia cheerfully, "just to cause a bit of a sensation. I want people to know I'm back, you see, and this is the sort of thing they expect from me. But those destructive little jaunts will just be detours. He's going to the desert, to find your lovely mother. He's drawn to her, like a magnet to metal, and his one desire in this world is to tear her limb from limb."

Eliza felt a pounding behind her temples. Nia was watching her with a curious little smile. She crawled across the floor to where the wounded half-hunter lay panting in weak gasps.

"Are you badly hurt?" she asked.

He struggled back into human form, and Eliza saw the nature of the wound on his chest. He was not bleeding in the ordinary way. He was leaking a sort of shimmering interplay of dark and light, his true form.

"Oh, Charlie," she whispered, her heart contracting painfully.

Nia rolled her eyes and, bored now her creature was gone, picked up another book.

"I'll be all right," Charlie managed to say.

Eliza nodded. There was no time to waste. She had to go after the thing, but it was obvious Charlie was too badly hurt to carry her or engage in any kind of further battle. She took the potion Swarn had given her out of her pocket.

"Drink this," she said, putting it to his lips.

"You might need it," he said faintly, turning his head aside. "It's really nay...that bad, Eliza."

"Stop it." She forced the mouthpiece between his lips and poured the thick mixture into his throat. He coughed and sputtered, but swallowed most of it.

"Disgusting," he gasped when it was done. "Like kissing a giant."

"Now you've got to get out of here," she said urgently. "Go, Charlie. Please."

"I willnay..." he began, and rolled onto his side.

"She's nay going to hurt me right now," said Eliza. "I'll get one of the dragons, aye. But you have to go first. Please."

"Dinnay go after it on your own, Eliza," said Charlie weakly, getting to his knees. "Get help. Get Swarn."

"Yes. And you fly clear, hide somewhere." Her voice cracked with desperation.

"Poor Smidgen," commented Nia. "Everything always seems so complicated for you. Too many attachments, that's your real problem. It makes you such an easy target."

Charlie began to change again as the shadow and light leaked from him. Wings strained from his back and his face lengthened into a great beak as he became a gryphon again. He limped across the battlefield of scattered books for the broken window, then looked back at Eliza over his shoulder. Nia was busy emptying another book and ignored them. She tossed it aside. *Thunk.*

Eliza gave a last look at Foss, frozen at the side of the room with his arms up in defense, and a powerful surge of anger pulsed through her, banishing all else.

"I'm going to kill that thing," she told Nia. "And then I'll come back for you."

"Oh, I wouldn't *kill* it, if I were you," said Nia breezily, picking up another book. Eliza lingered by the hole in the wall long enough to see Charlie take to the air, then turned and ran.

"Good luck, Smidgen!" Nia called after her.

CHAPTER

7

She took the stairs three at a time and burst out into the grounds. If she was right and the Emmisariae had already left, perhaps to seek her out in the desert, there might not be a dragon for her to escape on, but with the help of Swarn's potion Charlie would at least be able to fly to safety. She held the crystal around her neck in her fist and muttered as she ran, "Kyreth, help me, help me, help me!" Light poured out of it between her fingers. It became so hot she had to let go of it. It slowly dimmed and cooled again. There was no sign that her call had been heard.

She knew the dragons were kept in caverns beneath the Inner Sanctum and so she entered it a second time. There were several chambers branching off from the main hall, many of which were the private chambers of the manipulators of earth. Above one narrow doorway the characters were carved into the marble: *Hall of the Dragon*. Eliza entered the room. It was bare and plain but for a single pentagonal flagstone on the floor, which bore a mosaic dragon. Eliza knelt before it and tried to think what to do. She knew a few simple opening spells, but she doubted they would be much good in a place as deeply enchanted as the Mancer Citadel. She tried muttering them anyway. As she had expected, the dragon flagstone did not budge. She laid her hands on it and tried to use force but that was equally useless. A sense of her own powerlessness began to creep over her. She shook it away. Now was not the time to lose confidence. She knew another way into the caverns. She had gotten lost in the dungeons with Nell a long time ago. They had smelled the dragons down there.

Eliza ran across the grounds back to the north wing, wondering if Nia was watching her. As soon as she entered the dungeons she was assailed by the abominable stench of the Cra. She could hear their sickening hissing and lip-smacking. They were still held by the Mancers' barriers but they knew something was happening. She was glad of the darkness, glad to be spared the sight of them at least. Keeping one hand to the cold wall she ran through the maze of corridors, trying to remember her way. She was too frantic to manage a seeking spell or a light and had been going in circles for a while before she felt a gust of cool air and realized one of the larger caverns must be nearby. Once she found it, it was easy – a straight run back towards the Inner Sanctum underground. Halfway there the cavern forked in two and she went to the left, slowing down at the smell of sulfur.

Eliza tightened her grip on the hilt of her dagger. She knew very little about dragons, in fact. She knew they were highly intelligent and deadly. She knew they were impervious to most kinds of simple Magic. She knew they lived a very long time and were not easily mastered. The Mancer dragons were not as vicious as the wild dragons of the cliffs of Batt that obeyed Swarn but their loyalty was to the Mancers and she did not know how they would react to her. The dragon claw that served her as a dagger should, according to Swarn, enable her to command dragons, but she had never put this to the test.

She could feel their hot breath and hear the scraping of their metallic scales as they moved in the darkness. The sulfur of their breath stung her nostrils. She did not know the language of dragons, so she spoke in the Language of First Days and hoped they understood.

"Great beings," she began nervously, "I am the ward of the Mancers. I have –" and then she bumped up against something hard and screamed, leaping back. It was as if she'd run into the wall, but it wasn't a wall. She reached out and touched it. It was stone, a tall figure; she felt an arm, a hand. Her heart sank. She moved about the cavern slowly, feeling for more statues, and she found them. Five. The Emmisariae. They must have been planning to go the desert to find her when Nia froze them thus. But where was the Supreme Mancer? Had he heard her plea for help?

"Great Dragon," she said again in a high, thin voice. She could feel one of the massive beasts very nearby. "If you are willing to take me where I need to go, come with me to the Door."

Even as she said it, she realized she did not know the spells to open the vast iron door. There was no other way that she knew of for the dragons to get out. Charlie had gone. Suppose she was trapped here, with Nia and the Cra and the army of stone Mancers? Fear spread through her stomach, a cold sick ripple. But she began to walk back down the tunnel anyway and a hiss of smoke soared over her head. She heard the grating sound of scale on scale as more than one dragon lumbered to its feet, and the crash of claws on the stone floor of the cavern. They were coming with her. Not turning around, she walked back to the turn she had taken earlier and carried on straight. To her immense relief, the massive door at the end of the tunnel swung open with a groan as they approached, revealing a bright square of daylight. She did not know if it was the dragons performing this Magic, or even Nia sending her off on her quest, but it didn't matter. Eliza turned, and now she could see the dragons filling the cavern. The one nearest to her was staring at her intently, its head hanging low to the ground. Each of its gleaming, kaleidoscopic eyes was the size of her head.

"May I...get on?" she asked nervously. The dragon stared. She walked around its head, noting the steam that furled from its pulsing nostrils and the teeth like sabers curving over its powerful jawbone. Its neck was long and serpentine, gold-spiked. She placed a cautious hand at the base of its neck, just before it broadened out into muscled, scaled shoulders. On one of the scales she noticed a mark that seemed to have been branded on to it. It was the character for fire.

"You're Ka's dragon," said Eliza.

The dragon lifted its head ever so slightly, looking back at her, waiting. So she put her dagger away and took hold of one of the gold spikes with both hands. She braced her left foot against the creature's neck and heaved herself up and over, so she was seated at the base of the neck, between spikes, her back against the one behind her, holding on to the one ahead of her. As soon as she was settled, the dragon lumbered towards that square of light. The Mancer Citadel could move from place to place in Di Shang but for some years now it had been perched on the edge of a cliff in the arid plains approaching the Western Ocean. The door opened onto a dizzying drop into a canyon. The dragon leaped through the open door, joyfully stretched out its huge wings and pounded the air. The other dragons, letting out sharp, whistling screams, followed close behind. All five of them, including the dragon that carried Eliza, swooped down into the canyon and soared back up, embracing the wind and spitting fire. Unlike the wild dragons Swarn commanded, these dragons spent most of their time in a dark cavern. No wonder the open sky seemed to bring them such delight. Eliza, too, felt a great release in leaving the conquered Citadel behind. A part of her wanted only to go and hide or return to Tian Xia and beg Swarn for protection as Charlie had told her to. But she knew Nia was not lying when she said the monster she had made was going to find Eliza's mother. There was no time to go to Tian Xia, and hiding was not an option. It was not only her mother she had to protect. She was the Shang Sorceress. If the Mancers were all turned to stone there was only her to stop the thing before it hurt anyone. Nia knew her well and had created the perfect distraction.

As these thoughts raced through her mind, something struck her like a thunderbolt – *created*. I've *made* something special, Nia had said. Eliza couldn't be sure that the thing was not Illusion but if Nia thought Eliza might have Faery blood with which to defend herself against Illusion it seemed unlikely she would rely on it. The ravens had warned her about Nia's coming and about *Making*. Could it be that Nia had in fact *Made* a monster, just as that long ago wizard had Made the mortal dragons? If the thing was not an Illusion, what else could it be?

At her command, the dragons veered south over the parched earth. She kept an eye out for Charlie but did not see him and tried not to worry. Unlike her mother and all the people in the border towns between here and the desert, Charlie could take care of himself. He was a survivor, she told herself. The dragons dove in formation. Soon Eliza saw what they had seen. Nia's creature was flying low to the ground in an odd sort of zig-zag, roaring occasionally.

Eliza kept the Onbeweglich Cord always looped at the back of her coat. They had been a birthday present from Foss. While Foss had no doubt been right that it was excessive to use such powerful bonds on Abimbola Broom, they would be useful now. If Nia had Made this creature, then perhaps catching and killing it would hurt her in some way. Two of the dragons were making for it at a terrifying speed. When they were almost upon it they each spat a long blade of fire straight into it. The creature seemed to draw the flames into itself, absorbing the fire into its burning body, trailing flames through the air and burning even more brightly in the seams and cracks between its seared flesh. Eliza's dragon stayed above the others to give her a good view of what was happening. Fire would be of no use, obviously. The thing was already on fire; it was half made of fire. A third dragon dove into the thing and made to tear it apart with its vicious talons. The talons cut right through the monster but could not pull it apart. It was bonded tight by something else, something not physical. The burning flesh and bright, visible bone was severed in so many places and yet everything remained in place as if held together by some internal gravity. They had been flying low and the dragon hurled the burning beast to the ground. It tumbled and rolled and then rose upright with another roar, wings flexing. It was a roar of such unrelenting agony and rage that Eliza's heart clenched and a sob rose to her throat. Another dragon made a pass over its head. The beast leaped into the air and scraped its spiked fists against the scales of the dragon's belly. The dragon screamed and pounded its wings, rising out of reach, but the thing moved with it and drove several fists at once right into its chest. The other dragons all made for the thing at once and it fell away from them, spinning in flames as they breathed great balls of fire onto it. The hurt dragon crashed to the ground and threw its head back with a hideous scream. The monster was upon it in no time, slashing at its neck, and had to be pulled off by the three others while Ka's dragon circled anxiously overhead with Eliza on its back. What Eliza saw below her was a simple stalemate. The dragons were faster and stronger and outnumbered Nia's creation but the thing had one very clear advantage – it seemed to be indestructible. The dragons could tear it to pieces but it was already torn to pieces. They could burn it with fire but it was already burning. How could they destroy destruction embodied? They could delay it and hold it off but until they understood how it had been Made they could not kill it.

The hurt dragon was spitting blood now, thrashing its wings with rage. But Eliza knew enough from Swarn's tales of dragon-killing to know it was not near death yet.

"Down," Eliza told Ka's dragon and he dove straight for the raging beast. As they approached, she felt her breath drawn out of her, the air growing hot and thin and then unbreathable. This was not like killing the Cra. She could not make an error here. She gave herself over to her Deep Knowing, whirled the Onbeweglich Cord over her head and let them fly, holding one end in her hand. The lasso at the other end looped neatly over the monster's neck and Eliza pulled it fast. The dragon circled the thing at breakneck speed and Eliza wound the Cord around it. She had it, bound fast. But just as soon as she felt a surge of triumph the thing began to burn brighter inside, bleeding lava out between its cracks. It strained and strained and twisted and then burst free of the Cord, leaving the Magic rope she had used to lasso so many of the Cra in tatters. Ka's dragon rose quickly out of reach of the thing. It did not pursue them. Eliza drew in a deep shuddering breath of air.

A new plan formulated quickly in her mind and she gave her commands now. "Dragons of the Mancers," she called in the Language of First Days, fumbling for the right words, "Two of you must delay the monster. Drive it away from the...centres of living. One of you must go to the Xia Sorceress's former prison in the, um, land of snow. Bring me the Book of Barriers."

The wounded dragon was hunched on the stony ground now, staring up at her.

"Find refuge," she called down as Ka's dragon circled anxiously above it.

The dragons obeyed immediately, the injured dragon and one other veering north and two following the beast south. Nia's creature was bounding along the earth now, using it wings to glide several feet with each stride before touching the ground again with scalding hooves. The two dragons might be able to slow it down for a while, Eliza reasoned, but they would likely tire more quickly doing battle. It could hurt them but they could not hurt it. They would need help to stop it. The Mancers could not help her and the journey to Tian Xia would take too long but there were still some powers in Di Shang she could call on.

Ka's dragon looked back at her with one glittering eye.

"To Kalla," she told it.

While Eliza flew towards the capital on Ka's dragon, Nell was heading away from Kalla on a train to Elmount. It was one of the modern, high-speed *Confortare* trains. She had come out at the beginning of the semester on one of the old trains. It had been cramped and the air-conditioning had been broken but on the *Confortare* even the second class berths were relatively comfortable. A kindly attendant in a red blazer came around offering hot tea or coffee every hour or so. For the first few hours of the journey she enjoyed the view out the window of the world blanketed in snow, looking eagerly at the prosperous towns and cities they passed through. But now they were roaring along a black tunnel through the mountains and would be for some time.

End of term exams were finished at last and Nell was confident she had done well. Better, she hoped, than Oscar Van Holt, her main rival for top of the class. Now her mind was on other things, such as the outfit she'd bought in Kalla for Winter Festival, and whether Charlie and Eliza would be there or off on some adventure without her. Dearly as Nell loved her friends, it caused her no end of grief to be shut out of the Magic and excitement of their lives. Eliza was a Sorceress and Charlie was a Shade and their lives were entirely made up of strange adventures, whereas she, Nell, just had to go to school like an ordinary child. If they weren't in Holburg, Winter Festival would be entirely spoiled for her. She would only be able to think of what she was missing. But if they were there, they would tell her fantastic stories and Charlie would take her flying when everybody else was asleep.

With nothing to look at out the windows now, Nell opened a novel on her lap and pretended to read, while actually examining her fellow passengers. The train to Elmount was mainly full of people returning to the archipelago for Winter Festival. Elmount was one of those cities that islanders and vacationers passed through but where nobody actually seemed to live. Although of course there must be people on the train going home to Elmount as well. Nell shared her berth with an elderly couple and a strange-looking young man with a pale, narrow face and a mop of dark hair. Every time she looked at him, he twitched nervously and glanced at her, as if he could feel her gaze.

The elderly man was reading a newspaper he'd bought at the last stop. Now he folded it up and put it away, saying loudly to his wife, "Nothing new here! Abimbola Broom's trial and the Cra are still all over the front page, aye."

Nell brightened immediately, leaning towards them. "What's that about the Cra?" she asked. The woman looked disapproving, as if this was not a suitable subject for a young girl to take such an interest in, but her husband seemed quite happy to talk about it.

"Lah, you remember a couple of months back they *disappeared*. Mancers got them, that's the official report, aye. Almost all of them, all at once, which makes you wonder... Lah, of course we owe our very world to the Mancers and so it doesnay do to sound ungrateful, but if they could just round them all up like that, why didnay they do it before, I wonder?"

"I'm sure the Mancers have reasons for everything they do," said his wife placidly.

"Lah, that's what's in the *papers*," said the man cheerfully, ignoring his wife. "But at the *newsstand* they were saying there've been attacks all over the Republic just today, aye. No mention of *that* in the papers. Say what you will about Abimbola Broom, but the papers have gone downhill since he was put on trial."

"If it just happened *today*, how would it be in the papers already?" his wife asked pointedly.

"Attacks by the Cra?" asked Nell.

"Nobody knows," said the man smugly.

The young man emitted a high-pitched laugh that made them all jump.

"Except those who were attacked!" he said. "*They* know."

"Aye," said the elderly man gruffly, as if he did not think much of this contribution.

"Whatever it is, the Mancers will protect us," said his wife. "But it's probably nothing, if it's nay in the papers. Just gossip."

"You said yourself, it cannay be in the papers yet if it just happened!" the man said belligerently.

Nell looked out the window at the roaring blackness. Part of her was very excited, as always when *Something Was Happening*, but at the same time her heart was breaking. If *Something Was Happening*, Charlie and Eliza would almost certainly be in the thick of it and would not come to Holburg.

The door to their berth opened.

"Coffee?" asked the kindly attendant.

The elderly couple was sitting by the door and held out their cups to be filled first. When the attendant went to fill up the young man's cup, something strange happened. The top of the coffee pot had not been put on tightly enough and it came loose all of a sudden, hot coffee gushing out the top. It would surely have burned the young man's hand and gotten all over his lap. But the young man gasped a few words and the coffee seemed to leap back into the pot, the lid tightening itself firmly. It happened so quickly that only Nell and the young man were sure that it had happened at all. The attendant and the elderly couple tensed when the spill began and when it was averted they relaxed. The attendant poured the coffee and said apologetically, "Thought the lid was going to come off there." He tightened it a bit, unnecessarily, before refilling Nell's cup.

When she thought it over, Nell could not remember exactly what she had seen but, unlike the attendant and the elderly couple, she could not simply shake the strangeness away and forget it. She had seen *something*, after all, of that she was sure. She fixed her eyes on the young man, who drank his coffee quickly, looking out the window. His hands were trembling.

It was evening when they arrived in Elmount. The elderly couple had taken Nell under their wing and bought her dinner at a noodle shop by the port. They wandered around looking in bleak little shop windows until it was time for the boat to leave. They had arranged for cabins but Nell only had a Basic Passenger ticket so she bedded down in a hallway with everybody else who couldn't afford cabins. She lay awake as the boat rocked pleasantly beneath her. Eventually she slept a little but woke every time the boat stopped at one of the islands and other passengers stepped over her on their way to disembark. Early in the morning, she bought some bread for breakfast in the cafeteria and went up on deck. She walked up and down the deck, breathing in the sea breeze she had known all her life, watching people disembark at various islands to be embraced by their families. Then she saw the young man, bending into the wind with his threadbare coat clutched around him. He looked a very sad figure, with his untidy hair and too-narrow frame.

She approached him and offered him a piece of bread. He gave her a wary look, but he took the bread and devoured it as if he had been starving.

"Where are you going?" Nell asked, trying to sound friendly and nonthreatening.

"Stoot," he said.

"I'm going to Holburg," Nell said, although he hadn't asked. "I grew up there, aye. I'm a student in Kalla. Are you from Stoot?"

"Ye-es," he said vaguely, as if this might be a trick question.

Nell decided to be direct.

"You're nay from Stoot," she said firmly.

He stared at her, terrified.

"It's all right," she said. "I'm nay going to tell anybody. You're a wizard, are you nay?"

His eyes grew even wider and he didn't reply.

"Or praps nay a *wizard*, but you can do Magic. I saw what you did on the train, aye."

"This is my only pair of trousers," he said plaintively, by way of explanation. "If I got coffee all over them, what would I wear?"

"What's in Stoot?" Nell asked. "It's not one of the popular islands among vacationers."

His eyes brightened a little. "Coral!" he said, and then looked around anxiously.

"For spells," said Nell, and didn't wait for him to contradict her. "So *are* you a wizard?"

"Just a womi," he said shyly. "Not a wizard."

"Lah, it's good you averted that spill," said Nell. "It would have been a job to clean up."

He nodded. "Are you...?" he didn't finish his sentence and it took Nell a moment to understand what he was asking. She was delighted to be mistaken for a Tian Xia worlder, and was tempted for a moment or two to tell him that she was a witch.

"Human," she said regretfully. "But I've been to Tian Xia."

He looked as if he didn't believe her. Nell could see Stoot, a low cone of an island, growing nearer.

"Have you heard any rumours like what that couple was talking about?" she asked him quickly. "About attacks?"

He looked down at his feet. They were absurdly long. Looking at him now, Nell thought she should have known at first glance that he wasn't a Di Shang worlder.

"I dinnay know anything," he said.

"It concerns me a little," Nell explained. "My best friend is the Shang Sorceress...." She had been going to continue but he froze her with such a look of horror that she broke off in the middle of her sentence. Then he turned and fled. Nell stood staring after him for a moment before following.

"Wait!" she called. Passengers enjoying the bright balmy morning stopped to stare at them.

He ran indoors but there was nowhere to hide and she caught up with him in one of the second-class cabin corridors.

"Why are you running away?" she asked breathlessly. "Because of what I said about the Sorceress? She's very nice, really, she wouldnay be bothered about a harmless womi, whatever that is."

"Like a wizard," said the man, rabbity eyes darting here and there. "Only less so."

"But you see why I want to know what's going on?"

"Your friend should know," said the womi. "*She* should know."

"Know what?"

"Lots of crossings. I don't know *why* but I know that there are lots of crossings. It's a good time to be far out in the islands. Wouldn't want to be on the mainland now."

"Tian Xia worlders coming to Di Shang?" asked Nell, stunned

"I've got to go," he said. "We're almost at Stoot. Your friend is going to be busy. You shouldn't bother her about me."

"I'm nay going to turn you in," said Nell. "I just want to know what's happening."

"I don't *know*," he said, backing away from her. "Lots of crossings, that's all I know. I just want to be out of the way, see the coral. I'm not powerful, you know. Di Shang is a safe place usually but not right now."

Nell let him walk away from her swiftly. "Good luck!" she called after him, but he didn't reply.

The big boat didn't stop at Holburg, so Nell had to get off at Murda and pay one of the fishermen to take her across. From Murda, Holburg looked like a dense green hook or a beckoning finger laid flat on the surface of the water. The fishing vessel bobbed on the bright foaming waves and it was late afternoon when they docked in Holburg's harbour. Everybody who saw her as she made her way through Holburg Town stopped to say hello and asked for news of the city, so it took her some time to reach the dilapidated white house with chipping paint and a broken fence. There was not much winter to speak of in Holburg, just a pleasant cool wind, and the front door was wide open. She could hear the sound of the television inside and her brothers talking loudly over it. Nell was the youngest of five. Of her four older brothers, Danil and Som were still in school. Marik had graduated from high school last year and manned their father's cigarette and magazine shop now that their father had become one with the sofa. Alban, the eldest, had bought a fishing boat last year, married pretty Marti Somerset, and was building his own house. For now, the happy couple lived in Marti's uncle's van, whose engine had given out six years ago.

Nell dragged her bags into the front hall and called, "I'm back!"

"Nell's back!" roared Marik, in case anybody had missed her announcement.

Her mother Onni came bustling in from the kitchen to embrace her. Onni was a mass of pale flesh with fair, wispy hair and tiny, startled eyes. She had grown up on Holburg, a romantic, dreamy girl without much sense of the world beyond, and as a grown woman she seemed bewildered by, if not actively averse to, what had happened to her life. Nell felt a confused mixture of impatience and protectiveness towards her mother, while Onni was rather in awe of her clever and beautiful youngest child. She hugged and kissed Nell several times and then ushered her into the sitting room, where her father Gladd took up half the sofa.

Gladd had been a big noisy boy and had become an enormous silent man. He had a bit of brownish hair stuck to the top of his sweaty head. His chins rolled down his neck and became mounds of chest and further mountains of belly. He did not care to leave the sofa anymore and so there he remained. He was a bit puzzled by Nell's sudden fame as the first islander to win a scholarship to that fancy school in Kalla but it pleased him insofar as it must mean she was doing well. And so when he saw her he grinned. Nell kissed him on the cheek. He raised a fat hand to pat her hair.

Her brothers nodded and smiled shyly and dragged her bags up to her bedroom for her.

Ander Brady, the chief of police, was sitting in the tattered brown chair they referred to as "the guest chair," drinking a cup of coffee. He greeted Nell cordially and asked her about school. Ander, unlike most of the islanders, had actually been to the mainland and even to Kalla. It was well known by everybody except, apparently, Gladd, that Ander had long ago been very much in love with young dreamy Onni. Older than she, he had joined the army for a few years while she was still in high school, writing to her every week, but when he came back she was married to Gladd, for reasons nobody but Onni would ever know. Devastated, Ander had gone back to the military and become a war hero. Upon returning, he and Gladd struck up an unlikely friendship and he was the only person really who ever sat in the guest chair. Ander didn't look like a war hero to Nell. He was rather overweight, with a receding hairline, big pouches under his eyes and a shy but affable manner. Still, the fact remained that he had on his mantel more medals than anyone in Holburg had ever seen.

Nell politely told Ander a bit about her school. Onni stood behind her nodding enthusiastically as if to confirm what Nell was saying and Gladd stared open-mouthed at the television. Tiring quickly of her own story, Nell glanced at the television and saw a dashing, uniformed man speaking at a podium.

"Who's that?" she asked.

"Lah, that's General Malone!" exclaimed her mother, delighted to be able to provide some information. "You know, the one who disappeared for *nine years*!"

Nell looked even more closely when she heard that, realizing he must be the General Eliza had found in the Arctic.

"Something going on, aye," mumbled Gladd. It was not usual for Gladd to say something and so they all paused to take this in respectfully. Then Ander explained, "In the last twenty-four hours, they've confirmed a great many Tian Xia attacks. Nay just in the Republic, but all over Di Shang."

"And the Mancers?" asked Nell, who fancied herself a bit of

an expert on the mystical. After all, she was the only ordinary human in the Modern Age who had been to Tian Xia, even if she couldn't remember it. She had given up her memories in exchange for passage back and had regretted it ever since. It was terrible not to remember anything at all about the greatest adventure of her entire life.

"There's no word, aye," said Ander. He knew a thing or two about Tian Xia attacks and he was troubled.

"But we're quite safe *here*," said Onni. "Lah, nothing ever happens *here*. Will you stay for supper, Ander?"

"Oh, no. Mother's expecting me."

"Lah, you know she's welcome also, Ander!"

"No, no, she's poorly, I should get back, aye."

This was their ritual. Ander heaved himself up out of the guest chair and reached out a hand, which Gladd shook, mumbling something indiscernible.

"Same to you, Gladd, same to you," Ander said affably. Nell wondered if he actually knew what her father had said. "Good to have you back, Nell," said Ander as he made his way to the door in a slow shuffle, nodding to each of them in turn. "Boys, good evening. Thank you as always, Onni."

"Goodnight, Mister Brady," said Nell. He edged out the door and then broke into a stride that reminded Nell he had been strong and athletic once.

Supper was a raucous affair. Onni wanted to hear about Nell but Nell was tired after her journey and didn't have the energy to try to drown out her brothers. Alban and Marti came by after dinner and they all had some wine and became very jolly. Nobody remembered or cared that Nell was still a bit young for wine and so she got drunk for the first time in her life.

When her father had gone to sleep on the sofa, snoring so the floors trembled, and Alban and Marti had laid sleeping bags out on the floor in the hall, and the others had all gone to their beds, Nell sat by her bedroom window and breathed in the salty night air for awhile. She had never been drunk before and didn't want to sleep through the novel experience. So far, she just felt foggy-minded and a little sad, which wasn't terribly exciting. However, having witnessed adults behaving very stupidly when drunk, she was waiting to see if she herself would be suddenly compelled to do something idiotic. The town was silent. If she listened very carefully she could hear the pull of the sea. Then all of a sudden something fell out of the sky and crashed into the yard. She leaped to her feet and leaned further out the window, straining to see by the moonlight. The thing had wings and it was the size of a small car. It changed shape and became a boy staggering towards the house.

"Charlie!" she called. Charlie looked up at her and broke into a smile. Then his legs gave out beneath him and he collapsed on the lawn.

CHAPTER

8

$\mathcal{K}$yreth's hands had, over the course of nearly five centuries, done many things. His hands were credited with keeping the worlds apart. They were hands that could See, hands that could Open, hands that could Destroy. They were conduits for Great Magic and had built the greatest Barriers in the worlds. They were feared by many and respected by all.

Now, his hands were plunged into his marble desk past the wrist so he could not move them. Nia's white tiger watched him with inscrutable, iridescent eyes through the hole she had smashed in the wall. His mind was clouded by the Confusion. He could not bring his darting, fragmented thoughts together to summon the Magic he needed. He was still, however, the Supreme Mancer. Where other beings and perhaps other Mancers would be utterly lost in such a spell, unable to formulate a single coherent thought, Kyreth struggled mightily to clear his mind. Nia was a fool to leave him alone. If she believed that immobilizing his hands and baffling his mind were enough, she was mistaken. The Confusion sat like a mist over his brain. He needed to burn it off with clarity of thought and then he would be able to free his hands. Remembering who he was and what was happening was easy; maintaining a single train of thought was more difficult. His mind was like a wild horse he had to keep on track as it galloped to and fro. Had the Emmisariae escaped before Nia came? If so, and if they found Eliza first, all might still be well. Those five, with time to prepare and assistance from Tian Xia, would be a match for Nia. He wondered too what Nia was doing, where she was, how the Mancers were faring. He forced all these tangled dissonant thoughts away with a great blaze of energy. For a moment his mind was clear but it was not long enough to release his hands before the cloud converged again and scattered his thoughts in too many directions at once.

To become Supreme Mancer was not an easy thing. It required unusual ability and focus. It required perseverance. Kyreth had these. He did not let the spell take him. He did not become discouraged and allow the Confusion to sweep away his very self like a tidal wave. It had all the inexorable power of the tide coming in but Kyreth could hold off the tide and turn it back. Such was his power. Again, he swept aside the spell. He knew there would be no time to find words to free his hands and so he poured his Magic into force, giving his hands all the strength he could. The desk cracked down the middle, but held his hands fast. The tiger, still and watchful, did not move. Every now and then, the tip of his tail twitched.

Hours passed in struggle. Sweat poured down Kyreth's face and back. Piece by piece he destroyed the desk.

When Nia returned, he was slumped on the floor in an ungainly fashion, holding his head up with great effort. The desk was in pieces, yet his hands remained encased in blocks of marble still. His eyes were like dying embers, red with hatred. She stepped delicately into the study through the hole in the wall. She had not bothered to conjure any doors, simply tore her way through the Citadel's walls, and Kyreth longed to warn her that the Citadel had Magic of its own and would not tolerate such treatment without retaliating somehow. But he did not want to risk speaking. He could not be sure what would come out and would not give her the satisfaction of hearing him speak nonsense.

"Guess who I've just seen!" said Nia cheerfully, stepping over the ruin of the desk and crouching down before him. "Eliza! Such a treat! She looked very well, I thought. Oh, I know, you're disappointed, you'd hoped your Emmisariae might get to her first. But they're even more stuck than you are, you see. And Eliza wasn't with the Sorma anyway, so they wouldn't have found her. She's terribly like her mother, with the lies and rebellion, isn't she? Shall I tell you where she was? Or can you guess? She'd been in Tian Xia! Keeping in touch with Swarn and the Oracle. Obviously she doesn't think the Mancers can teach her everything she wants to learn. Clever girl. Oh, I can see you're very worried now. I'd think it was concern for dear Eliza if I didn't know you better. She's fine. I've given her something to do that will keep her busy and out of my way for a while. If she's as bright as I think, it won't actually get her killed, but she's rather unpredictable so it's difficult to say. It should tire her out at the very least. I don't want her putting up a fight and taking up loads of my time when I get back. Yes, that's right, we're going on a trip, Papa! Are you excited? Come on."

Kyreth was heaved to his feet like a puppet having his strings pulled and the blocks of marble fell away from his hands. At the same moment, the fog lifted from his mind. He stood towering over her with all his power. He knew at that moment that it was hopeless. His Magic was slow and he was alone. He was no match for her alone. Not anymore. She looked him in the eyes, waiting, with a slight smile, for him to understand how helpless he was, how little she feared him.

"It is me you want," he said hollowly. "Do your worst but let Eliza and the Mancers be. Return to Tian Xia and they will not pursue you."

"Such egotism!" said Nia. "It's true I've something particular in mind for you, Papa, given our long history, but I've no reason to harbour warm and fuzzy feelings for those that did your bidding. No, the Mancers must pay for what they participated in, and as for Eliza, she's far more mine than yours. You like to think you're protecting her but the truth is we *both* want to make use of her power. My way is more efficient, that's all. If you could do what I can, you would. Don't pretend otherwise. There is no moral high ground between you and me, and justice doesn't interest me, but retribution does. Now, tell me," and she stepped closer to him, touched a hand to his cheek, "when I was just a little girl, did you ever look at me and fear, even for a second, that I might be stronger than you one day and demand retribution?"

Kyreth said nothing.

"You didn't, did you?" whispered Nia. "It never even occurred to you. Such arrogance! Of course, you were very young then, hardly older than humans live to be. And so ambitious! You always wanted to be the Supreme Mancer. As soon as you were made an Emmisarius, free to leave the Citadel on your very own shiny dragon, you had plans. Yes, I know. But how did you *think* it would turn out? Did you really imagine you could woo my mother, that she would fall in love with you and willingly bear you a child? You weren't chosen to father the Shang Sorceress back then but you thought you would single-handedly take over the line of the Xia Sorceress. So what did my mother say to you when you propositioned her? Do you remember what her face was like? Did she laugh? Did she spit on you?"

Nia circled Kyreth slowly then grabbed his face between her two hands, pulling it down towards her own face.

"It must have been terrible," she hissed, her eyes inches from his. "Whatever she said or did, it must have cut you so deeply. And did you imagine that the child she bore unwillingly, cursing it in her womb, would be a true and loyal daughter to you? Did you think that? Or perhaps you only thought you would always be strong enough to keep me in check." She squeezed his head harder and shook it, then pressed her forehead to his. "But you were wrong, you were so wrong every time. You were wrong to think my mother could love you. You were wrong to think you could take by force what she would not give. You were wrong to think I would be the daughter you hoped for. And you were wrong, Papa, to think I would never be strong enough to make you pay."

With that she hurled him to the ground so he lay gasping amid the rubble of his desk. For a moment she stood over him, breathing hard. Then she leaned over and pulled him up by his arm.

"Come on."

The Sorceress and the Supreme Mancer crossed the grounds together, the white tiger loping ahead of them. They could see five bright specks in the southern sky.

"There goes Eliza with your dragons," said Nia. "Good for her. She'll figure out soon enough what I've made for her but if I know our Eliza she won't just give up. Do you know how I sent her hopping off that way? I threatened Rea. Such a loyal child, isn't she! But you don't know what that's like, of course. What is it that makes your daughters despise you?"

"Do not speak for Rea," said Kyreth. The words tasted of gunpowder in his mouth.

"Oh yes, your dutiful daughter *Rea*. But she wasn't keen on your choice of husband for her, was she? I don't imagine you were invited to her wedding with Rom. Oh, and then she did everything she could to keep your grandchild from you! Why do you suppose that is?"

"Rea is my true daughter," Kyreth said. He could not bid himself be quiet.

"Oooh, your *true* daughter!" cried Nia. They were almost at the dark wood. "Do you mean as opposed to me? What kind of daughter am I, then?"

"You are a perversion," said Kyreth. "A twisted and evil thing. A mistake."

Nia spun and took his throat in her hand, driving him to his knees at the edge of the wood. He choked for breath. The tiger circled them, tail lashing. Nia held him there for several minutes. The world began to shrink and spin and go black. Then she let go and he fell face-first to the grass, gasping for air.

"I came into the world," said Nia in a voice sharp and glittering as a newly forged blade, "helpless and misused. I made myself the greatest Sorceress that has ever lived, one of the most powerful beings in all of Tian Di. You will see how powerful I am, Papa, and then you will be proud of your little girl."

She turned and strode into the dark wood. Her Magic dragged him after her on his belly. Many-legged things scuttled over him and the low branches scratched his face. Soon they were on that silver shore and the Boatman emerged from the mist. Kyreth struggled to his feet.

The Boatman faced Nia. "Great Magic bars you from Crossing," he said in that voice like a blade scraping china. "I cannot take you."

"But you *can*, ghoul," said Nia. "And you shall."

She raised her hands. There came a flash so bright that Kyreth was blinded. The shore and the water and the line of dark trees were erased. There was only a white brilliance and the Language of First Days rolling across it like thunder, words of terrible power, as old as time. When Kyreth came to himself, the boat hung in a dazzling void and he was on it. Nia stood at the fore of the boat, whispering now, and her whispers were like wind in the sails, driving them through light into light, until the whiteness rushed upwards, blurring and thickening into a mist, and the sea emerged from it beneath them. She had broken the Magic that barred her from Tian Xia.

"There is an island between the worlds," said Nia to the Boatman, a little breathless. "You know where it is, for it was created by this being in the boat with me. Long ago, you took him there many times and took him away again. But you would not take me away when I begged you to. I had to learn to command you. Do you remember, Boatman?"

"I remember," said the Boatman.

"Take us there now."

Kyreth lay in the boat and gazed into the white mist that obscured everything. It was still possible that the Triumvira would stop Nia in Tian Xia but would they help the Mancers then? The alliances were fragile; he could not count on them. He shut his eyes and rested. He would need his strength for what was coming. He slept. In his dreams he saw again and again a golden-haired girl, green eyes full of loathing, backing away from him as he moved towards her.

"Papa." Nia's voice was soft in his ear. "We're here."

Though he could see nothing through the heavy white mist, Kyreth felt the stone tower he had built himself on a black wedge of rock he had called out of the water. What a day that had been, the exhiliration, for the first time testing the extent of his own power. He could hear the hounds of the Crossing baying all around the tower.

They disembarked, stepping onto the wet rock they could not see, for even their bodies were lost in the mist. Only Kyreth's eyes were visible, as the sun sometimes is on a foggy day, a haze of flame.

"Here is where my mother threw herself into the sea after you took me away from her," said Nia.

Kyreth shook his head and then remembered Nia could barely see him. "She did not want to raise you any more than she wanted to live," he said hoarsely. "I bound her with barriers throughout her pregnancy, kept her here, for your protection only."

"Barriers," said Nia in disgust. "This mist still makes me nauseous, centuries later, would you believe! Anyway, I haven't brought you here to avenge my mother. I never knew her and it was her own fool fault if she was too weak to take revenge and decided she preferred drowning instead. No, Papa, you're here because of what you did to *me*. Up we go."

Kyreth followed Nia into the tower. What choice did he have? Steps wound up to a single chamber at the top.

"Home sweet home," said Nia. "It was all sightless terror back then. The sound of the hounds all I had for friends..." She walked around the room as if in a trance, touching the walls she could not see. "You thought you could raise me to revere you. When that was an obvious failure, you thought to tame me like a little stray wildcat, break my spirit, and in that way make me your creature. But I wasn't like my mother, was I? I didn't give in so easily."

Her voice had been coming from across the room and so Kyreth was startled by her hand, cool on his cheek.

"What do you think I'm going to do to you?"

"I expect that you intend to kill me," he replied.

"And is there anything you'd like to say before I do? Any regrets you'd like to express?"

"I could not have predicted your nature," Kyreth said coldly. "I did the worlds a great wrong, unknowing."

"You did the worlds a wrong? What about *me*? What about my *mother*?"

"How little you understand," said Kyreth. "I had a vision. I knew the Mancers could be greater than we were. The Shang Sorceress has always been our greatest asset, our warrior. But imagine a Sorceress protecting either side of the Crossing! Two lines, the Shang Sorceress and the Xia Sorceress, guided by the Mancers. We should never have allowed our influence in Tian Xia to lapse. What I did was for a greater good, or would have been, if only you had been other than what you are. My single regret is that I did not see sooner what you were destined to become and snuff you out."

"Well, never mind," said Nia with a sigh. "I'm more interested in your suffering than your repentance. I wonder if you've ever known true fear? When I was just a small thing, you were all I knew of the world, and you meant me ill. Shall I show you what I mean?"

Now he felt her hands on either side of his face. His strength and certainties poured out of him like blood from a cut vein. He sank to the cold floor. Her voice seemed to come from the stone and the mist, a thousand voices in one, whispering, "Fear was my first lesson, my only lesson from you. I am its master now and will teach you to crawl before it. You will live in that moment when fear reaches its most terrible crescendo, the moment it turns your blood to ice, from now until your death."

As she spoke, terror swept through him, a mad, reasonless dread. He pressed himself against the wall, clawed at his chest. He could not see, he could not *see* what was coming, his matchless foe, his undoing. He tried to scream. His mouth opened wide but no sound came out of him.

"I am done with you," said Nia.

She turned and left the tower, breaking into a run halfway down the steps. She boarded the boat and was seized by a shudder that shook her from head to toe. Her tiger came and pressed against her. She buried her hands in the soft white fur of its neck.

"Go," she said to the Boatman. "To Tian Xia."

The Boatman obeyed her, as he had done centuries before, when she was just thirteen years old, crackling with a power that could no longer be contained and never to be mastered again.

CHAPTER

9

Nell ran down the stairs, jumping over Marti and Alban in their sleeping bags, passing her snoring father on the sofa, and out the battered screen door into the backyard. Charlie lay where she had seen him fall, breathing in shallow gasps. Something was wafting out of his chest like smoke.

"What's happening to you? What's the matter?" She knelt over him and put a hand to his clammy forehead.

"The Sorceress is free."

Nell's stomach executed a highly uncomfortable somersault.

"Where's Eliza?" she asked. When he didn't answer immediately, his head lolling to the side, she asked again, *"Where IS Eliza?"* and shook him by the shoulders, which made him gasp. A plume of the smoky substance poured from his chest. Nell pulled herself together and ran back inside for towels and water. She pressed the towels to his chest to try and stanch whatever was leaking out of him and raised him up so his neck and head were on her knees. She held the glass of water to his lips and he drank from it.

"She's nay hurt," he managed to say when he could speak again. "With any luck she's gone to Tian Xia...for help from the Triumvira."

"Why didnay you go with her?" demanded Nell. "You're hurt! You could have gone to the Cave, aye!"

Charlie shook his head and swallowed some more water. "No time. I would have...slowed her down. Couldnay have made the Crossing...like this."

"What happened to you? Why did you come *here?*"

He tilted his head back so he could look right up at her. "I'm dying, aye," he said. "I didnay want to be alone."

She looked down at Charlie, at his face white with pain but so very calm, and the moment seemed to stretch on forever. Then she tore her eyes away and looked up at the stars. Her mind worked quickly. A doctor would be useless and the doctor on the island was a drunk anyway. The Sorma might be able to help but then again, they might not. And how would she get to the desert, how would she find them without Eliza? Although she did not remember the Crossing to Tian Xia herself, she had forced Charlie and Eliza to tell her about it many times, how she had almost died on the way and how the healing cave had restored her to perfect health. The cave had healed Eliza's arm too, which had been crushed by a hound of the Crossing. The cave could save Charlie now.

"You're nay going to die, Charlie," she said firmly. "Just hold the towels to your chest and wait here."

"Dinnay go," he pleaded as she shifted him off her lap and back on to the grass. "It's all right, I'm nay scared. I've been around forever. Long enough, aye. I just didnay want to die in some dark corner without any friends."

"Charlie, *stop it.* I told you, you're nay going to die. Just wait. I'll be right back!"

"Nell!" he called after her, but she was off, running out the back gate and down the road to where Ander Brady and his mother lived.

The streets in Holburg were generally empty after eight o'clock and it was past midnight now. Everybody was sleeping. Her bare feet slapping against the road was the only sound besides the crickets in the gardens. When she reached Ander's house she ran straight up the front steps and rang the bell several times, then pounded on the door for good measure.

A light went on in one of the rooms and a few moments later Ander appeared at the door in his pajamas, looking sleepy and confused.

"Nell?" He squinted at her in the dark of the porch.

"I need help," Nell told him. "I need the helicopter and I dinnay have time to explain."

He frowned and rubbed his chin, then ducked his head at her and sniffed. "You've been drinking!" he said, appalled. "Your parents let you drink?"

"I dinnay think they really remember how old I am," she said impatiently. "Mister Brady, please listen to me. You know what we saw on the news, General Malone talking about Tian Xia attacks?"

Ander shook his head. "Come on, Nell. I've got to get you home."

"Aye, yes, walk me home, quick," she backed down the steps as he put on a pair of shoes and a light jacket over his pajamas and followed her. "So you remember what General Malone was saying?"

"Uh huh." In spite of himself he had to stride along very quickly to keep up with her.

"It's worse than they know. The Xia Sorceress is free. And – lah, it's complicated – but there's a being here now who is *good* and he's been hurt very badly. Di Shang doctors wouldnay be able to help him. I dinnay think even the Sorma could help him. But there's a place in Tian Xia that...heals beings when they're hurt or sick. And I need to get him there, aye."

"Do your parents know you're running around drunk in the middle of the night?" asked Ander.

"Of course they dinnay know!" snapped Nell. "Are you paying attention? There are ways into Tian Xia...a lot of ways, aye, and there's one not far from here. The only way to get there fast is to fly, but this being, he cannay fly now, because he's too badly hurt. But you can fly the helicopter, nay? The one for emergencies? You flew Missus Brock to the mainland hospital when she had a heart attack!"

They had reached the back gate.

"Let's get you inside," said Ander wearily.

Nell dragged him by the hand to where Charlie lay in the grass.

"You're back," said Charlie with a faint smile. "Good.

Who's that?"

"Mister Brady," said Nell. "He can help us."

"He's hurt?" Ander asked, kneeling swiftly. "You didnay wake up your ma?"

"She cannay fly a helicopter," said Nell.

Ander took the towels gently from Charlie's chest and looked for a long moment at the rippling fusion of gleam and gloom that bled from the wounds.

"What in the name of the Ancients is that?" he muttered.

"He's a Shade," said Nell, pressing the towels to the wounds again, though it did little good. "It means he can change shape. He's good, aye, and he helps humans. He helped to get rid of the Cra. But now he needs help. I'm nay drunk or crazy and I know exactly what to do. I just need you to fly the helicopter."

"Nell," said Ander, but she didn't let him finish.

"Whatever you're going to say, save it. I dinnay care. You're just trying to think of what you should do and he'll die while you wonder. We have to help him. I'm going inside to get a couple of things and when I get back, you need to carry him." Nell ran back into the house. Ander looked down at Charlie again.

"I cannay just take the helicopter," he said to Charlie apologetically. "I dinnay understand what's going on here. We should call somebody, I spec. Dinnay know who, though."

Charlie didn't waste his strength talking to Ander. He was trying to hang on until Nell reappeared.

It was a testament to her family's ability to sleep through anything that none of them woke as Nell tore through the house. She filled a school bag with bread and cheese and apples, two bottles of water and a half-empty bottle of brandy. Then she fetched her maps of the caves in Holburg from the stacks of papers in her bedroom. The tunnels had been built during the war for the islanders to hide in in the case of a Tian Xia attack. As children Nell and Eliza had known the entire complex by heart and had mapped it out. She placed these old penciled maps on the kitchen table with a note for her family, *Please check in on Missus Brady. Hide if you need to. Back soon.* Then she went back up to her room and added to the bag of food her three most prized possessions. These were the First Place Medal in the Kalla District Mathematics Competition she had won last year and the birthday presents Eliza and Charlie had given her when she turned fourteen. Eliza had gotten hold of a signed Cherry Swanson album *(Any friend of Eliza's is a friend of mine! Cherry S.,* she had written), and Charlie had brought back from Tian Xia a shard of black rock, embedded in which was the fossil of a tiny dragon no bigger than her hand. All of these she put in the bag. She ran back out to the yard, where Ander was massaging his temples with his thumbs and Charlie was quietly dying.

"Do you have anything valuable on you?" she asked Ander. "That watch! Is it valuable?"

"This?" He looked at his watch in surprise. "I dinnay spec so. It was my father's."

"Perfect," said Nell. "Pick him up. We have to hurry."

"Nell," said Ander again.

"Pick him up!" Nell all but snarled.

Without really knowing why he was letting a fourteen-year-old girl with alcohol on her breath boss him around in the middle of the night, Ander did as she said.

"Praps we should stop by the doctor," he suggested, following her out the gate.

"Dinnay be stupid," said Nell angrily. "You know just as well as I do that a doctor cannay heal a wound like that. We're saving his life."

Somehow that settled it for Ander. He had his doubts that Nell knew what she was doing, but she seemed to think she knew, at least. He himself hadn't a clue, but he held that action was better than inaction. And so he found himself wrapping the thing in blankets in the back of the helicopter, loading up with extra fuel and climbing into the front with Nell.

"I dinnay think you should come," he told Nell, knowing perfectly well it was useless.

"You'll nay find it without me," said Nell.

Ander put on his aviation headset and gestured for her to do the same. They fastened their seatbelts and he opened the throttle all the way. The helicopter had not been flown since Missus Brock's heart attack four years ago. It had been old and unreliable even then. But the rotary blades began their slow spin and, as they spun faster, the helicopter began to feel light, swaying slightly and giving a couple of awkward jerks. Then it lifted off the ground and Ander powered it forward. They skimmed along the alley for a few seconds then swooped upwards, leaving Holburg behind them.

"South!" shouted Nell, pointing.

In the back of the helicopter, Charlie tried to say Nell's name but the noise drowned him out. He couldn't hear his own voice. He could feel his life draining out of him. It seemed such a waste of effort, roaring off in this noisy machine. He just wanted her to sit with him while it all faded to black.

As Charlie was making his final desperate, wounded flight over the archipelago to Nell, powered only by Swarn's potion, Eliza was a few hundred miles southeast of Kalla, breaking into the Republic's top military command centre.

Flying across the country on Ka's dragon, she had tried to think of the ways it might be possible to get in touch with General Malone. She concluded that face-to-face was best. It could take hours or more to convince somebody to let her speak to him. Once he saw her he would remember her and would listen.

The dragon, with its mighty wings, was much faster than a gryphon. Still, it was dark by the time she caught sight of the command centre, a vast walled complex on a high plateau. She wished she'd had the foresight to mix up an invisibility potion while she'd been in the Citadel but it was too late now – she'd find no invisible eels to use in the wilds of Di Shang. She didn't dare fly too close, so she instructed the dragon to land east of the command centre, in the wooded foothills. She would have to go quite a distance by foot but a dragon approaching would be too obvious and would almost certainly be viewed as an attack. They would see *her* coming, too, but might hold off firing on a girl. From the foothills, she jogged down into the valley and then half-scrambled up onto the broad plateau. Once on the plateau she could not escape being seen and the important thing was speed. She sprinted straight for the high concrete walls. She was surprised to feel, as she approached, that they were protected by enchantment. The Mancers must have done this to help protect the complex from a Tian Xia attack. This would require more effort than she had thought. She pressed her hand to the wall, knowing full well that somebody would be watching her do so. The barriers were fairly simple. She made the symbol with her hand to conjure a door and then *pushed.*

She could feel the danger before she heard it and drew her dagger in a sweeping motion over her head, deflecting a hail of bullets. The wall groaned, a door opening into it. She created an empty space the size of a cupboard, stepped inside, and sealed herself in to catch her breath for a moment.

She didn't want to just emerge on the other side, where no doubt they would be waiting for her. She would have to walk through the wall a little ways. She closed her eyes. The wall was concrete and she could separate its parts in her mind – gravel, broken stone, sand, cement (which was oxidized lime and clay), and water. She needed to separate them, but in a precise enough way that the wall didn't just collapse on her. Her heart began to pound in her chest. She was not terribly good at separating elements and had certainly never done so while there was a risk of being crushed to death. She took a deep breath and let her Magic flow into the wall – *Undo, be pure, be what you were* – pulling element from element. For a moment, she was able to hold each part where she wanted and she felt space opening up before her – and then the fleeting thought, *Where's the sand?* interrupted the flow. The entire structure began to crumble. Without thinking she jammed the elements back together. The wall closed on her, concrete filling her ears, fitting itself around her limbs and face, pressing tighter and tighter around her. She could not move her hands to make a door and in a moment it would crack her into slivers. With her last ounce of strength she pulled the elements around her apart again and leaped forward as the wall around her loosened. She tumbled out of the wall in a small avalanche of sand and pebbles and slimy clay and water, and was fired on immediately. She rolled aside, gasping a simple barrier spell against metal. It would do for bullets but her barriers never lasted more than a minute or two. She had barely a moment to take in where she was. There were soldiers on the wall above her and soldiers running towards her as well, fast dark shadows. She ran straight for a squat concrete building in front of her while the wall collapsed behind her. No time to find the door, she would have to make one – she made the sign and leaped through the wall of the building as it opened and shut behind her.

She landed in an empty hallway. A siren was blaring now, alerting everyone to her presence. This was not at all how she had intended to find General Malone. The best thing to do would be to hide and send a seeking spell, which would be less visible than her. There was a supply closet in the hallway, so she stepped inside it and shut the door. Ignoring the sound of heavy boots outside, she sat cross-legged and spoke the spells of Seeking. Great beings could work these spells across vast distances but as yet Eliza was only able to seek within a radius of a few hundred feet. If General Malone were not nearby, she would have to move and try again.

The military complex spent the rest of the night and the early hours of the morning in a state of high alert. Something had breached the walls. It was impervious to bullets. It had vanished. They did not know what it was, except that it looked like a girl, and they did not know what it intended. It had emerged from the main wall and disappeared for ten or fifteen minutes inside the mess hall. Then it had suddenly emerged again and run into the armory. This had everybody most anxious. A sweep by Special Forces showed there was indeed a living thing inside the ceiling, although they weren't sure how it had gotten there. They fired a rocket straight into the ceiling and none of them heard or saw anything more for a further twenty minutes, when it was spotted again running for the Communications Tower.

General Malone's office was under heavy guard in case this was an assassination attempt. He was at his desk now, on the phone with a commander who told him that dragons had been sighted near the border. Reports were coming in from all over. This was the greatest influx of Tian Xia beings that Di Shang had seen since the arrival of the Xia Sorceress nearly half a century ago. Worst of all, the Mancers were nowhere to be found. The normal lines of communication yielded no response. Pilots were out looking for their Citadel but it could be anywhere in Di Shang. It was like looking for a needle in a haystack.

Quite suddenly the carpet under his feet shifted and then bulged. General Malone muttered, "Keep me posted," and hung up the phone. He backed away from the desk and drew his gun. The bulge in the carpet grew bigger, the carpet split, and a breathless girl with untidy hair crawled out from under his desk and looked up at him imploringly. She was wearing a dirty black robe and a dark green winter coat. He recognized her instantly.

"By the Ancients! Eliza Tok."

"Everybody's chasing me," she said, seeming rather hurt. "Would you tell them to stop?"

"*You* are what the entire complex is after? *You* breached our wall?"

"I needed to see you, aye."

General Malone went on the intercom. "Attention all personnel. The intruder has been found. The threat is eliminated. Resume your normal duties." He looked back at Eliza. She had grown a few inches. She looked older but not so different from when he had last seen her in the Xia Sorceress's web of Illusions.

"The outer wall will have to be rebuilt," he said. "We've shot up our own armory. The whole place is in uproar."

"I'm sorry," she said meekly.

General Malone wasn't sure if he wanted to scold her or laugh. He did neither.

"Perhaps *you* can shed some light on what's going on," he said. "Where are the Mancers?"

"The Xia Sorceress turned them all to stone," said Eliza. She didn't know what had happened to Kyreth but there was no point mentioning that now. General Malone stared at her in horror, speechless.

"She's free of the barriers but she's going to Tian Xia," Eliza continued. "We dinnay need to worry about her here, yet."

"Tian Xia worlders must know the Mancers are no longer defending Di Shang," said the General. "That's why so many are crossing over. The military...we can't handle a full-scale Tian Xia invasion without the Mancers."

There was a tap on the door.

"Enter," called General Malone.

Two guards opened the door.

"Everything all right?" asked one of them, looking warily at Eliza.

"Fine. Our intruder is...an old acquaintance of mine," said General Malone dryly. "She has a strange way of making a visit." He looked at Eliza again. "You do know I have a telephone, don't you?"

"I didnay know your number," said Eliza.

The General nodded to the Guards, who exchanged a look and shut the door behind them.

"I appreciate the information about the Mancers," said General Malone heavily. "Was that what you invaded a top military command centre to tell me?"

"No, there's something else," said Eliza. "There's a creature that the Sorceress *Made*, and if you kill it, it might...hurt her, or stop her. I'm nay sure. But it's connected to her. That's the one you need to go for, aye. Two of the Mancer dragons are following it now."

Eliza sat down on the floor abruptly and stopped talking. General Malone knelt at her side, touching her shoulder lightly.

"What's wrong?"

She shook her head. "I havenay eaten in a while. Nor slept. I came straight here."

The General nodded. "I'll have a bed made up. Let's get you some food."

He started to rise but she caught his sleeve with her hand. "First you have to send soldiers. It's heading for the border towns around Quan, aye. Going south. It might take a lot. Rockets, or...I dinnay know. It willnay be easy to kill."

General Malone patted her on the shoulder and helped her to her feet. "Consider it done, Eliza."

As she followed the General out into hall she seemed to hear the Oracle's voice again, almost hissing with pleasure. *Victory will only come at a price for you. You will cut out your own heart.* The first time they had met, she had told Eliza that she would lose all those she loved. Those words had haunted her ever since. According to the Oracle, Eliza was sure to meet a terrible end, the road ahead full of heartbreak and loss. *Yours is the lonely road,* the Oracle had said that first time. Now that Nia was free, surely that time had come, the time the Oracle was speaking of. But not everybody believed in prophecies. The Mancers believed the future to be undetermined and took prophecies more as warnings than as certain predictions. Eliza clung to this now and wished Foss were here to advise her. Now that the military was aware of Nia's creature and could prevent it from reaching her mother, she had to find a way to break Nia's spell on the Mancers. She couldn't face the battle ahead without them. But first, food and sleep.

CHAPTER

10

Nia climbed the black stone steps into Tian Xia, leaving the lake of the Crossing behind her while the nebulous boat faded to nothing. With this moment ever before her, she had been patient for years. She had prepared everything meticulously and at last the time had come for vengeance. For truly only revenge, the laying low of all those who had hurt and betrayed her, would give her any peace now. She reached the top of the steps and looked out over the red domed temples of the Faithful. She did not need to be patient any longer.

As she approached, black-robed figures massed in the fields and filled the catwalks on the outside of the temples, pointing at her. Soon they had all disappeared inside. Praying, no doubt. As if the Ancients were listening, as if they cared what happened here in the world they had left behind. The High Priestess descended a set of stairs from the Temple of the Nameless Birth and waited, alone, for Nia. Her eyes were like empty pools beneath her beaded hood. She bowed low as Nia approached and said in the Language of First Days, "The Ancients have allowed that the Great Sorceress has returned."

"Forsake the Ancients," said Nia curtly, pushing past her and climbing the steps. The fatalism of the Faithful irritated her to no end. She had never been able to share their beliefs, though she had endured the trials, sworn allegiance and donned the cloth simply out of gratitude for their protection once. They had been her first friends in the worlds, though she had not stayed with them for long, and so the Oracle's betrayal had stung all the more later on. It was the Oracle who had formed the Triumvira. It was the Oracle who had decided on banishment. She would pay for that now.

The chambers in the Temple were full of the Faithful chanting and praying. She could feel the power of their words joining and rising up. Such a waste of power. They were calling on beings too far away to hear or care. Nia passed them quickly, annoyed by their passivity. She descended the central spiral staircase and made her way swiftly along the dark, narrow passageway at the very bottom of the temple. None followed her. She stopped suddenly, shrugged off her coat, and drew from its scabbard a curved sword she had strapped to her back. She knelt on the cold floor and touched one of the flagstones lightly, whispering to it. It fell away without a sound. Nia leaped into the chamber. The Oracle stood against the wall, waiting for her.

"Somehow I knew you'd be huddled in a dark corner like a bug," mocked Nia. "It occurred to me that you *might* have moved quickly enough to gather your little cabal but clearly you're not as organized as I'd feared. Do you know, your people are all just babbling away up there. Not one of them tried to stop me."

"Destiny cannot be prevented," said the Oracle. "Though you will show me no mercy, I must tell you that I have never acted out of malice. I speak only the Truth given to me by the Ancients, Lords of us all."

"Calling yourself unmalicious shows a shocking lack of self-knowledge," said Nia. "And I don't know who is whispering answers in your ear but I'd be wary of assuming the future is set in stone. You'll never be a match for those who believe they can make the future what they will. But never mind. I'll ask you a question and you tell me the answer. When will the Oracle of the Ancients die?"

The Oracle closed her eyes and raised her head. A single tear slid down her cheek. "I have seen it," she said. "I am ready. You will strike my head to the ground with your sword."

"You *could* try to stop me," said Nia. "I don't know if that's crossed your mind. But I'm in a rush anyway, so thank you for being an idiot."

She stepped forward and swung her curved sword so it made an arc of light through the chamber. A great wail went up in all the temples as the head of the Oracle of the Ancients rolled to the earthen floor and her eight golden legs crumpled beneath her. Before her body had fallen, Nia had turned away and left the Chamber.

Violence hummed through her as she walked away from the temples, unsatisfied by that single swing of the sword. It was done, but it was not enough, it was not enough. She turned and looked back at the Faithful fleeing the Temples and her heart was taut like the strings of a violin. She threw her head back, flung out her arms, and called down a storm. Black clouds hurtled towards her across the sky and then they dove down, twisting into tornados. Great jagged swords of electricity leaped from the sky, turning everything white for a moment. Thunder drowned out her cries for more. The sky cracked and boomed, the wind howled, the rain descended in a roar. Nia found herself laughing as the temples were torn apart and burned and the earth was drenched. *This* was what she wanted. She could not hold within her all this rage and all this joy. Only nature was large enough to express it for her. She stood beneath the storm she had called until her heart was spent and soothed, and then a breeze swept it away and the day was quiet again, the harsh Tian Xia sky clear overhead. She was soaking wet but she felt better. She wiped the rain and tears from her cheeks, pulled back her drenched hair, and left the wreckage of the temples drying in the sun behind her.

Eliza woke suddenly. The room around her was dark and silent. At first she couldn't remember where she was. She sat up, heart racing, groping for her dagger, which she found under the pillow as always. Then it came back to her. She conjured a small light and looked around General Malone's bedroom. She was alone but when she opened the door she found a guard had been posted outside.

"Where's the General?" she asked the Guard. "How long have I been asleep?"

"A few hours," said the Guard, wary. "General's busy now."

"Tell him I'm leaving," said Eliza, striding off down the hall.

"Hold up, hold up!" the soldier called after her. "You can't just walk out. I'll get the General. You wait in his room."

Eliza hesitated. She didn't want to have to get out the way she'd come in but neither did she want to waste time here.

"I need to see him in ten minutes, aye, or I'm leaving," she said, folding her arms and facing the Guard. The Guard gave her an incredulous look.

"Is that right?" he said.

"I can walk through walls," Eliza told him. "Have you nay heard?"

The Guard gave a little shake of the head. "Just wait," he said, pointing at the bedroom.

Eliza went back in and sat down on the bed. It was half an hour before the General arrived.

"Planes are on their way," he told her. "They'll take care of this thing. But we can't hold off all of Tian Xia. We need the Mancers."

"I'll do my best to turn them back," said Eliza.

"I have a daughter your age," The General said, and he smiled a bit sadly. "I don't know what to think of you, Eliza. Your life is mighty strange."

Eliza nodded. "It really is, aye," she said.

The soldiers watched as the General escorted the girl to the edge of the plateau in his private car around midday. She climbed down to the valley by herself and headed for the foothills to find Ka's dragon. In spite of having slept and eaten, she was boneweary. The most important task for her now, if she was to undo anything Nia had done, was to discover exactly what Magic the Sorceress had wrought. This she could discover by Deep Seeing. The wall of the Library would show her what had been done to Foss. If the dragon that had gone north was successful and found the Book of Barriers in the Arctic, she ought also to be able to find how Nia performed the spell of Making. She did not trust that she would be strong enough to break Nia's spells or even to perform the Deep Seeing without Foss's help but she had to try.

The dragon Nia's creature had mauled lay in the grounds of the Citadel, glaring about with furious eyes. Ka's dragon landed near it, screaming out its greeting, and the hurt dragon released a piercing cry in reply. Eliza saw the symbol for wood branded into its neck. So this was Anargul's dragon, then. Eliza made straight for the Library in the north wing, her legs stiff and aching from the long, cold flight. She did not think Nia would still be here but her heart quickened nonetheless.

Nia was gone, but the Citadel was far from deserted. Word had spread rapidly through Tian Xia that the Great Sorceress Nia was free and the Mancer Citadel unguarded. A great many greedy giants, who more than any beings in the worlds loved to rule over the weak, had come to Di Shang to divide it into kingdoms among themselves. Cra had poured over the Crossing in great numbers, giving various treasures and powers to the Boatman in exchange, thinking to stay forever. Harrowghasters and half-hunters came – seeking easy prey – as well as curious or adventurous witches and such. The Mancer Citadel housed great treasures and objects of power. Unprotected by barriers, it drew all those that could scale its vast walls. Almost as soon as she entered the north wing, Eliza stumbled upon a cluster of mountain womi, muttering together and touching the wall in the hopes of finding a way into the Library. They were cloaked in heavy robes, hoods so large their faces were barely visible. When they saw her they leaped against the wall, first alarmed, then curious. Eliza did not pause. She was not going to worry about mountain womi at a time like this. Their bright little eyes peered at her as she passed them by and one made as if to grab her, but she drew her dagger and he jumped back. They muttered and followed her a little way, then lost interest and turned back to continue their futile assault on the Library wall. Nia had broken the barriers that surrounded the Citadel but the walls around the Library and the Treasuries were still full of their own Magic, which held fast against the intruders.

As she ran up the broad marble stairs she spotted one of the

Cra further up, tearing his nails along the carpet in an apparently random act of destruction. As soon as the thing saw her it emitted a hideous shriek and made away fast down the hallway on long black wings.

The Old Library was much as Eliza had last seen it. The great bookcases stood half empty, several of them toppled against their neighbours. She could not cross the Library without walking on the sea of books emptied by Nia that covered the floor. A chilly breeze came through the shattered window at the far end, the one Nia's creature had leaped through. A being no taller than Eliza, frizzle-haired and snaggle-toothed, with a nose like a little squashed turnip and brilliant deep blue eyes, was tapping Foss's stone arm in a curious way with a long knobby staff. Under his arm he clutched a tattered notebook.

"Who are you?" Eliza demanded in the common language of Tian Xia, approaching him with her dagger drawn. He squealed and stepped away from Foss. Eliza could not bring herself to look again at the stone figure of her teacher shielding his face. It was too painful. She turned her upwelling anger instead towards this intruder.

"I am Uri Mon Lil," he stammered, backing away from her as books slipped and slid beneath his feet. "I am the wizard of Lil. I intend no harm to...anybody, least of all you, whoever *you* might be...?"

He left this hanging as a question but Eliza saw no reason to answer him.

"Stop moving," she said angrily, and he stopped. It did not occur to her, at that moment, that a wizard was likely rather more powerful than she. Her fury carried her like a great wave and the wizard was so frightened by it that it did not occur to him, either, that she might not be equal to him in power. "Tell me what you are doing here."

The wizard hesitated, rather transparently trying to assemble a good story. Eliza pointed her dagger straight at his throat and ground out between her teeth, "The *truth*, Uri Mon Lil. I will know if you're lying." Of course, this was altogether untrue, but the wizard was rattled and believed her.

"Lil is an island in the Far Sea," he explained in a rush. "I have lived there many years. It is a beautiful place."

"I didnay ask you to tell me about your home town," said Eliza impatiently. "I want to know why you're *here*. You shouldnay *be* here."

"Of course, yes. Please don't interrupt me! It will be gone soon! I heard the Great Sorceress had defeated the Mancers and that many beings were crossing over. Oh dear, oh dear, it will be gone in a moment.... The Library of the Mancers is known in both worlds to contain the Deepest Secrets, the most ancient Texts. I feared the Cra or some other kind of stupid and malicious creature would burn the Citadel down and destroy the books. I came for the books but they are empty! Empty! Do you see? How will I help my poor Gautelen?" He sat down on a heap of books, dropped his staff, and burst into tears, which made it very difficult to keep pointing a dagger at him. Eliza hesitated, then lowered her weapon, still keeping a ready grip on it however.

"The Sorceress emptied the books," she said coldly. She wanted to know more about this wizard. It was dawning on her that if he could be trusted, she could greatly use his help in trying to break the spell on Foss. He did not seem very powerful (after all, he was afraid of *her*) but if he was really a wizard he would surely know quite a lot of Magic. The wizard continued to sob for a while but at last his tears subsided and he looked up at her with a face damp and crumpled with grief.

"I apologize," said the wizard. "Who are you?"

"I'll tell you, aye," said Eliza, making up her mind and putting her dagger back in her coat. "My name is Eliza and I am the Shang Sorceress."

"I see. And...I beg your pardon, but...who am I?"

Eliza stared at him. "You just told me you are Uri Mon Lil, wizard of Lil," she said.

"I see. And, excuse me for asking, but where are we?"

This was too much for Eliza to fathom. The little wizard seemed entirely earnest, looking up at her with eyes of the deepest, shining blue, still wet with the tears he had shed.

"Why are you asking me these questions?" she asked him, beginning to be afraid it was some kind of dupe.

The wizard shook his head pitifully. "I don't remember anything. I am so terribly unhappy and I don't even remember why." He looked around at the vast Library and the floor swamped with books. "By the Ancients! What a mess! What *happened* here?" He looked at the book in his own hands and opened it. "Ah!" he sighed. "Everything is explained here."

He became immediately deeply absorbed, turning the pages rapidly, sometimes gasping aloud and sometimes letting tears trickle down his wrinkled face and drip onto the pages. The pages were warped and worn and Eliza suspected he had wept over them a great many times.

"I see," he murmured when he had done. "It must be obvious to you that I am under a Curse. This is the work of the King of the Faeries and I shall forget it all again in twenty-nine minutes. How terrible." He looked up at Eliza with his head cocked on one side, his fear of her entirely gone. "How long have we known each other? You are not in my book."

"We just met a moment ago," said Eliza.

"Ah! I must write it down immediately." The wizard took a pen from the thicket of his hair. Peering over at his book Eliza saw instructions on the last page relating where he would find a pen and that he must write down any new and relevant information.

"You said you were Eliza, the Shang Sorceress?" he confirmed, writing it down with a brief description of her that she couldn't help reading upside-down, *young, funny face, big hair.* Except for the young part, it sounded just as much like a description of him, she thought indignantly.

"And are we friends? Or, on friendly terms at least?"

"That remains to be seen, aye," said Eliza. Crestfallen, the wizard wrote down *undecided relationship.*

"But you are a powerful Sorceress, are you not? I might have guessed that! You will drive the others from this place and, and, and..." he glanced at the stone figure of Foss. "It is one of the

Mancers, is it not?"

"He's my teacher," said Eliza. "I need you to help me break the Curse on him."

Uri Mon Lil leaped to his feet. Although he was spindly and bow-legged, with white hair exploding around a wizened little face, he was very spry. "Madam Sorceress, I am absolutely and one hundred percent at your service! It would be an honour to help you and the good and noble Mancers, Keepers of Knowledge, as my book calls them."

"Good," said Eliza. "Lah, if we have only twenty-nine minutes, tell me what you've just read. Why has the King of the Faeries done this to you?" Knowing what she did of this King, she was inclined to think well of the wizard for somehow incurring his wrath.

"Yes! These first pages explain to me that I married a Storm Seamstress from the Isles of Shol and our daughter, when she grew up, was the most beautiful woman in all of Tian Xia." Eliza looked at him doubtfully but he carried on as if he hadn't noticed. "Our daughter is a Storm Seamstress like her mother. Having a wizard for a father meant that her storms were in a class all of their own. Thunder like mighty drums, lightning that danced! She made wind that sang as it blew and ice crystals that rained down like diamonds falling from the sky! We were very proud of our strong and lovely daughter and imagined she would do great things. Word of her storms spread as far as the realm of the Faeries, on the opposite end of the world! The King of the Faeries called forth a storm from her to see it for himself. So taken was he with this storm that he summoned my daughter to his kingdom, that he might meet her. My daughter, as I said, is known to be one of the great beauties of the worlds. I knew what would happen if the King laid eyes on her. I had heard many things about this King. I had heard he was cruel and corrupt and I did not want him to marry my daughter. My daughter was frightened and begged me to help her, for refusing such a king would mean death. So before she went, I worked a spell to make her appear homely. Such a fool I was, to think I could deceive the

Faeries with Illusion! I knew little of Faeries, then, but they are *immune* to Illusion!"

Eliza nodded and rolled her eyes a bit, thinking that Lil must be very remote indeed if the wizard did not know *that*.

"The King saw through my spell," Uri Mon Lil carried on. "He saw my daughter in all her true loveliness and he declared that she would be his wife. My own wife and I despaired. We could not allow our daughter to be enslaved to such a being and so I tried again. I travelled to the realm of the Faeries, ostensibly to meet the King who had claimed my child. Once there, I had my daughter obtain a piece of his hair and I tried to cast a spell on *him*, a sort of...anti-love spell."

"There's no such thing as a love spell," said Eliza, "so how could there be an anti-love spell?"

"It is a form of Confusion made to work on the mind and affect the will," conceded the wizard, consulting his book again. "Again, I failed. When the King suddenly changed his mind about my daughter, his advisors realized that some Magic had been worked on him. I was put in a dungeon and they brought in a witch to break my spell. I felt sure I would be put to death for daring to cast a spell on the King of the Faeries, but my daughter Gautelen begged for my life and the King deemed it unseemly to murder his father-in-law. Instead, I was punished with this Curse and sent back to Lil. Every twenty-nine minutes, I forget...*everything*." He consulted his book again, reading rapidly, and then continued. "As you may know, the King of the Faeries may take as many wives as he pleases and selects which wife shall be queen for a hundred years. The King married my daughter a year ago and declared her the Queen of the Faeries, the first queen since the Xia Sorceress who is not, herself, a Faery. I have not seen her since. I came here hoping beyond hope that the great Books of the Mancers might teach me some way to free my daughter. To enable me to make this journey and keep my mission in mind, my wife made me this book, which I have been adding to. I gave a lock of my daughter's baby hair, all I had left of her, to the Boatman at the Lake of the Crossing. I thought I could give one

of the Books of the Mancers to return once I had found the solution but these books are empty, worthless, and there is nothing I
can do to help my daughter!" Uri Mon Lil's entire body sagged
with sorrow once again.

"If together we can free the Mancers," said Eliza, "I'm sure
they'll be grateful and willing to help you."

Hope lit up the tiny creased face of the wizard as she spoke
and his eyes shone. "Yes! Yes indeed! I will help you in whatever
way I can."

"Good. Do you know the spells of Deep Seeing?" Eliza asked.

Uri Mon Lil opened his book and glanced over the first page
again. "There are spells at the back," he said cheerfully, flipping
through the pages at the back of his tattered little book. "Let me
see, let me see. Simple Illusions. That's not right. Useful, though,
I'll bet. Flight with staff, aha!" He snatched up the knobbed staff
lying at his feet triumphantly. "I was wondering how I'd gotten
here! Moving objects large and small. Hum. Potions, quite a
number of potions." He turned a few more pages. "Simple barriers. Seeking. Oh dear, I don't think there's anything here about
Deep Seeing." His face fell. "Of course, I must have known how
to do it once. But I can't remember."

Eliza's mind was racing. "It doesnay matter if you cannay
remember," she decided. "You still have power, aye. I know how
the spell works and I'll teach it to you. Then we'll do it together."

She was a bit anxious, as they didn't have long before Uri
Mon Lil would forget again whatever she taught him. She led the
wizard to where Foss towered above them both in stone, and she
allowed herself to look at the figure closely for the first time. His
face was a mask of horror, his arms flung up, and she wondered
what his final thoughts had been. He had sent the summons for
her to return to the Citadel, hoping to protect her. How horrified
he must have been, then, when Nia appeared, and he realized that
in fact he was summoning Eliza to face her. She stepped around
Foss to the wall directly behind him and put her hands against it.

"We need to ask the wall to show us its memory. We're
looking for the moment in time, not very long ago, when this

Mancer was turned to stone."

"I see!" said Uri Mon Lil. "That sounds like a good idea."

"Then we want to break the spell," continued Eliza. "Put your hands over mine. We should be touching, aye, so our power works together instead of both of us just doing the spell at the same time."

Eliza told him the words. They pressed their foreheads to the wall and spoke the spell in unison. Eliza poured herself into the cold marble and into the past. It was as if she was falling through the wall, plunging into a great chasm. She felt the wizard's power envelop hers, steadying her, and the Library appeared before them, as if they were watching from inside the wall. They were behind Foss, who was chanting something in a loud and terrible voice. Bookcases were crashing against each other, books tumbling down in avalanches.

"It was you who designed the barriers, wasn't it?" Nia was saying, flicking her wrist at another towering bookcase so that it toppled out of her way. "Very creative, for a Mancer. I ought to come up with a special punishment just for you but I haven't time."

Foss called up a barrier around himself. Nia pulled it down with her hand.

"Too *slow*, silly," she said, almost affectionately. Then she pointed both hands at him, fingers stretched wide, and whispered, "*Stone*." There was a flash of light. Foss flung up his arms instinctively to protect himself.

Eliza trembled and then spilled in a thousand directions at once, coming to on the floor, shaking. The wizard was fanning her with his book and looking very anxious.

"Did you see?" he asked.

Eliza nodded. What she had seen horrified her but she was glad to know that the wizard was more powerful than he looked.

"How do we break it?" she asked him. "What kind of spell was it?"

Uri Mon Lil stared at her incredulously. "I've no idea," he said, and checked his watch. "Blast the Ancients! You're going to have to remind me of what's happened in just a minute..."

Eliza climbed to her feet. She felt a bit sick after the spell.

"Let's see if there are any books Nia didnay drain," she said. "We might be able to find something useful."

"Ye-es," the wizard looked around him in bewilderment. "Excuse me, but..."

"Read your book," sighed Eliza, tapping it, and she began to search through the empty books on the Library floor.

CHAPTER
11

Ander Brady swept the black water with the helicopter's search-light. The sickle of bare volcanoes rearing up out of the ocean were half-lit by the moon. The searchlight illuminated a wedge of barren rock not a hundred feet from one of the tallest volcanoes.

"That one," Nell said, pointing.

"You want me to land inside the volcano," Ander repeated for the third or fourth time, still not quite believing it. "And then some fellow in a boat comes and takes us to Tian Xia."

"Yes. And he's horrible-looking, aye, so brace yourself."

"I thought you didnay remember any of it."

"I remember the *journey*. I just dinnay remember anything while I was there."

Ander shook his head in bewilderment. Nell had never been like the other island children and she was indeed a close friend of Eliza Tok, who had been suddenly and dramatically taken from the island by Mancers a couple of years back. Still, it was hard to fathom that Onni and Gladd's daughter had been to Tian Xia. It had been enough of a shock when she got a scholarship to that school in Kalla.

"But you know the way to this cave."

"Aye, I can find it," said Nell confidently. She had required Charlie and Eliza to tell the tale of their Tian Xia adventures many times over in minute detail.

Ander skillfully poised the helicopter over the crater and descended into it, landing gently at the bottom. Unlike most craters, which filled in with dirt and mud, this one offered a broad opening into a rocky cavern where steaming water ran off into innumerable dark tunnels. The helicopter lights beamed off bits of damp black rock and then shut off. Ander cut the engines and the rotary wings slowed and hummed to a halt.

"Charlie? We're almost there. Can you hear me?" Nell scrambled into the back to check on the Shade. The cloudy substance was still pouring out from under the blanket she'd wrapped around his chest and she wished desperately that Eliza were here, or anybody who might know how to stop or slow a wound like this. Charlie's eyelids flickered open for a moment and her blood ran cold. His eyes were nothing like a boy's eyes anymore. They were clouded over, a cold, unsettling mix of mist and light.

"Just hang on a little longer, Charlie," she whispered in his ear. She climbed out the side door over him and Ander lifted the boy from the helicopter. They did not have to wait long before the ghostly boat emerged from the dark. Nell felt Ander stiffen beside her.

"Should've brought my gun," he muttered under his breath.

"I have been taking a great many beings from Tian Xia across to Di Shang these last days," said the Boatman, and they both cringed at his harsh, grating voice. "But humans crossing into Tian Xia? It is unusual." He pointed a single, pellucid finger at Nell. "I remember you."

"We want passage," said Nell. Much to her vexation, her knees seemed to have turned to water and were trembling so much she could barely stand straight. But she kept her voice as steady as she could. "We can pay."

"And so you must," said the Boatman, with a short laugh that sounded like somebody taking a knife to a window.

"Give him your watch, lah," Nell said to Ander.

"My da's watch?" Ander looked appalled.

"Charlie's dying," said Nell in a hard voice she had never used before. "You'll nay waste time wondering if his life is worth your watch."

Ander took off his watch and handed it to the Boatman.

"Passage for him," said the Boatman.

Nell reached into her bag and handed him her mathematics

medal and the Cherry Swanson album.

"Here's for me and Charlie," she said.

The Boatman grinned and wagged his head at her. "But you have brought me more than you are giving me."

Annoyed, she took out the fossilized baby dragon and thrust it towards him. He took it.

"You paid more last time," he said.

"I overpaid last time," said Nell levelly. "I thought you'd be glad I'm nay asking for credit."

At this, the Boatman threw back his head and rasped out his unspeakable laugh once more. Then he gestured that they could board.

"Is it true we can bring any inanimate object in our possession?" asked Nell, for Charlie had said something like this once.

"There is no price for a thing that has no will," conceded the Boatman.

Nell looked at the broad deck.

"Can you land the helicopter there?" she asked Ander.

He gaped at her. "You want to take a helicopter to Tian Xia?"

"How else are we going to get around?"

The Boatman watched with great amusement while Ander went back and started up the helicopter, hovering it over the boat and putting it down squarely on the deck. Nell pulled Charlie to the stern of the boat, wanting to stay as far as possible from the Boatman. Now that they were all on board, she began to feel better. Although she had told Ander that she remembered the Crossing and the hideous Boatman, her memory had kindly blurred just what an awful sight he really was and she was very annoyed with her knees for going wobbly on her. She hoped neither Ander nor the Boatman had noticed. The sails caught the nonexistent wind and they sailed fast through one of the caverns and out into the misty sea of the Crossing.

One of the things Nell did remember was being ill on the Crossing. It was the last thing she remembered before becoming exhausted and dehydrated and confused on the way back. Charlie had said that the first time was the worst and she hoped he was right. She was worried about Ander, too. But she could not dwell too much on how the journey might affect them. She had to look to Charlie. Cold sweat beaded on his skin and his breath was a slow, uneven rasp. She tried to prop him up comfortably and held his hand tight.

"You have to hang on, Charlie. I know the journey is hard but you have to stay with me. Can you hear me?"

He wheezed slightly in response. Ander sat with his back against the gunwale, hands clasped loosely between his knees, his expression fixed. It was impossible to tell what he was thinking. Since he was not forthcoming, Nell ignored him. She talked to Charlie, feeding him brandy in small doses and telling the most entertaining stories she could think of, inventing wildly whatever she thought might hold his interest. When his head began to drop she lifted it up and held it between her hands. He barely responded, except once when she mentioned Julian's name in passing. He made a sound like a gurgle. She paused and then tried again.

"Julian invited me to the Autumn Fire Dance last term," she told him. "He's a surprisingly good dancer, lah. I guess that comes from being athletic and coordinated."

Charlie's eyelids fluttered. Nell began to describe the dress she had worn to the dance and his expression went dead again.

"We danced and had punch," she tried desperately. "Julian looked very handsome, aye." She thought she saw a frown. "He kissed me when we were walking back to the dormitories."

At this, Charlie made another gurgle and one of his hands twitched.

"We kiss all the time," said Nell excitedly. "Even in a supply cupboard one time."

"What are you on about?" muttered Ander, frowning.

There was a crease between Charlie's eyebrows.

"Kissing and kissing," babbled Nell. The white mist closed over them.

"What's this?" came Ander's voice, a growl. "Cannay see a thing."

Nell squeezed Charlie's hand. It was cold and clammy and felt not altogether hand-like, as if the bones were going soft. She let go with a shiver. "I wish Eliza were here," she said. "It's funny, lah, she's so different in some ways from when I first met her but in other ways she's exactly the same. I remember her very first day at the school in Holburg; she corrected Mentor Frist's geography. I've loved her ever since. I dinnay think he ever forgave her, though."

Charlie made a sound that might have been a laugh. She stroked his face. His skin was dry and didn't even feel like skin. She was glad she couldn't see him. She set about repeating every amusing anecdote she could think of from Eliza's pre-Sorceress days, punctuating the stories by slipping a taste of brandy into his mouth. She stopped giving him brandy after she bumped one of his teeth with the edge of the bottle and it fell right out. Whenever she paused in her storytelling, she heard the hiss of the water under the boat. She was not sure how long they had been travelling when a wind swept down and the mist parted. She heard Ander draw in a sharp breath. The lake beneath them was a brilliant green, the sky above the colour of fire. In the distance, the dark shadow of the cliffs. Tian Xia. She felt nausea swirling up within her and she forced it down. She wouldn't get sick. She had to take care of Charlie.

"What am I doing?" muttered Ander to himself. He looked very pale. He turned accusing eyes on Nell, then went a little paler and staggered to his feet to vomit over the gunwale.

"You're going to be fine, aye," Nell told the Shade. Her voice sounded strange to her own ears, too nasal, somehow distant. "Once we get to the Cave, you'll be fine. Are you still awake? Are you listening to me?"

Charlie said nothing. He looked like a deflating balloon, his features soft and indefinite, his body losing its solidity. Like he was melting, coming apart. Her stomach convulsed. For a moment she thought she would be able to master it, that through sheer strength of will she could prevent the sickness from overwhelming her. Then she buckled over, clutching her stomach with a groan.

The boat raced on towards the dark cliffs, which loomed larger and larger. Her stomach lurched, knife-jabs of lightning pain shot through her bones, hot flashes and icy chills swept over her. She forgot about Charlie. She forgot about everything. She pressed her face to the boards and moaned, hands in her hair, helpless against the agony of it.

Ander was more experienced when it came to pain. He had fought many long years in the war and his body was a map of scars. In spite of being feverish, half-delirious, and wracked by stabbing pains, he dragged both Charlie and Nell into the helicopter as the cliff approached and the black zig-zagging steps opened up before them. He did not know if the awful shapes on the wall, glaring beasts and ominous watching things, were actually carved there or merely his own hallucinations, and he didn't bother himself about it. Nell was vomiting in the back of the helicopter as he started up the engine. As they soared up and over the wall, she leaned forward between the seats. Her damp hair stuck to her face, which was white as a sheet, and her pale lips trembled.

"Canyon," she croaked, and pointed.

At first this meant nothing to Ander. He followed her shaking finger and saw only a dark forest rising up to the right. Then he spotted the canyon snaking towards it, and he put the helicopter down on the edge of it. As soon as the rotary wings had stopped he yanked open the door, stumbled out of the chopper, fell to his knees and then flat on his stomach, where he lay still. Nell pulled open her door and fell out. She barely felt the impact as she hit the ground. Rust-coloured clouds flitted across the sky like smoke and the red sun beat down on them. She rolled onto her side with a gasp of pain and lifted her throbbing head. A good distance to the left, near the black cliffs, stood what appeared to be a great many ruins. Nell squinted, not quite trusting her eyesight. She knew these should be the Temples of the Faithful but Eliza had described them as rather beautiful and busy domes. These were collapsed, open to the sky, and deserted. She turned her head in the other direction. The canyon and the Ravening Forest. She crawled to where Ander lay on the red earth. His eyes were open and he was breathing, thank the Ancients. When he saw her, he said thickly, "What's happening to us?"

"Get Charlie," she said.

He staggered to his feet. Nell tried to do the same, but she couldn't, so she remained on her hands and knees. When she looked up, Ander had Charlie slung over his shoulder.

"I spec it's too late, Nell," said Ander.

Indeed, the limp, greyish form hanging over his shoulder did not look anything like a boy anymore. Something ink-black floated in long threads from the wet spaces that were once mouth and eyes. Nell looked away. She crawled along the edge of the canyon, and Ander followed after her.

Charlie must nay die, she repeated in her head, over and over, like a mantra. *Charlie cannay die.* Her hands and knees were numb. Her vision blurred and cleared and blurred again. She longed to lie down, to be still. But *Charlie must nay die*, she repeated. It felt like hours, though it was not nearly so long as that, before she found the narrow trail down the side of the canyon that Charlie and Eliza had told her about. She forced herself to move a little faster, though she could not rise from a crawl. And there, there it was, the dusty ledge, the dark craggy opening in the cliff. The walls and ground of the cave were fleshy and lightly furred.

She tried to speak and found she had no voice, so she pointed into the cave. Ander carried Charlie inside. Nell looked at him as he passed – his mottled grey flesh hung soft and boneless, and still the dark strands bled from the corners of his mouth and eyes – and quickly looked away again. As the rock face ground closed over Charlie, Nell's mind, too, shut tight. She curled into a ball right there on the stony ledge. Later she did not remember Ander carrying her back up the trail to the helicopter. He had learned long ago how to close his mind to pain and keep moving. There was a tent and various emergency supplies in the back of the helicopter. He pitched the tent in the small amount of shade the chopper offered, dragged Nell inside it, and then he too lay down at last and let this strange new world close around him.

When Nell opened her eyes, it was very dark in the tent. Her head was pounding and she was sore all over, as if she had been badly beaten. She sat up with a groan. Ander was still sleeping but she woke him to give him some water. The water refreshed them both and they crawled out of the tent. It was night. Bright comets slashed across the sky and three moons performed a slow circling dance together. To the south, the hanging gardens of the Sparkling Deluder twinkled and shone, changing shape, offering up wheels of glowing blossoms, cities of stars, leaping figures and spangled forests swaying in a gleaming breeze.

"Will you look at that," said Ander, his voice hoarse.

"It's beautiful," said Nell.

"You think so?" Ander looked around them and shuddered. "Looks a lonely, unfriendly sort of place, to me."

He made sandwiches with the supplies Nell had brought but she could only manage a few bites before her head began to spin and her stomach recoil. They slept again and it was day when they woke. This time they were both hungry. Ander prepared some packaged soup over a little camping stove.

"Lah, did you know it would be that bad?" he asked, handing her a bowl once it was ready.

Nell nodded. "But I passed out last time. I spec it's worse if you dinnay pass out."

"You should've told me, aye" said Ander.

"Sorry," said Nell. "It didnay seem like the most important thing at the time."

Ander gave a short laugh that was more of a snort. "That thing is lucky to have a friend like you."

"He's nay a thing," said Nell.

"Lah, what is he, then?"

Nell looked up at the sky. "It's complicated," she said.

"Lah, I've no doubt about that," said Ander. "But you've got me here, so why dinnay you try doing a little bit of explaining."

Camped on this deserted plain, with the Ravening Forest on one side and the ruined Temples on the other, Nell was more frightened and unsure than she had expected to be. To comfort herself as much as to fill him in, she told Ander the whole story of her forgotten journey with Charlie and Eliza. She felt better and better as she spoke. She sounded to herself like a hero in a storybook.

"So now what?" asked Ander when she was done. "I hate to say it, but I spec…look, Nell, your friend wasnay showing much sign of life when we put him in there. We cannay wait here for him to pop out again when he may nary do so."

"He'll be fine," Nell insisted.

"Praps so," said Ander doubtfully. "But then he can take care of himself, nay?"

"I spec so," Nell agreed. "Lah, you're right, we cannay just wait here. We've got to find Swarn."

"That witch you were talking about?"

"Eliza might be with her already, aye, but if she's nay there she'll definitely need Swarn's help. We should warn her."

Ander shook his head. "I dinnay think flying a chopper around a strange world full of beasties who can do Magic is a good plan at all, Nell. We've done what you came here to do, aye. Now it's time to go back."

"We have nothing left to pay for the way back," pointed out Nell. Ander stared at her in horror. Nell said nothing for a moment, rather enjoying the effect this had had. Then she said, "Swarn and other great beings can command the Boatman. So if we want to go back, aye, we'll need her help."

Ander gave her a look that was already becoming familiar.

"I couldnay tell you *everything* before we came," she protested. "There wasnay time!"

"Fine." Ander got to his feet and began to take the tent down. "Let's go find this witch."

As they passed over the Ravening Forest in the helicopter, Nell warned Ander that they might encounter dragons in the Dead Marsh. He gave her that look again and said, "What am I supposed to do if that happens?"

"Land," suggested Nell. "They'll probably just take us to Swarn. That's what happened last time."

This was very naïve of her. Dragons had a kind of Knowing beyond that of most other creatures. When they had found Eliza in the marsh more than two years ago, they knew enough to be curious, enough to know Swarn should be curious too. But Ander and Nell would be no more than a snack. Had they ventured into a marsh full of dragons in a helicopter they would have quickly met a fiery end.

Instead, what they found in the marsh was a slaughter. It was strewn with the broken bodies of dragons. Hundreds of them lay sinking in the muck, heads severed, hearts torn out. In the distance, a green light was burning.

"By the Ancients!" whispered Ander.

"There," said Nell, pointing at the green light. "Land over there."

Something around her heart was crumpling and cracking like egg shells but she wouldn't let herself think it yet, she wouldn't wonder about Eliza. The helicopter hummed over the final battlefield of the cliff dragons and Ander set it down on a large protruding hump of moss, a safe distance from what they could now see was a heap of leaping green flames. Nell knew perfectly well what this must be. Eliza had told her about Swarn's green fire that never went out. Her house was burning. Nell slid open the door of the helicopter and leaped out, sinking knee deep in the marsh.

"Hang on," Ander called after her. "Stick close to me!"

But Nell was already scrambling straight towards the burning house with one of the blankets from the helicopter wrapped around her.

The green fire gave off no smoke but it devoured the oxygen. As she approached, Nell found herself gasping for breath. The fire did not crackle; it burned in eerie silence, leaping hungrily over the ruins of the house. The roof had collapsed and was just a burning mass of bone and mud and scales now. Over her thundering heartbeat she heard a sound like a long hiss and then a spurt of pale green flame struck her.

The blanket caught fire and she dropped it in the mud, wheeling about, looking for her attacker. It was half-buried by the house, its long neck and head pinned to the earth, its bright eyes flitting about fearfully. It was a very small dragon, no bigger than the helicopter, and it had inexplicably tried to crawl into Swarn's house, perhaps deeming it a safe place from the slaughter of its elders. The heat of the green fire and the airlessness was more than Nell could bear for long but she quickly took in the main beams of the house, huge dragon bones that now pinned this smaller dragon.

The dragon spat feebly at her again. There were pools of green fire burning in wounds in its neck. She wetted the charred blanket in a muddy puddle and approached the dragon, steering clear of its great snapping jaws. The thing thrashed, terrified, as she tried to douse the green flames, but the marsh water and the blanket had no effect at all. She made her way back to the helicopter and Ander, who was looking around at the devastation in the marsh, dazed.

"Is there rope in the helicopter?" she asked him breathlessly.

"Rope?"

"Yes! Rope! What's the matter with you?"

This seemed to shake him out of his reverie.

"What's the matter with *you*, running around like that? We dinnay know who did this, what's going on. We should be getting out of here, not checking the place out."

Nell did not say the thing that was darting through her mind like poison, the sickening thought she could not catch and still – *My friend might be in there.* She said, "There's a dragon trapped by the house. I think it's a baby, aye. If we can pull off some of the roof beams it should be able to get free."

Ander squinted at the burning mass. "There's rope in the lifeboat," he said.

Nell looked at the compact little helicopter in surprise.

"What lifeboat?"

Ander opened the pilot's door and pulled a big tarpaulin square out from under the seat. This he let fall into the marsh. It was still linked to the helicopter by a thin rope, which he yanked. The tarpaulin square began to unfold and then inflate until a round rubber dinghy lay before them. He opened a flap in the dinghy and pulled out a bag of supplies. There was a knife, a flare gun, water-resistant matches, a tarpaulin for shade, whistles and a coil of sturdy rope.

"We need to tie this around the main supporting beam that's right across the dragon's back. Pulling that one aside should roll the others off, aye, and the dragon should be able to move," said Nell.

Ander glanced at the burning heap again. "Those are bones?" he exclaimed. "Lah, I hate to say it, my girl, but I'm just a policeman and I dinnay have superhuman strength. I'm nay going to be able to pull one of those off."

Nell rolled her eyes at him in exasperation and he said, "Oh, aye."

She set about tying one end of the rope firmly to the skids of the chopper while Ander started it up.

The helicopter rising into the air and settling very close by, agitated the poor trapped dragon terribly. It belched out smoke and fire and twisted its neck about in vain. Nell took the other end of the rope and raced in among the flames. The heat on her skin was scorching but she managed to climb up on the mound of bone and mud without actually touching any of the flames and fixed the rope around the largest of the roof beams. She ran back a safe distance and waved her arms at Ander. Her face felt hot and dry and she examined her clothes anxiously for any green fire but found none. Ander took the chopper slowly upwards. The mound of burning house began to shift. The great roof beam, perhaps the thighbone of a very large dragon, came loose and was pulled into the air by the helicopter. The other bones tilted and tumbled away. Nell had expected the trapped dragon to immediately take off, but it was slow to move. When the weight pinning it was lifted, it thrashed about a bit before dragging itself away from the burning rubble, then collapsed again. Nell approached cautiously, still keeping a safe distance from its head. The poor thing was covered in little pools of green fire and one of its wings was nearly torn from its body. Its leg, too, was badly broken. The creature was clearly in pain and very angry.

Nell circled the heap of burning rubble, more spread out now that the roof beams had rolled to the base of the mound. She took up a long yellowed tooth, half her own height, that had been part of the fence. She poked at the heap of flaming mud and scale with the tooth, but she knew she would not be able to properly excavate it. She saw a battered cauldron, half-melted, and bits of weapons. Swarn had not had a great many possessions. There were no signs, at least, that anyone had been inside. Alarm followed fast on the first rush of relief. There was no way to find them, now. Without them, there was no way to get back to Di Shang, unless they began to offer up memories or hopes or other parts of themselves that, she knew from experience, were too precious to part with. She looked at the dragon again. It lay in the marsh and clawed at the mud. Ander had landed and was untying the huge bone from the helicopter.

"Lah, we're done!" he shouted. "Let's get out of here!"

"We have to help it," she said, joining him by the helicopter.

"Only way I can think of is shooting the poor creature in the head," said Ander. "Though a gun wouldnay be much use against a dragon, come to think of it."

"If we can heal it, I'm sure it could lead us to Swarn," said Nell. "It looks as though she wasnay here when Nia came through. This must be Nia's doing, nay?"

"Who?"

"The Xia Sorceress."

"Oh, aye, you and she are on a first-name basis, are you?" Ander gave her an incredulous look. "I cannay tell if this is her handiwork or not."

"Who else would be strong enough to slaughter a marsh full of dragons?"

"Are you asking me or telling me?"

"Lah, it doesnay matter who did it. We need to find someone who can heal this dragon."

"We're nay getting it to that cave, I'll tell you that much. It's as big as the chopper as it is. I dinnay think there's much we can do for it."

The sky was darkening to a bloody crimson. The Irahok mountains loomed to the north, jagged and icy, and the dark shapes of slain dragons were scattered across the marsh in every direction. There was no sound but the rattling and rasping of the young dragon's laboured breath. Nell felt her knees go watery again. She had imagined arriving triumphantly in the marsh by helicopter and then being part of some great adventure with Eliza and Swarn. Instead, she was alone with a confused policeman in a marsh full of dead dragons and she didn't know what to do next. Well, she was fairly certain Eliza didn't go weak in the knees whenever she had a problem to deal with. She pinched herself hard on the arm and drew in a sharp, shuddering breath. The stories she had heard from Eliza and Charlie tended not to include many friendly Tian Xia worlders. The only beings besides Swarn and her dragons that had helped Eliza in any way were the Faithful.

"We'll go back to the temples," she decided. "Even if the Faithful are nay there, praps we can find some trace of where they've gone."

"What temples? Who? What are you talking about?" Ander ran his hands through his hair agitatedly. He had an awful sinking sense that he was being dragged deeper and deeper into something he did not understand or care to understand.

"By the lake of the Crossing. There were temples not far from where we landed, aye. They'd been attacked too, I think."

"It's a blur, lah. I wasnay feeling my best."

"We should go there now." She meant to sound decisive, confident, but everything she said came out in a high-pitched babble.

"It's getting dark," Ander commented. "But I dinnay fancy camping here."

The dragon let out a sudden roar of pain and dragged itself a little further on its belly. Nell shuddered and looked away.

"No, we have to hurry," she said. "We'll just have some food and go straight back. How are we for fuel?"

Ander refilled the engine from their supply and they left the dragon with its burning wounds and torn body behind in the marsh among the hundreds of dead dragons. They flew through the night, over the forest. Nell thought she could still hear the dragon roaring in pain long after they had left the marsh behind them. It was nearing dawn when Ander put the helicopter down by the ruined temples.

"Think we're seeing a sort of theme here," he commented, drinking from a bottle of water. "So you reckon this is your friend the Xia Sorceress's doing too?"

Nell took the bottle from him and finished it, then tossed it back into the helicopter.

"I spec so," she said. How glad she would be, right now, to lie down in her bed in Holburg or to watch television with her father! She straightened her shoulders and made for the temples. "Let's look around."

What they found, again, was tragedy. There were many bodies crushed by the collapse of the temples but if Eliza had been accurate about the numbers of the Faithful, most had escaped. Broken statues and painted walls lay crumbled in great heaps. Some of the temples had been reduced to rubble while others stood charred, with only sections caved in. Broken as they were, the temples were easy to climb. Nell wandered through the ruins, hoping to find someone alive. She peered into a room half open to the dawn sky, its remaining walls beautifully painted. Her eye was caught by a picture of a glittering sea-snake when somebody stepped in front of her, barring her view, and spoke in a language she did not understand. What she did understand very well, however, was that a narrow steel blade was pointed straight at her throat.

CHAPTER
12

Eliza had read a little of harrowghasters and heard some of Swarn's stories about them but she had never seen one. In this she could count herself lucky, for none who laid eyes on them and lived to tell of it had ever described it as a pleasant experience. Beings caught between life and death, they were among the most fearsome predators in Tian Xia. Emaciated and yet possessed of inhuman strength, with dank, matted hair and rotting skin the colour of a mottled bruise, they looked and smelled of death. They lived on the hearts of mortal beings and could stop the blood and breath of any living creature with a mere touch. After paralyzing their victims in this way, they cut out the heart, drank it dry and ate it. The story had it that, long before the separation of the worlds, the harrowghasters had been a tribe of noble and rebellious humans, until a malevolent Faery Cursed them into this terrible form for eternity. Beheading them or cutting out their withered hearts, widely considered a reliable way of killing any mortal creature, was of no use. They died only when deprived of heart's blood for a period of many months, growing gradually weaker until they fell into total decay. Beings with power kept them at bay with barriers and enchantments. Others stayed away if they could. During the war harrowghasters had crossed over in great hordes, moving through villages and leaving only corpses in their wake. Now fourteen of these monstrous creatures were walking the halls of the Mancer Citadel.

The Cra gave them a wide berth, swooping out of reach and staying close to the ceilings while the harrowghasters massed below, reaching vainly. The mountain-womi kept close together and managed brief Confusions and walls of fire to keep the harrowghasters away. However, two witches had been exploring the Citadel independently and the younger of the two was caught unawares and swarmed. She was left now slumped on the stairs, her bloody chest gaping open. The harrowghasters moved on, following the scent of life.

Eliza and the wizard of Lil had spent no more than an hour searching unsuccessfully for books not yet drained by the Sorceress. Eliza had twice had to remind Uri Mon Lil of who she was, who he was, and what they were doing. Once this was clear to him, he would set about the task with renewed zeal until he forgot again. Eliza smelled the harrowghasters before she saw them, the unmistakable waft of rotting flesh pouring from the hallway. She dropped the book she'd been examining and drew her dagger.

"Something is coming," she said to Uri Mon Lil. "Get behind me and find a spell in your book."

Uri Mon Lil was more than happy to dart behind Eliza.

"Spells are at the back of the book," Eliza reminded him.

"What am I looking for?" he asked, flipping pages frantically.

"Something useful," said Eliza as the harrowghasters swarmed into the Library, their clouded eyes lighting on the girl and the wizard. The stench was overpowering. Eliza spoke a simple barrier spell and the harrowghasters pressed themselves around it. Their lips had rotted away, leaving black-toothed hideous grins exposed, and they clacked their teeth now with eagerness. She could feel the barrier buckling under their strength and knew her skill was not enough to hold it long.

"You need to do the spell of flight," she said urgently to the wizard. "Flight with your staff. Quick."

Uri Mon Lil read the spell. As he finished, Eliza let her barrier crumble and Uri Mon Lil shot up into the air with his staff. Eliza darted between two of the harrowghasters, racing towards Foss's stone figure as if he could offer protection.

"Do something!" she shouted at the wizard, who was hovering way up near the ceiling, hanging over his staff and reading anxiously. The harrowghasters gave up on him and made for Eliza. For a minute or two she was able to fend them off with her dagger. She sliced off hands that reached for her, causing the harrowghasters to be a little more cautious, but there were too many of them to keep in her line of sight at all times. She stepped back and felt something like ice on her back, right between her shoulder blades, an awful cold grip that seemed to suck the air right out of her. The blood in her veins stopped flowing and a deathly heaviness sealed over her. Her eyes darted towards the dangling wizard but she could not make a sound, her lungs constricting violently.

Uri Mon Lil's book flew from his hands and hurtled across the room, striking the harrowghaster that had touched Eliza in the head. It was only a second but the blow knocked him slightly and his fingers left her back. Her blood began to flow again and air rushed into her lungs. She dove sideways, away from that deathly touch. The others descended on her, but before they could lay their hands on her all the books on the floor rose up and began to whirl about the room, battering the harrowghasters. A path through the storm of books cleared before Eliza, straight to the window. She could hear a voice chanting, and for a terrible moment she thought it was Nia. But then the voice cried, "Run, my girl!" and she saw her grandmother, Selva, by the hole Nia had blasted through the wall. The empty books rained down on the harrowghasters. Eliza grabbed Uri Mon Lil's book and ran to the window.

"Dragon of fire!" she shouted. Ka's dragon, waiting in the grounds far below, lunged into the air towards the window.

"Get down here!" Eliza called to the wizard.

"How?" he whimpered. The staff dove down towards her but remained several feet off the ground.

"Just stop flying," she shouted at him.

"I don't know how to stop!" he returned, but then a book struck him hard and he tumbled off his staff to the floor with a great wail. The staff darted back up to the ceiling. The harrowghasters were fighting through the books, some of them making for Eliza and Uri, some of them for Selva. Eliza grabbed hold of Uri Mon Lil and pulled him out the broken window with her. The two of them were caught almost immediately by Ka's dragon, who carried them out over the grounds under the darkening winter sky, nearly crushed in his talons, and set them down. Five of the harrowghasters hunched at the broken window, staring out after their vanished prey with dead eyes.

The Cra had been lying in wait. Since Eliza had returned to the Citadel, hundreds of them had been massing around the walls, bearing vast oily nets. When they saw that their nemesis had evaded the harrowghasters they surged up over the walls, shrieking. Ka's dragon was instantly caught in a vast net. Another net was dropped over Anargul's wounded dragon. Eliza knew that the weak enchantments of the Cra would not hold a dragon for more than a few moments but that was all the time such a horde of the Cra needed.

"Come on," she said, catching the wizard by the hand and running towards the Inner Sanctum for shelter.

"Oh, what is *happening*?" cried Uri Mon Lil, who had forgotten everything again and was very distressed to find himself fleeing an army of winged monsters without knowing why.

Looking up as she ran, Eliza saw above the shrieking Cra a great dark cloud descending. For one sickening moment she thought it was further armies of the Cra, numbers beyond what even the dragons would be able to repel, but as the cloud fell towards them and separated into individual shapes she understood. Something struck the back of her neck and she stumbled forwards. The Cra were all over her in an instant, knocking her to the ground on top of the cowering wizard. She felt sharp teeth and claws driving into her, strong arms trying to pull her over, but she clung to the wizard, shielding her chest and face and holding the book tight against her with one arm.

And then the ravens fell cawing on the Cra, attacking them with their hard, vicious beaks. The grounds of the Citadel had become a surreal battleground, black feathers flying. Ka's dragon tore his way out of the enchanted net and blazed fire in all directions, causing the Cra that could still do so to take flight. Eliza scrambled to her feet and pulled Uri Mon Lil into the Inner

Sanctum. They huddled in the hallway listening to the sounds of the battle outside, the screams of the Cra beating a retreat, and then quiet. They were both battered from the flying books in the Library and badly cut by the claws and teeth of the Cra.

"Are you all right?" Uri Mon Lil ventured, after they had sat and caught their breath a while.

"I'm fine," said Eliza, examining herself and concluding this was more or less true, since she was not bleeding heavily. "You?"

"I believe I am...not in mortal danger from these injuries," said the wizard.

Eliza smiled weakly. "Good. Then we're both all right."

"I'm so glad," said the wizard politely. "Do excuse me for asking, for this may strike you as a bit odd, but..."

"You dinnay know who you are or what's happening," Eliza finished for him. The wizard looked stunned by this.

"That is it, *precisely*. How did you know?"

"Everything is explained right here," said Eliza, handing him his book. "But we need to get out of here first."

She was getting slowly to her feet again, allowing herself to feel where it hurt now that she was safe, when a great scream came from Ka's dragon outside. Eliza ran out of the Inner Sanctum with the wizard close behind her. Both were momentarily paralyzed with horror by what they saw.

The harrowghasters were all over Anargul's dragon, who had only partially been able to get loose from the net the Cra had dropped. Ka's dragon was wheeling above them and sending down blades of fire but the harrowghasters did not burn. Anargul's dragon thrashed weakly for only a moment and then lay still. The harrowghasters began to burrow into the great beast's chest. A few others were feeding on the Cra left behind because they were too wounded to fly. It was a veritable feast for them. One of them spied Eliza and trudged half-heartedly in her direction.

"What is *that*?" cried the wizard. "It smells *foul*."

"You cannay let them touch you," said Eliza. "It's death if they do."

She did not need to call Ka's dragon. It swooped down and

Eliza and the wizard climbed onto its back, taking to the air well before the slothful harrowghaster reached them. In the shattered Library window she saw the dark-clothed figure of her grandmother raising a triumphant fist.

"Go north," she commanded the dragon. The dark cloud of ravens followed in their wake.

They flew north for a few hours before deciding to rest. It was an overcast night and great heavy snowflakes fell from the sky. Unable to see anything but the falling snow in the blackness, Eliza had the dizzying sensation that they were soaring ever upwards, and the ground suddenly firm beneath them gave her a shock when the dragon landed. The wizard built a little shelter out of dead tree branches by a frozen river while Eliza broke the ice and enchanted some fish to leap ashore and become a midnight supper. The mass of ravens settled quietly in the sparse, snow-covered trees.

Uri Mon Lil read his book over by the fire after they had eaten and then said, "According to my last entry, I was in the Library of the Mancers seeking a book that might be useful in my quest. There I met you, the Shang Sorceress." He gave her a slight bow here, which looked very odd sitting down. "Would you mind telling me what we are doing camping out in the snow now?"

"The Citadel wasnay safe," said Eliza wearily. Uri Mon Lil scribbled this down. "The books were all empty, anyway." She stretched and stared at the fire.

"I see." Uri Mon Lil looked around and said politely, "And this place is...?"

"Lah, just a place to rest," said Eliza. "Does your book mention harrowghasters?"

Uri Mon Lil flipped to the front and scanned the glossary of beings.

"Yes...here...oh my, they sound terrible. We haven't had a run-in with them, have we?"

"Aye, we have," said Eliza. "I wish I could forget all about it, too.

Does your book say that they feed on the hearts of living beings?"

"Yes, that's exactly what it says. Let me see..."

"So they wouldnay be interested in a ghost or a spirit, would they?" said Eliza.

Uri Mon Lil gave her an odd look. "What do you mean?"

Eliza shook her head. "It's nay important now. We need to get some sleep, aye. Let's take turns keeping the fire going. Here, I have an idea." She took his book and pencil from him and wrote on an empty page the following instructions, *KEEP THE FIRE GOING. Each time you forget everything and have to check your book, put a mark here. Once there are six marks, wake up Eliza.* Satisfied, she handed it back. "That way, your watch should be just about three hours, and then I'll take over for the next three hours."

"Ingenious!" agreed Uri Mon Lil. "Now, perhaps you could explain to me our *plan*. Have we got one?"

"Nay yet," said Eliza. "Stop asking questions – it's your watch and that means it's my turn to sleep."

Wrapping her coat tightly around her, she curled up before the fire.

Uri Mon Lil sighed. To his impressions of Eliza he added *surly*, then spent the remainder of his watch writing down many poetical descriptions of snow, which he was quite struck by. Eliza barely slept. She lay with her eyes squeezed shut while images of the shrieking Cra and the half-dead harrowghasters closing in on her reeled through her mind. Had it not been for Eliza's grandmother, they would not have made it out of the Library alive. The way the harrowghasters had made for her, too, told Eliza one thing for certain – Her grandmother was *alive*. Kyreth had lied to her.

The following morning, they spotted another dragon glinting gold in the sun – the one Eliza had sent north. Ka's dragon called out to it. It veered towards them and landed by the river, vast wings stretched out and gleaming. Standing in the snow by the smouldering fire, even with all her cares, Eliza was struck by the beauty of the scene – their rough little camp, the snow crisp and thick over the ground and the trees, and the brilliant dragon descending. When it came close to them, she saw by the brand on its neck that it was Trahaearn's dragon, and to her great relief, it had in its talons the Book of Barriers. Of course, when she opened it the Book was empty, drained of its knowledge by Nia, but that was of no great importance. All they needed was the object itself and the memory it would contain.

They worked the spell in the shelter by the river. The dragons took to the sky, their dark shadows wheeling across the snow and their scales shining in the morning sun, reveling in their freedom and power. Eliza and the wizard knelt on either side of the book, fingers entwined, and pressed their joined hands against it. Together they spoke the spell of Deep Seeing. They both felt the book giving way beneath their hands, the earth giving way beneath the spell, a tipping sensation as if the ground had suddenly tilted up vertically and they were sliding along it, and then they were swallowed by the book. It was the strangest sensation, as if they were liquid being poured down a spout and emerging as something entirely different.

Eliza was looking at Nia from an odd angle, as if lying on the floor looking up at the Sorceress. Nia's arms were raised above her head. She was pouring with sweat and clothed in flame, long bright ribbons of it dancing around her. The words she spoke were heavy with power and rooted in something deep and dark and secret – each one shimmered with pain, was edged in fire. She spoke the Language of First Days and yet there was something strange about it, something different. It was not the language normally used for spells. These were not commands or pleas or even complete sentences or words but rather the original roots of certain words, disconnected, as if she were naming things with no past or future. Flesh and bone and blood and sweat, rage and sorrow and fear and regret, these she called forth and each one began and ended in pain. The flames that licked her body fell away and formed a broad circle of smoke and ash. She stepped out of the circle and placed in the middle of it a pale, dead finger.

Eliza fell face first onto the book. Uri Mon Lil was staring at her with horror.

"Who are you?" he asked in a terrified whisper. "What are we *doing?"*

Eliza could have wept. Forgetting his purpose, he had pulled out of the spell. They would have to start over every twenty-nine minutes.

"It's important," she said. "It's important. We have to do it again."

She reached her hands out but Uri Mon Lil did not take them. She saw her hands were shaking and took a deep breath.

"You are a wizard under a curse," she said, struggling to control her voice. "There is no time to explain but please, you *have to help me*. We are performing a very important spell. Please trust me. I beg you." Tears rose to her eyes and she blinked them away angrily. Slowly, hesitantly, Uri Mon Lil reached out and took her hands.

"Teach me the words," he said in a low, uncertain voice.

They spent the day working the Magic. Every twenty-nine minutes Uri Mon Lil, forgetting their purpose, would withdraw from the spell in horror and they would have to begin again. The sixth time in, Eliza realized that the spell of Making had taken more than hours, more than days, in fact many months. They would need to skim through it like a book, looking for key moments, points of change. This was not easy but was in some way facilitated by the twenty-nine minute limit. They needed rest and timed these according to Uri Mon Lil's memory loss. Then they would re-enter the spell, emerging again a half hour later, shaking and appalled.

Nia shouted, flamed, raked the air with fiery hands. The finger on the ground split open, began to grow. The bone branched out into a skeleton with many arms. The flesh formed the body within and around it. Fire and smoke threaded through the creature like nerves and veins. It had no heart or internal organs. It lay in the circle of ash, massive and unmoving, lifeless. Nia had not *Made* anything yet, only changed the shape of the finger. Eliza remembered that awful moment more than two years ago when Nia had sliced off Rea's little finger before letting her go. Had she been planning this since then? This monster was her mother's very flesh and bone, changed and ravaged, but what animated it?

They slept poorly that night and began again at dawn. Although Uri Mon Lil could not remember any of it, they were developing a rhythm together, entering the spell more surely and easily each time. His hands and his power remembered, even if his mind did not. Each time she explained to him what they were doing he seemed more accepting of it.

Nia knelt on the ground and cupped her hands together. She whispered into a small opening between her thumbs. Eliza could not hear what she said and yet she felt it, a pure horror and a vengeful rage. She was half-relieved every time Uri Mon Lil's concentration faltered and the spell spat them out. Then she would look into the wizard's terrified, bewildered face and explain, as best she could, again and again and again. Nia's hair began to fade and whiten, thin lines spidered across her face, and always she remained in the same posture, whispering hoarsely. The inaudible words radiated an unendurable level of pain, wrath and fear.

Then Nia opened her hands and a rough ball of what looked like black metal lay cupped in her palms. *Kwellrahg*, she named it. She pressed it to her chest. Her flesh and bone opened up around it and closed over it. *Kwellrahg*, she said again, hoarsely, and the monster on the ground came to life, surging up and then crawling down her throat, shrinking as it did so, passing into her like a horrible shadow. When it was done she stood up unsteadily. Her face was drawn and hollow-eyed, her white hair lank and wet with sweat, but she was lit from within somehow with a pale light of triumph. With a shriveled, shaking hand she undid the locket around her neck, opened it, and looked into the tiny mirror. She breathed deeply as her youth and beauty were restored to her. Then she turned her head and looked, or so it seemed, straight at the girl and the wizard spying on her much later through the book. And she smiled.

Eliza lay in the snow by the burnt-out fire. She was soaked through with sweat that was fast becoming cold. She saw the dragons moving together on the opposite side of the bank in the dark. Shivering, she pulled herself together and rekindled the fire.

Uri Mon Lil was sound asleep and she left him that way for a while. Her mind felt as if it had been shoveled out. It was a tremendous effort just to think.

Had Nia known they might be watching? If so, why had she left the Book of Barriers behind? Perhaps she had wanted Eliza to know what she now knew – Nia had Made the Kwellrahg, true, but she had Made it out of Rea's flesh and bone, Rea's terror and fury in defeat. It was possible that killing the Kwellrahg would hurt Nia in some way, though she couldn't be certain. It was also possible that it would hurt Rea, or worse. Rea was weak and could not take much.

The military was hunting the monster right now under General Malone's orders. She had to go to the desert; she had to stop them. But she felt helpless, too helpless to move. The day's Magic had emptied her. She watched the stars and tended the fire until a faint light appeared on the horizon to the east and she ached with the desire for sleep. Uri Mon Lil was always very frightened when woken and she thought hazily that it must be awful not to know who or where one was. She left him with the book open before him and slept dreamlessly.

She woke when the sun was already high in the sky. Ka's dragon was keeping the fire alive with his breath. She was terribly hungry but so worn out from the previous day's Magic that it took her a long time to charm a single black trout to leap out into her hands.

After they had eaten, she brought Uri Mon Lil up to date. Panic was closing on her now. The Kwellrahg was bent on destroying her mother and so she had to protect her mother from it. But harming the thing could harm her mother. How could she fight a foe she couldn't hurt?

"You say this is the Book of Barriers?" said Uri Mon Lil, flipping through the empty pages. "Pity there's nothing in it. It feels as if it must have been powerful, once."

"You can feel that?" asked Eliza, interested. "That's more than I can. I spec you must be a prize strong wizard when you have your memory."

"According to my book, I was," agreed Uri Mon Lil. "But

there's no way of knowing how much of that was self-aggrandizement. I don't know if I was the type of wizard to brag. I should hope not but there's no way to be certain, is there?"

One of the ravens perched in the trees swooped low over Eliza's head suddenly and landed next to her in the snow. She had almost forgotten about them. Uri Mon Lil paid no attention to it and continued chattering about what wizardry might do to one's ego. Eliza looked at the bird and the bird looked back. There was something in those small black eyes that she recognized.

"There are rather a lot of those birds around here, aren't there?" commented Uri Mon Lil, looking at the trees along the river, dark with ravens. He shuddered a little, for it was an unsettling sight.

Eliza reached for the bird, touched its feathers, its beak. For one giddy moment she felt herself within the bird, looking back at a puzzled, frightened girl. At the same moment, she and the bird spoke. In unison, they said, "The Sorma." Then the bird took off and Eliza was returned to herself.

"That was odd," said the wizard, frowning at her. But Eliza's mind felt like a flower opening suddenly. A sense of what to do next began coming to her in fragments.

"Are you...all right?" asked Uri Mon Lil, looking carefully at Eliza and then anxiously consulting his book for anything on possession by ravens.

"We need a barrier spell," said Eliza with sudden urgency. "And we can retrieve it from the memory of this book."

"Oh good," said the wizard brightly. "How will we do that?"

"With the same spell we used yesterday, aye," said Eliza.

"Ah," said the wizard. "And what spell would that be?"

"Dinnay worry," said Eliza, taking the book from him impatiently. "We're quite good at it together."

"Oh, I'm so glad," said the wizard. "What do we need a barrier *for*?"

Eliza ignored the question. There was too much to explain and he would forget it all soon in any case. "Something strong but simple will do, aye. It doesnay need to resist Magic, only physical forces like metal or fire. It needs to be large, though. We need to be able to cast it over a wide area, maybe multiple areas."

"I see."

"We can find the time when that spell was being written in the book," said Eliza. "All the books could be restored that way! You said it felt powerful, aye. *They remember* what was in them once and this spell can reveal it."

"And..."

"No time to explain anymore, Uri Mon Lil. We've probably only got twenty minutes left as it is. Take my hands."

CHAPTER

13

The being holding a sword to her throat was the loveliest being that Nell had ever laid eyes on. He was tall and slim, dressed in silk clothes and a feathered cape and soft leather boots. His hair and skin had a kind of inner luminescence, so that he seemed made of light rather than flesh. In symmetry and charm and beauty his face was too perfect to describe. He stood on the ground before her and yet there was something in his stance that made her think of flight, as if in fact he was lighter than air on his feet, unutterably graceful even without moving. At the same time there was a weight and a stillness to him, a sense of something ancient and unmoving. She was so taken aback, so enchanted by his appearance, that she forgot to be afraid of the point of his sword, which nearly grazed her throat.

"You must be a Faery," she breathed.

He spoke again in the strange, beautiful language. When she did not reply, he said, "What are you?"

Although he was not speaking Kallanese, the intent behind his words was unmistakable. It was a strange sensation to hear entirely unfamiliar words and yet have no doubt as to their meaning.

"Nell," she stammered. "I mean, that's...Why can I understand you? Can you understand me?"

The Faery looked scornful. "You know what I am. Do you not know I have the power to understand you and to make myself understood when I wish to be?"

She was going to reply when something hurtled into the Faery through the open ceiling and he was knocked to the ground. Whatever had flown into him changed shape as it knocked him back and became a half-hunter, growling and slavering, short swords grasped in hairy fists. The Faery managed an elegant kick and a twist, bucking the half-hunter off him so it staggered backwards. Before it had time to leap at him again, a golden net burst from the Faery's hand and ensnared the beast. Nell watched all this too stunned to move, but as the Faery drew his sword and made for the half-hunter, she came to her senses.

"Stop!" she shouted, throwing herself against the Faery with all her might.

For a moment they all froze, the half-hunter in the net, the Faery with his sword poised for a killing blow and holding Nell with his other arm. Then the Faery stepped back, keeping Nell at arm's length.

"I have never heard of a nell," he said coldly. "Why does your half-hunter attack me?"

"*You* attacked *me*," said Nell. "Or, at least, you pointed your sword at me in a not very friendly way. And Nell is my name, aye."

She knelt and untangled the net around the half-hunter.

"Is that you, Charlie?"

It was. The half-hunter became a rather sheepish-looking Charlie. He pushed his hair out of his eyes and smiled at her. Nell crushed him in a hug.

"I didnay expect you to get well so quickly!" she cried, looking him over for any signs of injury and finding none. "I wasnay sure you would get well at *all*. I thought you might be...lah, Charlie, you looked terrible, and there was something like smoke, but it wasnay smoke, just pouring out of you." She found she was sobbing quite unexpectedly and wiped the tears hastily from her cheeks.

Ander Brady appeared at the opening Nell had come through. He held his jacket over his arm. His pajamas were wrinkled and filthy with marsh water. The Faery swiveled and pointed his sword at Ander.

"What's this?" Ander asked, looking at the Faery in amazement.

"Are you also a nell?" the Faery demanded, beginning to feel outnumbered.

"I'm an Ander," said Ander, frowning. "Look who's better," he added to Charlie.

"We're Di Shang worlders," explained Nell eagerly, letting go of Charlie. "At least, Ander and I are. Charlie is...something else, aye." She was wracking her brains trying to decide if Faeries were good or not. They were the villains of human history but that was a long time ago. Eliza had only ever spoken of the King of the Faeries, who was an equivocal case but ostensibly allied with Swarn. They were certainly no friends of Nia, which surely put them all on the same side, or so she hoped.

"Di Shang worlders?" said the Faery wonderingly. "Human, then." He bent to look more closely at Nell, examining every inch of her face with great studiousness. He reached out and pressed his fingers to her cheek, as if testing the texture of her skin, then took a strand of her hair between his fingers and rubbed it a little, drew it close to his face, and sniffed it. Nell stood very still and let him, though she wasn't sure why.

"What are you *smelling* her for?" Charlie drawled, getting to his feet.

"You smell...very nice," said the Faery, letting go of her hair and glaring at Charlie a little.

"That cannay be true," laughed Nell. "We've just been in the Dead Marsh."

"Did you see Eliza?" asked Charlie immediately.

"Who is this fellow?" Ander asked, pointing at the Faery.

"What are you doing in Tian Xia?" asked the Faery.

For a few minutes there was a great deal of talking all at once, and every now and then the Faery swished his sword in the air impatiently. Once Charlie had explained to Nell everything that had happened between his visit to Ariston Hebe with Eliza and his sudden appearance in her backyard in Holburg, Nell told him that Nia had already been to the marsh and slaughtered the dragons. The Faery interrupted her sharply.

"Is the Warrior Witch living?" he demanded.

"I spec so," said Nell. "But I dinnay know."

"And you are friends of hers?"

"Yes. Sort of...friends of a friend."

The Faery paced a bit and then said to Charlie mistrustfully, "I have heard of beings like you, who can change shape without the use of Illusion or Glamour. In the stories the Faeries tell, such beings are spies and renegades, loyal to no one."

"That's fair," Charlie conceded, at the same moment as Nell protested, "Charlie's *very* loyal."

"Listen, we're looking for this witch because we need someone who can command the Boatman to take us back home, aye," said Ander. "As Nell here tells it, only the great beings can do that. But if you're a Faery, praps you can help us."

"We *cannay* go back yet!" protested Nell. "We've got to find Swarn! And Eliza! And we have to help that poor dragon!"

"I am looking for the Warrior Witch also," said the Faery. "My name is Jalo. I am the second son of Nikias. Word came to us in the Faery Realm that the Sorceress Nia had defeated the Mancers with a powerful Curse. His Majesty the King of the Faeries could not risk summoning his allies in the usual way, for such Magic would lead the Sorceress to us immediately. Our Kingdom is hidden and ten of us were sent in quiet and secrecy to bring the Oracle of the Ancients and the Warrior Witch Swarn to the safety of the Faery Realm. I found the body of the Oracle in a cavern below one of these temples. I fear the Sorceress may already have slain the Warrior Witch as well, if what you say is true."

"We can help you!" cried Nell. "There's a dragon in the marsh that's nay dead yet, only injured. But it cannay fly. If we can heal it somehow, I'm sure it could lead us to Swarn, aye. Wherever she is."

Jalo hesitated. "I was commanded to return instantly when I found the Oracle," he said, "and I have found her."

"But the other Faeries willnay know where to find Swarn if she's hiding somewhere," said Nell, "and there's nay time to run back and forth getting word to whomever. Do you know any Magic for healing? The dragon is hurt very badly."

The Faery considered this a moment. "There is a witch in the mountains who is said to be a great healer. We could go to her. My myrkestra is outside but cannot carry so many."

"Dinnay worry," said Nell. "We have a helicopter."

Jalo's myrkestra was a grey and white bird half the size of a gryphon. He instructed it in his own tongue to wait for them in the Dead Marsh. Then he circled the helicopter with interest.

"It is not beautiful," he decided.

"I've got to say no to this," Ander said to Nell, glancing a bit anxiously at the Faery. "I'm glad to see your friend is better, aye, and that's what we came here for. But your parents are going to be worried sick, and my poor ma..."

"Mr. Brady, this is very, very important!" sputtered Nell. She couldn't bear to turn back now that they might actually be able to save the poor suffering dragon and perhaps even help in the great battle to come. "My parents are fine, they're taking care of your mother, she's fine, everybody's fine! But dinnay you see, we can really do something good if we help this Faery find Swarn!"

"I just dinnay see how he needs our help," said Ander. "He can do this on his own."

"You will guide me to this dragon once we have found the means to heal it," said the Faery impatiently. "Now, please – my Myrkestra is on its way to the Dead Marsh already. I wish to see how your Flying Machine works."

Something about the Faery's manner made it impossible to refuse, although later Ander could not have said why this was so. And so he found himself piloting the helicopter north towards the Irahok mountains with a shape-shifter, a Faery and the stubbornest girl he'd ever met, in the back.

"It is a very noisy Magic!" Jalo shouted to Nell as they lifted off. "And I do not understand it! I had been told Di Shang worlders possessed no Magic at all!"

"It's nay Magic," Nell shouted back. She had become fascinated by engines recently and so was quite content to bellow a very detailed explanation to the Faery as they flew north. The

Faery was astounded and full of questions. Every now and then he leaned forward to give directions to Ander but for the most part he focused on Nell and her descriptions of the various flying machines in Di Shang. Charlie looked out the window, bored and wishing he'd opted to fly himself.

"It has been said that the Ancients gifted humans with ingenuity instead of Magic," commented Jalo. "It would seem that the end result is almost the same! You have learned to make *nature* do the work of Magic!"

They left the ruined temples and the lake of the Crossing behind them and flew over rolling green plains in which the ugly stone fortresses of the Giants towered. From the air they could see for miles, the great jagged mountains cutting across the horizon to the north and the Ravening Forest a fringe of green in the east.

"Are you really Immortal?" Nell asked Jalo.

"We are," he said. "There are two realms inhabited by Faeries – the Kingdom in Tian Xia and another that we call the Far Realm. A Faery can go there only when he or she has fulfilled the allotted time in this realm, however long that may be. They say the Faery knows when the time has come to go. I often wonder what I will find in this Far Realm but none return and so we do not know."

"So Faeries cannay die from illnesses or injuries?" Nell asked.

"Great Magic is required to kill a Faery. There are stories from long ago but it is difficult to say if they are true. I have heard it said that humans live only a hundred years or so. Is this true?"

Nell laughed and said, "A hundred years is a very long time for a human! Most dinnay live to be quite so old as that."

The Faery regarded her with stupefaction. "Such a brief time!" was all he said for a while. "And then?"

"Some humans believe in an afterlife. Some believe there's nothing at all."

"What do you believe?"

Nell shook her head. "I dinnay know. Nobody *knows*."

"How long will *you* live?"

Nell laughed again. "Humans dinnay know when they're going to die," she said. "It just happens, sometimes very suddenly. If I'm lucky, aye, I'll live to be an old woman of a hundred. But I could die this afternoon."

Jalo looked horrified at this. "Is it so easy to die?"

"I hadnay thought of it as *easy*, but I spose it is," said Nell. "Compared to other beings, we do die very easily."

"Are you not afraid?"

"I spec we learn not to dwell on it too much," said Nell thoughtfully. "Or praps we get used to the idea. It's just how it is. I hate to think that I'll disappear from the worlds, not be Nell anymore, praps not be anything at all. But then, we wouldnay cherish our lives so much if we didnay know how short a time we have."

"How fragile and noble humans are!" said the Faery, deeply moved. He looked at her tenderly. "I cannot imagine it. While you are with me, I will do my utmost not to let you die."

Nell laughed but she was rather touched, too. "Thank you," she said. "That's comforting."

They were passing over the land of the giants. One of the unwieldy fortresses was under siege, smoke and fire pouring out of it. Brutish giants surrounded it, swinging great blades and hurling boulders at each other.

"Look!" Nell cried, waking Charlie, who had gone to sleep.

"Giants are always at war," Charlie said, unimpressed.

"True enough," Jalo concurred, but Nell watched the battle until they had left it behind them.

"There is a rarer sight," Jalo said suddenly, softly, touching her arm and pointing out the window. She had to crane her neck to look up where he was pointing and saw only a streak of deep crimson flashing by them.

Charlie looked pleased. "They say a sighting is good luck," he said.

Jalo nodded and smiled.

"What was it?" asked Nell.

"The Vermilion Bird of the Sparkling Deluder," said Jalo. "It flies over all of Tian Xia. Nobody knows why. Keeping watch, perhaps."

The foothills rose up gradually into the ferocious mountain range that ran as far as the eye could see from east to west, icebound peaks lost in swirls of cloud. The Faery leaned forward and told Ander where to set down in a clearing on a snowy mountain.

"There is a cave somewhere here!" Jalo shouted as they bundled out of the chopper. The wind was fierce and the ground slippery. "Wait for me by your helicopter and I will find it. Please be careful not to die." With that, he disappeared among the thick pines.

Ander wrapped himself in blankets and took a nap in the helicopter, while Charlie and Nell wandered about the clearing a bit to stretch their legs. They had been flying all day and the light was beginning to fade from the sky.

"I dinnay know why you jumped on Jalo that way," Nell told him. "It made for an awkward beginning."

"I saw him pointing a sword at you," protested Charlie. "It looked to me like you were in danger and I was helping."

"I wasnay in danger. He was just a bit nervous at first," said Nell. "You should check before you go leaping on someone, aye. He might have cut you into bits with that sword if I hadnay stopped him."

"Lah, that's twice you've saved my life then," said Charlie. He glanced at her from the corners of his eyes. "I'd resigned myself, you know. I couldnay have made the Crossing without you. I was just hanging onto your voice."

Nell shushed him. She had just become aware of a pair of bright eyes watching them from a dark hump she had, until then, assumed was the stump of a tree.

"What?" asked Charlie, aggravated. "I'm trying to say thank you, lah."

"That tree stump has *eyes*," Nell hissed at him. "Over there. *Look*."

Charlie gave the stump a long look. Then, before Nell could stop him, he scooped a handful of snow, packed it into a tight ball in his fist, and pegged it straight at the stump. The stump leaped aside with an angry cry and at the same moment reared up to its full, stringy height. It had brown crinkled flesh rather like a toad's, but it moved so quickly, bounding towards them, that it was hard to make out much else except that it was bigger than them and had bright staring eyes. Nell turned with a shriek and ran among the trees. For several minutes she could hear the thing, whatever it was, galumphing after her, letting loose odd war-like shouts and yelps as it went. Then Nell realized she could only hear her own screams and footsteps crashing through the snow. She stopped running.

"Why did you run off like that?" Charlie was at her side, having flown after her as a bird.

"Why did *you?*" demanded Nell. "You could have turned into something scary and made it go away."

"I didnay want to lose you," he said, laughing. "You took off at such a clip! Come on, we should get back to the helicopter."

But neither of them moved. They could see their breath pluming out into the cold, dark air as the last of the daylight faded from the sky and night fell and the trees soared up all around them, black and ominous. The silence and the falling darkness made Nell think back on her conversation with the Faery about how easily humans can die. A twig cracked somewhere nearby and she tensed.

"Did you hear that?"

"Look!" Charlie pointed, and Nell saw that a wavering light was moving among the trees, coming towards them.

"No, no, no," she hissed at Charlie, who had started to go towards it. "Lights in forests are *bad*, nay? You always hear stories about travellers lured deeper into the woods by mysterious lights and so on."

"I've nary heard any stories like that," said Charlie as the light came closer. A tall dark shape was following the light, keeping close to the trees so it was difficult to see what it was.

"This time, dinnay go running off," said Charlie. "Stay close to me."

"Why dinnay you change?" said Nell. "Become a dragon or

something!"

"Lah, I want to see what it *is* first," he replied. The light emerged from between the trees, a glowing sphere, and circled them slowly as if it was having a good look at them. The dark shape following it hid behind a tree.

Charlie called out something in the common language of Tian Xia. The light darted close to their faces and then retreated. A being stepped from behind the tree. It was the stump-thing, stretched out and gangly, with a black cloak pulled around it. It had a bit of colourless hair sticking out of its scalp in wisps but otherwise its face was like a long, shriveled bean with brilliant eyes. Mouth and nose appeared to be mere gaps in the face, darker than the darkness. It spoke in a rattling voice like autumn leaves underfoot and Charlie replied. Then the thing turned, its ball of light zipping on ahead.

"Come on," said Charlie. "She's a witch. Prolly the one we're looking for."

"She?" muttered Nell, but she followed them. Gradually the trees grew thinner and they came to a rocky outcrop with branches piled before an opening. The witch removed the branches and the light bobbed inside, then whizzed back out and circled the witch's head in a panic. The witch began to gibber angrily. Jalo stepped out of the cave.

The stump-like creature Charlie had thrown a snowball at was in fact the very being they had come in search of – a witch named Heilwig. The witch had heard the helicopter long before it landed and had been watching to see what would emerge. She was not at all pleased that Jalo had found her cave and made himself at home there without an invitation, but after many soothing apologies the witch calmed down. They all entered the cave after being formally and pointedly invited and Heilwig set about building a fire. The cave was a large, cool dome, insulated with woven rugs and straw mats. A sleek, bright-eyed mink bared its teeth at the visitors and then leaped to Heilwig's shoulders, draping itself around her neck like a living fur scarf.

"Get the other human from the helicopter," Jalo told Charlie, keeping his eyes on the witch.

Nell glanced at Charlie a bit nervously, for Jalo had said this in a very kingly way and, although he was accommodating, Charlie didn't like to be bossed around. Charlie looked for a moment like he was going to refuse.

"I'll go," Nell offered, although she didn't want to miss a moment of what was going to happen in the cave.

"No, it's fine, I'll go," Charlie grumbled, and he disappeared out the entrance. Heilwig and the Faery conversed in low voices, not bothering to include Nell.

Ander and Charlie returned with provisions from the helicopter, the last of the food that Nell had packed. Nell made sandwiches, which delighted Heilwig. She ate three in a row with great gusto, not saying thank you or even looking at Nell when she handed them over. The Faery declined politely, but Nell caught him giving the bread a look of quiet distaste.

"I wonder what your parents are going to say to me when I get you back," brooded Ander, rubbing his unshaven chin with his hand. "I reckon I'm going to be in a lot of trouble, aye."

"Dinnay be silly," said Nell. "We *had* to help Charlie, and now we have to find Swarn and Eliza."

"And you're sure they're together?"

"No," Nell admitted, "but I spec they will be."

"And how are we going to help when we find them? Seems to me that you and I will just be in the way. You should be with your parents, aye. This is nay our fight."

"Of course it's our fight!" protested Nell. "This is *everyone's* fight. What will become of the worlds if Nia is nay stopped? It will be chaos, aye, and nobody will be able to stop Tian Xia worlders from crossing over. Humans will be like slaves again."

"Aye, sure it's important," said Ander calmly. "But what can *we* do *here?* We should be taking care of our families in Di Shang, Nell, that's where *we* belong."

Nell stared angrily at the fire. She knew he was right. Now

that Charlie was better and Jalo was involved, she and Ander were not going to be of much use to anybody. But she couldn't bear to go home to make decorations and cakes for Winter Festival, all the while wondering if the dragon was still alive, if they had found Swarn, if Eliza was with her and safe. She knew herself to be powerless, but all the same she could not allow herself to be relegated to the sidelines yet again. She was involved this time and she would stay that way. Ander looked at Nell, her eyes bright with tears, jaw clenched, and he sighed.

"We'll stay with them until we find your friend," he said. "Just so you can see she's OK. Then we go back. We dinnay belong in this world." With that he lay down on his side and went to sleep. Relieved, Nell turned her attention to the conversation between Jalo and the witch.

"What are they saying?" she whispered to Charlie.

"Swarn is still alive," Charlie said. "Heilwig saw her two days ago, aye. Swarn is trying to get witches to join with her to fight Nia but none are willing."

"Why are they nay willing?" asked Nell, appalled.

"Witches are pretty solitary. They stay neutral in most disputes," said Charlie. "From their perspective, pitting themselves against Nia is just a form of suicide. Swarn is nay likely to find many in Tian Xia willing to join this fight."

"Is Heilwig going to come and help the dragon?"

"She's nay coming with us," said Charlie. "But she'll make a potion. She needs one night to gather and prepare the ingredients. Right now they're negotiating payment. Jalo was offering Faery treasure, but she wants Magic, aye. Some kind of Illusion."

"Tell them the dragon is nay just hurt, he's on fire – it's a magic fire, I spec – green, and he had little burning bits all over him," said Nell.

Charlie interrupted the witch and the Faery to tell them this. It seemed to perturb Heilwig quite a bit. She muttered to herself, scratching at her head and wriggling in a strange way before resuming conversation with the Faery.

Nell wasn't aware of having fallen asleep, but she woke in the morning to find Charlie and Ander also sleeping on the floor of the cave. The Faery Jalo was watching the witch grind something to powder with a pestle and mortar, chanting in a low sing-song as she did so. Her singing voice was surprisingly lovely, altogether unlike the gravelly rattle of her speech. Nell sat up and watched, fascinated, as the witch took a little black kettle from over the fire and poured a liquid bright as quicksilver into the bowl of powder. She poured it in slow circles, singing, and stirred the mixture into a gleaming paste. She drew a circle with her finger on the stone floor, placed the bowl in the centre of it, then clapped her hands over it three times, making sharp, guttural exclamations with each clap. The paste began to steam. She drew the steam up with her hands and began to shape it. The paste was dissolving fast, becoming a silky white smoke that obeyed the movement of her fingers and the direction of her breath. She spoke to it as she shaped it and Nell saw that it was taking the shape of a dragon. Soon the smoke dragon was fully formed and spread its wings out. The witch threw back her head and began to bay like a hound, waking Ander and Charlie, who watched open-mouthed as she performed the rest of the spell. The Faery calmly handed the witch a jeweled gourd he'd had at his side. She took it and held it up to the dragon, speaking a command. The dragon dis-integrated into elegant white threads that poured into the gourd. Heilwig stopped it up and handed it to the Faery. She spoke to him at length and he nodded, listening carefully.

"We need some of the dragon's blood and fire for this to work," Charlie translated quietly to Nell. "We add it to the mix, say a spell, then we treat his wounds with the potion."

Nell touched Heilwig on the arm and said, "Thank you."

The witch looked at her like she was an unpleasant insect and did not reply.

CHAPTER
14

Alvar, Lord of the Faery Guard and Second Advisor to His Majesty, Malferio, the King of the Faeries, wandered through a fragrant garden, enchanted by the colourful songbirds his daughter's mother-in law, Tariro, had sent as a gift. Tariro's eldest son, Cadeyrn, was a gifted lad, quick with his sword and his wits alike. Alvar had approved of the match for his daughter. Indeed, he could not have hoped for better. His daughter was not a great beauty, nor was she particularly talented or clever. All she had was her rank and she was lucky it had been enough for the likes of Cadeyrn or, more accurately, for Cadeyrn's mother. Tariro herself was not nobly born, but nobody remembered that these days.

The garden was Illusion, though well done, but the birds were real, captured by Tariro's servants from an island in the Far Sea. Their song was exquisite, their feathers far brighter and softer than any of the birds in the west. He thought he would like a coat made of such feathers and wondered if there was some way he could ask her for more birds. He would write her a letter, reassuring her that Cadeyrn was indeed moving up as quickly as was seemly, and include a subtle hint of how lovely such a coat would be. Perhaps a poem of thanks, with a line about how the birds wore feathered coats beyond what could be dreamed of in the humble Faery Court. Yes, she was clever, she would pick up on that.

He left the Illusion of the garden intact, hoping he would have time to return later. A path appeared under his feet and he followed it downhill into a valley of towering ash-grey trees whose pale branches reached towards a stormy white sky. Wind lashed the trees but did not touch Alvar. Victims of Malferio's insane purges were bound to the trees by silver chains. They hung their heads or shouted Curses they could not complete or moaned into the wind. Alvar walked among them, as he did every day. Some of them were old friends but he did not meet their eyes. He could do nothing for them now. He walked here as a reminder. As a warning.

The sky flashed and shook and the trees groaned, their pale, leafless fingers shuddering. Something was moving further in among the trees. Alvar reached for his sword. No, it must have been a trick of the light, the wind throwing shadows. There was no one here. He walked further and then froze. There was a sound on the wind like a bright, ringing laugh. He saw the flash of a cloak moving behind one of the trees in the distance.

"Show yourself!" he called. Again he heard the echo of sweet laughter, like a girl's. He peered among the trees and the hanging bodies of old comrades. There, again, too quick for him to be sure – gleaming hair, a swirling robe.

And a voice behind him. "Alvar."

Witchery. He did not turn around. How could there be a witch loose in the Traitor's Wood? He should summon the Faery Guard at once, but....

"Wait," said a voice in his ear, a voice he knew.

She stepped out from behind a tree several paces away.

"Wait, Alvar. Hear me out before you act."

She was as beautiful as ever. So lovely that his heart seemed to stumble and pause. Her cloak was silver-white, her satin dress a brilliant green flecked with gold, like her eyes. Her hair tumbled over her shoulders in shining curls and the look on her face was caught somewhere between pleading and laughter.

"It would be treason to speak with you," he said. "I could find myself hanging from one of these trees."

Nia looked around and shuddered. "I don't know why you come here; it's very morbid of you. But you won't end up this way, Alvar. You're far too clever. And if you listen to me, everything might be different." She paused, her smile trembling slightly. "No more Traitor's Wood."

"If I am so clever," said Alvar, "why have I not yet summoned the Guard?"

Nia shook her head. "I am a match for all of you now, Alvar. You should hear what I've come to say."

The trees swayed and the wind screamed around them, touching neither. Alvar felt strangely calm. So, Nia had come. To him. There were only two possibilities now. Malferio and the Faeries would destroy her at last or she would destroy Malferio. And he, Alvar, would fall with one or rise with the other. If he spoke to Nia now, his life would depend upon her success. Centuries ago he had been a member of a secret society in favour of assassinating the King and his dangerous Queen. The society had never gained the support it needed for an undertaking so vast as the murder of another Faery and it was disbanded altogether once Nia left the realm and the worst of the purges were over. The fact that Alvar was still free and in a position of prominence showed that the King did not know of the society. The fact that Nia was here now suggested that perhaps she did. Or perhaps she only knew that the thought of her death, even when he had worked for it, had always grieved him. Perhaps she knew he had seen nothing lovelier in all his thousands of years than the flash of her eyes.

Alvar had done terrible things in his life, things he took no pride in. But he could never be called a coward. It had come to this and he was glad.

"Come," he said, and held out his hand. The relief on her face was plain. As she came closer he saw around her neck Chiranjivi's Mirror, the gift of Faery Immortality to a mortal, and a shining vial that, he knew, contained Malferio's blood. Her hand in his was soft and warm. A sandy path opened among the trees and they took it out of the wood, which fell away behind them. They emerged under a gentle sky, rose-coloured, tinged with gold. Emerald waves lapped against the sandy shore. Behind them chrysanthemums bloomed, heavy-headed on their stems.

"Very pretty," said Nia. She looked up at him coyly through a fringe of dark gold lashes. "You called me Queen once. Does that seem funny, now?"

"Not funny," said Alvar, but he smiled. "How did you find us?"

She frowned. "Don't insult me. I'm not a fool and neither are you. That's why I came to see you first. The allegiance of the Faery Guard is yours, Alvar. You carry a great deal of influence. Others will listen to you. You have to make my case for me."

"I thought you were a match for all of us."

"There's no need for an all-out war. I have no grudge against the Faeries. In fact, I'm rather fond of Faeries. But I have a matter to settle with your king. Whether the Faeries rally around him or not, I *will* destroy him. If you can persuade the Faery Lords to overthrow him, it will all be very simple. If not, I will have my way in the end anyway, but I will count you in particular my enemy."

"You do not need to threaten me," said Alvar. "You smell wonderful. What is that?"

"It's a human-made perfume, would you believe," she said with a laugh. "They're surprisingly good at some things. Are you listening to me, Alvar?"

"It is a difficult thing you ask," he said.

The waves darkened and rose up, the sky began to tremble, and he looked at her in surprise.

"Not so difficult," she said. A wave crashed against the shore, and the water that splashed them was cold. "Perhaps you would prefer that both he and I were dead, but this cannot be. It will all be over in a day or so and I promise you I will be the victor. This king of yours is not well loved. His marriage to me left him very unpopular as we both know. The Faeries will support his exile. In return I will swear by the Oath of the Ancients never to enter the Realm of the Faeries again. You can accept my proposal now or you can wait for me to give you a demonstration of my power and accept it later. What will you do?"

"It is not enough," said Alvar. "The Faeries will not back it."

"The Festival of Light, when the Faeries swear allegiance, is the day after tomorrow. I will give the Faeries every reason to turn on their king, I promise you. Overthrown, he is in *your* power, and you must promise me his expulsion. Do not put my question aside again. What will you do?"

The waves were dark giants now, the sea black, the sky red. The chrysanthemums were growing, swaying, winding upwards. Nia's eyes shone.

"Tell me what you wish me to do," said Alvar.

To Eliza's partial relief, the ravens did not follow when they flew south again. They found the Special Forces deployed by General Malone well before nightfall. It appeared that the General had not taken entirely seriously her assessment of the threat. He had sent a pitifully small troop to deal with the Kwellrahg and they had not fared well. When Eliza and Uri Mon Lil found them, they were in various stages of regrouping at the edge of the Great Sand Sea, just south of the border.

Uri Mon Lil needed reminding of what he was to do, but he then did it so flawlessly and effortlessly that Eliza was deeply impressed. She was able to make a simple barrier around herself quickly enough, but this! Soaring overhead on a dragon, this spindly little wizard with his wild hair, bright eyes flashing terribly, his arms above his head, used the spell they had retrieved from the Book of Barriers to enclose the hapless troops below in invisible cells. It was sheer luck that had brought her such an ally and Eliza was flooded with gratitude. The barriers would last a day or so at the most, but long enough, Eliza hoped, for her to do what needed to be done without interference. The troops thus contained, they flew on, looking out for the Kwellrahg. They did not have to look for long. It was staggering along the ground several miles beyond the military encampment, wings scorched and hanging useless after the battering it had received from rockets and artillery fire. Aysu and Obrad's dragons were still pursuing it, circling overhead but keeping their distance. Eliza called the dragons together, glad to have the advantage of speed over the Kwellrahg. They were well beyond any inhabited areas and so they let the beast be and flew into the desert.

They had left behind them that morning a wintry, snow-covered plain, and now flew over an expanse of burnt sand. Claimed by no country or kingdom, the Great Sand Sea was home only to the Sorma. For thousands of years, cut off from the rest of the world, the Sorma had travelled in small tribes from one oasis to another. It was said that they could bring any being back from the very brink of death and that they could tame any creature, however fierce, however wild. After her rescue from Nia's Arctic prison, Eliza's mother Rea had been in desperate need of healing, and so it was to the vast loneliness of the desert and to his people the Sorma that Eliza's father Rom Tok had brought her. Ten years of torment had left Rea deeply scarred within and broken without. Nia had stripped her of her power and her memory and these could not be returned to her. The Sorma could not replace all that she had lost; they could not give her back the strength she once had. But they could tame her wild terror. They could give her new strength and ease the pain. With the Sorma, Rea seemed to find some degree of peace. She could not remember how she had loved her husband once but she came to love him again. When she was with him, Eliza thought she seemed almost happy.

Rea's relationship with her daughter was not so easily rebuilt. They remained careful with one another, both wishing for a closeness they had no idea how to work towards. Eliza spent most of her time with the Mancers in their Citadel, deep in her training as a Sorceress. It was not a journey her mother could make and Rom did not like to leave her, so Eliza saw her parents only when she came to the desert. It was always a joy and a wonder to see her mother alive. All through her childhood some part of her had longed for this woman of whom she had no memory, only a photograph. Now Rea was here, but she remained a stranger, a fantasy come inexplicably to life. Rea herself had trained with the Mancers and with Swarn; she had had a Guide, married and borne a child in secret, fought with Nia, but she remembered none of it. Her Guide had left her. And so Eliza could not turn to her mother for advice or answers to her many questions about the strange life she had been called to. She could not ask her mother why she had tried to hide her from the Mancers. All Rea had known and been belonged to Nia now. In a sense, Nia contained Eliza's mother, or at least that part of Rea that had been, once, Eliza's mother. Rom and the Mancers spoke sometimes of how powerful Rea had been, how full of life and joy. But all Eliza knew was the enfeebled stranger in the desert who hung off her father's arm and woke them all in the night with her screams.

When she watched her father and Rea together, holding hands, she was glad for him. But she was excluded from their happiness, such as it was. Excluded by her mother because, much as Rea would have liked to be close to her daughter, she did not know or understand her. Excluded by her father because their relationship as it had been before was changed forever. It was this that grieved her most. He had been the strong one, he had made the decisions, protected her and cared for her, once. When the Mancers came for Eliza they had reached a point, too soon and all at once, where she was beyond his protection. Now, at the age of fourteen, she had power, she made her own decisions, and had proved she was more than capable of taking care of herself. Rea, once among the greatest of the Shang Sorceresses, was the one who needed taking care of. And so Eliza's father took care of Rea and nobody took care of Eliza anymore. She knew it was absurd to want her father to treat her like a child or anything less than what she *was*, but the change had happened so suddenly and so traumatically. The life she had known had been over in a flash when the five Emmisariae of the Mancers descended on Holburg. Eliza knew that life was change and nothing ever remained the same, but still, the years in Holburg with her father, in the cottage near the sea with its garden and beehives, remained a sort of golden period in her memory, a perfect world before the storm struck.

As dusk fell they crossed the flat sandy plains, aiming for a bright hump on the horizon. There began the dunes, vast mountains of sand shaped by wind. They flew over great ridges that swept in creamy curves down into deep valleys, all of it gold in the setting sun. As the sky darkened and the moon rose, these same magisterial dunes shone ghostly white. The desert appeared endless and unchanging, although its valleys and cliffs and ridges were being constantly remade by the wind. There were no landmarks to speak of but Eliza knew exactly where her father's tribe would be wintering. She had learned on her first journey to the Great Sand Sea that she possessed what all the Sorma possessed – an unwavering sense of the desert. This desert had claimed vast armies in the past, protecting the southern countries for centuries from the powerful northern invaders. No explorer had ever crossed it successfully without a Sorma guide. But Eliza could not be lost here. She *knew* the desert and it recognized her as one of its own. It would not lead her astray.

For all that, she would never love the desert. The only place that had ever felt like home to her was Holburg, with its dense green woods, sandy beaches and trees heavy with fruit, all cradled tenderly by the bright blue sea. She was restless in the desert and ill at ease with the Sorma. Though they were welcoming, she felt like an outsider. Their ways were not familiar to her, would always be exotic and only half-understood. She longed for water and colour.

It was night and the desert sky was bright with stars when the young Shang Sorceress, the wizard of Lil, and the four surviving dragons of the Emmisariae reached the Sorma camp. The camp was on the fringes of an oasis, an island of green in the desert, rich in dates and olives and freshwater springs. Here they would spend several weeks stocking up on food and water before moving on, following their sense of the desert to another oasis that would feed them and provide water.

Almost all of the tribe had retreated to their tents for the night but a few fires still smouldered. The vast dunes loomed all about the oasis, a startling oval of life and birdsong. But whereas the sea as Eliza knew it was full of life, the Great Sand Sea surrounding this island was sterile and deadly. The four dragons set down at the edge of the camp, where an old woman was waiting.

Her grey hair was wound up on top of her head and she wore billowing, colourful fabrics which swept around her in a style that looked effortless but was, in fact, very complicated. Her forehead was marked with the blue teardrop that indicated she was an Elder. Her name was Lai, and she was Eliza's paternal grandmother.

"Greetings, Grandmother," said Eliza, bending to kiss her hand and then kissing her on both cheeks. Uri Mon Lil slid off the dragon's neck and stumbled up behind Eliza.

"Where are we?" he asked.

"Someplace safe," said Eliza a bit curtly, for she was getting tired of explaining things.

"I dreamed you were coming," said Lai, smiling and revealing a row of perfect white teeth. "But in my dream, it was you alone. I did not know you would come with another being and so many dragons. Something is wrong, yes?"

"Yes," said Eliza. "Is my father sleeping?"

"He is. Shall I wake him?"

"No, it can wait until morning."

"You will need refreshment. Come, and your friend, too."

Eliza and Uri Mon Lil followed Lai to a broad tent outside of which an old man was sleeping.

"Your Grandfather always means to count the stars," commented Lai, stepping over him. "But he falls asleep every night before he reaches a hundred. I will bring him in later."

Inside, she poured them each some strong tea and proffered a bowl of dates. They ate and drank gratefully. Uri Mon Lil, who could not understand what they were saying, furtively consulted his book. He was most distressed to discover that he had an unhappily married daughter, was stricken by a terrible Curse, and had gotten himself involved in something very complicated and dangerous with a surly young Sorceress, with whom his relationship was alarmingly described as "uncertain."

"Is it true that the Sorma can heal any being, even those on the brink of death?" asked Eliza.

Lai nodded her head. "This is true. Perhaps you are wondering why your mother remains weak. We cannot heal her because your mother is not wounded. It is not injury she suffers, but a lack. It is not a question of healing, but of wholeness."

"I'm not talking about my mother," said Eliza.

Lai raised her eyebrows and waited.

"A being who suffers...you could ease the pain? Even if the suffering were caused by Magic?"

"I know nothing of Magic," said Lai. "But we can ease pain and heal the wounded."

"And is it true that the Sorma can tame any beast, however wild?"

"This is also true."

"Then I need your help," said Eliza.

CHAPTER
15

Gautelen Mon Lil Mon Shol was half Storm Seamstress, half witch. She was seventeen years old and until a year ago she had been happy. For one year now, though she lived as a queen in the heart of the Faery Kingdom, a place whose beauty outstripped any other place in the worlds, her heart felt like a stone sinking fast through dark water. When she woke in the mornings and remembered where she was, she wished with all her being that she could return to her dreams and never have to walk through another waking day as Queen of the Faeries. All the beauty around her, all the beauty of her husband, was dead to her. The world of Illusion was a prism of glittering despair. Because the lives of her parents depended on her obedience, she performed her duty as Queen and as wife, but she did so with her teeth clamped tight over a rage she would not once have believed herself capable of. When the Faeries asked for a storm, she lit up the sky with colour and sound and they were delighted. She could not give them the storm she longed to make – the hail of destruction, the bolts of flame, the wind that screamed all her despair. But just such a storm had been called for a few days earlier, from a power greater than she had ever known. She had given it with all her heart, feeling in the demand for it a fury that matched her own. That storm had given Gautelen some small relief and she was still weary from it.

She had spent the morning walking in a desultory manner through the Illusions her Faery attendants provided to entertain her when the king was busy. A diamond bridge spanned a starry night sky, but she barely noticed her surroundings. Bored, she napped in a flower as large as a house. On a hillside brilliant with heather overlooking a white city of spires and towers, birds serenaded her and sat on her shoulders, but they were not real and she paid them no mind. It was all false, false, and the wondrous sights had no effect on her. Lying back in the heather, for a moment she thought she smelled the sea. She sat upright immediately, filled with longing. The birds scattered, frightened by something. The heather around her turned black.

Yes, there was salt on the breeze. The Faeries who attended her looked confused. Something glinted further down the hill, like a window of light suddenly opening. Gautelen leaped to her feet and ran towards it. It was a long mirror. She scowled at her reflection as she approached it. Her bright silk robe and the jewels that decked her arms and throat and hair disgusted her. The diamonds around her neck were like shackles. She fingered the brilliant gems, her anger working a slow burn in her, then tore them from her throat and threw them to the ground. She pulled the jewels from her hair also, until she stood before the mirror with diamonds, emeralds, sapphires and gold scattered on the ground at her feet, hair disheveled, the fury she could not act upon throttled in her throat.

"I hate you," she said in a trembling voice to her reflection. As soon as she had spoken, another woman appeared behind her in the mirror, a lovely women in a robe that matched her own, still decked with jewels, but this woman was fair-skinned with golden hair.

"I'm sorry, but I can't let that pass," said the woman. Her voice was honey-sweet and smooth. "Hate is a confusing emotion, I know, but it's important to keep it focused on those who have deserved it. *Never* misdirect it at yourself, you poor girl. That is an amateur's mistake."

Gautelen looked behind her in alarm, but she was alone on the hillside. The charred heather had risen up in a twisted wall, separating her from her attendants.

"Am I going mad?" she asked unhappily.

"Far from it, your Majesty." The apparition in the mirror stroked her wild hair but Gautelen could not feel the touch.

"Everything is about to come out right. Now promise me you'll never say such a thing to yourself again!"

Gautelen was baffled but not particularly afraid. What did she have to fear?

"I promise," she said.

"Good girl. You're young and you've led a sheltered life," said the apparition. "When it comes to hate, you are terribly inexperienced. So take it from one who has been at this game a great deal longer than you – self-hatred is a fool's capitulation. Revenge is the only relief."

The apparition stepped out of the mirror onto the hillside, a flesh-and-blood woman, and Gautelen knew beyond a shadow of a doubt that her closed and dreary world was about to be blasted wide open. She spent her days surrounded by beauty that did not touch her, but this woman's beauty made her ache with unshed tears, revived the near-dead memory of joy. Perhaps it was because she was powerful and free and Gautelen was not. Or perhaps it was because she brought with her a rush of hope Gautelen had not felt since before her wedding day.

"I was Queen of the Faeries too, once upon a time," said the woman with a knowing smile. Then Gautelen understood whom it was that stood before her.

"You are the Xia Sorceress," said Gautelen in a whisper. "That was your storm I sent."

"And it was magnificent. I thank you," said Nia. "The storm spoke to me, Gautelen. It told me that you and I were meant to help each other. How do you like the Realm of the Faeries, your Majesty?"

Gautelen did not reply. Her heart was racing, her mouth suddenly dry. She had heard many terrible stories about this Sorceress, who had terrorized Tian Xia for three hundred years before being banished by the Triumvira. It was widely known that the Sorceress was barred forever from Tian Xia by the most terrible Magic and that the Mancers had imprisoned her in their world with the most powerful barriers. Yet here she was. It could not be Illusion or trickery. She was too real. Gautelen knew she should be afraid, but what she felt was elated. She had endured this imprisonment for a year, and every word the Sorceress spoke was a promise of freedom. Gautelen would gladly have followed her to the end of the worlds.

"I know how you feel, little one," said Nia, taking Gautelen's chin in her hands. Gautelen stared into the Sorceress's eyes, brilliant green flickering with gold light. "I know *exactly* how you feel."

And then Gautelen could hold her tongue no longer. "I hate him," she declared vehemently, tears springing to her eyes. "I want him to die!"

"That's right, *him* you hate," Nia laughed. "I'm afraid he cannot *die*, dearest, but he will suffer, I promise you that."

"You hate him too," Gautelen whispered.

"Yes," said Nia, as tenderly as if she was confessing love. "I am going to destroy him, and then you will be free. But I cannot fight all the Faeries if they choose to stand by their king. I must ensure that they do not. Will you help me?"

"I'll do anything you ask," said Gautelen fiercely. "Anything."

"Good girl. We will help each other." Nia held out a hand to her. Gautelen dropped to her knees before the Sorceress and kissed the hand rapturously.

"Now," said Nia, stroking her cheek, "let's fix your hair. You look a fright."

Rumours abounded among trolls, centaurs and other mountain-dwellers about the mysterious new creature spotted in the skies of Tian Xia, a roaring, flying thing with giant eyes. Quite unaware of the confusion they were causing, Ander, Nell, Charlie and Jalo flew southeast in the helicopter, over the mountains and the slate-grey cliffs of Batt, which formed a towering, ragged cleft along the northernmost edge of the Dead Marsh. Jalo's myrkestra was waiting for them by the ruins of Swarn's house.

Nell and Ander had arrived the first time when the slaughter was still fresh. Now the stench of dead dragons was overpowering. Jalo had to work an Illusion so that they smelled only lilies in order for them to be able to get out of the helicopter. Even spared the smell, it was a terrible sight to see.

"She's completely insane," said Charlie hoarsely, looking around at the miles of broken dragon bodies. "Why would she do this?"

The young dragon lay motionless by the still-burning house and, when she saw it, Nell was afraid that they were too late. But as she approached its golden eyes flicked in her direction and a weak puff of smoke came from its nostrils.

"We need something that will catch fire easily," said Nell. "Like dry bracken."

"I have a fire stick," said Jalo, taking out a slender black rod that he kept next to his sword.

"What is that?"

"It feeds the flame without burning down," he said. "It's a very useful item. It can be used for a fire that will never go out or a torch."

"Good. We just need to get the dragon to breathe on it, aye. Can you talk to dragons?"

"Not these dragons," said the Faery.

"Lah, give me the gourd," said Nell, and he handed it to her. "Blood will be easy to get. He's covered in wounds."

The dragon did not even lift his head as Nell went to examine his torn wing. The blood there was congealed, no longer running freely. Deep black pits full of green fire had formed in his side and on his back.

"We have to cut him," said Nell, a lump coming to her throat.

"You should not be so close," said Jalo, drawing his sword and joining her. "Remember how easily you die. Let me do this."

Charlie and Ander hung back together, watching.

"She's quite a girl, aye," said Ander, rubbing his stubbled chin ruefully. "She's just a kid, but somehow...lah, there's no telling her what to do, is there?"

"No, I spose not," said Charlie gloomily. "Do you think he's handsome?"

"What? Who?" asked Ander. "The Faery?"

"Yes," said Charlie. "I mean, I spec he is, obviously. He's a

Faery."

Ander gave Charlie an incredulous look. "Praps...I'm no judge, but I'd say so..." he faltered.

"Nary mind," said Charlie crossly.

Jalo cut into the dragon's wound with his sword. The dragon shuddered but did not otherwise protest. Nell quickly unstopped the gourd and caught the bright red running blood with it. Obtaining the flame was more difficult. The dragon was so weak that he could not be angered to fight, and none of them had the heart to torment him.

"We need to show him what we're doing," decided Nell. She approached the dragon's head, which made Jalo nearly apoplectic with anxiety for her. She placed her hand on the rough, dry scales between its eyes and looked into them.

"We're trying to help you, aye," she said softly.

"He doesn't understand you," said the Faery. "Get *back*. He could still be dangerous."

"He can understand this," said Nell, stroking the dragon between his eyes and looking at him intently. "Become a dragon, Charlie, and breath fire on the stick."

Charlie obeyed, becoming a dragon roughly the same size as the injured one. Jalo held up the fire stick and Charlie breathed a thread of flame onto it. Immediately it flared. The hurt dragon watched with its golden eyes, not moving any other part of itself. Nell pointed to the fire on the stick and then held up the gourd. She stroked the dragon between the eyes again. Jalo quenched the fire stick with a word and she held it towards the hurt dragon. The dragon stared at it balefully.

"Please," Nell entreated the dragon. "*Please* try. I know you're in pain, but *please* try."

They repeated the same demonstration a number of times, to no avail.

"He's too badly hurt," Charlie concluded. "We're going to have to frighten him, and even then I'm not sure he's got the strength to fight back. What should I turn into? What are dragons afraid of? Bigger dragons?"

Nell's eyes filled with tears. She stroked the dragon's nose. "We cannay," she said. "He's been through too much already."

"Lah, do you want to help him or not?" asked Charlie.

"If you want my opinion, this thing's done for," said Ander, who had kept back and watched in silence until now. "Kindest thing you can do now is cut its head off with that sword."

"No!" shouted Nell. She turned towards the dragon desperately. "Nobody's going to cut your head off! I promise!"

The dragon lifted its head an inch or two off the ground and opened its jaws. All that came out was smoke.

"Try again," Nell said encouragingly.

The dragon looked at her forlornly, then belched forth a tiny ball of red fire that the Faery skillfully caught as the flame rolled out over its tongue. The fire stick flared and Nell unstopped the gourd again. Jalo plunged the fire stick into the mix and the potion burst out of the gourd in silver swirls. Hurriedly, Jalo spoke the words the witch had taught him and the bright swirls fluttered over the dragon, dousing the green fires and settling into his wounds. The dragon's eyes closed.

The spell took much of the day. The dragon remained very still as the potion melted into light that moved like little eddying pools in his wounds. Jalo and Nell passed the time by comparing passages of Faery poetry and human poetry.

"They make you memorize all that stuff at that fancy school?" Ander asked, impressed by the long recitations Nell was capable of.

"We dinnay *have* to memorize them," said Nell, "but I have a good memory, and some of these I wrote papers on, so I've read them over and over. Lah, this one's old but it's a classic, aye. It's by Lapto, about the creation of Di Shang."

She recited it in full and the others listened.

Ander shook his head. "I never read much poetry. I spec I've been missing out."

"But human poetry seems so often to amount to mere stories in verse," said Jalo. "Surely the point of poetry is that it is...like *music* made of words. Listen, here is another poem by Shira."

"All you've done is poems by Shira," complained Charlie.

"Well, yes, she is our greatest poet. Listen carefully and you will hear how the rhythm builds a sensory impression of water."

"What is the poem called?" Nell interrupted.

"We don't title our poems," said Jalo a little primly. "The subject ought to be self-evident. As in this case. You could not possibly think the poem to be anything but water in words. To name it would be superfluous."

He recited, and the other three listened in awe. His words swept away the terrible surroundings. They could feel the cool ripple, the silken depths. It was like having one's mind immersed in a shining pool. When he had finished, none of them spoke for a while, not wanting to shake the feeling the poem had left them with.

"It's very different from human poetry, aye," Nell conceded at last. "Will you teach it to me?"

Jalo looked pleased and was about to reply when the little dragon lifted its head and rose to its feet. Light poured off it in rivulets and streams. It stretched its wings out, raised its head, and wailed. It was a cry of such wrenching grief that they were all frozen where they stood for a moment. Then the dragon lowered its head and looked at Nell.

"It worked!" she cried.

Without thinking she ran to it and placed her hands on its bright, scaled face. The dragon kept its eyes steady on her and there was something like kindness in its gaze.

"Now let's see if it will lead us to Swarn," said Nell.

The fuel reserves were getting low, so they agreed to leave the helicopter in the Dead Marsh. The Faery rode his myrkestra, Charlie flew as a gryphon with an anxious Ander clinging to his back, and Nell, feeling triumphant, rode the dragon. She was sure Eliza would be very impressed when she heard how Nell had gotten Charlie to the healing cave, enlisted the Faery's help and saved the dragon. She imagined over and over again how she would tell the tale. "At first, the Faery seemed more inclined to kill us then help us, but it wasnay too hard to win him over. I just explained how essentially we were all on the same side..."

The dragon led them west, towards the Sea of Tian Xia, following the descent of the sun. They stopped for a couple of hours in the foothills where trolls lived and the myrkestra and Charlie hunted rabbits, which they cooked over a fire and shared. Jalo kept watch while the others slept all too briefly. Before it was light he woke them again to continue the journey. The dragon seemed impatient to carry on, certain of its destination. Beyond the land of the Giants the earth was webbed with thousands upon thousands of glittering rivers. Long graceful boats plied the rivers but Nell could not make out what kind of beings guided the boats. They passed over the rivers, which eventually merged into several large rivers, over dramatic waterfalls and twisted rock formations, until they reached a thick forest of black trees. Over this was the Sea of Tian Xia, clear as glass.

They veered north and were flying along miles of rocky coastline when a thick purplish fog closed about them, eclipsing everything, sound as well as sight. Nell could not see her own hands clutching the spiked neck of the dragon, nor could she hear the wings of the dragon beating the air anymore. She called out to the others but her voice was swallowed by the fog. The dragon cried out then and though its plaintive cry was also muted it carried a little further. Nell assumed at first that the dragon's cry was to help the others follow what they could not see. It continued to cry out for a long time, until there came a returning cry, a shrill and terrible sound from somewhere ahead of them. The fog parted like curtains, revealing the grey, ridged sea below and the wooded coast. A dragon twice the size of the one Nell rode was circling above a windy bluff, screaming. A white-haired figure stood on the bluff holding a glittering spear.

The dragons landed on the bluff, soon followed by the gryphon and the myrkestra. Swarn came striding to meet them. Although Nell did not know it, the witch was changed. Her strong, dark face was hollow and gaunt and her eyes burned even more fiercely than before. She looked mistrustfully at the little group, then said to Charlie, "Where is Eliza?"

"We thought she was with you," said Charlie. Nell's heart plummeted.

Swarn looked around. "We cannot talk here. Come, among the trees." She stopped and pointed at the Faery. "You cannot enter the witches' forest."

"No," said the Faery, looking in alarm at the trees.

"Why cannay you?" asked Nell.

"It was Faeries that Cursed the witches who make up the trees of this wood," said Swarn, her voice steely. "But they retain a power of their own and no Faery may enter."

"Lah, you just wait here," said Charlie to Jalo cheerfully.

"Wait!" said Nell. "He's helped a lot. He should be part of any discussion, aye. Why do we need to go in the forest?" She didn't much like the look of the dark trees either.

"It is not safe out in the open," said Swarn. She thought for only a bit, then gestured for them all to follow. "I invite you, Faery, and you are under my protection for the moment."

Jalo didn't seem to find this very comforting, but he followed Swarn and the others in among the trees. The mist fell behind them like a wall and the trees formed a tight circle around them. It was as if they stood at the center of a fortress made out of forest and fog.

"Tell me what has happened, Shade," said Swarn.

"The Mancers have been turned to stone," said Charlie. "Praps you already know that. Eliza and I found Nia in the Citadel, draining all the books. And she made this...monster. To keep Eliza busy, out of the way, she said. The monster was going to find Eliza's mother. I was hurt and I couldnay help her. I thought she'd come find you, aye. I didnay think she'd be crazy enough to go after it by herself, but if you havenay seen her, I spec that's what she's done."

"By herself?" echoed Nell faintly. "Why would she do that?"

Charlie shrugged unhappily. "You know how she is about her family."

"You say Nia *Made* a monster?" Swarn asked.

Charlie looked puzzled. "Lah...it came out of her mouth. It was disgusting, actually. Will you come back to Di Shang with us? We've got to find Eliza, help her."

"Eliza will be safe until Nia returns to Di Shang for her," said Swarn. "Nia would not wish her dead, not yet. We can help her best by stopping Nia, though I confess I am at a loss. Tell me how you came to be in the company of a Faery and one of my dragons."

The Faery stepped forward at this. "I am Jalo, second son of Nikias," he introduced himself. He described his own meeting with Nell and the scene of slaughter they had encountered in the Marsh. Swarn listened with an impassive face but Nell saw her knuckles whiten around the spear. "The King of the Faeries awaits you in the Realm of the Faeries, that you may join forces against Nia," he concluded.

"I sought the King," said Swarn tersely. "He has hidden himself behind a great wall of Illusion. I thought he did not mean to fight."

"He is protecting his people," said Jalo. "But he has sent out a number of his best soldiers to find his allies and bring them to him. The Oracle is dead, the Mancers incapacitated, but I have found you. I can take you to him. We should not scatter our force but rather work together in an organized fashion. The Curse on the Mancers must be broken and they and the Shang Sorceress must all be brought to the Realm of the Faeries. Our kingdom is impenetrable; we can fight the Sorceress from there."

"Then I should go to Di Shang," said Swarn. "Perhaps I can break the Curse on the Mancers."

"You should not go alone," said Jalo. "It will be safer if you are accompanied by some members of the Faery Guard. Curses are Faery Magic, after all. Come to the Faery Realm and consult with the King. We must agree on a battle plan. I cannot speak for my King until he knows all that I know."

"I'll go back to Di Shang to help Eliza, then," said Charlie.

"How will you find her?" demanded Swarn. "The Faery is right. We need to co-ordinate our efforts. I have no doubt there will be a role for you, too. I think that Eliza is safe for the time being."

"Then we'll all go together," said Nell hopefully.

"Yes," said Jalo. "And quickly."

Ander looked at Nell. She avoided his gaze and he said nothing. It was agreed. The trees parted, the fog dissolved and Jalo on his myrkestra led the group across the Sea of Tian Xia to the legendary, hidden Realm of the Faeries.

CHAPTER
16

The winter sojourn at the oasis was a busy time for the Sorma. They hunted and plucked birds and put every part of them to practical use – skins and feathers for clothing, bags and camel saddles; meat sliced and dried and salted and then tightly packed for the long months of travel ahead; bones and beaks turned into needles and fastenings. They dried dates and pickled olives and edible plants. They collected fresh water and repaired tattered tents and worn clothing. When they set off again, it would be with supplies enough to last them their journey to another oasis. The scarred, angry-looking camels roamed freely, eating plants and drinking from the streams, and their flabby humps grew full and firm again.

Eliza met with the Council of Elders at dawn. She had bathed in one of the springs and changed into clean clothes in the Sorma style, a colourful tunic over loose trousers. The Elders sat cross-legged in a semi-circle in the Council Tent, listening carefully while she explained everything. Spoken out loud, her plans sounded flimsy and reliant on too many uncertainties, even to her. But her grandmother said simply, "We will help you," and the others said *Arash*, it is agreed.

The Healers and the Spirit Speakers were called. Eliza sent the dragons circling over the dunes to keep a lookout for the Kwellrahg. She then wrote out a page of instructions for Uri Mon Lil, describing the spell of Deep Seeing and asking him to look in the Book of Barriers for the Sperre-Tahora, a complex barrier spell usually only cast by Mancers to contain a particular, named being and its Magic.

When Rom and Rea woke and emerged from their tent they were delighted to find Eliza in the camp. Even engulfed in her father's bear hug, Eliza's task weighed on her. There was no safe harbour for her, not even here. She noticed that Rea's face looked lined and pinched.

"Are you all right?" she asked her mother shyly.

Rea nodded and managed a tight smile.

"You dinnay look well," said Eliza.

"She hasn't been sleeping lately," said Rom, supporting her with his arm. "A bit of a relapse, in terms of...pain."

"I know," said Eliza. "I mean, I know why."

She explained it to them over breakfast in their tent. Rea flexed her hand, looking at the space where her little finger was missing.

"I don't understand why she made it out of *me*," she said when Eliza had finished.

"Having it come after you was the best way to make sure I'd go after it," said Eliza. "It's linked to Nia through the Magic of Making but linking it to you as well is a sort of protection for her. She must have known I would figure it out, aye. I dinnay dare hurt it and so I cannay use it to hurt her."

"Do you suppose it could provide a way to...help Rea? Get back her strength?" asked Rom, stirring the fire restlessly.

"I dinnay think so," said Eliza. "She's kept the power for herself. She just used the flesh and the suffering to forge the connection she wanted. I suppose in theory we could get your finger back, but I wouldnay know where to begin."

Rea laughed weakly. "It sounds like too much trouble," she said. "My finger is the least of what's been cut away from me."

"Are you sure this wizard is strong enough to do what you say?" Rom pressed on. "He seems...not very wizardly."

Eliza shrugged. "I've never met a wizard so I dinnay know about that. But he has power and he's all we've got."

"I can't imagine what it's like to forget everything *every twenty-nine minutes*," sighed Rea. "It puts my situation in perspective, doesn't it?"

Eliza hugged her knees and rocked back and forth a bit

before the dying fire. "I just wish it was already happening. Waiting is horrible."

"Game of chess?" suggested Rom, and Eliza smiled.

Eliza and her father played chess through the morning. The concentration of it soothed her somewhat. After lunch she took a walk through the oasis, checking on the preparations of the Sorma and Uri Mon Lil's progress with the spell. Finally, too restless to stay in the camp, she called back Ka's dragon and he bore her up over the oasis and north along the dunes. Half a mile away, soaring over the lip of a golden dune, they spotted the Kwellrahg, flaming wings hanging, climbing with fierce determination up the steep sandy slope. Ka's dragon veered in a sharp circle, letting out a warning cry, and made back for the camp.

"It's coming!" Eliza called to the Sorma as soon as the dragon landed. She ran to where Uri Mon Lil was rereading her instructions to him.

"Is it ready?" she demanded. He gave her a startled look.

"Never mind who I am," she snapped, picking up his book and reading the spell. It was complete. Relief washed over her. "I'm sorry," she apologized immediately. "I'm *very* nervous. Thank you for doing this."

"Not at all," said Uri Mon Lil amiably. "But I appear to be preparing a very difficult *barrier* spell...to hold...some kind of beast. It seems an odd thing for me to be doing."

"It's a very good thing for you to be doing," said Eliza, "and I'm grateful, aye. Come on."

The Healers and the Spirit Speakers stood at the edge of the camp, waiting.

"Eliza," said Rom, taking her arm. "If it doesn't work..."

"It will," she said, and hugged him fiercely. Then, without thinking about it, she hugged Rea too.

"It should be me doing this," Rea whispered in her ear. "It was *my* battle."

"You did your part," said Eliza. "It's my turn now."

The Sorma Elders had formed a semi-circle before the camp. Uri Mon Lil was at the centre of it with his book open to the Sperre-Tahora. Rom helped Rea to a position next to the wizard and Eliza stepped aside, dagger at the ready should anything go wrong. They waited until the Kwellrahg appeared, dark and flaming, over the edge of the dune.

Spying the Sorma camp, the Kwellrahg extended its tattered wings wide, showering sparks, and crossed the sandy expanse at a gallop.

"By the Ancients," murmured Rea, leaning heavily against Rom. He glanced anxiously at Eliza.

When it was only as far away as the length of a playing field, Eliza could hold herself still no longer. The closer the Kwellrahg was, the easier it would be for Uri Mon Lil to cast the Sperre-Tahora. But she could not risk the creature falling on her mother first.

"Now Uri!" she said.

He raised one arm, fingers outstretched, and called out the ancient words of the Sperre-Tahora. Eliza felt power rolling off him in great waves. He seemed to grow, not in size precisely but in another kind of stature. The Kwellrahg slowed, not because the spell was working yet but because it understood something was about to happen and didn't know what. It tossed its great horned head about, vomiting smoke, uncertain. Its flaming eyes took in the enemy before it, Uri Mon Lil casting the spell, Eliza with her dagger drawn, the rows of Sorma, trying to determine which among them posed the greatest threat. Then its eyes fell on Rea again and it regained its purpose, making for her in a mad bolt as if recognizing the chance was close to slipping away. Rom wrapped his arms around his wife. They all felt the air around them sucked away as the Kwellrahg drew near. Rea could not look away but when the Kwellrahg was almost upon them Rom turned his head in horror, rasping, "Eliza! Stop it!" Eliza started forward just as something flew from the wizard's hand and struck the Kwellrahg. It stumbled and the force that had struck it ballooned out around it, only visible as a shimmer in the air. Once it was enclosed, they could all breathe again. The Kwellrahg roared, hurling its battered, burning form against the barrier.

"How long will the barrier last?" Eliza asked Uri Mon Lil.

"I've no idea," he answered. "I'll stay close, in case it needs to be redone."

Eliza nodded. "Go back to your tent," she said to Rom and Rea. "You dinnay need to see the rest of this."

Eliza joined the Sorma forming a circle around the trapped Kwellrahg. Her heart hammered against her ribs as if it were trying to break free and for a moment she imagined that it might burst out of her, a black raven, and take to the sky. The Kwellrahg's fear and desperation had infected her. She wanted to scream at the Sorma to hurry. The urgency of the task overwhelmed her, made her knees fold under her. She felt her grandmother's arms around her, holding her up, drawing her back into the circle. The Kwellrahg roared again and battered the barrier, which shuddered but did not break. The Sorma observed it quietly.

"This being is made of fear and anger and feeds on the same," said Lai quietly. "At its core there is something that draws such emotion to it like a magnet. Can you feel it?"

"Yes," whispered Eliza.

"That is what holds it together," said Lai. "Its flesh and bone are so imbued with rage and terror that although it is burned and severed, the parts cannot fall away from the core. So it remains whole, in a sense, drawn tight around that centre. We cannot heal it, Eliza, because it was never whole. We can only try to add elements to it that will soothe it somewhat. But first *you* must tame it. Do you know why the Sorma can tame any beast?"

"No," said Eliza.

"Because we can control our fear. You can master an animal physically by using its own strength against it. This is easily learned. But you must master the will of the beast as well. It must know, without a doubt, that you are stronger, that you can punish or protect it. For the beast to believe this, you must show no fear. Are you afraid, Eliza Tok?"

"Yes," said Eliza.

"Then you are not ready."

"But we don't have time..."

"There is time. We have much to prepare. Go and ask your Aunt Ry for some tea. Rest."

Eliza nodded. She marvelled at how calm the Sorma seemed, standing so close to the Kwellrahg, their eyes still as stones, their breathing steady.

She went to find her aunt in the camp.

Aunt Ry, her father's eldest sister, often wandered into the desert by herself, to find little pools of water or tiny oases, returning with herbs, roots and fungi whose purpose she seemed to understand instinctively. When Eliza found her, she was playing with her five-year-old son in the shade. She had kind eyes and a heart-shaped face. Like most of the Sorma women she kept her hair cropped close, which complemented her dramatic eyes and cheekbones. Eliza was very comfortable with Ry, for she saw so much of her father in her.

"Grandmother told me to ask you for some tea," said Eliza. She felt strangely leaden, as if she too were enclosed in a kind of barrier that kept her at a distance from the world and everyone in it.

Ry looked deeply into her eyes, taking Eliza's chin between her thumb and forefinger. She nodded and said, "Come with me."

Eliza followed her to her tent and waited while Ry brewed the tea, watching those strong, supple hands at work. The tea was thick and black and very bitter, but Eliza drank it all. It left her thirstier than before. Ry was talking to her and the words ran together, making no sense. Her aunt's face was kind and concerned, but Eliza felt she was looking at it from a great distance. There was somewhere else she needed to be.

She heard her own voice as if it was someone else's thanking Ry thickly, awkwardly, and she stumbled back out into the sun. It was too bright. If only she could drink the sun, bring dark and quiet. The Sorma moving about the camp made her claustrophobic. She couldn't breathe. She walked away from the tents, into the desert, to put space between herself and the camp, herself and the Kwellrahg, herself and the awful thing required of her.

She followed the Kwellrahg's tracks up the dune and over the edge, and she kept walking, climbing up the steep dunes until she lay panting on their ridges, then staggering down them into hot, sandy valleys. The camp was hidden from view. She could see only the rolling hills of golden sand around her and the sky, a vast blue dome arcing overhead. The sun blazed vengefully. Though she was pouring sweat, she climbed another dune and over the peak of this one she saw something strange. In the valley below was a tree. It had a great big knobbed trunk and powerful branches twisted out every which way, like a strong hand with many muscular fingers reaching for the sky. It was the Lookout Tree from the southern cliffs of Holburg. She ran down the dune towards it, heart in her throat. As she got closer to it she saw there was somebody in the tree, perched on the very branch she and Nell used to sit on to look out over the archipelago.

She stood beneath the tree and looked up. The figure on the upper branch was a small boy, only about four or five years old. He had tight dark curls and liquid eyes and his little legs were swinging. He looked back down at her.

"Hello," said Eliza.

"I can see *everything* from up here," said the little boy in a piping voice. "You can't see much at all from down there, can you?"

Eliza looked around her. The desert curved up towards the sky and the sky curved down towards it so they formed a perfect sphere and the sun burned a hole at the top of it all.

"No, I cannay see very much," she answered. "Where am I?"

The little fellow kicked his legs vigorously and said, "This is the edge of things. You've got to go back."

She felt a terrible weariness gathering behind her eyes. "I'm too tired," she told him. "I need to rest for a while."

"No rest for the wicked!" piped the little fellow. "You've got to go back. You're allowed to come this far, exactly. This is the farthest. That's how Magic works."

Eliza squinted up at him. He was looking at her quite imperiously. "I'm a Sorceress," she told him. "What do *you* know about Magic?"

He laughed a ringing little laugh. "I know *everything* about Magic. I know where it ends."

"Where?" asked Eliza.

"Here!" he said. "That's why you've got to go back."

She sat down and leaned against the trunk of the tree. It was so familiar against her back. If only she could see the islands, if only she could run back to town and their little house and have a glass of water. If only she could leap into the sea. The little boy regarded her from above and then asked, "Why are you sad?"

"So many reasons," said Eliza, but she couldn't weep. Her body was too parched, too dried up, even to squeeze out a tear or two.

"You've got to go back," said the boy again, more kindly. "But you can take something with you, if you like."

"What should I take?" asked Eliza, leaning her head back to look up at him.

The boy cackled wildly. "You look funny upside down."

She pulled a face, and he cackled more.

"You're funny. I *like* you."

"My name is Eliza," she said.

"I *know* that," he said a bit impatiently. "But it doesn't mean anything. It's just a word your mother and father picked out to call you, but they didn't know anything about you then and they still don't."

"What's your name?" asked Eliza.

The boy hesitated, then said, "I *like* you, but you're a bit stupid. Do you like birds?"

"I dinnay know," said Eliza. "I like some birds."

"How can you do anything if you don't know?" demanded the little boy crossly.

"I dinnay understand you," said Eliza. "I dinnay know where I am."

This seemed to send the little boy into a rage.

"Pay attention!" he shouted at her. "Why don't you *pay attention?* You are *very* stupid, and *quite* ugly and you don't *pay attention!*"

"You said you liked me, lah," said Eliza, almost tempted to laugh at this sudden tantrum.

"I don't like you at all," he returned snootily. "You're a stupid girl and I'm bored of talking to you. This is the edge of things and you've got to go back. Are you going to take something with you or not?"

"Yes," she said. She looked at the brilliant sky. Innumerable black dots swam before her eyes before becoming ravens. She looked up at the tree and it was full of ravens too, perched silent on every branch.

"They shouldn't *be* up here," the boy shouted down at her. "I don't *want* them up here."

Birds began to burst out of the sand like black plants suddenly sprouting all over the dunes. They walked towards her, leaving streams of little bird tracks behind them. She leaned against the tree with her legs splayed out and birds sat on her legs and on her shoulders and her head. She was dizzy with thirst. The ravens made odd rattling sounds in the backs of their throats. There were so many of them that it was quite deafening. She covered her ears and looked around at them. They regarded her most intelligently, filling the sphere of sand and sky. In the rattling, a sort of conversation emerged among them.

Power flows, of course it does. How did she carry it? Next to her heart. The centre is the strongest. We are all made of Flow. How will you bear it? Little girls grow up, there is nothing unusual in it. You cannot protect them, you cannot protect yourself. What will you call it? There is power in the names of things. Who can you trust? The worlds will have their way, in the end, in the end. You don't understand, you can't see the whole picture. So many secrets, kept for so long. She loves you, you know. She is in your heart. Of course she is. Of course.

Eliza was terribly thirsty now. She touched the sand but it was too dry, she could not drink it. She touched the sky but it gave her nothing. And so she told the ravens, I'm thirsty, I think I might die of it, and they became a black river that flowed into her mouth, quenching her thirst at last. The little boy in the tree scowled down at her. "Now go back," he said, and she did so.

CHAPTER
17

Dusk fell as they flew across the Sea of Tian Xia. For a while, Nell could see all the islands sprinkled around the coast like little jewels and it reminded her of home. But there were fewer islands as they flew on and the sky darkened until she could see nothing but the brilliant Hanging Gardens of the Sparkling Deluder far to the south. She dozed on the dragon's back, coming to every few minutes with a start. Suppose she fell off? How long was the fall to the sea below? The steady *schoom, schoom, schoom* of the dragon's wings lulled her out of consciousness. The odd thought crossed her mind that it would take them years to reach the Realm of the Faeries and she would return home an old woman. No, that was ridiculous. She laughed, and the sound of it was strange in the empty night sky. She had no sense of how many hours had passed when the moon suddenly illuminated an inhospitable looking land far below, lava fields crumbling to the very shore and red volcanoes flaming brightly. Rivers of fire flowed between black craggy cliffs and quenched themselves in the sea. They flew into this hell and as they did, Jalo began to sing.

The song caught them each like a hook to the heart, even Swarn. It seemed to contain all the joy and all the sorrow and all the beauty of the worlds, giving voice to everything they had no words for. Their vision blurred with tears and they forgot or did not care that they were aloft in a fiery, dangerous land. Nell felt herself soaring on the music alone; it bore her up and filled her, made her complete in a way she had never known and yet, at the same time, undid her entirely, pulled her apart. She knew she could not bear for it to end, would never survive the loss of this song, yet she also longed for it to end, to release her, let her be. And now the song was calling to them, *Come, come, come*, and they did, how could they not? *Follow, follow, follow*, what else could they do, what would be left of them without this music? It carried them gently, effortlessly, and laid them down, murmuring, *Sleep, sleep, sleep*, and it was with gratitude that they succumbed. Oblivion swept over them.

Nell woke to voices, her heart still aching with the music she had heard. She opened her eyes and blinked, confused. Trees heavy with emerald green moss surrounded her. The moss hung in elegant fringes from the branches and encased the trees entirely. Through the branches twined over her head, she saw a pale sky. She sat up and petals spilled off her. She had been lying in a bower of moss and flowers. She rose and followed the voices she had heard. She found her friends in a clearing among the trees. Ander and Charlie were sprawled on elegant divans arranged around a low table laden with bowls of fruit and cakes, eating with deep concentration. Swarn sat cross-legged on the ground, back straight, and did not touch the food. There was no sign of Jalo, but another Faery in a brightly feathered cloak was leaning against one of the trees and watching them with his arms folded, an amused expression on his face.

"You're the last to wake up," said Charlie, pointing out the obvious. Charlie looked the way he always did, but in this lovely setting Nell noticed how bedraggled and unwashed Ander was, and she suspected she looked just as bad.

She smiled brilliantly at the Faery, hoping she didn't actually smell bad. "Hello. I'm Nell."

"Please eat," said the Faery, not bothering to introduce himself in return. "Jalo is speaking with his mother. He will come for you when they are finished."

Needing no further prompting, Nell sat down on one of the divans and tucked into the fruit. There was a plate of what looked like dark bread but when she put it in her mouth it melted to a thick, sweet liquid almost like molasses.

"Where are the dragons?" she asked Swarn.

"They are stabled," said Swarn. A reluctant smile tugged at the edges of her mouth. "The first dragons of the cliffs of Batt ever to enter the Realm of the Faeries, I'd wager. And I must thank you for saving the injured one. These two insist it was your doing."

"Oh!" Nell was a little surprised by that, but pleased. "Aye-anytime."

"There are only two left now," said Swarn. "They will be the parents of the future generations."

"Lah, what *happened* in the marsh?" asked Nell.

Swarn's face closed. For a moment Nell thought she would not answer and was afraid it had been a terrible thing to ask. Then Swarn said, "Nia blindsided me. I was not ready. I knew I could not defeat her by myself and so I called the dragons to hold her off. They gave me time to escape and seek friends, though I found none. I did not think she had the power to destroy them all. I did not think she would do so. I should have stayed and died with them."

"You'll be much more helpful alive," Charlie pointed out, but Swarn looked away, scowling at their idyllic surroundings.

Nell dropped the subject and looked up at the Faery.

"Is there anywhere we could have a bath?" she asked.

The Faery, who had been listening to their conversation with undisguised fascination, started at being spoken to directly.

"Of course," he replied. "Jalo instructed me to...yes, you must all bathe."

"Thank the Ancients!" said Nell. "I've been in these same clothes for *far* too many days in a row now."

Ander looked ruefully at the grimy pajamas he'd been wearing since Nell had come banging on his door in Holburg.

"I think a bath would suit me, too," he said. "Wonder if I could get a shave?"

Nell grinned at him, for in a week he had very nearly grown a full beard. Unlike his hair, it was quite grey.

"This way," said the Faery to Nell and Swarn, pointing. A

path of bright pebbles appeared, winding among the trees. The Faery directed Charlie and Ander along another path that appeared as soon as he pointed at the ground. Nell hurried along the path, Swarn following behind her. She could hear running water now. The path led directly to a shining pool hidden by trees that grew close together. At one end of it, a waterfall spilled over a tall, rocky cleft. Moss hung wet and gleaming over the rocks.

"Oh!" cried Nell, enchanted. She stripped off her filthy clothes and leaped into the water. It was pleasantly cool and clear as glass. She stood beneath the waterfall and let the water rush over her, pounding in her ears. When she emerged, blinking the water out of her eyes and laughing, Swarn was sitting in the water, her clothes lying on the bank. Nell was startled to see that her strong brown body was a map of scars. She sat in the water with more dignity than Nell would have imagined a naked person could possess.

"I hope we are right in turning to the Faeries for help," said Swarn crisply. "Your friend seems sincere enough but I have never trusted Faeries and am loath to do so now. Malferio in particular is slippery, unpredictable."

"I dinnay see that we have a choice," said Nell, to which Swarn nodded curt agreement. Nell sat on the bank letting herself dry off. Two silvery white dresses, impossibly soft to the touch, were laid on the ground for them, the sleeves and hems adorned with tiny, fragrant flowers. She stifled a laugh trying to imagine Swarn wearing such a thing. When she was more or less dry, she slipped into the smaller dress. It fit her perfectly.

"Do you think it's safe to explore a bit?" Nell asked.

Swarn did not answer immediately and when she spoke, it was not to answer Nell's question. "I am not afraid to die," she said. "But I fear for Eliza. Even if the Faeries give her sanctuary, I wonder if it is enough. She is so young, her potential still untapped. It grieves me to think –"

"Dinnay think it, then," said Nell sharply. "Eliza's going to be fine, aye. We have a plan!"

"Do we?" Swarn asked dryly.

"*Yes!* The Faeries help us get safely back to Di Shang, you break the Curse on the Mancers, we find Eliza, and then all together we crush Nia! Lah, praps not *we.* There's not much I can do. But it's a good plan, aye."

Swarn smiled at Nell for the first time with something nearly approaching warmth.

"Eliza loves you dearly," she said.

"I know," said Nell. "She's my best friend."

The witch slipped under the water and began to swim slow circles around the pool. Nell could hear Charlie and Ander talking in the opposite direction from the clearing and so she ran through the trees to find them. There was a bright glimmer between the trees and then the woods were gone, as if they had never been there at all. Nell stumbled slightly, startled. She was on a bamboo walkway on a lake. The lake shone silver and dazzling butterflies swooped among the waterlilies. The walkway met with several others, criss-crossing the water. White flowers were twined around the bamboo railings. She looked behind her but there was no sign of the mossy wood. The lake was ringed by tall mountains and at the top of the nearest mountain perched a castle with long, delicate spires. Unearthly music echoed across the water.

"Hello, Nell!" Ander and Charlie were walking towards her. Ander had shaved off his rough beard and looked quite transformed. They were both dressed in the brightly feathered vests and silk trousers the Faeries wore. The sight of Ander in particular dressed as a Faery made Nell laugh.

"It doesnay quite suit you, Mister Brady," she said.

"But your dress suits you very well," Ander said with a smile. He waved his hand at their surroundings and added, "Quite something, all this, lah! Nary thought I'd see the like."

"Listen, I know you must be upset with me," said Nell in a rush. "But we couldnay ask Swarn or Jalo to take us home when time is so short. You understand, nay? We'll go back to Di Shang when Swarn goes. And lah, a chance to see the Realm of the Faeries..."

Ander shook his head. "I've given up trying to thwart you, Nell," he said. "I'm beginning to see you are not like other children."

"I'm hardly a child; I'm nearly fifteen!" Nell protested. Charlie snickered a little at that.

"Lah, sure, whatever you say. Fifteen to me sounds like a kid, aye. What I mean is that most of us lead pretty ordinary lives because, when you come down to it, we're pretty ordinary people. The ones who have grand adventures and are at the centre of things are mostly those who have some kind of special gift or talent, like your friend Eliza. Then there are people like you, who have something else...I dinnay know what to call it, exactly, but I'll say this, you've got more energy than anyone I've ever met." Ander looked at her rather fondly for a moment and then continued, "You remind me of your ma, except you've got this energy she never had. When she was a girl, oh, by the Ancients, she had the prettiest laugh you've ever heard. Dinnay hear it much these days. She wouldnay say it, wouldnay know how to, but life has been a disappointment to her. There she was, all those years, thinking it was going to be beautiful and that it would just happen. But it never happened. I dinnay think you can imagine what that's like, or how many adults are not much more than the sum of their broken dreams, all the things they wished for then just buried inside themselves somewhere." Ander laid his big, meaty hand on her shoulder, crushing the flowers on her dress. "You're a rare one, all right, and everything your ma should've been." At this, he got a bit teary, and turned and strode off abruptly.

Nell and Charlie looked at each other.

"That was strange," said Charlie.

"Should we follow him?" asked Nell, taken aback by his speech.

Charlie shook his head. "Let him be a bit, aye." He reached over to tear one of the flowers off the railing, then stopped himself. "Today's the first day of Winter Festival, nay?"

"So it is!" exclaimed Nell. "My parents are prolly out of their minds, aye. And we're missing the Day of Regrets! Have you ever celebrated Winter Festival, Charlie?"

"Sure. I used to pose as a traveller from someplace friendly so they'd include me. I never was one for the Day of Regrets, though. I'd usually show up on the third day for the feast, aye. That's when it starts to get good."

"I like the idea behind the Day of Regrets, but in practice it always seems a bit false," Nell agreed. "Nobody ever wants to talk about their *real* regrets, on Holburg anyway, so they make things up half the time."

"Lah, since it's the Day of Regrets, let's start with you. What do you regret?"

Without agreeing to walk, they both began strolling in the opposite direction from where Ander had gone.

Nell thought hard. "Sometimes I regret giving up my memories of the first time we came to Tian Xia, but I dinnay know how else we would have gotten away, and now that I'm here I feel it's being made up for. Praps I regret not being more patient with my parents. But that's a bit feeble, nay? What about you?"

"I regret failing Eliza," said Charlie solemnly. "I regret every time I've failed her. I regret...lah, there are a lot of things I regret."

"I spose I'd have more if I'd been alive as long as you," said Nell, trying to be kind. "And I dinnay think it's fair to say you've failed Eliza. She wouldnay think so."

Charlie shook his head and grinned at her. "If you lived a thousand years, I doubt you'd have a single real regret. It's not your nature."

"What do *you* know about my nature?" Nell laughed.

"I know you pretty well."

"I spec you do. But lah, unless you're going to tell me all the stories of all your regrets from all your thousands of years, I spose that's the end of our Day of Regret Ceremony. Without the procession and the ashes and the Shedding of Tears. And we've already broken the fasting rule by having breakfast, aye. I completely forgot about it."

"I'm sorry you're missing it because of me," said Charlie.

"Oh, but I'd *much* rather be here!" exclaimed Nell. "The Realm of the Faeries! Everything seems so perfect, more beautiful than it *should* be, in a way. It's wonderful but a little disturbing at the same time, dinnay you think so? Like it's nay real or like there's some dark side to it all we cannay see with the naked eye. Do you feel that, too?"

Charlie nodded. "I dinnay feel exactly safe here. Praps it's just knowing we'd never find our way out without one of *them*."

"Lah, but Jalo's trustworthy."

Charlie shrugged non-committally.

"Of *course* he is," said Nell. "Think how much he's helped us already! I just wish Eliza were here too. I'd imagined the three of us together over Winter Festival."

"What about Julian? Did he go somewhere else for Winter Festival?"

Charlie asked this with studied casualness. Nell paused. Since getting on the train in Kalla she had not thought of Julian at all, except to babble embarrassing stories on the Crossing to keep Charlie awake.

"No," she said slowly. "I mean, yes. He went home, aye. He lives in Bled. It's not far from Kalla."

Life at Ariston Hebe seemed impossibly remote, though she had left only a week ago. She had been so preoccupied with so many things, with sports and tests and hairstyles and Julian, but all of that had melted to insignificance the moment Charlie crashed into the backyard, half-dead.

"It seems so trivial, aye," she said, with a disconcerted half-laugh.

"What?" asked Charlie. "Julian? I thought he seemed sort of...lah, trivial is a good word but praps it shouldnay be applied to a person."

"No, I dinnay mean him. I mean all of it. School, everything."

Nell watched the butterflies batting about in the sweet-smelling air and tried to imagine going back to school after Winter Festival, seeing her friends again, and Julian. But if Nia was not stopped the worlds would be changed. Without the Mancers, Tian Xia beings would keep on pouring into Di Shang. What would become of her safe and happy life at Ariston Hebe?

Would the changes reach as far as Holburg?

"Your problem is you're hooked on adventure," said Charlie. "You're never happier than when the worlds are in peril, aye."

"That's nay true," said Nell, thinking how terrified she had been when it was just her and Ander in Tian Xia. She didn't admit that to Charlie, though. "If any of us is *really* hooked on adventure, it's you. Eliza says you cannay stay in one place for more than a day or so without getting restless."

"Then it's my problem too," agreed Charlie. "I think you're worse than I am, though."

She punched him on the arm. He mimed pain, then said, "There's no point picking a fight with me, lah. You know I could turn into a dragon and eat you."

Nell laughed, and they stopped walking at a curve in the bridge to watch several luminescent swans glide by. They stood in silence for a while, lost in their own thoughts. Nell was thinking about Ander's surprising speech about her mother when Charlie said, half-reluctantly, "Did Eliza ever tell you that, when we were trapped in the Arctic, she saw my true form?"

Nell looked at him, startled. "No! I didnay know you *had* a true form. I just thought that you...lah, I dinnay know what I thought. I spose I nary did think about it."

"I should've known she wouldnay tell even you," said Charlie.

"She can keep a person's secrets, aye," agreed Nell, not wanting to pry further, curious though she was.

Then Charlie leaned a bit closer to her and said, "I want to show you. So I dinnay have anything else to say on the Day of Regrets."

Nell stared at him, unsure how to reply. One moment he was Charlie, so very familiar, the way he stood, the slant of his shoulders, the curve of his mouth and the way his eyebrows pointed up just slightly at the tips. And then he wasn't Charlie anymore. He dissolved into a luminous wave entwined with its own shadow. It was light and darkness and everything in between, snaking towards her, and in it she could almost see something happening, but it was something beyond what she had words or thought for.

It slipped around her neck and pressed itself to her cheek, and it was like touching something that cannot be touched – the way water would feel if it wasn't wet, or fire if it wasn't hot. It crossed her lips and she inhaled it. As it streamed into her lungs the world was briefly changed, everything was different, and she felt within herself infinite possibilities of life and being. Then she exhaled, and the wavering billow took shape, became Charlie again.

For a long moment he held her gaze and she found herself unable to look away or speak. Then they both became aware of footsteps approaching rapidly.

"Enjoying the water promenade, I see!" said Jalo cheerfully.

Nell forced herself to look away from Charlie to the Faery. He was dressed even more splendidly than before.

"The King has decreed that an elite squadron of the Faery Guard will escort the witch and the rest of you to Di Shang and the Mancer Citadel, leaving at dawn tomorrow. A place has been selected for the witch to prepare her Magic and I've taken her there."

"Why tomorrow?" asked Nell. "We should go as soon as Swarn is ready!"

"I'm afraid there's no question of leaving tonight," said Jalo solemnly. "It is the Festival of Light, when we swear allegiance to the King, and *all* Faeries must be present. It only happens twice a year. I'm sure it will be interesting for you."

Nell wanted to argue but sensed it would do no good. In any case, she was feeling disoriented. "Thank you," was all she managed.

"My mother Tariro owns a number of the Faery Mines, of which I'm sure you've heard," Jalo continued. "Perhaps you would enjoy a tour? They are quite spectacular, really."

"We'd love to," said Nell, looking at Charlie. He looked back at her a bit sadly.

"Sure," he assented.

CHAPTER
18

Rea woke up screaming. Instantly she was in Rom's arms, his mouth against her ear, his voice telling her, *It's just a dream, it's a bad dream*, his body strong and close. But this was no dream. She had lost herself and would never find herself again. All she had been, all she had loved and fought for, all she had known and believed had been taken from her. Her entire *life*, her *daughter*. That tremendous power she had relied on, *revelled* in, had proved in the end insufficient, buckling and breaking before a greater power. She knew the horror of defeat, of finding one's strength wanting. She had seen it again in the Kwellrahg's eyes, her own fear, her own rage, her own absolute helplessness. She remembered only this – that Nia had broken her, torn her away from herself, stripped her down to next to nothing. All that remained was this lost ghost of what she had been, and she would walk the world so, always. It was not enough to have so little of oneself. It was not enough on which to try to build a new self. It was not enough even to have the ones you loved around you still when the full richness of that love and all its history was lost to you. It was no dream, the thousands of losses, her *self* yanked out of her piece by piece. She screamed until her voice gave out. Ry made her drink some mixture she choked on, the Sorma gathered to sing to her, burning herbs around the tent, and Rom clung to her and rocked her back and forth – but it meant nothing at all. They could not help her. Nia had been stronger and Rea had lost the battle. She had lost everything.

When Eliza returned to the camp, a circle of five Sorma spirit-speakers were gathered around the Kwellrahg, just outside the barrier. Three of them sang in low voices while one kept up a steady drumbeat and another played a wooden flute – a soaring, brilliant sound that swooped and spun over the gentle voices and the deep rhythm of the drum. Ry had placed three bowls of herbs on the ground around the barrier and they were burning now, their fragrant smoke pouring over the beast, who twitched restlessly, angrily.

"You feel better," said Lai when Eliza joined them. It was not a question so Eliza did not answer it. She felt the pull of the Kwellrahg, the nightmares and panics it sought to draw from her. She gave them up willingly, let the burden of fear fall from her. She remembered what Nia had said about fear. True freedom is the freedom from fear. Eliza had faced before the loss of all she loved, all she was, and now she would face it again. She knew what had to be done. She knew she might fail but that was barely the point. It was just a matter of doing, now.

"I'm ready," she said, and stepped into the barrier. The air went out of her lungs.

Swarn had taught Eliza what the Sorma knew also – in battle, balance trumps strength. What she had understood as an idea, yet struggled to enact with her body, became now her physical nature. A profound change had taken place in the desert by the tree. She did not need to untangle its meaning yet. She knew simply that she could rely on her Magic, that it would not let her down.

The Kwellrahg lunged at her and she swung aside, letting it crash against the barrier. She drove her dagger into its side and withdrew it. The monster was slowed and disoriented by the herbs of the Sorma, its innate viciousness quelled somewhat by their music. It stumbled and roared but it could not strike her with its powerful spiked fists, it could not catch her. She circled it for hours, letting it fall again and again, jabbing it with her dagger and dancing out of its reach. Whenever her lungs began to ache she leaped out of the barrier to draw in a breath, for the Sperre-Tahore contained the Magic of the beast, including its ability to draw the oxygen out of the air around it.

She did not meet the force of the Kwellrahg with force of her own, but with her dagger pulled it in the same direction it was lunging, so its own momentum brought it crashing forward into the sand. She rallied. When it was losing its balance or staggering away, she used all the force she had to push it back. Again and again she drove it down to the ground, then let it rise again. The Kwellrahg grew ragged and weary and furious. The barrier was weakening but she spared no thought for that. Lava flowed from the beast's many wounds. The vast dome of sky overhead faded to black and the stars appeared, countless numbers of them sprinkled across the darkness. She stumbled slightly in the sand and stepped outside the barriers quickly.

"I need to rest," she said. The spirit speakers were waiting with a spiked harness. They went to work immediately. She watched for a moment, pitying the beast, as they skipped about it, quick on their feet, steady on the moving sand. It was not difficult for them to fix the harness around the Kwellrahg. The spikes carried a soothing drug that flowed when the harness remained loose. But they also held a pain-inducing poison that was activated by excess pressure. Any beast ensnared by the contraption learned quickly to obey the pull of the harness, to maintain the flow of the soothing drug and to avoid the poison.

Eliza walked a little ways in the dark and then sat down on the cooling sand. She closed her eyes and felt her mind take flight on dark wings. She flew with a great flock along a canyon by night. They were of one mind, turning and dipping together. It was electrifying, the power of her own wings bearing her up, her sheer lightness in the air. She had always been a passenger, too heavy for the sky, borne up by another. Now she truly understood the joy of flight. She swooped up along the great white wall of the Mancer Citadel and saw below the dead dragon in the grounds, a few of the Cra creeping this way and that. Somewhere here, her grandmother Selva was kept alive, in secret. This was something to do with the

Gehemmis she had read about. The Mancers and their books, the Mancers and their secrets, the Mancers and their dominion over Di Shang – her grandmother and her mother and how many before them had sacrificed themselves to serve the Mancers. It was a noble heritage, Foss told her, but, dearly as she loved him, she could no longer agree. She veered away from the Citadel.

She wanted to find Charlie but encountered only fire and a terrible clashing sound when she sought him. Wings scorched, she flew back, then told herself, *No, I cannot be burned.* She flew through the fire into the deepest mist. There was nothing here. *But that's not true*, she thought. *Something is here.* She flew into a tempest, where hail and wind assailed her, forced her back. But the storm was unreal. She drove through it into a wood full of snakes and thick webs and throttling vines. There was no up or down, no ground or sky, only the tangle of beast and branch and a slithering furious darkness that wrapped around her throat and squeezed-but she would not be strangled. *There is no Guardian here, and I will pass.* She found herself in a deep, mossy wood. Charlie and Nell were both there, asleep on beds of flowers, breathing softly. Swarn sat by a tree, her face buried in her hands. How had they all come to be in this place together? She wanted to go to them, ask them what had happened, but a wind came and caught her unguarded, swept her away. She fought it with all her might, blown across a landscape of strange, swirling rock formations to the wall of a great castle, where Nia stood alone, looking out into the night. The wind blew her into Nia's oustretched hands.

"You've found your Guide," said Nia, "and space won't trap you now. But you're not really *here*, Eliza. Can you feel this?" She snapped the wings of the bird and let it drop towards the ground, but there was no ground. Eliza plummeted and opened her eyes. The desert was dark and she could hear the furious roar of the Kwellrahg. She could still feel the broken wings on her back where there was nothing. She didn't know what it meant but there was no time to think about it. First things first – the Kwellrahg. She had to get back to it.

They fought through the night and as the sun rose over the edge of the sandy horizon. Eliza held the reins to the Kwellrahg's harness in one hand, her dagger in the other. As the day grew brighter the terrible beast regarded Eliza with flaming eyes, groaning pitifully as if to say, *Just let me be.* She felt all the forces of the universe aligned with her, flowing through her. She was not tired. She was not afraid. The barrier weakened and fell away. The Kwellrahg's Magic was faltering too – the air around it was breathable, if thin. The Kwellrahg groaned deeply. She drove her dagger into it again and again, tears blurring her vision. She thought of the Cra, the countless numbers of them she had cut down with this very blade, the stink of their blood and the terrified screams of their deaths. She thought of Abimbola Broom. "I have two daughters," he'd said, his face a desperate mask. And yet she had brought him to the Mancers to face punishment instead of to the Sorma for a chance at redemption. She remembered her grandmother. "No pity?" Where *was* her pity, then? She had been so sure, so righteous. Where had that righteousness come from? And where was it now? Her pity for the Kwellrahg washed through her, overwhelmed her. Distracted, distraught, she stumbled in the sand. A flash of fear cleared her mind and she readied herself for the blow the Kwellrahg would surely land.

But the Kwellrahg was hunched before her, silent, unmoving. All its will to fight had left it. She led it this way and that with the harness and it followed wearily. She forced it to climb the dunes after her, to crawl along the burning desert floor at whatever speed she determined. She brought it to lay on its belly before the Sorma.

"Now we will do what we can to ease its pain," said her grandmother.

"Not yet," said Eliza. "I'm not finished. I need the wizard."

A bewildered Uri Mon Lil was brought to her.

"I do apologize –" he began, but Eliza cut him off with an exhausted smile.

"Dinnay apologize. Help me to rename this thing."

"Ye-es," he said hesitantly, his eyes fixing on hers. There was something so commanding in her gaze that he asked no more questions.

Eliza put her hands on either side of the Kwellrahg's burning face. The sky went black with ravens and the air filled with the sound of beating wings. In this moving darkness she spoke to the Kwellrahg in the Language of First Days, while Uri Mon Lil knelt in the sand and gave all his own power to her task. It was not a spell or anything he understood. She was taking possession of the beast and he simply channeled his power into the tremendous Magic that flowed all about them. Sometimes the Kwellrahg snarled and tried to writhe out of her grasp, but mostly it lay very still and seemed to be listening. The sun completed its journey from east to west and disappeared from view. In the darkness the ravens rattled, *Name him Urkleis, name him, take him, name him, name him Urkleis.*

It was like entering the earth, being buried alive in its hot centre. She had to wrestle a thing she could not get her hands on, a dark tangle. She saw it with her mind's eye but could hardly move towards it. The thing wheeled about freely while she was trapped, her mouth and eyes stopped. Her fingers felt like mud; how could they grasp? She heard her own voice and the words she spoke somewhere else, somewhere on a sandy strip on the surface of a tiny world, but they were such small words and the universe was endless and empty and uncaring. The dark swirling thing she had to catch was falling away from her, fast, and she would be alone out here, utterly alone. She was afraid, she burst the solid mass around her and it became an avalanche, sweeping her away, to a place where she would spin forgotten forever. The wizard's Magic held her as the avalanche poured over her and that voice of a girl kept speaking, determined. Now she could move, and she dove through empty black space after the thing she could feel but no longer see. It had eternity within which to flee her. The wizard's Magic carried her like a current in space and she called the thing to her and it came, Nia's spell, it slithered and mocked and bound her hands and filled up her ears with its gleeful clamour. It was stronger than her, stronger by far. It twisted about her and squeezed, like an anaconda. *See if you pop. See what comes out. See what you are made of, little girl.*

"What's happening to her?" Rom asked his mother, horrified. The sky was full of screaming ravens. Eliza knelt in the sand in a cloud of beating wings, her hands clenched around the head of the felled Kwellrahg, her eyes rolled back in her head. She was gasping for breath as if someone was strangling her, her body rigid and shaking. Choked words burst out of her intermittently. The wizard knelt by her, eyes closed, brow furrowed, while the Sorma looked on in awed silence.

"She is working Magic," said Lai.

"Stop her," said Rom. "It's hurting her!"

The Sorma looked uncertain. Rom pushed past them to his daughter, tried to catch her by the shoulder and shake her free. A charge like electricity surrounded her and sent him stumbling back, rattled to his very bones. The ravens swarmed about him, shrieking angrily. He could not lay a hand on her.

"Eliza!" he shouted. "Come back to me!"

She was choking now, not breathing at all, her arms and hands twitching in tiny spasms, as if something unseen was squeezing out her last breath.

"Eliza!"

He felt a hand on his trouser leg and looked down. Rea had crawled after him from the tent and he hadn't heard her. She looked up at him, hollow-eyed.

"Don't distract her," she said. "You can't help."

Rom stared at his wife and then back at his struggling daughter. Again, he thought, once again I am of no use at all to Eliza.

The snarl of darkness swallowed Eliza, pressing hard on her heart. Inside it, she could feel the deep Magic, too intricate, too complete for one such as her to unravel. Always, in the end, she came up against her own limits, and that was where she would remain now. In the place where she could do nothing because she was not strong enough. The thing carried her beyond space, to a place that was not a place but rather collapse. *I'm going to leave you by the river, little girl.* What river? *A thick darkness that will carry you between the paws of the Guardian and then no more, no more, no more.* She is almost relieved. *Look at that unhappy man in the desert, he is worried about his daughter. He doesn't understand how vast it is, what a brief sliver of life we have in any case.* Her tooth snags what feels like a loose thread, she takes it between her teeth and pulls. *I won't go to the river. You were not Made perfect. She is only a Sorceress after all, strong though she may be. I can unravel you.* The thing twists about her neck like a noose and hangs her from the top of the universe but she doesn't need to breathe anymore. She only needs to pull the thing between her teeth until the noose loosens, comes at her like a snake. They fall into the wizard's Magic and he holds them fast as they struggle there. She pulls the name, she pulls it and pulls it, beyond endurance, this is all there is. And, at last, a slackening, a kind of surrender. The Kwellrahg gives it up with a groan or a sigh. The young Sorceress lies flat on the sand, hands still gripping it, and the ravens cover her like a blanket. No, she cannot sleep, not yet. She hears her own voice again, good, she knows the words, she knows them, they are part of the fabric of everything. She takes the name and gives him another. Then he belongs to her.

"Silver is the best conduit," said Lai. In a basket they had tens of silver needles threaded with silver fine as hair. The ends of these threads were wound through rough gemstones.

"What will the stones do?" asked Eliza.

"They are not all stones," said Lai. She picked up a rough shard of something black. "This is petrified wood, for calming fear. Here, amethyst and jade for quieting and soothing. Lapis for cooling and drawing out heat. For quieting temper, coral.

Serpentine is for healing. We are ready."

All night the Sorma toiled on the thing Eliza and Uri Mon Lil had named the Urkleis. At times he began to struggle or groan but Eliza stopped him with a sharp command and he obeyed her. With the silver needles and silver thread, the Sorma bound his torn flesh and broken bones. Each needle in the end found its way to his centre and was driven into the black rock Nia had made, the life-giving core of the Urkleis. The healers burned herbs and sang as they worked. The Urkleis became more and more docile, until at last as dawn broke he moved not at all. As the positive and soothing elements the Sorma introduced flowed through the beast, the flesh and bone began to fall away from the centre. Soon his body was a burning heap. Eliza reached into the fire and took out the hard rock, the thing Nia had made and that she had renamed. She removed the silver needles and put it in her pocket.

"Bury the body with the gems, somewhere safe," said Eliza to her grandmother.

"It shall be done," said Lai, and the Sorma said "*Arash.*"

CHAPTER
19

Tariro greeted the human visitors graciously and granted them permission to visit her mines. She had never seen humans before and she was interested but not much impressed. The man was unpleasant to look at, ill-shaped, with lines on his face and tufts of grey in his hair. She assumed this was the result of his age; she had heard that advancing years ravaged human bodies and minds in terrible ways, making them weak and confused and prone to illness until they died and decayed. She did not like the boy, either. He pushed his hair out of his eyes and looked wary, without showing any of the amazement that was written so clearly on the faces of the other two humans. There was something not quite right about him, though she could not put her finger on it. The man and the girl, to her satisfaction, stared in awe at the giant carved pillars soaring skyward to a vaulting roof, at herself seated on an ornate throne at the top of a flight of marble steps, gleaming with jewels, her fine dress spread out around her, the cliff plunging behind her. But though she found herself disliking the old man and the boy, it was the girl she watched anxiously as the little group made their way down the mountainside. If human age was a horrifying sight to the ageless faeries, human youth was tantalizing. This girl was in the full bloom of it, fresh-faced and glossy-haired, glowing with that strange combination of fragility and passion that marked all mortals. There were many songs and stories about Faeries who fell in love with young mortals and, although the lesson was always that these unions ended badly, their attraction remained undeniable. There was something so moving in their inevitable deaths, and they seemed so very much of the earth, so real. She saw Jalo's pleasure in this young girl, the tenderness of his gaze on her when she curtseyed awkwardly to Tariro. They were to leave tomorrow – good. She could not allow her promising younger son to fall in love with a human girl.

Tariro was in any case distracted by other matters and was glad to see them go. Her husband, Nikias, had been summoned with great secrecy by Alvar, Lord of the Faery Guard, and had been gone for two days now. Tariro had invented a pretext to visit Leanda, the wife of the First Advisor Emyr. Leanda told her that Emyr was away tending to business for a short while but Tariro sensed her anxiety. Something was afoot and Tariro hated not knowing what. Her only consolation was that Leanda did not know what it was either.

Although the Faery Kingdom was very much a patriarchy, Tariro was one of the rare female Faeries to have obtained a degree of power in her own right. Though she did not herself come from an important family, she had made her connections wisely. Her wit, her intelligence and her non-threatening charm won her a place in circles to which someone of her rank would not normally have access. She listened sympathetically as her new friends discussed matters of finance and court intrigue and later she would privately make a suggestion or two that revealed her to be a tactical genius. Many prominent Faeries increased their wealth and stature, or destroyed an enemy, through her counsel and remained grateful thereafter, believing that they alone were the fortunate recipients of her startling wisdom. Because she was a useful friend to have, she was invited to important parties, and exceptions to the usual hierarchies were made to include her. Her friends made her careless promises. She remained gracious, humble, unassuming. Everybody secretly owed her a favour and everybody thought they were the only one. Then, with manoeuvres so subtle that nobody was entirely sure how it had happened, she had taken over the goldmines of Sim and the diamond mines of Harrah, and then all of the silver mines that did not belong to the king, becoming one of the wealthiest and most influential Faeries in the Realm. It was whispered that she had forged allegiances with witches and had access to potions that were strictly forbidden. Besides that, whoever controlled silver was not to be crossed. Her marriage to the High Lord Nikias had confirmed her as a rising star, a fixture in the Faery Court. Though technically she and Nikias should have been allowed only a single son, she was wealthy enough to pay the tax on another. Jalo was born and the odds of a child of hers rising to prominence were increased. Cadeyrn, both in his career and in his marriage to Alvar's daughter, did her credit. But her younger son, Jalo, had an energy and cleverness to him that made her hope for even greater things. Her ambition for herself and for her sons was boundless. Now it was clear some great intrigue was taking place and that she was excluded from it. As soon as Jalo and his humans had left, she called for her faithful spy, Miyam.

"What have you heard?" she asked.

"Madam, all of the High Lords have gathered at Alvar's Castella."

"Does the King know?"

"The spies he thinks to be his have been in Alvar's pocket for centuries now. He knows nothing."

Tariro breathed a sigh of relief. This sounded to her like treason and Malferio was nothing if not ruthless when it came to treachery. His marriage to Nia three hundred years ago had led to the most terrible purges the Faery Kingdom had ever known as he struggled to hold on to his power. It was bold indeed of him to have married another outsider last year and to declare her Queen. He was over-confident, and something was happening. Nikias was too slow to ensure his own advantage in whatever changes came. He should have consulted her or at least arranged for a spy to bring her word of the proceedings.

"What are they discussing?"

"I do not know. Nobody but the High Lords themselves have been present at these meetings. But there is more, My Lady."

"Tell."

"Alvar has a visitor."

"Who is it?"

"Nobody knows. She has not showed herself but she is staying in His Majesty's Wing in the Castella."

Tariro drew her breath in sharply. Every Castella had a wing for the King, reserved for him alone in case he decided to visit. "You say *she*. How do you know this?"

"One of the guards has seen them together."

"Is she a Faery?"

"No. Perhaps human."

"Did this guard say what she looked like?"

"Only that she was very beautiful and she seems to have Alvar's ear."

"Forsake the Ancients," murmured Tariro. "Find a pretext to go to Nikias. I must know everything. And send me the Gem-Weaver."

The Faery Mines were legendary throughout Tian Xia. In a Realm of Illusion, they were one of the few realities. The ores and gems within them were the finest in the worlds, both in beauty and in magical properties. As the little group approached the mines, the towering mountains all around them became, in the blink of an eye, rocky hillocks. It did not seem so much a change as a shift in perception, like realizing something you thought was far away is in fact very close, the distant mountain merely a boulder at your feet.

The mine-openings were guarded by Faeries in black silk with glinting spears. Watchful raptors glided overhead. The guards parted for Jalo, however, and so Nell, Charlie and Ander followed him into the dark tunnels beneath the rock. In one of the mines, gold hung luminous as starlight from the ceiling, like tapered stalactites, and in another, diamonds the size of boulders sparkled in the walls and on the damp stone floors.

"Still spooked?" Charlie asked Nell quietly.

"What do you mean?" asked Nell, startled.

"You said you thought this place had a kind of dark undertone to it, before."

"Oh! Yes. Yes. It does."

"What did you think I meant?" Charlie sounded hurt.

"I dinnay know. I'm sorry." She sighed, wondering what to say to make things normal between them again. Part of her wished she could forget what had happened on the lake. It had been such a strange and powerful feeling and she had been unprepared for it. "I'm glad you showed me, Charlie." She didn't have to explain what she meant. But she wasn't telling the whole truth and he knew it.

"It's nay really a big secret. I just thought...because we're friends..." he trailed off.

"I know," she said.

"Come this way!" called Jalo. "Look!"

They followed him down a long glittering tunnel made entirely of diamonds.

"The correct use of diamonds can increase the power of a Curse exponentially," said Jalo cheerfully, waving his fire stick so the light at the end of it leaped off the glittering walls.

"Your mother seems partial to them," said Charlie. Jalo gave him a sharp look. Charlie looked back blankly. His hair had fallen over his eyes again.

"Are you hungry?" Jalo asked Nell and Ander. "I have heard that humans and animals suffer greatly from hunger and must eat frequently."

"That's true," said Charlie feelingly. Nell and Ander agreed that they were hungry as well. Jalo led them out of the mine shaft and they found themselves in a clearing at the top of a hill. The hillside was covered with silver-leafed olive trees and the sky was pale blue with wisps of white cloud, like the sky of Di Shang.

"Does this make you feel at home?" Jalo asked Nell. To her surprise, the familiar sky made her want to weep. She wondered how her parents were. They must be beside themselves with worry for her.

"Yes," she managed. "Thank you."

A blanket was laid with soft bread and cheese and bowls of olives. There was a jug of wine as well, and four jewelled goblets.

"Dinnay know that you two should be drinking this stuff," said Ander to Charlie and Nell as they filled their goblets happily.

"I'm much older than you are," said Charlie indignantly.

Nell sipped at the goblet. The wine was smooth and rich. Every mouthful made her feel warmer, calmer, kinder. She looked at Charlie and felt a smile stretch wildly across her face. He gave a short laugh and looked away, down the hillside.

They remained there, eating and drinking and talking languidly, until peals of bells broke open the sky. The olive trees swayed and bent as if beneath a great wind, though the air was still. Black-clothed guards strode into the clearing. Tariro swept behind them in an elaborate scarlet dress.

"It's time," she said to Jalo, and then looked at the others. "Are you bringing them, too?"

"I'm sure they would be interested..." Jalo began. Nell watched him a bit pityingly. He seemed afraid of his mother. She couldn't imagine what that must be like.

Tariro waved her hand as if to say she didn't care and just hearing about it was a bother.

"I'll arrange for an extra morrapus," said Jalo humbly.

The morrapus was an orb of silk fixed around a delicate gold cage the size of a small room. The bottom was filled with cushions for the comfort of the travellers. Snowy-plumed myrkestras pulled it through the air. Jalo rode in his mother's morrapus. Swarn, Ander, Nell and Charlie rode together in another. It did not feel like flying at all, but more like floating. Ander began to feel quite nauseous as they bobbed through the air and had to huddle at the bottom of the morrapus with his head between his knees.

"Did you have any luck today, preparing the spell?" Nell asked Swarn.

"What spell?" scoffed Swarn. "There is nothing to prepare. I do not yet know what Nia has done to the Mancers or if I can break it. I must see them before I can try to do anything at all."

"But Jalo said they had given you a place to work," Nell said, perplexed.

"A polite way of saying they kept me confined. They did not

want me wandering freely. You may be considered harmless, but I am not."

Swarn's jaw was set and she did not seem to want to talk any more. Nell pulled the silk away from the gold webbing so she could see out. The sky was full of billowing silken morrapi of every colour imaginable. They flew over narrow spiralling mountains with shining bridges, miles long, slung between them. She could see foaming waterfalls and breath-taking gorges, dark, gleaming lakes surrounded by thick woods, and high in the mountains, hundreds upon hundreds of castles with swooping rooftops, their brilliant tiles shining in the golden light.

The morrapi were converging on an enormous, sheer white rock that towered over the mountains. Nell felt again that unsettling perceptual shift, as if the mountains were only jagged stones, the castles upon them mere toys. A strangely beautiful structure covered the flat top of the rock, its intricate walls and elegant curved rooftops giving the impression of a giant bird about to take flight. The morrapus landed within the outermost walls, in a crowd of silken orbs and white myrkestras. Jalo rushed to help Nell out. He led her and her companions through the crowds toward a pair of giant crimson doors, Ander staggering queasily, Swarn and Charlie looking guarded. They had to wait to file in past rows of long-legged silver-hounds. Nell felt the cold nose of one of the hounds touch her hand as it sniffed her, searching for silver. She looked into its bottomless eyes and shuddered. The lean hounds moved past them, down the line.

"It is forbidden for any but the Faery Guard to carry silver," Tariro explained coolly.

"As you have seen today, our Kingdom is a place of absolute beauty," Jalo enthused to Nell, not registering her distaste for the silver-hounds. "And as such, it suits you very well!"

Nell thanked him and did not say what she thought of that. She noticed Tariro give her a sharp look, however. Through the crimson doors, they followed a long passageway, taking many turns, and then came to another set of giant doors guarded by silver-hounds and guards bearing spears. Beyond this, more twisting corridors led to yet another set of doors and the same thing again. By the time they came to the innermost wall, Nell had no idea how to find her way back out, which was more than a little disconcerting. They entered a vast courtyard full of thousands upon thousands of Faeries standing in orderly blocks. Lily petals covered the ground like snow. A broad petal-strewn path led from the crimson doors, between the Faery formations, to a pyramid of steps lined by rows of the Faery Guard. At the top of the stairs, two thrones stood side-by-side on a platform. This was the High Step, Jalo explained to Nell in a whisper. Slender bridges were slung from the High Step out to separate, garlanded platforms that seemed to hang in the air, forming a semi-circle around it. Each of these platforms held at least thirty or forty Faeries in fantastic, colourful dress.

"Come, you are guests of my family and you will watch from our dais," said Jalo. The sky was emptying of the last morrapi as they made their way up the steps of the pyramid to the platform just below the High Step and crossed one of the bridges to a dais shared by several noble families. While Ander, Charlie and Nell attracted a few curious stares, most of the Faeries looked at Swarn. She had refused the fresh attire offered by the Faeries, sticking to her worn leather and wolf-skin vest, though they had not allowed her to bear any weapons to the ceremony. Tariro had somehow ended up walking next to her, as if they were particular companions, and this caused a great deal of whispering. Jalo introduced Nell and the others to his father, Nikias, who struck Nell as rather dunderheaded for a Faery.

The air crackled and rippling waves of colour swept across the sky, accompanied by music like the song Jalo had sung when they first entered the Realm of the Faeries. Faeries dressed in yellow came around with trays of exotic delicacies and crystal glasses of heady wine. The sky went suddenly black and figures edged in gold danced across it, enacting Faery Legends to the rhythm of a terrifying drumbeat. In one of these displays, Nell thought she was witnessing the Mancers fleeing Tian Xia. In another, a being made of stars gave a Faery two boxes. The Faery opened the boxes and then, across the sky, Faeries danced and fought.

"There is a legend," Jalo explained to Nell when she asked him what it meant, "that the Sparkling Deluder in the south long ago gifted the Faeries with Music and Envy, shaping our destiny forever."

"What about the Mancers?" asked Nell.

Jalo smiled wryly. "To you, they are great protectors, but to us, they are something else. They were the scribes of the Faeries in the Early Days."

"When humans were slaves," said Nell.

"Yes," Jalo admitted, "but for the Faeries, that time is still widely considered a golden age. The rise of the Mancers as a separate power is regarded as a kind of betrayal."

"What do *you* think?" asked Nell.

Jalo smiled at her again but he did not have time to reply before a great noise drowned out any possibility of conversation. The sky began to crackle with lights, as if it were splitting open and some heretofore hidden luminescence was breaking through. The Faeries stomped their feet and clapped their hands in unison. The sound was deafening and shook the whole courtyard. Nell put her hands over her ears, looking around her. The dais was shaking and swaying. The Faeries looked transported with an almost mad joy.

"Welcome the King!" shouted the Faeries. "Welcome the King! Welcome the King! Welcome the King!"

The crimson doors at the end of the compound swung open and a morappus as bright white as the Di Shang moon came billowing through it behind a huge, gold-eyed myrkestra. The Faeries erupted into applause. Drums thundered and the sky flashed white and gold. The King of the Faeries emerged from the morappus in a cloak of crimson feathers that trailed on the ground. His tunic and pantaloons were made of threads so radiant he seemed to be clothed in light. On his brow sat a band of the finest Faery gold. The King's new wife stepped out of the morrapus after him and, with hands joined, they proceeded towards the pyramid, climbed slowly to the High Step, then turned and bowed to the shouting mass of Faeries.

Nell was surprised to see that the Queen did not look like a Faery at all. She was taller than the King and her hair formed a dark halo around her lovely face. In contrast to the fair-skinned Faeries, her skin was black and shone like burnished ebony. She had a regal face – high forehead and slanted cheekbones, a strong jaw and full lips. Her long eyes were the colour of fire. She wore a simple white robe and a shawl of gold thread. The first and second Advisors left their respective daises, crossing the swinging bridges with flawless balance and grace to flank the King and Queen.

Malferio spoke to the assembled masses, "Since the Ancients Made Tian Di, the Faeries have wrought in the west the first and the only Great Civilization! Poetry, music, beauty, war, all of these belong to us! We, with the power of Illusion, are the true heirs of the Ancients! Still we flourish, and crush all our enemies beneath our heels! On this night, we celebrate the greatness of the Faeries and the inviolable sanctity of the Faery monarchy!"

Wild applause carried on for several minutes. Then it was Queen Gautelen's turn to say a few words. Her voice was powerful and carried easily across the grounds.

"Today you swear allegiance to your King and thus to me, his Queen. You expect that I will make humble thanks for your welcome and express my admiration for the Faeries and my joy at being made your Queen. But I will disappoint you, for my loyalty and my gratitude and my admiration are spoken for already, by my own people. I have been married one year now, but still this King of yours has not fulfilled his promises to me."

The King did not immediately register what she was saying. Then his face went white with fury and he grabbed her by the arm, pulling her back sharply. Gautelen shouted out the rest while struggling free of his grasp. "Now I demand publicly that his part of our bargain be discharged! A Kingship, recognized by the Faeries, must be given to my father, the wizard of Lil. Immortality must be granted to the Storm Seamstresses of Shol. My people are to be given the protection of the Faery Guard against any outside threat. I am your Queen and I –"

The King pinned her arms behind her back and hissed a single word in her ear. She fell silent but her look was triumphant. She had said enough. There was an awful hush throughout the courtyard. Nobody dared to make a sound. The King looked out over the crowd, his expression part anger, part incredulity. Emyr, the First Advisor, stepped forward with a slight bow and murmured something in his ear. The King nodded, appearing relieved, and Emyr spoke.

"Her Majesty Gautelen, Queen of the Faeries, came to me with these demands and asked that I compel the King to make good on his promises. Of course, I cannot and shall not do any such thing. However, the High Lords agree that marriage to outsiders should not be entered into by Faeries in position of authority and that an outsider must never be made Queen again. I propose that this be made law and that the King's current marriage be dissolved."

This was met with startled silence, and then a slight smattering of applause that died out quickly. The King's expression had changed slowly to disbelief and then horror as Emyr spoke and he began to understand the full breadth of the situation. He closed a hand over his First Advisor's shoulder. Even those at the back of the courtyard could see Emyr turn white.

"I made no promises to this lying Storm Seamstress, though that is beside the point," Malferio snarled. "I am your *King* and this is nothing short of treason. I hereby command the execution of this faithless Queen and the immediate arrest of Emyr, First Advisor."

A buzz of voices set up in the courtyard. Gautelen raised her chin slightly, as if daring anyone to lay hands on her. Emyr looked desperately at Alvar. The Faery Guard lining the pyramid in rows moved on the King's command, but Alvar halted them with a gesture. They obeyed him instinctively, for such was their practice. It did not occur to them for a moment or two that they had obeyed him in defiance of their king.

"I must inform the Faeries that the Sorceress Nia broke free of her Di Shang prison a matter of days ago and defeated the

Mancers," announced Alvar in his powerful baritone. The crowds fell silent again. "She has killed the Oracle of the Ancients and she has infiltrated the Realm of the Faeries. Two days ago I found her waiting for me in the Traitor's Wood."

The King blanched. "That is impossible –" he began. Alvar continued as if the King had not spoken.

"Years ago, this King of ours, in the madness of passion, gifted the Sorceress Nia with immortality and his own blood. Thus she became a terrible threat to us. We remained loyal to him in spite of this. He learned nothing from his mistakes and has arrogantly married another outsider, who has also shown herself to have interests entirely unaligned with those of her subjects, the Faeries."

The King interrupted by drawing his sword.

"You are speaking lies!" he shrieked, pointing his sword at Alvar. "This is treason! High treason! Guards, take him away!"

The Guards hesitated a moment. The King of the Faeries swung his sword at Alvar, who neither flinched nor stepped aside. Immediately one of the Guards leaped forward, fending off the blow with his own sword. A tremor went through the crowd. The Guard in question seemed appalled at what he had done, but after a brief, stunned moment, the other Guards applauded him. The King dropped his sword and began to tremble.

"This is Nia's work," muttered Swarn.

"Quite right," whispered a voice in her ear. Swarn spun around, reaching for the dagger that was not at her belt, but nobody was there. A muttering swept through the crowds as the crimson doors swung open again. The Sorceress Nia entered the courtyard on the back of a white tiger. She wore a glittering dress of jewels, diamonds, emeralds and rubies all woven together, sparkling in her hair and around her neck. Bands of gold were fixed around her arms. Though the outfit must have been tremendously heavy, she held herself as if it was weightless. Nobody spoke or moved as the tiger loped easily among the Faeries and climbed the steps of the pyramid between the rows of the Faery Guard to the High Step, where Nia dismounted and faced the

King. As she stepped up, Gautelen stepped down and away, her eyes meeting Nia's briefly.

The King of the Faeries watched her progress across the courtyard with an expression of pure disbelief. When she stood before him, he reached his hands out to her and said simply, "My dear."

"I told you I would come," said Nia, not taking his hands. "There will be no pleasantries this time, Malferio. This is the hour for revenge, and you will pay for what you did to me."

He shook his head slightly and reached for her again. "Nia, it is not too late for us."

"It was too late," said Nia, "the first time you told me *No*." She regarded him coldly for a moment and then turned and faced the Faeries. Her voice rang clear and sweet across the courtyard. "I have made an offer to the High Lords and they have accepted. I swore by the Oath of the Ancients that I would never return to the Realm of the Faeries if this king, Malferio, be deposed and exiled."

Malferio's face twisted. "You will not give in to this!" he screamed at the throngs of Faeries. "I am your King! It is your duty to defend me!"

"This King has brought danger to his subjects and shame on the Faeries, forcing us into unwelcome alliances," said Alvar. "We must end his reign tonight. Though the penalty be death of my Immortal Self, I hereby withdraw my allegiance to the King Malferio and nominate Emyr, the First Advisor, to succeed him!"

The other High Lords applauded from their daises while the Faeries watched, stunned and uncertain.

"Guards!" the King shouted, desperate. Nia plucked the crown from his head.

"Don't make a scene, my love," she said to him. "It isn't dignified."

Emyr stepped forward and Nia handed him the crown.

Nell had been watching all this with mounting horror, unable to understand what was being said but grasping the situation well enough. Now she found her voice and plucked at Swarn's sleeve.

"Is that...?"

"That is her," said Swarn, her voice devoid of emotion.

Nell felt sick to her stomach. "Lah, then *do* something!" she hissed.

"What can I do?" Swarn asked dryly. "If the Faeries wish to depose their King it is not my business. They have thrown their lot in with Nia and it is best that we leave quickly and quietly. Where is your friend, Jalo?"

Nell looked around, but he was not at her side anymore. She spied him standing with a hand on his sword hilt, by his mother's side, near the front of the dais. Tariro was talking rapidly in his ear. His face was very white.

"I'll talk to him," she said.

"Don't draw attention to yourself," hissed Charlie.

For a moment the scene on the High Step was pandemonium. The Guards had made clear their allegiance to Alvar but found themselves unable to take hold of their King until Malferio broke every Faery law by beginning to Curse Alvar. Immediately the Faery Guard closed around him. Alvar himself bound the deposed King's wrists in silver chains and took his sword. Bound in silver, he could neither speak a complete Curse nor work Illusion.

"You will suffer for this, Alvar. You and all you love will suffer for eternity. I promise you," hissed Malferio.

Alvar met his eyes calmly and did not reply. Emyr and his trembling wife seated themselves in the thrones on the High Step.

"Now is the moment when allegiance should be sworn!" cried Alvar to the Faery throng. "Let us swear allegiance to a king who will not betray us, a king with the interests of the Faeries always in his heart! His Majesty, King of the Faeries, Emyr!"

At first only the High Lords and their startled, frightened wives spoke the Oath of Allegiance, but, after a fierce look from Alvar, the Faery Guard joined in all together, and within seconds the entire host of Faeries in the courtyard were swearing allegiance to the new King.

Emyr rose.

"I thank you from the bottom of my heart," he said with all

the gravitas befitting a king. "My life's honour is to lead you. I name High Lord Alvar as my First Advisor, and as second Advisor I name High Lord Nikias."

Thunderous applause broke out among the Faery Guard as Alvar bowed deeply to the new King. Nikias seemed quite stunned, but a number of others noticed the satisfied look on Tariro's face, registered that Nia's dress was made of Faery jewels, and drew their own conclusions.

"Are there any requests for the new King?" called Alvar.

Nia, who had stood aside throughout this with her eyes fixed on Malferio like a hawk's on a mouse, stepped before him now and bowed low.

"Your Majesty, I humbly beg that the criminal Malferio be exiled and given to me."

"It is done," nodded Emyr. Malferio looked at his bound wrists and at the High Lords carrying on with the ceremony as if he thought he might wake up at any moment. Nia's tiger growled, circling him hungrily.

Gautelen stepped back onto the High Step next and bowed before Emyr.

"I ask permission to return to my home of Lil," she said, her voice shaking with emotion.

"It is done. I dissolve the bond of marriage between you and the former king. Tomorrow you will go home with an escort of the Faery Guard."

Gautelen bowed again, amber tears of joy falling from her eyes.

Nell was struggling to reach Jalo's side through the crowd on the dais but Tariro saw her first and stepped in the way, gripping her arm firmly.

"These are Faery matters," she hissed. "Do not try to sway Jalo, little girl. It will end badly for all of you."

"I need to talk to him," begged Nell. Tariro was dragging her towards the edge of the dais and her grip on Nell's arm burned. As she pulled her right to the edge of the dais, Nell realized with horror that Tariro meant to throw her over.

"Charlie!" she cried, but it came out strangled. The strength of the Faery overpowered her entirely and she could do nothing to free herself.

"You need to *disappear*," said Tariro.

A brown hand on Tariro's bejeweled arm stopped her. Tariro let go instantly and Nell fell at the Faery's feet, gulping for air.

"Your part is done," said Swarn. "We will leave peacefully."

"Sooner," said Tariro, "is better. The escort is ready."

"It is late and we need rest," said Swarn. "We will go at dawn, as arranged."

Tariro looked about to protest but Swarn held her gaze a moment and Tariro thought better of it. She nodded assent. "Dawn," she said.

Still sprawled on the ground between Swarn's legs, Nell saw Nia crossing the swaying bridge to the dais and approaching them. The Faeries stepped out of her way hurriedly, creating a path directly to Swarn.

"Swarn," Nell gasped to warn her, but Nia was upon the witch before she had a chance to prepare herself. They stood eye-to-eye for a moment and a hush fell over the Faeries. Even the ceremony on the High Step halted as they all watched to see what the Sorceress Nia would do to Swarn, the Warrior Witch.

"It's tempting to satisfy our audience and have a tremendously dramatic battle right here and now, isn't it?" said Nia lightly. "But I think they've had enough excitement for one night, and I don't like to take my eyes off of that snake for too long." She glanced back at Malferio, who was watching, his hands chained, as if it were a preview of his own end. Her tiger guarded him closely.

"I had to trap him," Nia continued, "like a little rat. I had to come into his hole after him. But I think I can count on your honour, Swarn. An admirable quality, if that's the sort of thing one admires. If I ask you to meet me at the Hall of the Ancients the day after tomorrow, will you come?"

"I will come," said Swarn. And then, as if she could not help herself, she said through gritted teeth, "Your slaughter of the dragons was unnecessary and barbaric."

Nia raised her eyebrows and laughed at that. "I just wanted to see what it was about killing them *you* always seemed to enjoy so much," she replied. "I've concluded it's a vastly overrated pleasure. I was surprised and disappointed, though, at the way you scurried off. I trust I won't be disappointed again?"

"You will not," said Swarn.

Nia nodded and cast a brief glance at Nell and Charlie and Ander, who had grouped around Swarn. "The company you keep," she said, with a roll of her eyes. With her gown of jewels clinking and twinkling she strode back to the High Step. The white tiger pounced, its great mouth closing over Malferio's head. As he screamed threats and showered incomplete Curses upon all his former subjects, the tiger dragged him down the steps after the Sorceress, across the petal-strewn courtyard, and out the crimson doors, which opened before them and closed with a thunderous bang. Thus ended the reign of Malferio, King of the Faeries for a thousand years.

CHAPTER
20

"You'll come back soon, won't you?" asked Rom, hugging his daughter goodbye. The question was taut with fear.

"Soon," she said.

"It's the Day of Forgiveness, you know," he added, and almost managed a smile. Eliza had lost track of the days and was faintly surprised to find Winter Festival already upon them. The Sorma did not celebrate it the way Northerners did.

"I'd forgotten," she said.

"Forgive me." His voice broke on the word *forgive*.

"For *what?*" asked Eliza, incredulous.

"For not being able to protect you or do this for you," he said.

Eliza shook her head, not sure if she wanted to laugh or cry. "This is just the way it is," she said. She had long since forgiven him for letting her childhood go. What other choice had either of them had?

"How is Ma?" she asked. "Is she still...?"

Rom nodded. "She's quieter now. Not sleeping yet."

"It's my fault. What we did to Nia's beast. I broke it the way she was broken."

"She's strong, Eliza. Like you. She'll be all right."

Eliza embraced her grandmother and grandfather and all her aunts and uncles and cousins, and Uri Mon Lil shook hands with them all. Then they mounted their dragons and flew north, leaving the Great Sand Sea and the remains of the Kwellrahg's body behind them.

It was early afternoon when they reached the Citadel. The

grounds looked black from above, filled with waiting ravens. As they landed, Eliza felt the Citadel recognize and welcome her. She realized, to her surprise, that it almost felt like home. She was terribly tired and she wanted to run to her bedroom, lie down and sleep. But that was impossible. The body of Anargul's dragon lay collapsed in the grounds, surrounded by ravens, and it grieved Eliza to see such a noble creature lying dead. The bodies of the Cra were also scattered here and there, their hearts cut out. Eliza did not look at them.

"What has happened here?" whispered Uri Mon Lil, looking around. "Oh, this is a dreadful place." He looked at Eliza fearfully.

"Wait here with the dragons," said Eliza. "I willnay be long."

Eliza made her way through the empty halls of the Treasury. Finding the place she sought, she laid her hand against the cold marble of the wall. Before she had even whispered a spell, a door opened before her. The Citadel was on her side, inviting her into the large, torch-lit room. The Vindensphere sat, unharmed, on a black cushion atop a round, stone table. She wrapped it in her coat and left the room. The Citadel allowed her to go – she was no thief. This was the will of the Citadel, also.

Uri Mon Lil was hiding in the woods, cowering, when she returned.

"You're safe," she told him when she found him. "But you have to come with me."

"Where are you taking me?" he asked.

She managed a smile. "Home."

She led the terrified wizard and the dragons into the dark wood in the northwest corner, the wood that led to the Crossing. The tangle of trees made way for the huge dragons and in no time they found themselves on the silvery shore where Eliza had first crossed over. This was where Kyreth had summoned the Hound of the Crossing to test her power.

She was so changed from those days. She was not that girl anymore.

She spread her arms wide and the water trembled when she

spoke. Ravens screamed in the wood behind them.

"My power spans the worlds and that between the worlds, my power spans the skies and seas of Tian Di, my power is undivided. Where I walk is the ground and what I speak is the truth. The tide will come to me when I beckon, the moon will sink when I point to the horizon. Here I demand a bridge, here where I stand, here I call upon the Boatman of the Crossing, passage to be mine."

The Boatman came slowly into view.

"Welcome, Sorceress," he said.

Eliza found herself, for the first time, looking into his eyes. She understood then that he was not a being like other beings in the worlds. He was not of the worlds. He was timeless, death-less, lifeless. He was a being like that little boy in the tree — a Guardian who maintained the limits of the worlds. But this was one boundary she was permitted to cross, one Guardian she could command, and he would obey her. He saw her recognition and smiled his ghastly smile. "I've been waiting for you," he said.

The dragons sat, bright and hulking, at the centre of the deck. Eliza and Uri Mon Lil sat aft, watching the hissing sea race by. Eliza was bone-weary, longing for sleep, but she was afraid that if she slept she would wake up without this new power that coursed through her, that she would wake up just Eliza again and not be up to the thing she had to do. She clutched the Vindensphere in her lap. She would not use it yet. She could not waste any of her strength.

"Quite an adventure," Uri Mon Lil commented once he had read through his notes and added the fact that they were returning to Tian Xia. "It says here that you are a Sorceress."

"True," she said, for the first time in her life feeling it to be so.

"And that our relationship is...undetermined." He looked at her inquiringly.

"That's an old entry," she said, and laughed for the first time in days. "You'd better change that to friend."

Uri Mon Lil beamed at her. "I *thought* so," he said.

Nia and Malferio stood on a red-black lava field that crumbled into a grey sea. Behind them, dark peaks spat flame. He stumbled back on the uneven stones, but for every step back he took, she took one forward, maintaining their proximity. His wrists were still bound with silver.

"You can't kill me," he snarled. "Your life depends on mine. Whatever you do to me, you must leave me alive, and one day I will have *my* revenge. Bear that in mind, Nia. Whatever you do to me one day will be showered back upon you tenfold, I swear by the Ancients!"

"Yes, the Ancients," said Nia. "Swear by them if you want to. They don't care for you, Malferio, nor for any of us. They did not stop me from beheading their Oracle and they will lend no power to your pleas for mercy. That is what you're begging for, really, isn't it? That I will show some mercy?"

After a long silence, Malferio tried to scream a Curse. But it perished in his mouth, leaving him with aching teeth and a burnt tongue. Nia stepped towards him.

"Go on, beg. It would please me, I think."

"I can give you anything," Malferio said hollowly, his eyes bright with hate. "Name it."

"You can give me *nothing*," hissed Nia, pushing him down on his knees before her. "You are not a king any longer, Malferio. I wear your blood, your immortality, and there is nothing I want from you except to bring about your absolute defeat and degradation. To grovel before me will be your final gift to me. Crawl."

Malferio fell flat on his belly, possessed by something he could not resist, and writhed on the ground.

"I will be your end, Nia," he gasped out. "Remember that. You will suffer for this. All who took part will suffer for this. I will be your end!"

"Hush now," said Nia. "I wonder how many beings you have Cursed in your day? What do you think? It would be impossible to count, I imagine. I learned Curses from the Faeries, among other things. Would you like to hear the one I've prepared for you? You can measure it according to the Curses you have cast and see how it holds up." She knelt next to him and her voice softened. "You will live forever, Malferio, as the Faeries do, but you will never cross over to that other unknown land. You will wander Tian Xia, forever banished from the Realm of the Faeries. You will be spurned by all other beings, who will sense the Curse upon you and flee. Whatever you touch will burn you, from now and forever. Whatever you taste will be dust, from now and forever. All you look upon will be colourless shadow, full of dire threat, from now and forever. Every sound that reaches your ears will do so in a terrible clamour, grating, whining, from now and forever. Every smell that reaches your nose will be the most appalling, sickening stench it will reduce you to nausea, from now and forever. Whatever visions or dreams you see will be loaded with terror, from now and forever. You will have no friends, none will take pity on you, from now and forever. Malferio, I rob you of the power of Illusion. I rob you of the power of the Curse. I rob you of all your lesser powers, too, that you may live weakened and helpless, from now and forever. Such is your Curse."

Her heart pounding, with rage or joy or grief – she could not tell – Nia unchained him and walked away quickly, without looking back once at the Faery collapsed at the edge of the churning sea.

Nell woke with the dizzying, horrible sense of not knowing where she was or how she had come to be there. This was followed quickly by a more actual vertigo when she pulled aside the curtains surrounding her soft bed, leaped out, and found herself atop a circle of stone soaring above shining cities nestled between mountains, forests and rivers and, far in the distance, the silver glint of the sea. She clutched the bedpost, reeling, her feet inches from the drop down to the glittering half-real Realm of the Faeries. The last thing she remembered was the pandemonium following Nia's exit from the Festival of Light. *What are we going*

to do now? She had asked Swarn. And she remembered the witch's face, lined and fierce and somehow sad. Her half-smile as she said, *I think you'd best take a rest.* A quick motion, something stinging in her eyes. And now.

"What by the Ancients is going on?"

Charlie's voice. She peered around the bedpost to see there were two more ridiculous four-poster beds atop the floating slab of stone. Charlie had gotten out of his and was staring around with a slightly sick expression rather like her own must have been just a moment ago. Ander groaned from within the third bed, waking up.

"Swarn did this to us," said Nell.

"Lah, of course she did," said Charlie ruefully. "How are we going to get down?"

"I dinnay fancy jumping," said Nell, peering again at the long drop down to the beautiful miniature world. "Why would she do this, Charlie?"

"I spec she just wanted us safe and out of her way," said Charlie. "While she took care of her own business, aye."

"Lah, there's a view to wake up to," muttered Ander, emerging from his bed and not looking particularly surprised. "They must get bored, dinnay you think, living forever and knowing none of it is real? You'd get jaded prize quickly, I should think."

"Swarn has gone to fight Nia," Nell told him. She sat on the edge of her bed and buried her face in her hands. Charlie sat down next to her.

"She made a choice, aye," said Ander. "We can nay like it, but it's her battle."

"She'll lose it," said Nell. "And there will be nobody left to help Eliza."

The stone circle began to move lower, until they were floating among the green mountains. It carried them towards a large balcony carved out of the side of a mountain, with waterfalls running on either side of it, and settled down there. Jalo was waiting for them.

"I trust you slept well," he began, but Nell cut him off.

"Did you know that Swarn had left?" she asked.

He nodded, taken aback. "She left after the ceremony, with

her dragons."

"So you just left us to sleep in some fancy prison?" she cried.

Jalo looked offended. "I couldn't wake you. She had done something to you. She swore it was harmless and you would wake in the morning. I thought you would enjoy waking up to a view of our beautiful realm. It was no prison."

"I'm sorry, lah," said Nell, shaking her head. "Everything has gone wrong. We came here to get help, we had a *plan*, and now Swarn has gone running off to get killed and I dinnay know what to do."

"Surely it is not your fight," Jalo said soothingly.

"Of course it is," said Charlie. "Once she kills Swarn, Eliza is next on her list."

"And without the Mancers, Di Shang worlders will be prey to any Tian Xia monster that wants to cross over. There willnay be anywhere safe anymore," added Ander.

Jalo looked from Nell to Charlie to Ander, and then said, "There is one place that is safe. The Faery Kingdom. In exchange for Malferio, the Sorceress has sworn by the Oath of the Ancients never to return here. The Oath is unbreakable. As long as you are here, you are safe. We can send emissaries to bring your friend here too. Nia will not be able to reach her."

Nell thought about this for a long moment. "I dinnay know if Eliza would agree to hide," she said at last, "but it's her only chance."

"Then it is done. You must not go."

Nell shook her head. "I cannay just...abandon my family," she said. "Eliza should come here to be safe from Nia, but there are people who need us."

"Agreed," said Ander immediately. "If it is to be the way it was during the long war, I know I'll be needed. I would never let anything happen to your family, Nell."

"And I may not be much good where Nia is concerned, but I can certainly protect people against your average Tian Xia beastie," added Charlie.

Nell smiled tearfully at them. "Then we have a solid plan B," she said.

"Good for us!" said Charlie. "What's plan A?"

"We cannay give up on the worlds just yet," she said. "Nia has been attacking her enemies one by one because she knows she cannay take them on all together. Swarn is nay dead yet, and praps the Mancers can still be helped. We *have* to convince the Faeries to help Swarn or to help break the spell on the Mancers. The Faeries are still our best chance. *Together* they're far more powerful than Nia, nay?"

Jalo shook his head. "A deal has been made," he said. "Peace has been struck with the Sorceress. We cannot fight her."

"You dinnay have to," insisted Nell. "You just have to...help her enemies a little. Please, Jalo. We need to speak to the new king."

"You should forget these matters and stay here," said Jalo again. "You will be made comfortable, I will see to it. You could be the first Engineer of the Faeries, teach us to build flying machines. If you want to bring your family also..."

Nell smiled ruefully. "I dinnay think your mother wants us here," she interrupted him, refraining from adding that Tariro had tried to throw her off the dais the night before. Now that Swarn was not here to offer protection, she wanted to move somewhere safer as soon as possible.

Jalo flushed slightly and said nothing. She felt rather badly for raising what must be a thorny family issue. "It doesnay matter," she said. "I'm asking *you* for help, Jalo. Please."

He met her eyes and nodded firmly. "I will do whatever I can to help you," he declared.

"We have to speak with the King. Our first plan is still a good one. We just need his approval."

"He is newly crowned," said Jalo, "and thus terribly busy..." He saw Nell's face curve down into an angry frown and sighed. "I will try."

"You're the son of the Second Advisor now," pointed out Charlie. "You must have some influence."

"Yes," said Jalo darkly. "I suppose I do."

The King's Castella was in uproar, with so many morrapi coming and going that from a distance it looked like a tiny castle in a snow globe. The vast household and many belongings of Emyr, the new King, were being transported in. The King was speaking with his two advisors in a pleasant pavilion in the Royal Gardens when Jalo arrived.

"It is a pleasure to see you, Jalo," said Emyr, in a somewhat *too* Kingly way. "We have just been discussing your brother's promotion!"

"Ah," said Jalo, bewildered.

"Head of the new King's Guard," said Emyr brightly. "Splendid, eh? Of course, there will be a fine position for you, as well, should you wish it."

He beamed at Nikias, who looked delighted and more than a little out of his depth.

"I thank you, Your Majesty," said Jalo, bowing. "If I may...I have come to see you regarding an important matter. The peace that has been made with the Sorceress Nia."

Emyr sighed. "We had no choice, Jalo. It is for the best."

"The best for whom?" Jalo asked this rather heatedly, then calmed himself. "The Faeries too may find themselves reaping some of the chaos to come if Nia is not stopped. Though she herself may not enter this Realm again, there is no telling what an unbalanced world will lead to. The Warrior Witch is not strong enough to fight Nia alone, but with the help of the Faeries..."

"We have sworn an oath!" said Emyr. "The battle with Nia was always Malferio's, not ours. We are well rid of it. Let the witch and the Sorceress settle matters between them alone."

"What of the Mancers?" Jalo pressed on. "I volunteer personally to lead a small group of Faeries to Di Shang. Perhaps we may recruit some witches or wizards to assist us and try to break the Curse upon them. This need not be an official mission, but rather one that is close to my own heart, as it will lead to the protection of my friends. May I have your permission to do this, your Majesty?"

"Jalo!" exclaimed Nikias. "Don't be ridiculous."

Alvar responded gravely. "Why would Faeries help Mancers, Jalo? There has never been friendship there. It is best you stay here. There is much to do in building this new kingdom and we could use a fine mind such as yours."

"I beg you to reconsider," said Jalo stiffly, directing his words to Emyr rather than Alvar. Alvar looked annoyed and stepped back, shooting a hard glance at an anxious Nikias.

"It is not in our interests," said Emyr simply. "The humans should leave and let that be the end of it. You should concern yourself with Faery matters, as befits your rank. Enough trouble has come to us from relations with outsiders."

"Your Majesty," began Jalo, his throat suddenly quite dry. "Think of the havoc Nia's victory will lead to..."

"I have spoken, Jalo," said Emyr harshly, leaning forwards. "Do not shame your mother and father by asking me again for what I have already refused."

Nikias looked quite alarmed by this. Jalo bowed deeply and left them.

Nell could see as soon as Jalo returned what the outcome had been. She grabbed his hands and looked up into his sad, handsome face.

"So they willnay help," she said. "But *you* can help us, Jalo. Take us to the Hall of the Ancients. We can rescue Swarn, aye, get her to the Citadel. It might still be possible."

"I dinnay recommend going anywhere *near* Nia," said Charlie. "We need to get to Di Shang quickly, find Eliza, and bring her back here where she'll be safe."

"I agree," said Jalo unhappily. "I fear there is little we can do for the witch. And I think your Sorceress friend will have to keep a low profile here. Outsiders are going to be particularly unpopular for a while to come."

"We cannay abandon Swarn. She's our friend too!" cried Nell. "Sort of, lah. We dinnay need to fight Nia, just grab Swarn and get out of there."

"She's made her choice, aye," said Charlie. "She went to fight Nia on her own."

"It's the wrong choice!" Nell shouted at him. "She'll be killed, and there will be nobody to help Eliza, nobody to free the Mancers. We have to help her."

"I'm with Nell on this one," Ander spoke up firmly. "I dinnay know the witch well, but we've made a journey together and I know you dinnay leave your comrades to get killed."

Nell realized she was still holding on to Jalo's hands and let go. "We need to leave right away," she said.

"Even if she is still alive, I don't see how we will help Swarn," said Jalo a little peevishly.

"You're a Faery, lah," said Nell. "Dinnay you have any powers?"

"Illusion won't work against her, because she wears the King...Malferio's blood," said Jalo. "I suppose I could try a Curse."

"What kind of Curse?"

"I don't know. Blindness, Terror..."

"What about both? Blind and terrify her and we'll whiz off with Swarn, aye."

"She would break my Curse. She is very strong," said Jalo.

"But praps not soon enough!" said Nell. "All we need is a little time."

"She'll strike before he gets the Curse out," protested Charlie. "You dinnay know anything about Nia, Nell. We cannay best her."

"Then we arrive once the battle has begun," said Nell. "She'll be busy fighting Swarn. We surprise her with a Curse she wasnay expecting, then fly like mad for the Crossing."

Ander looked at her admiringly. "You'd be good in the military, aye," he said.

Nell grimaced at that. "Will you do it, Jalo?" She saw him hesitate and added, "You're nay afraid, are you?"

Jalo stiffened. "If I can be of service in any way, it will please me greatly."

Nell looked at Charlie.

"If it goes wrong, I'm nay staying to fight," he said. "I'll head

CHAPTER
21

Swarn had returned to the marsh for her weapons, where she saw firsthand the devastation Nia had wreaked. She could not kill Nia, who had the immortality of the Faeries, but she could make her suffer and she meant to. With a curt word, she put out the enchanted fire that still smouldered on the ruined house and then searched the smoking rubble for her two best spears and her bow and arrow. She had hoped to arrive at the Hall of the Ancients before Nia, to prepare herself, but the journey was long and it was late morning on the day they had appointed when she left the dragons in the mountains and sent them east. They were the last of the dragons of the cliffs of Batt, the fiercest race of mortal dragons in Tian Di. She would not risk their lives in this battle. Alone, she began the long trek up the mountain.

When she arrived it was close to nightfall. The Hall of the Ancients loomed on the peak, far above the swirling sea of cloud, a dark stone tower inscribed with runes and ancient symbols. Its entrance ways were various, many of them secret, unseen by those who did not know them. But Swarn knew the place well, knew the rune to touch that would open the base into a door. She made her way along the cool, dark tunnel to the inner wall, which parted before her with a groan. She stepped into the circular Hall. Nia was already there, her tiger pacing restlessly. From the grottoes above, worn statues of the Early beings looked down on them – Dragon, Faery, Mancer, Mage, Demon, Man and Beast.

"I was afraid you weren't going to come after all," said Nia. "And what about your dragons? You haven't brought them?"

Swarn heaved one of her spears straight at Nia, immediately

followed by the other. The first was too quick for Nia to dodge but she caught it, staggering backwards with a gasp. The second she managed to avert, but she could not immediately break or cast aside the other – it stuck firm to her hands. Swarn raised her bow and sent a volley of arrows at Nia, who broke the spear and raised up a barrier. The first arrow drove through the half-erected barrier and caught her in the shoulder. Swarn closed her eyes and her ears, shut off her worldly senses to protect herself against Illusion. She had to rely on her instinct. She took an enchanted knife from her belt and hurled it. She felt it knocked aside, hitting no mark. It skidded back to her across the stone floor. She could feel Nia's Magic pressing around her, seeking to disarm her, but Swarn's weapons were powerful and her control of them absolute. The spear that Nia had dodged returned to her hand. She felt Nia move, swiveled accordingly, and hurled the spear again. Nia caught it and struggled with it. Fearing she might break this second spear too, Swarn caught up the knife on the ground before her and dove into Nia, knocking her backwards. They landed hard on the floor, Swarn on top, the spear between them pressing into Nia's ribs. Swarn resisted the temptation to open her eyes, to smell or listen. Her knife was inches from Nia's face, but Nia had a grip on her wrist and the grip burned. Never mind. Swarn had been burned before, and badly. This was nothing to dragon flame.

"I will cut that pretty face off before you kill me," Swarn hissed. "For Audra, for Rea and for the dragons."

The tiger was upon her then, tearing at her arm with its powerful jaws. She switched the knife to her other hand, swung it towards the tiger's neck, but before she could cut its throat a tremendous force threw her back towards the wall. She struck it hard and all the air went out of her, but she managed not to drop the knife. For a moment her senses burst open, but the instant she smelled fire she clamped them shut again. She felt Nia approaching with the spear, wrestling with its Magic. She wanted to use Swarn's own weapons against her, just to show off, but it would take her time to pervert such strong enchantments and this was to Swarn's advantage. Her right arm had been torn badly by the tiger and was of little use to her now. With her left hand she hurled the knife again towards Nia. The arrows had come back to her quiver. Blocking the pain from her savaged arm as best she could, she fired off a second volley, these ones toward the tiger, but they were all sent off course and the knife too clattered to the ground. Swarn felt her concentration clouding and quickly repelled the Confusion. Slow, she was slow not to have known it was coming before it began. She lunged forward, laying hands on the spear Nia held. For a moment they wrestled for it and, because the spear was hers and all its power yearned towards her, Swarn won. She tried to drive it into her enemy but her hands began to fumble it suddenly. Again she had to pour all her power into fending off the Confusion.

"You look silly running around with your eyes closed and your face all pinched that way," said Nia. "I don't *have* to use Illusion, you know."

Swarn felt something hurtling towards her. She opened her eyes and saw only a fog, thick and white, and then the thing struck her and she crashed to the ground, stunned. It was one of the carvings come loose from the wall. The stone head of a dragon.

"The Ancients would call it sacrilege," rasped Swarn. "You murder their Oracle, desecrate their temples, destroy the Hall they built!"

"The Ancients don't *care*," Nia replied, and another great statue, this of a Mage, broke free of the wall and flew across the Hall, slamming into Swarn. The Confusion pressed hard against her mind. She forced it out, and as she did so she was struck yet again. This time she felt her ribs cave in beneath the blow. She gasped for air and pain shot through her. She accepted the pain this time. She could not hold off the pain as well as the Confusion. Somehow Nia had her spear again and she wasn't sure how it had happened. With all her will she tugged it towards her, and it pulled Nia to her. She wrenched the spear away.

"I *will* kill you with your own spear eventually," said Nia in her ear. "The only question is how close to dead you'll be when I get to it."

Swarn cleared her mind with an agonizing breath. It was nearly hailing slabs of stone and statues now. She locked her mind on one and caught hold of its flow, swung it round towards Nia. It shattered in the air before it struck the sorceress and Swarn felt a crushing blow to the back of her neck. She was flat on the stone floor, and opened her eyes without meaning to. Flames sprang up around her. She leaped above them, hanging onto her spear, which hovered in the air at a gasped command. Balancing on her spear, she reached into her pocket and hurled a sleeping powder at Nia. Nia brushed the potion from her, but it slowed her for a moment, and Swarn's spear shot from under her, straight for Nia's heart. She tried to dodge it but wasn't quick enough and the spear went through the same shoulder that had taken the arrow wound. Nia cried out in rage and pain as the spear's enchantment coursed through her bloodstream. Without her spear to stand on, Swarn had plunged into the flames below, but crawled free of them, rolling over to put them out. She could smell her own flesh sizzling.

Nia wrenched the spear from her shoulder, shuddering violently. She tried to hurl the spear at Swarn but it would not go, so she battered the witch with stones, half-burying her in them. Dazed, Swarn lay beneath the heap of rock and for a moment she could not move. It was all the time Nia needed. Clutching the spear with her two hands, she fought it to the finish. It broke with a thunderous clap and she gave a yell of triumph. Swarn was slowly, painfully, pulling herself out from under the rubble. The Confusion came upon her so quickly and powerfully that it took her whole. She fell back, bewildered, lost. Nia smiled, then heard her tiger growl warningly. Something large and white was flying towards her, and she heard the words of a Curse. Her vision began to cloud and a thread of icy fear wove its way into her blood. A Faery. She shook off the Curse with an angry shout, then hurled the bottom half of the broken spear into the myrkestra, which plunged straight to the ground, dead. The Faery rolled upright immediately, drawing his sword and beginning the Curse again. A dragon was coming at her from the other direction, pouring fire from its mouth. Nia pointed a finger in either direction and spoke two spells at once. She sent the dragon and its two passengers flying back into the wall and baffled the Faery's tongue so he could not finish the Curse. The next instant, Jalo found himself bound with the same silver chains that Alvar had put on Malferio, and Charlie was no longer a dragon but trapped in the form of a cockroach.

"There," Nia said a little breathlessly, smiling at Jalo and shrugging off the last clinging shadows of the unfinished Curse. "Isn't it convenient I hung onto those chains, you naughty pact-breaker. Won't your new king be cross when he hears what you're up to?"

Nell was sprawled on the floor, banged up and winded from the dragon suddenly flying into the wall – this had not been in any way part of their attack plan. The cockroach scuttled to Nell's side. She had not for a moment really believed they would fail – she didn't have much experience with failure – and so she was slow to realize what was happening. Ander had spent a long time in the army, however. He had not really believed they would succeed and was quick to assess the new situation. He saw that Nia had neutralized the two new attackers who posed any kind of practical threat – the Faery and the Shade – and would now turn her attention to the witch. He knew what she would do even as she did it and he acted without thinking. The mission, after all, was to help the witch, to get her out of here. He was already up on his feet and running when the other half of the broken spear left Nia's hand. He knocked it to the ground, picked it up and turned on the Sorceress. And then it was hard to say what happened, but the spear shaft was in her hand again rather than his and a moment later it caught him full in the chest. Nell could see the point of it come out his back, but it didn't register, even as he staggered and then fell back amid the broken statues cluttering the ground.

Nia said, "That was rather heroic. Pointless, but heroism usually is."

Rising to her feet was painful and her balance was off, but

Nell stumbled over to where Ander lay impaled, staring about him in a startled sort of way. Nia watched them, interested.

"Mr. Brady," said Nell thickly, "are you all right?"

It would occur to her later, when she had time to process it all, that this was probably the single stupidest thing she had ever said in her entire life. Ander Brady was not all right. He had a spear through his chest and would be dead in moments.

"Hello Nell," said Ander, which was also an odd thing to say under the circumstances, but Ander would have no time to think about it later. He gave a sputtering little cough, gasped down one last breath, and then his eyes glassed over and he stopped breathing altogether.

Nell stood next to him, unable to think for a moment. Then she walked over to where the Faery had dropped his sword, picked it up, and looked at Nia with bleak hatred.

"Nell, don't," Jalo begged her, his face white and stricken.

But Nia was laughing. "*You* are *adorable!*" she exclaimed. "What in the worlds are you and that man *doing* here?"

"I'm Eliza's friend," said Nell, and she ran at Nia with the sword.

She found herself sitting down hard. The sword was in Nia's hand, who twirled it at her threateningly and then said, "That makes perfect sense. Where *is* Eliza, anyway? I hope she's still having fun with the present I Made her. I haven't had a chance to look in on her, I've been so busy, but no doubt she's hard at work. I'm quite eager to see how much she's figured out. She's an original, isn't she, our Eliza?"

"Are you going to kill me now?" asked Nell dully. The cockroach was racing across the rubble-strewn hall towards her, as if he might protect her in insect form.

"Oh, no!" said Nia. "You get a free pass, my girl. I'm not about to go killing Eliza's friends off. She'd think I was being malicious and, oddly enough, her opinion matters to me. *He* wasn't a friend of hers, was he? I didn't really mean to kill him but he did get in my way."

Nell looked at Ander again, lying back with the spear in him.

She could not weep or feel sorrow or fear or anything at all really, beyond a hazy sense of nothing being quite real. She looked around the Hall. The shattered statues, the dead myrkestra, the Faery bound in silver, his face a mask of misery, and Swarn sitting on the pile of rocks, eyes darting about but settling nowhere, her mouth hanging open. The cockroach reached her and crawled onto her hand. She watched Nia go to the myrkestra and pull the lower half of the spear out of it with a hideous sucking sound that made Nell want to throw up.

"I should snap her out of it for this last bit," commented Nia to Nell. "It's no good killing someone when they aren't even aware you're doing it. It takes away the whole point of revenge."

Nell tried to get up but couldn't. Something was stopping her, something she had no way of fighting. She curled a hand around the cockroach and looked away. She didn't want to watch. Nia stepped carefully through the rubble and waved the end of the spear before Swarn's face. Swarn's eyes cleared. She drew in a painful gasp of air and stared up at Nia.

"You're a better match for me than your sister was," said Nia, sounding quite friendly.

Swarn glanced at the spear, her face showing nothing.

"Last words?" asked Nia. "Something like *I'm sorry* perhaps?"

"I'm not sorry," rasped Swarn.

"Those are the last words I would choose, too," said Nia approvingly, and drove the broken spear down towards Swarn's heart. It glanced aside, and Swarn laughed weakly. Nia looked very put out.

"How can there be *deeper* enchantments on it?" she asked petulantly. "How long do you *spend* on your weapons? Never mind. I'm not inflexible. If I have to kill you with a Faery sword instead, so be it. It's not as poignant, but it'll serve." She tossed aside the shaft of the spear and pointed the sword at Swarn. "They say you have to pierce a witch straight through the heart and then burn her to be certain she's dead. Burning and drowning, those are the most popular, aren't they? But we'll begin with the heart. Then I'll burn you to cinders and drown the pieces on my way back to

Di Shang. I don't want you coming back for me."

She lunged for Swarn again. Again the sword glanced away.

"Barriers!" cried Nia. "I know a thing or two about barriers, you sad sack."

She pressed her hand against the barrier. Swarn kept her eyes fixed on Nia's face.

"It's strong," said Nia, then stood up straight, looking around her in surprise. "Too strong for you to have done it just now, weak as you are. Who is there?"

Nell looked up just in time to see ravens pouring into the hall, filling the great vault with the sound of their wings. The tiger gave a full-throated roar, driving the ravens up to the top of the vault, where they swarmed and screamed.

"Eliza!" shouted Nia. "Spare me your feathered friends! Come out and say hello!"

The wall opened and Eliza stepped through it, dagger in hand. She did not cast a glance towards her friend – even when Nell called out to her – or the Faery in chains, or even the dead man. She fixed her gaze on Nia.

"What are you doing *here*, Smidgen?" said Nia irritably. "Can't you see I'm busy killing this witch?"

"I'm done with the Kwellrahg," said Eliza.

"You *can't* be."

Eliza said nothing.

"You didn't kill it," said Nia. "And you didn't make that barrier by yourself, either – it's too strong for you alone. Who is with you? You didn't find a stray Mancer I missed, did you?"

"No," said Eliza. She looked around at the hall briefly. "You've made a mess, aye," she said.

"Yes," said Nia happily. "The Hall of the Ancients! You can really feel it here, can't you? Their vast indifference. You and I are all that's left of their long-ago, too-slight pity."

"How profound," said Eliza.

Nia raised an eyebrow. "Sarcasm doesn't suit you, Smidgen. What are you *up* to? Where is the Kwellrahg?"

"Usually I'm impatient and you want to talk," commented Eliza.

"Oh, have you come to *talk?*" asked Nia, thoroughly annoyed now and keeping one eye on Swarn. "What would you like to talk *about?*"

"You're the only one who knows everything my mother used to know," said Eliza. "You have so many of the answers I want."

Nia rolled her eyes. "Answers are over-rated. They wouldn't satisfy you anyway. Now, I can see you've made all kinds of progress in the last few days, as your noisy flock up there attests. I'm obviously good for you. But if you want to sit down and have a long chat, do you mind if I kill the witch first? I didn't kill your charming little friend by the way, even though she started waving a sword at me. How's that for generous?"

"I willnay let you kill Swarn," said Eliza.

"You're going to stop me, are you? I'm fascinated. You're actually a bit creepy when you're being cryptic and calm. Well, let's see who you've brought with you."

Nia turned her back on Eliza and made her way towards Swarn. Nell found she was able to move again. Immediately she scrambled to her feet and ran to Eliza to embrace her. Eliza gestured her aside, barely looking at her, murmuring, "Not yet, not yet." Nell stepped back. Nia was pressing on the barrier around Swarn with her palms. She laughed and turned, beckoning. The wall opened again and Uri Mon Lil found himself stumbling out into the hall.

"A wizard!" said Nia. "Under a *Curse*, no less. What odd friends you have, Smidgen."

The ravens started to descend and the tiger roared again, sending them all flapping back up, shrieking noisily.

"Well. Are you going to tell me what you've done with the Kwellrahg?" asked Nia. "Or are you going to make me guess?"

Eliza drew the rock out of her pocket and held it out on her palm to show the Sorceress. A flicker of alarm crossed Nia's face.

"How in the worlds did you manage that?" she asked. "You can't possibly have broken my spell."

"I didnay break anything," said Eliza. "I added things."

"But *what?*" Nia's gaze was fixed on the dark rock.

"It's nay Magic," said Eliza. "You wouldnay understand."

Nia laughed shortly at that, then held her hand out and spoke its former name, *Kwellrahg*. It didn't budge. Nia paled slightly.

"The renaming was Magic," Eliza admitted.

"How clever you are, Eliza," Nia said quietly. "Much cleverer, as it turns out, than me. But what will you do with it?"

Eliza did not reply. She kept her eyes steady on Nia, her mind closed firmly against the Sorceress. They were at a stalemate until one of them acted.

"I could kill you easily," said Nia, her voice still very soft. "It would take me half a second."

"I know," said Eliza. "But what a waste of power that would be."

"Yes," said Nia, a smile tugging at her lips. "Precisely. Oh, Eliza, what *are* you thinking?"

Nia made up her mind. She spun around and made for Swarn. She uttered a powerful spell that left the barrier in tatters instantly and snatched up the broken spear shaft again. As soon as Nia used her Magic, Eliza whispered her command to the core of the Urkleis. Nia arched backwards with a sudden, startled cry as Magic poured out of her, drawn to the Urkleis. She swung to face Eliza, understanding now, and raised the spear, but it was too late. The Urkleis drew Nia's Magic towards it in a great rush that made the Hall tremble and, at the same time, poured her Magic back at her. Her own Magic met itself in an unbreakable deadlock and Nia, whose physical form and strength were made up so entirely of Magic, was pinioned midrun, her body rigid with the effort of tearing herself free, arms out, the fingers of one hand spread, the other hand clutching the broken spear.

"Eliza," she said, her voice strained. "Don't do this to me."

Eliza shut her out, keeping her eyes down now. She knew if she but looked at Nia she would relent. As Nia had done in the Arctic, Eliza whispered the name, *Urkleis*, and pressed the dark rock to her chest, just above her heart. It was excruciating. Flesh and bone pried themselves apart to make way, and closed again around the stone.

"Well done," breathed Uri Mon Lil.

For a moment, none of them moved. Then the cockroach became Charlie, Swarn rose slowly to her feet, and Nell threw her arms around her best friend.

"So *you* are the Shang Sorceress," said Jalo, with deep respect.

CHAPTER

22

The ravens had all disappeared now. Nia's tiger paced around his Mistress in circles, snarling at the group. Nia struggled to speak, but she could not move her tongue.

Eliza unchained the Faery. They gathered around the body of Ander Brady.

"Is that the police chief from Holburg?" asked Eliza, shocked.

Nell bent down to close his staring eyes and Swarn pulled the end of her spear from his body. Jalo removed his cloak and laid it on the ground. Together they lifted the large man onto it and wrapped it around him.

They made their camp on the mountainside. It was a cold night but Jalo created a roaring bonfire with his firestick and they gathered around it.

"Is it customary to...burn your dead?" asked Jalo.

"We'll take him back to Holburg," said Nell. "He should be cremated and buried there. Nay here." She said *here* with real loathing, as if no place could be as barren or as heartless as this place.

"Today is the Day of Feasting," said Nell sardonically. None of them was hungry.

"It's almost tomorrow," said Eliza.

"The Day of Dancing," said Nell. She began to laugh, then

stopped abruptly and closed her eyes.

There was a distant rumble of thunder. In the ruined Hall at the top of the mountain, Nia's tiger let out a desolate roar.

There was a storm off to the north, moving away from them, further into the distance. Nell and Charlie fell asleep wrapped in blankets by the fire. Uri Mon Lil nodded off in the middle of updating his book and, at last, Jalo dozed as well.

Eliza looked at Swarn. Her clothes were soaked in blood, particularly around her right shoulder, and her face was swollen and bruised. She sat very still.

"Are you injured badly?" asked Eliza quietly.

"Yes," said Swarn. "But I'll live. What is the Magic you did?"

"The main bit wasnay Magic at all," said Eliza. "I used the Sorma techniques of taming and healing – that was how we disassembled the monster. That was enough to stop it from doing any harm, but I remembered what you told me about the wizard who Made the dragons and was absorbed by them. I was gambling that anything a being Makes could draw Magic from its Maker. You and the Mancers taught me that the Magic in the worlds is what was left here by the Ancients, the Magic of their Making, but I'm nay even sure..." Here Eliza took a deep breath, and then she said, "I'm nay sure the Ancients left Tian Di. I think maybe Tian Di absorbed them."

Swarn listened but said nothing.

"I've felt how *alive* the worlds are with mysterious powers that...lah, it seems true, but I spose it doesnay matter. If I could control the thing Nia Made, I thought I could control her Magic. Praps not use it myself but at least direct its flow. I got the idea of a deadlock from Wennot's Sixth Law. Only her own Magic would really be strong enough to bind her."

"Wennot?" inquired Swarn.

"A Di Shang scientist. Equal and opposite force...something Nell told me about."

"Her pride was her downfall, as is often the case," mused

Swarn. "She couldn't resist performing the Magic of Making, dangerous as it was. You must keep the Urkleis safe, Eliza."

Eliza could feel it in her chest, a hard, bitter lump, aching.

She said, "The Oracle told me that victory would only come for me with sacrifice. She said I would cut my own heart out."

Swarn nodded slowly, staring at the fire. "I doubt that is meant literally," she said. "You could try to interpret it, but sometimes hints of the future are best left alone. Have you sacrificed much for *this* victory?"

"It doesnay feel like a victory," said Eliza.

Swarn nodded again and let the subject drop. "You have brought the Vindensphere," she said. "How did you take it from the Citadel?"

"It was easy to take, aye," said Eliza. "I think the Citadel knew what I meant to do with it."

"What do you mean to do with it?"

"I have to find Kyreth. I dinnay know if Nia has killed him, but if he's alive he might be the only one who can break the Curse on the Mancers."

Swarn gave Eliza a long, steady look, as if weighing something. "You asked me once why your mother hid you from the Mancers and I did not tell you," she said at last. "I thought the knowledge would be a burden, as it was for her. She learned something from the Oracle that broke her heart, Eliza."

"What was it?"

Even as she asked she realized that she knew what Swarn would say.

"Kyreth is Nia's father," said Swarn heavily. "You should know everything, Eliza, before you seek him out."

Jalo, Charlie and Nell wandered among the trees. Eliza, Swarn and Uri Mon Lil were working some Magic together and had asked for no distractions.

"It's cold," said Nell.

"We could be at the seaside in summertime," suggested Jalo,

looking at the bare trees and the snowy crags overhead.

"No," said Nell, shuddering. "I've had enough Illusion."

"It's the Day of Dancing," Charlie reminded them, doing a half-hearted little jig.

Nell laughed a little, then said, "It feels strange to laugh, aye. My throat hurts, like I've been coughing all night."

"You look terrible," Charlie agreed.

"Not at all!" said Jalo indignantly. He took Nell by the arm and drew her aside. Charlie scowled and stuffed his hands into his pockets.

"Soon, we will be going our separate ways," he said. "But meeting you has been an honour and a delight, Nell. I hope it will not be the last we see of each other."

"Aye, we'll keep in touch," said Nell vaguely.

"In that spirit, I have a gift for you." From a pocket in his vest, he produced a gold ring with a white crystal embedded in it.

"Oh," said Nell, taken aback. Charlie craned his neck to see.

"It is one of my family crystals," said Jalo. "Crystals are used for summoning. If ever you need my help, turn the crystal and call my name. I will come find you."

"Thank you," said Nell. "Lah, I wish I had something to give you." Then it struck her. "You should take the helicopter! It's still in the Dead Marsh, aye! There's enough fuel to get you to the sea of Tian Xia, I'm sure. And if you do run out of fuel...lah, you're an Immortal, so I'm sure you'll be all right."

"The helicopter is a fine gift," said Jalo, smiling down at her. "I hope that I will see you again, Nell."

"Who knows," she said. She stood on tiptoe to kiss his cheek. His skin was cold.

"I am very sorry about your friend," he added.

A light rain began to fall.

As the sun crossed the sky somewhere behind the swathe of heavy cloud, Swarn stood in the rain and let loose a wrenching cry in the language of the dragons. The Mancer dragons became alert and restless, scanning the horizon. They all sheltered among the trees as the rain came down and at last they heard an answering cry. The two cliff dragons, rust-red and terrible to behold, came hurtling towards them out of the grey sky.

They said their farewells on the mountainside. Uri Mon Lil was going to the Realm of the Faeries with Jalo, who had promised that his Curse would be lifted by the most skilled practitioners. Having heard that his daughter had been released to return home, his face was lit with joy.

"You will always be welcome in Lil," the wizard said to Eliza, clasping her hands and pumping them up and down. "And if ever you need a wizard's help again, I hope that you will call on me."

"Thank you," said Eliza warmly. "And if you ever need a Sorceress's help, the same applies."

Uri Mon Lil's face creased with smiles. "I look forward to remembering you without the help of my book."

"That will be nice," agreed Eliza.

Swarn said her farewells curtly. Her dragon lay flat to enable her to climb onto its neck. She did so slowly and with difficulty, but they all knew better than to help her.

"What will you do now?" asked Eliza.

"Bury the dragons," said Swarn. "Rebuild my home."

She did not look back as the dragon beat its great wings and took off, flying back in the direction of the Dead Marsh.

"Wait, Jalo!" cried Nell as the Faery was about to follow, sitting in front of the wizard astride the young dragon whose life Nell had saved. "Can I...may I have your fire stick?" she asked humbly.

He gave it to her without question, and then they took to the air.

The three friends made the journey back to the Crossing with two Mancer dragons and a dead man. The Faithful were beginning to trickle back to their temples.

"It is all as the Ancients will it," said Rhianu to Eliza. "Now we will rebuild."

Eliza commanded the Boatman and he came.

"Lah," said Charlie, impressed. "How about that!"

"We have one stop to make," she said darkly.

It felt as if he were splitting in two. Half of him stepped out of the shadows and the other half remained. The shadows clung to his back, tugging at him. He saw before him a young girl with wild curly hair, looking at him very coldly. A pocket in the mist had opened around them.

"Eliza," he said, when he had found her name inside the part of him that knew her. The shadows curled around his shoulders, wove up his spine, pulling. Back that way was only a mad, helpless terror. He knew because half of him lived there, would always live there.

But the half of him emerging remembered power. Hungered for it.

"We couldnay break the Curse," said Eliza in a hard little voice. "It's too deep for that and the Faeries will nay help you. All I can do is give you clarity."

"Yes," said Kyreth, understanding this immediately. "Of course. Clarity." He clung to it. It was all he had. It was the thin cord between him and the power. The story returned to him piece by piece.

"I know everything," said Eliza. "I know what you did to her mother. I know what you did to her. I thought about leaving you here, but I need you to break the Curse on the other Mancers. It's a simple Curse, I think, but I couldnay ask more of Swarn. She was so...broken. We all are."

"Yes," said Kyreth. His mind was creeping among the parts of the story he knew like a rat in a half-finished house. Something was changed about Eliza. She carried a great weight. She had found her Guide, too. "Good," he said. "Good girl."

Eliza looked outraged at this. "Come on," she said. "We need to go back to the Citadel."

Kyreth followed her down the winding steps. "And Rea?" he asked. "No harm has come to Rea?"

Eliza told him and he listened. Her words were like little darts. She was so angry, so angry. It didn't matter. She didn't understand. Rea was safe. The mist kept opening before the girl. Kyreth's eyes met the Boatman's as he stepped aboard. Yes, home, they would go home. Away from this awful place. He barely took in the other passengers, the dragons. He shuffled to the bow and sat down. Eliza said something but he wasn't listening now. If he let go of himself for an instant he would tumble backwards into that void. Eliza's spell of clarity was weak, but what could he expect of one so young? She'd had some help; he felt two other wills at work, soldering this feeble spell. It was just enough that he could get a grip on the world and cling to it, hold tightly and see out of the prison Nia had made for him, the mad fear that pulled him back and pulled him back. Now they were going home, back to the Citadel, and he would be stronger there. The Mancers would refine the spell. He just had to hang on long enough to get there.

"I'll join you as soon as I can," Eliza promised Charlie and Nell once they were all safely in the grounds of the Citadel. She hugged them both tightly.

"I just noticed," said Nell, smiling tearfully at Eliza. "You're wearing it."

"What?" said Eliza, and then her eyes widened as she remembered the flowery bra. "Oh. Yes. I spec I've gotten used to it." She looked tenderly at her best friend, her pale tear-streaked face and the hollows under her eyes. "You need rest, Nell."

"You too," said Nell.

Charlie became a gryphon. He bore Nell on his back and held Ander's body, wrapped in the Faery cloak, in his great talons. They soared up into the welcoming Di Shang sky.

The few intruders that still lingered in the Citadel fled as soon as they saw the Supreme Mancer had returned. Kyreth barely glanced at the dead dragon in the grounds. He went straight to the Inner Sanctum. He seemed to stand straighter there, his eyes brightening. Eliza watched him for a while, struggling to work Magic in spite of the powerful Curse that still clung to him. He was strong enough and she could not help him, so she went to the Library and waited.

It was late in the day, on the Day of Songs, when the stone cracked and fell away. Foss looked around at the ruin of the Library and saw Eliza catapulting into him.

"I can only presume," he said, catching her in his long arms, "that everything has come out right."

"Yes," said Eliza, beaming up at him. "It has!"

He cupped his huge hand around her cheek tenderly. "Poor Eliza, I see that you have borne the worst of it. I called you back here – a terrible mistake, but I had no time to undo it!"

"It came out right," said Eliza. "Except for the books, lah. She drained the books, Foss." She picked one of the empty books up to show him and he flipped through it sadly.

"Recovering the stolen words of these texts is a project that will go beyond my lifetime," he said. "Destruction is a quick matter, whereas rebuilding – ah! But at least I have a clever assistant to help me begin!"

"Foss," she said, and then her eyes filled with tears and she could not continue.

"What is it?" he asked her gently, resting a hand on her shoulder.

She swallowed the lump that had come to her throat and said

in a voice that shook only a very little, "I'm leaving and I'm nay coming back this time. I just wanted to say goodbye to you."

Foss looked stunned. He said simply, "Why?"

"There are...many reasons," she said. "But mostly...I've learned some terrible things about Kyreth. I cannay stay here. Nay with him."

Foss took this in and then said, "Tell me."

When she had told him everything, he said, "If you wish to go, you must go quickly. You will not be allowed to leave if the other Mancers learn of your intent."

Eliza took the crystal Kyreth had given her from around her neck and pressed it into his hand.

"It was an evil act," said Anargul to the assembled Mancers on the following day. The Emmisariae sat at a long stone table in the Inner Sanctum. The rest of the Mancers were seated around the walls. Kyreth sat in a chair before the table, his eyes terrible. "It was a very great evil and one he kept secret from all of us. It has been costly, too. The worlds have suffered terribly from the wrath of the Xia Sorceress."

"You misinterpret his actions," said Obrad, glancing at Kyreth. "Though it cannot be denied the result was catastrophic, he acted with noble intentions. Had Nia been malleable we would have had a powerful Sorceress on either side of the Crossing, protecting it."

"But he told us nothing of this," said Anargul. "He acted in secrecy, risking the balance of the worlds. When he became Supreme Mancer he did not own up to any responsibility. And what of Nia's mother? Was not a terrible crime committed against her?"

"We do not know that," said Obrad.

"She killed herself," pointed out Aysu softly.

"That is not proof of anything but an unhinged mind," said Obrad.

"Trahaearn," said Aysu. "What say you?"

Trahaearn raised his head slowly. "He did wrong and kept secrets. For this he should be punished. And yet in his years as Supreme Mancer he has been a strong and wise leader. For this he should be rewarded. I do not know what justice is, in this case."

"Ka," said Aysu, "What say you?"

"I agree with Trahaearn," said Ka. "Though I do not condone what he did, I do not wish to see His Eminence cast out from the Mancer fold. He is one of the greatest Mancers in all our long history and Nia has punished him soundly for what wrong he did. But he cannot lead us anymore. Even if we forgive his wrongs, he is too much impaired. We cannot break a Curse as strong as the one Nia has laid on him and the Faeries will never come to our aid."

"Anargul?" asked Aysu.

"He should be cast out," said Anargul shortly. She did not look at Kyreth.

"Obrad?"

"I accept whatever is the will of the Mancers, but in my own heart I feel that His Eminence is the greatest leader the Mancers have known since Karbek and should not be lightly cast aside."

"Then let us say he has earned our friendship and our help through the centuries and we shall give it to him," said Aysu gravely. "He shall stay among us and we shall do what we can for him, but he shall not be called Supreme Mancer anymore."

"That title must fall to you, Aysu," said Ka. The others murmured their assent.

"Then Foss will take my place among the Emmisariae as Manipulator of Water," said Aysu. "Foss, will the Shang Sorceress accept this arrangement? Will she return to us?"

"I do not know," said Foss.

"As Emmisarius, you must seek her out and hear her thoughts on this," said Aysu. "If she refuses, she must be persuaded. The Shang Sorceress cannot sever ties with the Mancers, nor dictate how we deal with our own."

She looked out at the assembled Mancers.

"Do the Mancers accept what we have spoken?" she asked.

Kyreth half-listened to what was being said, the Mancers voicing their approval that he should be deposed. Aysu would be Supreme Mancer. It was laughable, that. Even in the throes of this Curse, he was stronger than Aysu. It didn't matter. He had his own battle to tend to, the constant struggle against the shadows of dread that sought ever to draw him back to the tower where his other half waited, utterly lost. There were ways to break even a Curse as powerful as this one. The simplest way was to kill the one who has Cursed you. His mind worked slowly, slowly, but it worked. Lost in shadow, still he could see in the dark. He could see, he could think, he knew what to do. They would not cast him out. Though they did not say why, it was because they feared him. And rightly so.

Aysu stood before him now, demanding his acceptance of her authority. He closed his mind to her and bowed.

Ander Brady's funeral was held on the Day of Stories, the sixth and final day of Winter Festival. All the islanders came and, instead of the usual stories, they told stories about Ander. They burned his body on a pyre at the northern tip of the island. His bones were buried and stories told over them and the ashes scattered into the sea, as was the custom in the Archipelago. Nell placed Jalo's firestick at the grave, where it would always burn. She had been welcomed back to the island with tears and relief, but Eliza was given a wide berth. They all remembered her, that odd little Sorma girl who had lived among them a few years before being whisked away by Mancers. She was taller now and, though she dressed like an ordinary girl, there was something alarming about her. She carried a long wooden staff. They noticed an unusual number of ravens flocking about the island, settling in the trees and on rooftops. It was her kind that had led to such a bad, untimely end for Ander, they muttered, and it was only by luck that dear Nell had survived.

As the night grew late and the stories began to dwindle, Alban invited Nell and her friends to come roast marshmallows at the beach with him and Marti. They ate marshmallows until they all felt a bit sick, and Marti fell asleep while Alban strummed his guitar.

"I dinnay feel like I should be happy about anything. I feel like I dinnay have the *right*," said Nell, lying on her stomach on the sand and staring into the fire. "But I cannay help it. I'm so *glad* that I'm alive and that you two are alive. We made it home. Di Shang is safe. But Ander is dead and..." she broke off and left the sentence unfinished, swallowing hard.

"I spec we all feel that way," said Charlie. "We *are* lucky to be alive. Of course we're happy about it."

Nell closed her eyes to stop her tears. She could still see the flames dancing on the inside of her eyelids. Within seconds she was asleep.

"What are you going to do, Eliza?" asked Charlie.

"I dinnay know," said Eliza. "I havenay slept in days, so I spose I'll rest here a while if Nell's family will have me. Then, if you're up for it, I've got to take Uri Mon Lil's staff back to him. It was still floating up in the corner of the Library, aye. Foss had to get it down for me. I'd like to check on Swarn, too. Make sure she's all right."

"I go where you go, Cap'n."

"*Please* dinnay call me that."

"Cannay help it. So you're really nay going back to the Citadel?"

She shook her head.

"Good. I nary liked that place."

Eliza looked at him fondly. The firelight cast leaping shadows across his face.

"You should have told me how badly hurt you were," she chided him. "I'd nary have left you alone if I'd known."

"There wasnay time," he said. "I couldnay help you anymore but I didnay want you stuck helping me."

"But Charlie, lah, you might have *died*."

"We all might have died."

She cast her eyes down at the fire and said, "I dinnay know what I'd do without you."

He put his arm around her and gave her a squeeze. "Let's nary find out," he said.

Leaving the others by the fire, Eliza walked along the dark beach. Small waves lapped at her ankles, quick and urgent as if trying to get her attention, the frothy fringe of the vast ocean. The Urkleis was lodged in her chest like an inescapable horror, Nia's terrible will turned against itself and frozen. Her ravens circled over her head. They did not need to speak to her; she understood the warning they carried. She could turn her back on the Mancers, maybe, but not on what she was. She would have to find her own path now. She turned around and looked back at the fire, a bright glow down the beach where her friends slept. Water washed over her feet – *swish, swish, swish*. The tide was coming in.

Chapter
23

Malferio, once King of the Faeries, stumbled through a haze of pain and fear and foulness. He did not know these lands. He did not know where he was. But every bird and beast, every blade of grass meant him ill, he knew that much. His mind was fixed in a grinding rage on she who had laid this Curse on him. If he could tear out his own life to end hers, he would do it.

He came to a foul-smelling river with dangerous currents. It did not burble pleasantly the way the rivers he had once known had done. It screamed. He fell on his knees, exhausted, and the ground cut into him. He could hardly breathe for the stench of the air.

A figure was approaching. Fear pressed in on him. He was powerless and despised and so he feared all beings. He tried to see through the shadows that clouded his vision. It was something almost fiery in the dreary landscape. Something bright white. He tried to back away but his limbs were too weak.

"Help me!" he screamed, and scooped up a handful of dirt. It burned his hand and he threw it at the being. "Help me!"

The being knelt at his side and he saw who it was.

"Help me," he whispered again.

"I will help you, Malferio," said Kyreth.

ACKNOWLEDGEMENTS

My thanks and my love to the family and friends who have been on my side for so long that my side wouldn't exist without them: Jonathan Service, for making me maps and always believing I can be a better writer than I am; Gillian Bright, for cheering me on; Mick Hunter, for making everything possible and never (seriously, not once!) complaining; David Egan, who gets my stories so well because he grew up inside so many of them; Michael and Janice Egan, not only for reading drafts of the book but for putting me up and putting up with me for chunks of writing said drafts; Jordan and Joshua Egan, for their enthusiasm when I most needed it; my grandmother, Kato Havas, for her support, honesty, and invaluable criticism from the first novel I ever wrote at age six to my current work-in-progress; and my parents, for more than I could possibly say.

Heartfelt thanks are also due to Laura Peetoom, for editing the book and for always being so completely right, and to all the wonderful, talented people at Coteau Books, for taking a chance on me in the first place and for turning my stories into such beautiful books.

ABOUT THE AUTHOR

Catherine Egan made her debut as a fantasy novelist with the bestselling first book in this series, *Shade and Sorceress*. Her short fiction has appeared in many literary journals in the United States and Canada. A world traveller, she now lives with her family in New Haven, CT. Readers can follow Catherine's experimental Twittertales – stories told in three tweets a day – on Twitter: @ByCatherineEgan or by visiting her website at www.catherineegan.com.